The Martins Of Cro' Martin
Vol. II

by

Charles James Lever

The Martins Of Cro' Martin
Vol. II
by Charles James Lever

ISBN: 978-93-63053-38-0

Published by

DOUBLE 9 BOOKS

2/13-B, Ansari Road
Daryaganj, New Delhi – 110002
info@double9books.com
www.double9books.com
Tel. 011-40042856

ABOUT THE AUTHOR

Charles James Lever was an Irish author and storyteller who lived from August 31, 1806 to June 1, 1872. Anthony Trollope said that Lever's books were like his conversations. Lever was born on Amiens Street in Dublin. He was the second son of architect and builder James Lever and went to special schools. He had many adventures at Trinity College, Dublin, from 1823 to 1828. It was there that he got his medical degree in 1831. Some of the stories of his books are based on these experiences. The character of Frank Webber in the book Charles O'Malley was based on Robert Boyle, a friend from college who later became a priest. Lever and Boyle made extra money by singing original songs in the streets of Dublin. They also pulled off a lot of other jokes, which Lever wrote about in more detail in his books O'Malley, Con Cregan, and Lord Kilgobbin. Before he really started studying medicine, Lever went to Canada on an emigrant ship as an untrained surgeon. He has used some of what he learned in Con Cregan, Arthur O'Leary, and Roland Cashel. When he got to Canada, he went into the woods and joined a Native American group. But he had to leave because his life was in danger, just like his character Bagenal Daly did in his book The Knight of Gwynne.

CONTENTS

CHAPTER I
MR. HERMAN MERL

This much-abused world of ours, railed at by divines, sneered down by cynics, slighted by philosophers, has still some marvellously pleasant things about it, amongst which, first and foremost, *facile princeps,* is Paris! In every other city of Europe there is a life to be learned and acquired just like a new language. You have to gain the acquaintance of certain people, obtain admission to certain houses, submit yourself to ways, habits, hours, all peculiar to the locality, and conform to usages in which—at first, at least— you rarely find anything beyond penalties on your time and your patience. But Paris demands no such sacrifices. To enjoy it, no apprenticeship is required. You become free of the guild at the Porte St. Denis. By the time you reach the Boulevards you have ceased to be a stranger. You enter the "Frères" at dinner hour like an old habitué. The atmosphere of light, elastic gayety around you, the tone of charming politeness that meets your commonest inquiry, the courtesy bestowed upon your character as a foreigner, are all as exhilarating in their own way as your sparkling glass of Moët, sipped in the window, from which you look down on plashing fountains, laughing children, and dark-eyed grisettes! The whole thing, in its bustle and movement, its splendor, sunlight, gilded furniture, mirrors, and smart toilettes, is a piece of natural magic, with this difference,—that its effect is ever new, ever surprising!

Sad and sorrowful faces are, of course, to be met with, since grief has its portion everywhere; but that air of languid indifference, that look of wearied endurance, which we characterize by the classic term of "boredom," is, indeed, a rare spectacle in this capital; and yet now at the window of a splendid apartment in the Place Vendôme, listlessly looking down into the square beneath, stood a young man, every line of whose features conveyed this same expression. He had, although not really above twenty-four or twenty-five, the appearance of one ten years older. On a face of singular regularity, and decidedly handsome, dissipation had left its indelible traces. The eyes were deep sunk, the cheeks colorless, and around the angles of the mouth were those tell-tale circles which betray the action of an oft-tried temper, and the spirit that has gone through many a hard conflict. In figure he was very tall, and seemed more so in the folds of a long dressing-gown of antique brocade, which reached to his feet; a small, dark green skull-cap, with a heavy silver tassel, covered one side of his head, and in his hand he held a handsome meerschaum, which, half mechanically, he placed from time to time to his lips, although its bowl was empty.

At a breakfast-table covered with all that could provoke appetite, sat a figure as much unlike him as could be. He was under the middle size, and slightly inclined to flesh, with a face which, but for some strange resemblance to what one has seen in pictures by the older artists, would have been unequivocally vulgar. The eyes were small, keen, and furtive; the nose, slightly concave in its outline, expanded beneath into nostrils wide and full; but the mouth, thick-lipped, sensual, and coarse, was more distinctive than all, and showed that Mr. Herman Merl was a gentleman of the Jewish persuasion,—a fact well corroborated by the splendor of a very flashy silk waistcoat, and various studs, gold chain, rings, and trinkets profusely scattered over his costume. And yet there was little of what we commonly recognize as the Jew in the character of his face. The eyes were not dark, the nose not aquiline; the hair, indeed, had the wavy massiveness of the Hebrew race; but Mr. Merl was a "Red Jew," and the Red Jew, like the red partridge, is a species *per se*.

There was an ostentatious pretension in the "get up" of this gentleman. His moustache, his beard, his wrist-buttons, his shirt-studs, the camellia in his coat,—all, even to the heels of his boots, had been made studies, either to correct a natural defect, or show off what he fancied a natural advantage. He seemed to have studied color like a painter, for his dark brown frock was in true keeping with the tint of his skin; and yet, despite these painstaking efforts, the man was indelibly, hopelessly vulgar. Everything about him was imitation, but it was imitation that only displayed its own shortcomings.

"I wonder how you can resist these oysters, Captain," said he, as he daintily adjusted one of these delicacies on his fork; "and the Chablis, I assure you, is excellent."

"I never eat breakfast," said the other, turning away from the window, and pacing the room with slow and measured tread.

"Why, you are forgetting all the speculations that used to amuse us on the voyage,—the delicious little dinners we were to enjoy at the 'Rocher,' the tempting dejeuners at 'Véfour's.' By Jove! how hungry you used to make me, with your descriptions of the appetizing fare before us; and here we have it now: Ardennes ham, fried in champagne; Ostend oysters, salmi of quails with truffles—and such truffles! Won't that tempt you?"

But his friend paid no attention to the appeal, and walking again to the window, looked out.

"Those little drummers yonder have a busy day of it," said he, lazily; "that's the fourth time they have had to beat the salute to Generals this morning."

"Is there anything going on, then?"

But he never deigned an answer, and resumed his walk.

"I wish you'd send away that hissing teakettle, it reminds me of a steamboat," said the Captain, peevishly; "that is, if you have done with it."

"So it does," said the other, rising to ring the bell; "there's the same discordant noise, and the—the—the—" But the rest of the similitude would n't come, and Mr. Merl covered his retreat with the process of lighting a cigar,—an invaluable expedient that had served to aid many a more ready debater in like difficulty.

It would be a somewhat tedious, perhaps not a very profitable task, to inquire how two men, so palpably dissimilar, had thus become what the world calls friends. Enough if we say that Captain Martin,—the heir of Cro' Martin,—when returning from India on leave, passed some time at the Cape, where, in the not very select society of the place, he met Mr. Merl. Now Mr. Merl had been at Ceylon, where he had something to do with a coffee plantation; and he had been at Benares, where opium interested him; and now again, at the Cape, a question of wine had probably some relation to his sojourn. In fact, he was a man travelling about the world with abundance of leisure, a well-stocked purse, and what our friends over the Strait would term an "industrial spirit." Messes had occasionally invited him to their tables. Men in society got the habit of seeing him "about," and he was in the enjoyment of that kind of tolerance which made every man feel, "He's not *my* friend,—*I* didn't introduce him; but he seems a good sort of fellow enough!" And so he was,—very good-tempered, very obliging, most liberal of his cigars, his lodgings always open to loungers, with pale ale, and even iced champagne, to be had Ifor asking. There was play, too; and although Merl was a considerable winner, he managed never to incur the jealous enmity that winning so often imposes. He was the most courteous of gamblers; he never did a sharp thing; never enforced a strict rule upon a novice of the game; tolerated every imaginable blunder of his partner with bland equanimity; and, in a word, if this great globe of ours had been a green-baize cloth, and all the men and women whist-players, Mr. Herman Merl had been the first gentleman in it, and carried off "all the honors" in his own hand.

If he was highly skilled in every game, it was remarked of him that he never proposed play himself, nor was he ever known to make a wager: he always waited to be asked to make up a party, or to take or give the odds, as the case might be. To a very shrewd observer, this might have savored a little too much of a system; but shrewd observers are, after all, not the current coin in the society of young men, and Merl's conduct was eminently successful.

Merl suited Martin admirably. Martin was that species of man which, of all others, is most assailable by flattery. A man of small accomplishments, he sang a little, rode a little, played, drew, fenced, fished, shot—all, a little—that is, somewhat better than others in general, and giving him that dangerous kind of pre-eminence from which, though the tumble never kills, it occurs often enough to bruise and humiliate. But, worse than this, it shrouds its possessor in a triple mail of vanity, that makes him the easy prey of all who minister to it.

We seldom consider how much locality influences our intimacies, and how impossible it had been for us even to know in some places the people we have made friends of in another. Harry Martin would as soon have thought of proposing his valet at "Brookes's," as walk down Bond Street with Mr. Merl. Had he met him in London, every characteristic of the man would there have stood out in all the strong glare of contrast, but at the Cape it was different. Criticism would have been misplaced where all was irregular, and the hundred little traits—any one of which would have shocked him in England—were only smiled at as the eccentricities of a "good-natured poor fellow, who had no harm in him."

Martin and Merl came to England in the same ship. It was a sudden thought of Merl's, only conceived the evening before she sailed; but Martin had lost a considerable sum at piquet to him on that night, and when signing the acceptances for payment, since he had not the ready money, somewhat peevishly remarked that it was hard he should not have his revenge. Whereupon Merl, tossing off a bumper of champagne, and appearing to speak under the influence of its stimulation, cried out, "Hang me, Captain, if you shall say that! I 'll go and take my passage in the 'Elphinstone.'" And he did so, and he gave the Captain his revenge! But of all the passions, there is not one less profitable to indulge in. They played morning, noon, and night, through long days of sickening calm, through dreary nights of storm and hurricane, and they scarcely lifted their heads at the tidings that the Needles were in sight, nor even questioned the pilot for news of England, when he boarded them in the Downs. Martin had grown much older during that same voyage; his temper, too, usually imbued with the easy indolence of his father's nature, had grown impatient and fretful. A galling sense of inferiority to Merl poisoned every minute of his life. He would not admit it; he rejected it, but back it came; and if it did not enter into his heart, it stood there knocking,—knocking for admission. Each time they sat down to play was a perfect duel to Martin.

As for Merl, his well-schooled faculties never were ruffled nor excited. The game had no power to fascinate *him*, its vicissitudes had nothing new or surprising to him; intervals of ill-luck, days even of dubious fortune might occur, but he knew he would win in the end, just as he knew that though there might intervene periods of bad weather and adverse winds, the good ship "Elphinstone" would arrive at last, and, a day sooner or a day later, discharge passengers and freight on the banks of the Thames.

You may forgive the man who has rivalled you in love, the banker whose "smash" has engulfed all your fortune, the violent political antagonist who has assailed you personally, and in the House, perhaps, answered the best speech you ever made by a withering reply. You may extend feelings of Christian charity to the reviewer who has "slashed" your new novel, the lawyer whose vindictive eloquence has exposed, the artist in "Punch" who has immortalized, you; but there is one man you never forgive, of whom you will never believe one good thing, and to whom you would wish a thousand evil ones,—he is your natural enemy, brought into the world to be your bane, born that he may be your tormentor; and this is the man who *always* beats you at play! Happily, good reader, you may have no feelings of the gambler,—you may be of those to whom this fatal vice has never appealed, or appealed in vain; but if you *have* "played," or even mixed with those who have, you could n't have failed to be struck with the fact that there is that one certain man from whom you never win! Wherever he is, there, too, is present your evil destiny! Now, there is no pardoning this,—the double injury of insult to your skill and damage to your pocket. Such a man as this becomes at last your master. You may sneer at his manners, scoff at his abilities, ridicule his dress, laugh at his vulgarity,—poor reprisals these! In his presence, the sense of that one superiority he possesses over you makes you quail! In the stern conflict, where your destiny and your capacity seem alike at issue, he conquers you,—not to-day or to-morrow, but ever and always! There he sits, arbiter of your fate,—only doubtful how long he may defer the day of your sentence!

It is something in the vague indistinctness of this power—something that seems to typify the agency of the Evil One himself—that at once tortures and subdues you; and you ever hurry into fresh conflict with the ever-present consciousness of fresh defeat! We might have spared our reader this discursive essay, but that it pertains to our story. Such was the precise feeling entertained by Martin towards Merl. He hated him with all the concentration of his great hatred, and yet he could not disembarrass himself of his presence. He was ashamed of the man amongst his friends; he avoided him in all public places; he shrunk from his very contact as though infected; but he could not throw off his acquaintance, and he nourished in his heart a small ember of hope that one day or other the scale of fortune would turn, and he might win back again all he had ever lost, and stand free and unembarrassed as in the first hour he had met him! Fifty times had he consulted Fortune, as it were, to ask if this moment had yet arrived; but hitherto ever unsuccessfully,—Merl won on as before. Martin, however, invariably ceased playing when he discovered that his ill-luck continued. It was an experiment,—a mere pilot balloon to Destiny; and when he saw the direction adverse, he did not adventure on the grand ascent. It was impossible that a man of Merl's temperament and training should not have detected this game. There was not a phase of the gambler's mind with which he was not thoroughly familiar.

Close intimacies, popularly called friendships, have always their secret motive, if we be but skilful enough to detect it. We see people associate together of widely different habits, and dispositions the most opposite, with nothing in common of station, rank, object, or pursuit. In such cases the riddle has always its key, could we only find it.

Mr. Martin had been some weeks in Paris with his family, when a brief note informed him that Merl had arrived there. He despatched an answer still briefer, asking him to breakfast on the following morning; and it was in the acceptance of this same invitation we have now seen him.

"Who's here just now?" said Merl, throwing down his napkin, and pushing his chair a little back from the table, while he disposed his short, fat legs into what he fancied was a most graceful attitude.

"Here? Do you mean in Paris?" rejoined Martin, pettishly,—for he never suffered so painfully under this man's intimacy as when his manners assumed the pretension of fashion.

"Yes,—of course,—I mean, who's in Paris?"

"There are, I believe, about forty-odd thousand of our countrymen and countrywomen," said the other, half contemptuously.

"Oh, I've no doubt; but my question took narrower bounds. I meant, who of *our* set,—who of us?"

Martin turned round, and fixing his eyes on him, scanned him from head to foot with a gaze of such intense insolence as no words could have equalled. For a while the Jew bore it admirably; but these efforts, after all, are only like the brief intervals a man can live under water, and where the initiated beats the inexperienced only by a matter of seconds. As Martin continued his stare, Merl's cheek tingled, grew red, and finally his whole face and forehead became scarlet.

With an instinct like that of a surgeon who feels he has gone deep enough with his knife, Martin resumed his walk along the room without uttering a word.

Merl opened the newspaper, and affected to read; his hand, however, trembled, and his eyes wandered listlessly over the columns, and then furtively were turned towards Martin as he paced the chamber in silence.

"Do you think you can manage that little matter for me, Captain?" said he at last, and in a voice attuned to its very humblest key.

"What little matter? Those two bills do you mean?" said Martin, suddenly.

"Not at all. I 'm not the least pressed for cash. I alluded to the Club; you promised you 'd put me up, and get one of your popular friends to second me."

"I remember," said Martin, evidently relieved from a momentary terror. "Lord Claude Willoughby or Sir Spencer Cavendish would be the men if we could find them."

"Lord Claude, I perceive, is here; the paper mentions his name in the dinner company at the Embassy yesterday."

"Do you know him?" asked Martin, with an air of innocence that Merl well comprehended as insult.

"No. We 've met,—I think we 've played together; I remember once at Baden—"

"Lord Claude Willoughby, sir," said a servant, entering with a card, "desires to know if you 're at home?"

"And won't be denied if you are not," said his Lordship, entering at the same instant, and saluting Martin with great cordiality.

CHAPTER II
MR. MERL

The French have invented a slang word for a quality that deserves a more recognized epithet, and by the expression *chic* have designated a certain property by which objects assert their undoubted superiority over all their counterfeits. Thus, your coat from Nugee's, your carriage from Leader's, your bracelet from Storr's, and your bonnet from Madame Palmyre, have all their own peculiar *chic*, or, in other words, possess a certain invisible, indescribable essence that stamps them as the best of their kind, with an excellence unattainable by imitation, and a charm all their own!

Of all the products in which this magical property insinuates itself, there is not one to which it contributes so much as the man of fashion. He is the very type of *chic*. To describe him you are driven to a catalogue of negatives, and you only arrive at anything like a resemblance by an enumeration of the different things he is not.

The gentleman who presented himself to Martin at the close of our last chapter was in many respects a good specimen of his order. He had entered the room, believing Martin to be there alone; but no sooner had he perceived another, and that other one not known to him, than all the buoyant gayety of his manner was suddenly toned down into a quiet seriousness; while, taking his friend's arm, he said in a low voice, — "If you 're busy, my dear Martin, don't hesitate for a moment about sending me off; I had not the slightest suspicion there was any one with you."

"Nor is there," said Martin, with a supercilious glance at Merl, who was endeavoring in a dozen unsuccessful ways to seem unaware of the new arrival's presence.

"I want to introduce him to you," said Martin.

"No, no, my dear friend, on no account."

"I must; there's no help for it," said Martin, impatiently, while he whispered something eagerly in the other's ear.

"Well, then, some other day; another time—"

"Here and now, Claude," said Martin, peremptorily; while, without waiting for reply, he said aloud, "Merl, I wish to present you to Lord Claude Willoughby,—Lord Claude, Mr. Herman Merl."

Merl bowed and smirked and writhed as his Lordship, with a bland smile and a very slight bow, acknowledged the presentation.

"Had the pleasure of meeting your Lordship at Baden two summers ago," said the Jew, with an air meant to be the ideal of fashionable ease.

"I was at Baden at the time you mention," said he, coldly.

"I used to watch your Lordship's game with great attention; you won heavily, I think?"

"I don't remember, just now," said he, carelessly; not, indeed, that such was the fact, or that he desired it should be thought so; he only wished to mark his sense of what he deemed an impertinence.

"The man who can win at rouge-et-noir can do anything, in my opinion," said Merl.

"What odds are you taking on Rufus?" said Martin to Willoughby, and without paying the slightest attention to Merl's remark.

"Eleven to one; but I'll not take it again. Hecuba is rising hourly, and some say she 'll be the favorite yet."

"Is Rufus your Lordship's horse?" said the Jew, insinuatingly.

Willoughby bowed, and continued to write in his note-book.

"And you said the betting was eleven to one on the field, my Lord?"

"It ought to be fourteen to one, at least."

"I 'll give you fourteen to one, my Lord, just for the sake of a little interest in the race."

Willoughby ceased writing, and looked at him steadfastly for a second or two. "I have not said that the odds were fourteen to one."

"I understand you perfectly, my Lord; you merely thought that they would be, or, at least, ought to be."

"Merl wants a bet with you, in fact," said Martin, as he applied alight to his meerschaum; "and if you won't have him, I will."

"What shall it be, sir," said Lord Claude, pencil in hand; "in ponies—fifties?"

"Oh, ponies, my Lord. I only meant it, just as I said, to give me something to care for in the race."

"Will you put him up at the 'Cercle' after that?" whispered Martin, with a look of sly malice.

"I'll tell you when the match is over," said Willoughby, laughing; "but if I won't, here 's one that will. That's a neat phaeton of Cavendish's." And at the same instant Martin opened the window, and made a signal with his handkerchief.

"That's the thing for *you*, Merl," said Martin, pointing down to a splendid pair of dark chestnuts harnessed to a handsome phaeton. "It's worth five hundred pounds to any fellow starting an equipage to chance upon one of Cavendish's. He has not only such consummate taste in carriage and harness, but he makes his nags perfection."

"He drives very neatly," said Willoughby.

"What was it he gave for that near-side horse?—a thousand pounds, I think."

"Twelve hundred and fifty, and refused a hundred for my bargain," said a very diminutive, shrewd-looking man of about five-and-thirty, who entered the room with great affectation of juvenility. "I bought him for a cab, never expecting to 'see his like again,' as Shakspeare says."

"And you offered the whole concern yesterday to Damre-mont for fifty thousand francs?"

"No, Harry, that's a mistake. I said I 'd play him a match at piquet, whether he gave seventy thousand for the equipage or nothing. It was he that proposed fifty thousand. Mine was a handsome offer, I think."

"I call it a most munificent one," said Martin. "By the way, you don't know my friend here, Mr. Merl, Sir Spencer Cavendish." And the baronet stuck his glass in his eye, and scanned the stranger as unscrupulously as though he were a hack at Tattersairs.

"Where did he dig him up, Claude?" whispered he, after a second.

"In India, I fancy; or at the Cape."

"That fellow has something to do with the hell in St. James's Street; I 'll swear I know his face."

"I've been telling Merl that he's in rare luck to find such a turn-out as that in the market; that is, if you still are disposed to sell."

"Oh, yes, I'll sell it; give him the tiger, boots, cockade, and all,—everything except that Skye terrier. You shall have the whole, sir, for two thousand pounds; or, if you prefer it—"

A certain warning look from Lord Claude suddenly arrested his words, and he added, after a moment,—"But I'd rather sell it off, and think no more of it."

"Try the nags; Sir Spencer, I'm sure, will have no objection," said Martin. But the baronet's face looked anything but concurrence with the proposal.

"Take them a turn round the Bois de Boulogne, Merl," said Martin, laughing at his friend's distress.

"And he may have the turn-out at his own price after the trial," muttered Lord Claude, with a quiet smile.

"Egad! I should think so," whispered Cavendish; "for, assuredly, I should never think of being seen in it again."

"If Sir Spencer Cavendish has no objection,—if he would permit his groom to drive me just down the Boulevards and the Rue Rivoli—"

The cool stare of the baronet did not permit him to finish. It was really a look far more intelligible than common observers might have imagined, for it conveyed something like recognition,—a faint approach to an intimation that said, "I'm persuaded that we have met before."

"Yes, that is the best plan. Let the groom have the ribbons," said Martin, laughing with an almost schoolboy enjoyment of a trick. "And don't lose time, Merl, for Sir Spencer would n't miss his drive in the Champs Elysees for any consideration."

"Gentlemen, I am your very humble and much obliged servant!" said Cavendish, as soon as Merl had quitted the room. "If that distinguished friend of yours should not buy my carriage—"

"But he will," broke in Martin; "he must buy it."

"He ought, I think," said Lord Claude. "If I were in his place, there's only one condition I 'd stipulate for."

"And that is—"

"That you should drive with him one day—one would be enough—from the Barrière de l'Étoile to the Louvre."

"This is all very amusing, gentlemen, most entertaining," said Cavendish, tartly; "but who is he?—I don''t mean that,—but what is he?"

"Martin's banker, I fancy," said Lord Claude.

"Does he lend any sum from five hundred to twenty thousand on equitable terms on approved personal security?" said Cavendish, imitating the terms of the advertisements.

"He 'll allow all he wins from you to remain in your hands at sixty per cent interest, if he doesn't want cash!" said Martin, angrily.

"Oh, then, I 'm right. It is my little Moses of St. James's Street. He was n't always as flourishing as we see him now. Oh dear, if any man, three years back, had told me that this fellow would have proposed seating himself in my phaeton for a drive round Paris, I don't believe—nay, I 'm sure—my head couldn't have stood it."

"You know him, then?" said Willoughby.

"I should think every man about town a dozen years ago must know him. There was a kind of brood of these fellows; we used to call them Joseph and his brethren. One sold cigars, another vended maraschino; this discounted your bills, that took your plate or your horses—ay, or your wardrobe—on a bill of sale, and handed you over two hundred pounds to lose at his brother's hell in the evening. Most useful scoundrels they were,—equally expert on 'Change and in the Coulisses of the Opera!"

"I will say this for him," said Martin, "he 's not a hard fellow to deal with; he does not drive a bargain ungenerously."

"Your hangman is the tenderest fellow in the world," said Cavendish, "till the final moment. It's only in adjusting the last turn under the ear that he shows himself 'ungenerous.'"

"Are you deep with him, Harry?" said Willoughby, who saw a sudden paleness come over Martin's face.

"Too deep!" said he, with a bitter effort at a laugh, — "a great deal too deep."

"We 're all too deep with those fellows," said Cavendish, as, stretching out his legs, he contemplated the shape and lustre of his admirably fitting boots. "One begins by some trumpery loan or so; thence you go on to a play transaction or a betting-book with them, and you end — egad, you end by having the fellow at dinner!"

"Martin wants his friend to be put up for the Club," said Willoughby.

"Eh, what? At the 'Cercle,' do you mean?"

"Why not? Is it so very select?"

"No, not exactly that; there are the due proportions of odd reputations, half reputations, and no reputations; but remember, Martin, that however black they be now, they all began white. When they started, at least, they were gentlemen."

"I suspect that does not make the case much better."

"No; but it makes *ours* better, in associating with them. Come, come, you know as well as any one that this is impossible, and that if you should do it to-day, I should follow the lead to-morrow, and our Club become only an asylum for unpayable tailors and unappeasable bootmakers!"

"You go too fast, sir," exclaimed Martin, in a tone of anger. "I never intended to pay my debts by a white ball in the ballot-box, nor do I think that Mr. Merl would relinquish his claim on some thousand pounds, even for the honor of being the club colleague of Sir Spencer Cavendish."

"Then I know him better," said the other, tapping his-boot with his cane; "he would, and he 'd think it a right good bargain besides. From seeing these fellows at racecourses and betting-rooms, always cold, calm, and impassive, never depressed by ill-luck, as little elated by good, we fall into the mistake of esteeming them as a kind of philosophers in life, without any of those detracting influences that make you and Willoughby, and even myself, sometimes rash and headstrong. It is a mistake, though; they have a weakness, — and a terrible weakness, — which is, their passion to be thought in fashionable society. Yes, they can't resist that! All their shrewd calculations, all their artful schemes, dissolve into thin air, at the bare prospect of being recognized 'in society.' I have studied this flaw in them for many a year back. I'll not say I haven't derived advantage from it."

"And yet you'd refuse him admission into a club," cried Martin.

"Certainly. A club is a Democracy, where each man, once elected, is the equal of his neighbor. Society is, on the other hand, an absolute monarchy, where your rank flows from the fountain of honor,—the host. Take him along with you to her Grace's 'tea,' or my Lady's reception this evening, and see if the manner of the mistress of the house does not assign him his place, as certainly as if he were marshalled to it by a lackey. All his mock tranquillity and assumed ease of manner will not be proof against the icy dignity of a grande dame; but in the Club he's as good as the best, or he'll think so, which comes to the same thing."

"Cavendish is right,—that is, as much so as he can be in anything," said Willoughby, laughing. "Don't put him up, Martin."

"Then what am I to do? I have given a sort of a pledge. He is not easily put off; he does not lightly relinquish an object."

"Take him off the scent. Introduce him at the Embassy. Take him to the Courcelles."

"This is intolerable," broke in Martin, angrily. "I ask for advice, and you reply by a sneer and a mockery."

"Not at all. I never was more serious. But here he comes! Look only how the fellow lolls back in the phaeton. Just see how contemptuously he looks down on the foot-travellers. I'd lay on another hundred for that stare; for, assuredly, he has already made the purchase in his own mind."

"Well, Merl, what do you say to Sir Spencer's taste in horseflesh?" said Martin, as he entered.

"They're nice hacks; very smart."

"Nice hacks!" broke in Cavendish, "why, sir, they're both thoroughbred; the near horse is by Tiger out of a Crescent mare, and the off one won the Acton steeple-chase. When you said hacks, therefore, you made a cruel blunder."

"Well, it's what a friend of mine called them just now," said Merl; "and remarked, moreover, that the large horse had been slightly fired on the—the—I forget the name he gave it."

"You probably remember your friend's name better," said Cavendish, sneeringly. "Who was he, pray?"

"Massingbred,—we call him Jack Massingbred; he's the Member for somewhere in Ireland."

"Poor Jack!" muttered Cavendish, "how hard up he must be!"

"But you like the equipage, Merl?" said Martin, who had a secret suspicion that it was now Cavendish's turn for a little humiliation.

"Well, it's neat. The buggy—"

"The buggy! By Jove, sir, you have a precious choice of epithets! Please to let me inform you that full-blooded horses are not called hacks, nor one of Leader's park-phaetons is not styled a buggy."

Martin threw himself into a chair, and after a moment's struggle, burst out into a fit of laughter.

"I think we may make a deal after all, Sir Spencer," said Merl, who accepted the baronet's correction with admirable self-control.

"No, sir; perfectly impossible; take my word for it, any transaction would be difficult between us. Good-bye, Martin; adieu, Claude." And with this brief leave-taking the peppery Sir Spencer left the room, more flushed and fussy than he had entered it.

"If you knew Sir Spencer Cavendish as long as we have known him, Mr. Merl," said Lord Claude, in his blandest of voices, "you'd not be surprised at this little display of warmth. It is the only weakness in a very excellent fellow."

"I 'm hot, too, my Lord," said Merl, with the very slightest accentuation of the "initial H," "and he was right in saying that dealings would be difficult between us."

"You mentioned Massingbred awhile ago, Merl. Why not ask him to second you at the Club?" said Martin, rousing himself suddenly from a train of thought.

"Well, somehow, I thought that he and you did n't exactly pull together; that there was an election contest,—a kind of a squabble."

"I 'm sure that *he* never gave you any reason to suspect a coldness between us; I know that *I* never did," said Martin, calmly. "We are but slightly acquainted, it is true, but I should be surprised to learn that there was any ill-feeling between us."

"One's opponent at the hustings is pretty much the same thing as one's adversary at a game,—he is against you to-day, and may be your partner to-morrow; so that, putting even better motives aside, it were bad policy to treat him as an implacable enemy," said Lord Claude, with his accustomed suavity. "Besides, Mr. Merl, you know the crafty maxim of the French moralist, 'Always treat your enemies as though one day they were to become your friends.'" And with this commonplace, uttered in a tone and with a manner that gave it all the semblance of a piece of special advice, his Lordship took his hat, and, squeezing Martin's hand, moved towards the door.

"Come in here for a moment," said Martin, pushing open the door into an adjoining dressing-room, and closing it carefully after them. "So much for wanting to do a good-natured thing," cried he, peevishly. "I thought to help Cavendish to get rid of those 'screws,' and the return he makes me is to outrage this man."

"What are your dealings with him?" asked Willoughby" anxiously.

"Play matters, play debts, loans, securities, post-obits, and every other blessed contrivance you can think of to swamp a man's present fortune and future prospects. I don't think he is a bad fellow; I mean, I don't suspect he'd press heavily upon me, with any fair treatment on my part. My impression, in short, is that he'd forgive my not meeting his bill, but he'd never get over my not inviting him to a dinner!"

"Well," said Willoughby, encouragingly, "we live in admirable times for such practices. There used to be a vulgar prejudice in favor of men that one knew, and names that the world was familiar with. It is gone by entirely; and if you only present your friend—don't wince at the title—your friend, I say—as the rich Mr. Merl, the man who owns shares in mines, canals, and collieries, whose speculations count by tens of thousands, and whose credit rises to millions, you'll never be called on to apologize for his parts of speech, or make excuse for his solecisms in good breeding."

"Will you put up his name, then, at the Club?" asked Martin, eagerly. "It would not do for *me* to do so."

"To be sure I will, and Massingbred shall be his seconder." And with this cheering pledge Lord Claude bade him good-bye, and left him free to return to Mr. Merl in the drawing-room. That gentleman had, however, already departed, to the no small astonishment of Martin, who now threw himself lazily down on a sofa, to ponder over his difficulties and weave all manner of impracticable schemes to meet them.

They were, indeed, very considerable embarrassments. He had raised heavy sums at most exorbitant rates, and obtained money—for the play-table—by pledging valuable reversions of various kinds, for Merl somehow was the easiest of all people to deal with; one might have fancied that he lent his money only to afford himself an occasion of sympathy with the borrower, just as he professed that he merely betted "to have a little interest in the race." Whatever Martin, then, suggested in the way of security never came amiss; whether it were a farm, a mill, a quarry, or a lead mine, he accepted it at once, and, as Martin deemed, without the slightest knowledge or investigation, little suspecting that there was not a detail of his estate, nor a resource of his property, with which the wily Jew was not more familiar than himself. In fact, Mr. Merl was an astonishing instance of knowledge on every subject by which money was to be made, and he no more advanced loans upon an encumbered estate than he backed the wrong horse or bid for a copied picture. There is a species of practical information excessively difficult to describe, which is not connoisseurship, but which supplies the place of that quality, enabling him who possesses it to estimate the value of an object, without any admixture of those weakening prejudices which beset your mere man of taste. Now, Mr. Merl had no caprices about the color of the horse he backed, no more than for the winning seat at cards; he could not be warped from his true interests by any passing whim, and whether he cheapened a Correggio or discounted a bill, he was the same calm, dispassionate calculator of the profit to come of the transaction.

Latterly, however, he had thrown out a hint to Martin that he was curious to see some of that property on which he had made such large advances; and this wish—which, according to the frame of mind he happened to be in at the moment, struck Martin as a mere caprice or a direct menace—was now the object of his gloomy reveries. We have not tracked his steps through the tortuous windings of his moneyed difficulties; it is a chapter in life wherein there is wonderfully little new to record; the Jew-lender and his associates, the renewed bill and the sixty per cent, the non-restored acceptances flitting about the world, sold and resold as damaged articles, but always in the end falling into the hands of a "most respectable party," and proceeded on as a true debt; then, the compromises for time, for silence, for secrecy,—since these transactions are rarely, if ever, devoid of some unhappy incident that would not bear publicity; and there are invariably little notes beginning "Dear Moses," which would argue most ill-chosen intimacies. These are all old stories, and the "Times" and the "Chronicle" are full of them. There is a terrible sameness about them, too. The dupe and the villain are stock characters that never change, and the incidents are precisely alike in every case. Humble folk, who are too low for fashionable follies, wonder how the self-same artifices have always the same success, and cannot conceal their astonishment at the innocence of our young men about town; and yet the mystery is easily solved. The dupe is, in these cases, just as unprincipled as his betrayer, and their negotiation is simply a game of skill, in which Israel is not always the winner.

If we have not followed Martin's steps through these dreary labyrinths, it is because the path is a worn one; for the same reason, too, we decline to keep him company in his ponderings over them. All that his troubles had taught him was an humble imitation of the tricky natures of those he dealt with; so that he plotted and schemed and contrived, till his very head grew weary with the labor. And so we leave him.

CHAPTER III
A YOUNG DUCHESS AND AN OLD FRIEND

Like a vast number of people who have passed years in retirement, Lady Dorothea was marvellously disappointed with "the world" when she went back to it. It was not at all the kind of thing she remembered, or at least fancied it to be. There were not the old gradations of class strictly defined; there was not the old veneration for rank and station; "society" was invaded by hosts of unknown people, "names one had never heard of." The great stars of fashion of her own day had long since set, and the new celebrities had never as much as heard of her. The great houses of the Faubourg were there, it is true; but with reduced households and dimly lighted salons, they were but sorry representatives of the splendor her memory had invested them with.

Now the Martins were installed in one of the finest apartments of the finest quarter in Paris. They were people of unquestionable station, they had ample means, lacked for none of the advantages which the world demands from those who seek its favors; and yet there they were, just as unknown, unvisited, and unsought after, as if they were the Joneses or the Smiths, "out" for a month's pleasuring on the Continent.

A solitary invitation to the Embassy to dinner was not followed by any other attention; and so they drove along the Boulevards and through the Bois de Boulogne, and saw some thousands of gay, bright-costumed people, all eager for pleasure, all hurrying on to some scheme of amusement or enjoyment, while they returned moodily to their handsome quarter, as much excluded from all participation in what went on around them as though they were natives of Hayti.

Martin sauntered down to the reading-room, hoping vainly to fall in with some one he knew. He lounged listlessly along the bright streets, till their very glare addled him; he stared at the thousand new inventions of luxury and ease the world had discovered since he had last seen it, and then he plodded gloomily homeward, to dine and listen to her Ladyship's discontented criticism upon the tiresome place and the odious people who filled it. Paris was, indeed, a deception and a snare to them! So far from finding it cheap, the expense of living—as they lived—was considerably greater than at London. It was a city abounding in luxuries, but all costly. The details which are in England reserved for days of parade and display, were here daily habits, and these were now to be indulged in with all the gloom of solitude and isolation.

What wonder, then, if her Ladyship's temper was ruffled, and her equanimity unbalanced by such disappointments? In vain she perused the list of arrivals to find out some distinguished acquaintance; in vain she interrogated her son as to what was going on, and who were there. The Captain only frequented the club, and could best chronicle the names that were great at whist or illustrious at billiards.

"It surely cannot be the season here," cried she, one morning, peevishly, "for really there isn't a single person one has ever heard of at Paris."

"And yet this is a strong catalogue," cried the Captain, with a malicious twinkle in his eye. "Here are two columns of somebodies, who were present at Madame de Luygnes' last night."

"You can always fill salons, if that be all," said she, angrily.

"Yes, but not with Tour du Pins, Tavannes, Rochefoucaulds, Howards of Maiden, and Greys of Allington, besides such folk as Pahlen, Lichtenstein, Colonna, and so forth."

"How is it then, that one never sees them?" cried she, more eagerly.

"Say, rather, how is it one doesn't know them," cried Martin, "for here we are seven weeks, and, except to that gorgeous fellow in the cocked hat at the porter's lodge, I have never exchanged a salute with a human being."

"There are just three houses, they say, in all Paris, to one or other of which one must be presented," said the Captain—"Madame de Luygnes, the Duchesse de Cour-celles, and Madame de Mirecourt."

"That Madame de Luygnes was your old mistress, was she not, Miss Henderson?" asked Lady Dorothea, haughtily.

"Yes, my Lady," was the calm reply.

"And who are these other people?"

"The Duc de Mirecourt was married to 'Mademoiselle,' the daughter of the Duchesse de Luygnes."

"Have you heard or seen anything of them since you came here?" asked her Ladyship.

"No, my Lady, except a hurried salute yesterday from a carriage as we drove in. I just caught sight of the Duchesse as she waved her hand to me."

"Oh, I saw it. I returned the salutation, never suspecting it was meant for *you*. And she was your companion—your dear friend—long ago?"

"Yes, my Lady," said Kate, bending down over her work, but showing in the crimson flush that spread over her neck how the speech had touched her.

"And you used to correspond, I think?" continued her Ladyship.

"We did so, my Lady."

"And she dropped it, of course, when she married,—she had other things to think of?"

"I 'm afraid, my Lady, the lapse was on *my* side," said Kate, scarcely repressing a smile at her own hardihood.

"*Your* side! Do you mean to say that you so far forgot what was due to the station of the Duchesse de Mirecourt, that you left her letter unreplied to?"

"Not exactly, my Lady."

"Then, pray, what do you mean?"

Kate paused for a second or two, and then, in a very calm and collected voice, replied,—"I told the Duchesse, in my last letter, that I should write no more,—that my life was thrown in a wild, unfrequented region, where no incident broke the monotony, and that were I to continue our correspondence, my letters must degenerate into a mere selfish record of my own sentiments, as unprofitable to read as ungraceful to write; and so I said good-bye—or *au revoir*, at least—till other scenes might suggest other thoughts."

"A most complimentary character of our Land of the West, certainly! I really was not aware before that Cro' Martin was regarded as an 'oubliette.'"

Kate made no answer,—a silence which seemed rather to irritate than appease her Ladyship.

"I hope you included the family in your dreary picture. I trust it was not a mere piece of what artists call still life, Miss Henderson?"

"No, my Lady," said she, with a deep sigh; but the tone and manner of the rejoinder were anything but apologetic.

"Now I call that as well done as anything one sees in Hyde Park," cried the Captain, directing attention as he spoke to a very handsome chariot which had just driven up to the door. "They're inquiring for somebody here," continued he, as he watched the Chasseur as he came and went from the carriage to the house.

"There's a Grandee of Spain, or something of that kind, lives on the fourth floor, I think," said Martin, dryly.

"The Duchesse de Mirecourt, my Lady," said a servant, entering, "begs to know if your Ladyship will receive her?"

Kate started at the words, and her color rose till her cheeks were crimsoned.

"A visit, I suspect, rather for you than me, Miss Henderson," said Lady Dorothea, in a half-whisper; and then turning to her servant, nodded her acquiescence.

"I 'm off," said Martin, rising suddenly to make his escape.

"And I too," said the Captain, as he made his exit by an opposite door.

The folding-doors of the apartment were at the same moment thrown wide, and the Duchess entered. Very young,—almost girlish, indeed,—she combined in her appearance the charming freshness of youth with that perfection of gracefulness which attaches to the higher classes of French society, and although handsome, more striking from the fascination of manner than for any traits of beauty. Courtesying slightly, but deferentially, to Lady Dorothea, she apologized for her intrusion by the circumstance of having, the day before, caught sight of her "dear governess and dear friend—" And as she reached thus far, the deep-drawn breathing of another attracted her. She turned and saw Kate, who, pale as a statue, stood leaning on a chair. In an instant she was in her arms, exclaiming, in a rapture of delight, "My dear, dear Kate,—my more than sister! You would forgive me, madam," said she, addressing Lady Dorothea, "if you but knew what we were to each other. Is it not so, Kate?"

A faint tremulous motion of the lips—all colorless as they were—was the only reply to the speech; but the young Frenchwoman needed none, but turning to her Ladyship, poured forth with native volubility a story of their friendship, the graceful language in which she uttered it lending those choice phrases which never seem exaggerations of sentiment till they be translated into other tongues. Mingling her praises with half reproaches, she drew a picture of Kate so flattering that Lady Dorothea could not help a sense of shrinking terror that one should speak in such terms of the governess.

"And now, dearest," added she, turning to Kate, "are we to see a great deal of each other? When can you come to me? Pardon me, madam, this question should be addressed to you."

"Miss Henderson is my secretary, Madame la Duchesse; she is also my companion," said Lady Dorothea, haughtily; "but I can acknowledge claims which take date before my own. She shall be always at liberty when you wish for her."

"How kind, how good of you!" cried the Duchess. "I could have been certain of that. I knew that my dear Kate must be loved by all around her. We have a little *fête* on Wednesday at St. Germain. May I bespeak her for that day?"

"Her Ladyship suffers her generosity to trench upon her too far," said Kate, in a low voice. "I am in a manner necessary to her,—that is, my absence would be inconvenient."

"But her Ladyship will doubtless be in the world herself that evening. There is a ball at the Duchesse de Sargance, and the Austrian Minister has something," rattled on the lively Duchess. "Paris is so gay just now, so full of pleasant people, and all so eager for enjoyment. Don't you find it so, my Lady?"

"I go but little into society!" said Lady Dorothea, stiffly.

"How strange! and I—I cannot live without it. Even when we go to our Château at Roche-Mire I carry away with me all my friends who will consent to come. We try to imitate that delightful life of your country houses, and make up that great family party which is the *beau idéal* of social enjoyment."

"And you like a country life, then?" asked her Ladyship.

"To be sure. I love the excursions on horseback, the forest drives, the evening walks in the trellised vines, the parties one makes to see a thousand things one never looks at afterwards; the little dinners on the grass, with all their disasters, and the moonlight drive homewards, half joyous, half romantic,—not to speak of that charming frankness by which every one makes confession of his besetting weakness, and each has some little secret episode of his own life to tell the others. All but Kate here," cried she, laughingly, "who never revealed anything."

"Madame la Duchesse will, I 'm sure, excuse my absence; she has doubtless many things she would like to say to her friend alone," said Lady Dorothea, rising and courtesying formally; and the young Duchess returned the salutation with equal courtesy and respect.

"My dear, dear Kate," cried she, throwing her arms around her as the door closed after her Ladyship, "how I have longed for this moment, to tell you ten thousand things about myself and hear from you as many more! And first, dearest, are you happy? for you look more serious, more thoughtful than you used,—and paler, too."

"Am I so?" asked Kate, faintly.

"Yes. When you're not speaking, your brows grow stern and your lips compressed. Your features have not that dear repose, as Giorgevo used to call it. Poor fellow! how much in love he was, and you 've never asked for him!"

"I never thought of him!" said she, with a smile.

"Nor of Florian, Kate!"

"Nor even of him."

"And yet that poor fellow was really in love,—nay, don't laugh, Kate, I know it. He gave up his career, everything he had in life,—he was a Secretary of Legation, with good prospects,—all to win your favor, becoming a 'Carbonaro,' or a 'Montagnard,' or something or other that swears to annihilate all kings and extirpate monarchy."

"And after that?" asked Kate, with more of interest.

"After that, ma chère, they sent him to the galleys; I forget exactly where, but I think it was in Sicily. And then there was that Hungarian Count Nemescz, that wanted to kill somebody who picked up your bouquet out of the Grand Canal at Venice."

"And whom, strangely enough, I met and made acquaintance with in Ireland. His name is Massingbred."

"Not the celebrity, surely,—the young politician who made such a sensation by a first speech in Parliament t'other day? He's all the rage here. Could it be him?"

"Possibly enough," said she, carelessly. "He had very good abilities, and knew it."

"He comes to us occasionally, but I scarcely have any acquaintance with him. But this is not telling me of yourself, child. Who and what are these people you are living with? Do they value my dear Kate as they ought? Are they worthy of having her amongst them?"

"I 'm afraid not," said Kate, with a smile. "They do not seem at all impressed with the blessing they enjoy, and only treat me as one of themselves."

"But, seriously, child, are they as kind as they should be? That old lady is, to my thinking, as austere as an Archduchess."

"I like her," said Kate; "that is, I like her cold, reserved manner, unbending as it is, which only demands the quiet duties of servitude, and neither asks nor wishes for affection. She admits me to no friendship, but she exacts no attachment."

"And you like this?"

"I did not say I should like it from *you!* said Kate, pressing the hand she held fervently to her lips, while her pale cheek grew faintly red.

"And you go into the world with her,—at least *her* world?"

"She has none here. Too haughty for second-rate society, and unknown to those who form the first class at Paris, she never goes out."

"But she would—she would like to do so?"

"I 'm sure she would."

"Then mamma shall visit her. You know she is everything here; her house is the rendezvous of all the distinguished people, and, once seen in her salons, my Lady—how do you call her?"

"Lady Dorothea Martin."

"I can't repeat it—but no matter—her Ladyship shall not want for attentions. Perhaps she would condescend to come to me on Wednesday? Dare I venture to ask her?"

Kate hesitated, and the Duchess quickly rejoined,—"No, dearest, you are quite right; it would be hazardous, too abrupt, too unceremonious. You will, however, be with us; and I long to present you to all my friends, and show them one to whom I owe so much, and ought to be indebted to for far more. I 'll send for you early, that we may have a long morning together." And so saying, she arose to take leave.

"I feel as though I 'll scarcely believe I had seen you when you have gone," said Kate, earnestly. "I'll fancy it all a dream—or rather, that my life since we met has been one, and that we had never parted."

"Were we not very happy then, Kate?" said the Duchess, with a half-sigh; "happier, perhaps, than we may ever be again."

"*You* must not say so, at all events," said Kate, once more embracing her. And they parted.

Kate arose and watched the splendid equipage as it drove away, and then slowly returned to her place at the work-table. She did not, however, resume her embroidery, but sat deep in reflection, with her hands clasped before her.

"Poor fellow!" said she, at length, "a galley-slave, and Massingbred a celebrity! So much for honesty and truth in this good world of ours! Can it always go on thus? That is the question I'm curious to hear solved. A little time may, perhaps, reveal it!" So saying to herself, she leaned her head upon her hand, deep lost in thought.

CHAPTER IV
A VERY GREAT FAVOR

Amongst the embarrassments of story-telling there is one which, to be appreciated, must have been experienced; it is, however, sufficiently intelligible to claim sympathy even by indicating,—we mean the difficulty a narrator has in the choice of those incidents by which his tale is to be marked out, and the characters who fill it adequately depicted.

It is quite clear that a great number of events must occur in the story of every life of which no record can be made; some seem too trivial, some too irrelevant for mention, and yet, when we come to reflect upon real life itself, how many times do we discover that what appeared to be but the veriest trifles were the mainsprings of an entire existence, and the incidents which we deemed irrelevant were the hidden links that connected a whole chain of events? How easy, then, to err in the selection! This difficulty presents itself strongly to us at present; a vast number of circumstances rise before us from which we must refrain, lest they should appear to indicate a road we are not about to travel; and, at the same time, we feel the want of those very events to reconcile what may well seem contradictions in our history.

It not unfrequently happens that an apology is just as tiresome as the offence it should excuse; and so, without further explanation, we proceed. Lady Dorothea soon found herself as much sought after as she had previously been neglected. The Duchesse de Luygnes was the great leader of fashion at Paris; and the marked attentions by which she distinguished her Ladyship at once established her position. Of course her unquestionable claim to station, and her own high connections rendered the task less difficult; while it imparted to Lady Dorothea's own manner and bearing that degree of dignity and calm which never accompany an insecure elevation.

With such refinement of delicacy, such exquisite tact, was every step managed that her Ladyship was left to suppose every attention she received sprung out of her own undeniable right to them, and to the grace and charm of a manner which really had had its share of success some five-and-thirty years before. The gloomy isolation she had passed through gave a stronger contrast to the enjoyment of her present life; and for the first time for years she regained some of that courtly elegance of address which in her youth had pre-eminently distinguished her. The change had worked favorably in her temper also; and Martin perceived, with astonishment, that she neither made injurious comparisons between the present and the past, nor deemed the age they lived in one of insufferable vulgarity. It would scarcely have been possible for Lady Dorothea not to connect her altered position with the friendship between Kate Henderson and her former pupil; she knew it, and she felt it. All her self-esteem could not get over this consciousness; but it was a humiliation reserved for her own heart, since nothing in Kate's manner indicated even a suspicion of the fact. On the contrary, never had she shown herself more submissive and dependent. The duties of her office, multiplied as they were tenfold by her Ladyship's engagements, were all punctually acquitted, and with a degree of tact and cleverness that obtained from Lady Dorothea the credit of a charming note-writer. Nor was she indifferent to the effect Kate produced in society, where her beauty and fascination had already made a deep impression.

Reserving a peculiar deference and respect for all her intercourse with Lady Dorothea, Kate Henderson assumed to the world at large the ease and dignity of one whose station was the equal of any. There was nothing in her air or bearing that denoted the dependant; there was rather a dash of haughty superiority, which did not scruple to avow itself and bid defiance to any bold enough to question its claims. Even this was a secret flattery to Lady Dorothea's heart; and she saw with satisfaction the success of that imperious tone which to herself was subdued to actual humility.

Lady Dorothea Martin and her beautiful companion were now celebrities at Paris; and, assuredly, no city of the world knows how to shower more fascinations on those it favors. Life became to them a round of brilliant festivities. They received invitations from every quarter, and everywhere were met with that graceful welcome so sure to greet those whose airs and whose dress are the ornaments of a salon. They "received" at home, too; and her Ladyship's Saturdays were about the most exclusive of all Parisian receptions. Tacitly, at least, the whole management and direction of these "Evenings" was committed to Kate. Martin strictly abstained from a society in every way distasteful to him. The Captain had come to care for nothing but play, so that the Club was his only haunt; and it was the rarest of all events to see him pass even a few minutes in the drawing-room. He had, besides, that degree of shrinking dislike to Kate Henderson which a weak man very often experiences towards a clever and accomplished girl. When he first joined his family at Paris, he was struck by her great beauty and the elegance of a manner that might have dignified any station, and he fell partly in love,—that is to say, as much in love as a captain of hussars could permit himself to feel for a governess. He condescended to make small advances, show her petty attentions, and even distinguish her by that flattering stare, with his glass to his eye, which he had known to be what the poet calls "blush-compelling" in many a fair cheek in provincial circles.

To his marvellous discomfiture, however, these measures were not followed by any success. She never as much as seemed aware of them, and treated him with the same polite indifference, as though he had been neither a hussar nor a lady-killer. Of course he interpreted this as a piece of consummate cunning; he had no other measure for her capacity than would have been suited to his own. She was a deep one, evidently bent on drawing him on, and entangling him in some stupid declaration, and so he grew cautious. But, somehow, his reserve provoked as little as his boldness. She did not change in the least; she treated him with a quiet, easy sort of no-notice,—the most offensive thing possible to one bent upon being impressive, and firmly persuaded that he need only wish, to be the conqueror.

Self-worship was too strong in him to suffer a single doubt as to his own capacity for success, and therefore the only solution to the mystery of her manner was its being an artful scheme, which time and a little watching would surely explain. Time went on, and yet he grew none the wiser; Kate continued the same impassive creature as at first. She never sought,—never avoided him. She met him without constraint,—without pleasure, too. They never became intimate, while there was no distance in their intercourse; till at last, wounded in his self-esteem, he began to feel that discomfort in her presence which only waits for the slightest provocation to become actual dislike.

With that peevishness that belongs to small minds, he would have been glad to have discovered some good ground for hating her; and a dozen times a day did he fancy that he had "hit the blot," but somehow he always detected his mistake erelong; and thus did he live on in that tantalizing state of uncertainty and indecision which combines about as much suffering as men of his stamp are capable of feeling.

If Lady Dorothea never suspected the degree of influence Kate silently exercised over her, the Captain saw it palpably, and tried to nourish the knowledge into a ground for dislike. But somehow she would no more suffer herself to be hated than to be loved, and invariably baffled all his attempts to "get up" an indignation against her. By numberless devices—too slight, too evanescent to be called regular coquetry—she understood how to conciliate him, even in his roughest moods, while she had only to make the very least possible display of her attractions to fascinate him in his happier moments.

The gallant hussar was not much given to self-examination. It was one of the last positions he would have selected; and yet he had confessed to his own heart that, though he 'd not like to marry her himself, he 'd be sorely tempted to shoot any man who made her his wife.

Lady Dorothea and Kate Henderson were seated one morning engaged in the very important task of revising the invitation-book,—weeding out the names of departed acquaintance, and canvassing the claims of those who should succeed them. The rigid criticism as to eligibility showed how great an honor was the card for her Ladyship's "Tea." While they were thus occupied, Captain Martin entered the room with an open letter in his hand, his air and manner indicating flurry, if not actual agitation.

"Sorry to interrupt a privy council," said he, "but I've come to ask a favor,—don't look frightened; it's not for a woman, my Lady,—but I want a card for your next Saturday, for a male friend of mine."

"Kate has just been telling me that 'our men' are too numerous."

"Impossible. Miss Henderson knows better than any one that the success of these things depends on having a host of men,—all ages, all classes, all sorts of people," said he, indolently.

"I think we have complied with your theory," said she, pointing to the book before her. "If our ladies are chosen for their real qualities, the men have been accepted with a most generous forbearance."

"One more, then, will not damage the mixture."

"Of course, Captain Martin, it is quite sufficient that he is a friend of yours—that you wish it—"

"But it is no such thing, Miss Henderson," broke in Lady Dorothea. "We have already given deep umbrage in many quarters—very high quarters, too—by refusals; and a single mistake would be fatal to us."

"But why need this be a mistake?" cried Captain Martin, peevishly. "The man is an acquaintance of mine,—a friend, if you like to call him so."

"And who is he?" asked my Lady, with all the solemnity of a judge.

"A person I met at the Cape. We travelled home together—saw a great deal of each other—in fact—I know him as intimately as I do—any officer in my regiment," said the Captain, blundering and faltering at every second word.

"Oh! then he is one of your own corps?" said her Ladyship.

"I never said so," broke he in. "If he had been, I don't fancy I should need to employ much solicitation in his behalf; the—they are not usually treated in that fashion!"

"I trust we should know how to recognize their merits," said Kate, with a look which sorely puzzled him whether it meant conciliation or raillery.

"And his name?" asked my Lady. "His name ought to be decisive, without anything more!"

"He's quite a stranger here, knows nobody, so that you incur no risk as to any impertinent inquiries, and when he leaves this, to-morrow or next day, you 'll never see him again." This the Captain said with all the confusion of an inexpert man in a weak cause.

"Shall I address his card, or will you take it yourself, Captain Martin?" said Kate, in a low voice.

"Write Merl,—Mr. Herman Merl," said he, dropping his own voice to the same tone.

"Merl!" exclaimed Lady Dorothea, whose quick hearing detected the words. "Why, where on earth could you have made acquaintance with a man called Merl?"

"I have told you already where and how we met; and if it be any satisfaction to you to know that I am under considerable obligations—heavy obligations—to this same gentleman, perhaps it might incline you to show him some mark of attention."

"You could have him to dinner at your Club,—you might even bring him here, when we're alone, Harry; but really, to receive him at one of our Evenings! You know how curious people are, what questions they will ask:—'Who is that queer-looking man?'—I 'm certain he is so.—'Is he English?'—'Who does he belong to?'—'Does he know any one?'"

"Let them ask me, then," said Martin, "and I may, perhaps, be able to satisfy them." At the same moment he took up from the table the card which Kate had just written, giving her a look of grateful recognition as he did so.

"You 've done this at your own peril, Miss Henderson," said Lady Dorothea, half upbraidingly.

"At *mine*, be it rather," said the Captain, sternly.

"I accept my share of it willingly," said Kate, with a glance which brought a deep flush over the hussar's cheek, and sent through him a strange thrill of pleasure.

"Then I am to suppose we shall be honored with your own presence on this occasion,—rare favor that it is," said her Ladyship.

"Yes, I 'll look in. I promised Merl to present him."

"Oh, you need n't!" said she, peevishly. "Half the men merely make their bow when they meet me, and neither expect me to remember who they are or to notice them. I may leave your distinguished friend in the same category."

A quick glance from Kate—fleeting, but full of meaning—stopped Martin as he was about to make a hasty reply. And, crumpling up the card with suppressed passion, he turned and left the room.

"Don't put that odious name on our list, Miss Henderson," said Lady Dorothea; "we shall never have him again."

"I 'm rather curious to see him," said Kate. "All this discussion has imparted a kind of interest to him, not to say that there would seem something like a mystery in Captain Martin's connection with him."

"I confess to no such curiosity," said my Lady, haughtily. "The taste to be amused by vulgarity is like the passion some people have to see an hospital; you may be interested by the sight, but you may catch a malady for your pains." And with this observation of mingled truth and fallacy her Ladyship sailed proudly out of the room in all the conscious importance of her own cleverness.

CHAPTER V
A LETTER FROM HOME

While this discussion was going on, Martin was seated in his own room, examining the contents of his letter-bag, which the post had just delivered to him. A very casual glance at his features would have discovered that the tidings which met his eye were very rarely of a pleasant character. For the most part the letters were importunate appeals for money, subscriptions, loans, small sums to be repaid when the borrower had risen above his present difficulties, aids to effect some little enterprise on whose very face was failure. Then there were the more formal demands for sums actually due, written in the perfection of coercive courtesy, subjecting the reader to all the tortures of a moral surgical operation, a suffering actually increased by the very dexterity of the manipulator. Then came, in rugged hand and gnarled shape, urgent entreaties for abatements and allowances, pathetic pictures of failing crops, sickness and sorrow! Somewhat in contrast to these in matter—most strikingly unlike them in manner—was a short note from Mr. Maurice Scanlan. Like a rebutting witness in a cause, he spoke of everything as going on favorably; prices were fair, the oat crop a reasonable one. There was distress, to be sure, but who ever saw the West without it? The potatoes had partially failed; but as there was a great deal of typhus and a threat of cholera, there would be fewer to eat them. The late storms had done a good deal of mischief, but as the timber thrown down might be sold without any regard to the entail, some thousand pounds would thus be realized; and as the gale had carried away the new pier at Kilkieran, there would be no need to give a bounty to the fishermen who could not venture out to sea. The damage done to the house and the conservatories at Cro' Martin offered an opportunity to congratulate the owner on the happiness of living in a milder climate; while the local squabbles of the borough suggested a pleasant contrast with all the enjoyments of a life abroad.

On the whole, Mr. Scanlan's letter was rather agreeable than the reverse, since he contrived to accompany all the inevitable ills of fortune by some side-wind consolations, and when pushed hard for these, skilfully insinuated in what way "things might have been worse." If the letter did not reflect very favorably on either the heart or brain that conceived it, it well suited him to whom it was addressed. To screen himself from whatever might irritate him, to escape an unpleasant thought or unhappy reflection, to avoid, above all things, the slightest approach of self-censure, was Martin's great philosophy; and he esteemed the man who gave him any aid in this road. Now newspapers might croak their dark predictions about the coming winter, prophesy famine, fever, and pestilence; Scanlan's letter, "written from the spot," by "one who enjoyed every opportunity for forming a correct opinion," was there, and *he* said matters were pretty much as usual. The West of Ireland had never been a land of milk and honey, and nobody expected it ever would be,—the people could live in it, however, and pay rents too; and as Martin felt that he had no undue severity to reproach himself with, he folded up the epistle, saying that "when a man left his house and property for a while, it was a real blessing to have such a fellow as Scanlan to manage for him;" and truly, if one could have his conscience kept for a few hundreds a year, the compact might be a pleasant one. But even to the most self-indulgent this plan is impracticable; and so might it now be seen in Martin's heightened color and fidgety manner, and that even *he* was not as much at ease within as he wished to persuade himself he was.

Amid the mass of correspondence, pamphlets and newspapers, one note, very small and neatly folded, had escaped Martin's notice till the very last; and it was only as he heaped up a whole bundle to throw into the fire that he discovered this, in Mary's well-known hand. He held it for some time ere he broke the seal, and his features assumed a sadder, graver cast than before. His desertion of her—and he had not blinked the word to himself—had never ceased to grieve him; and however disposed he often felt to throw upon others the blame which attached to himself here, he attempted no casuistry, but stood quietly, without one plea in his favor, before his own heart.

The very consciousness of his culpability had prevented him writing to her as he ought; his letters were few, short, and constrained. Not all the generous frankness of hers could restore to him the candid ease of his former intercourse with her; and every chance expression he used was conned over and canvassed by him, lest it might convey some sentiment, or indicate some feeling foreign to his intention. At length so painful had the task become that he had ceased writing altogether, contenting himself with a message through Kate Henderson,—some excuse about his health, fatigue,-and so forth, ever coupled with a promise that he would soon be himself again, and as active a correspondent as she could desire.

To these apologies Mary always replied in a kindly spirit. Whatever sorrow they might have cost her she kept for herself; they never awakened one expression of impatience, not a word of reproach. She understood him thoroughly,—his easy indolence of disposition, his dislike to a task, his avoidance of whatever was possible to defer; more even than all these, his own unforgiveness of himself for his part towards her. To alleviate, so far as she might, the poignancy of the last, was for a while the great object of all her letters; and so she continued to expatiate on the happy life she was leading, her contentment with the choice she had made of remaining there, throwing in little playful sallies of condolence at her uncle's banishment, and jestingly assuring him how much happier he would be at home!

In whatever mood, however, she wrote, there was a striking absence of whatever could fret or grieve her uncle throughout all her letters. She selected every pleasant topic and the favorable side of every theme to tell of. She never forgot any little locality which he had been partial to, or any of the people who were his favorites; and, in fact, it might have seemed that the great object she had in view was to attach him more and more to the home he had left, and strengthen every tie that bound him to his own country. And all this was done lightly and playfully, and with a pleasant promise of the happiness he should feel on the day of his return.

These letters were about the pleasantest incidents in Martin's present life; and the day which brought him one was sure to pass agreeably, while he made vigorous resolutions about writing a reply, and sometimes got even so far as to open a desk and ruminate over an answer. It so chanced that now a much longer interval had occurred since Mary's last letter, and the appearance of the present note, so unlike the voluminous epistle she usually despatched, struck him with a certain dismay. "Poor Molly," said he, as he broke the seal, "she is growing weary at last; this continued neglect is beginning to tell upon her. A little more, and she 'll believe—as well she may—that we have forgotten her altogether."

The note was even briefer than he had suspected. It was written, too, in what might seem haste, or agitation, and the signature forgotten. Martin's hand trembled, and his chest heaved heavily as he read the following lines:—

"Cro' Martin, Wednesday Night

"Dearest Uncle,—You will not suffer these few lines to remain unanswered, since they are written in all the pressure of a great emergency. Our worst fears for the harvest are more than realized; a total failure in the potatoes—a great diminution in the oat crop; the incessant rains have flooded all the low meadows, and the cattle are almost without forage, while from the same cause no turf can be cut, and even that already cut and stacked cannot be drawn away from the bogs. But, worse than all these, typhus is amongst us, and cholera, they say, coming. I might stretch out this dreary catalogue, but here is enough, more than enough, to awaken your sympathies and arouse you to action. There is a blight on the land; the people are starving—dying. If every sense of duty was dead within us, if we could harden our hearts against every claim of those from whose labor we derive ease, from whose toil we draw wealth and leisure, we might still be recalled to better things by the glorious heroism of these poor people, so nobly courageous, so patient are they in their trials. It is not now that I can speak of the traits I have witnessed of their affection, their charity, their self-denial, and their daring—but now is the moment to show them that we, who have been dealt with more favorably by fortune, are not devoid of the qualities which adorn their nature.

"I feel all the cruelty of narrating these things to you, too far away from the scene of sorrow to aid by your counsel and encourage by your assistance; but it would be worse than cruelty to conceal from you that a terrible crisis is at hand, which will need all your energy to mitigate.

"Some measures are in your power, and must be adopted at once. There must be a remission of rent almost universally, for the calamity has involved all; and such as are a little richer than their neighbors should be aided, that they may be the more able to help them. Some stores of provisions must be provided to be sold at reduced rates, or even given gratuitously. Medical aid must be had, and an hospital of some sort established. The able-bodied must be employed on some permanent work; and for these, we want power from you and some present moneyed assistance. I will not harrow your feelings with tales of sufferings. You have seen misery here—enough, I say—you have witnessed nothing like this, and we are at but the beginning.

"Write to me at once yourself—this is no occasion to employ a deputy—and forgive me, dearest uncle, for I know not what faults of presumption I may have here committed. My head is confused; the crash of misfortunes has addled me, and each succeed so rapidly on each other, that remedies are scarcely employed than they have to be abandoned. When, however, I can tell the people that it is their own old friend and master that sends them help, and bids them to be of good cheer,—when I can show them that, although separated by distance, your heart never ceases to live amongst them,—I know well the magic working of such a spell upon them, and how, with a bravery that the boldest soldier never surpassed, they will rise up against the stern foes of sickness and famine, and do battle with hard fortune manfully.

"You have often smiled at what you deemed my exaggerated opinion of these poor people,—my over-confidence in their capacity for good. Oh—

take my word for it—I never gave them credit for one half the excellence of their natures. They are on their trial now, and nobly do they sustain it!

"I have no heart to answer all your kind questions about myself,—enough that I am well; as little can I ask you about all your doings in Paris. I'm afraid I should but lose temper if I heard that they were pleasant ones; and yet, with my whole soul, I wish you to be happy; and with this,

"Believe me your affectionate

"Mr. Repton has written me the kindest of letters, full of good advice and good sense; he has also enclosed me a check for £100, with an offer of more if wanted. I was low and depressed when his note reached me, but it gave me fresh energy and hope. He proposed to come down here if I wished; but how could I ask such a sacrifice,—how entreat him to face the peril?"

"Tell Captain Martin I wish to speak to him," said Martin, as he finished the perusal of this letter. And in a few minutes after, that gallant personage appeared, not a little surprised at the summons.

"I have got a letter from Mary here," said Martin, vainly endeavoring to conceal his agitation as he spoke, "which I want to show you. Matters are in a sad plight in the West. She never exaggerates a gloomy story, and her account is very afflicting. Read it."

The Captain lounged towards the window, and, leaning listlessly against the wall, opened the epistle.

"You have not written to her lately, then?" asked he, as he perused the opening sentence.

"I am ashamed to say I have not; every day I made a resolution; but somehow—"

"Is all this anything strange or new?" broke in the Captain. "I'm certain I have forty letters from my mother with exactly the same story. In fact, before I ever broke the seal, I'd have wagered an equal fifty that the potatoes had failed, the bogs were flooded, the roads impassable, and the people dying in thousands; and yet, when spring came round, by some happy miracle they were all alive and merry again!"

"Read on," said Martin, impatiently, and barely able to control himself at this heartless commentary.

"Egad! I'd have sworn I had read all this before, except these same suggestions about not exacting the rents, building hospitals, and so forth;

that *is* new. And why does she say, 'Don't write by deputy'? Who *was* your deputy?"

"Kate Henderson has written for me latterly."

"And I should say she 's quite equal to that sort of thing; she dashes off my mother's notes at score, and talks away, too, all the time she 's writing."

"That is not the question before us," said Martin, sternly.

"When I sent for you to read that letter, it was that you might advise and counsel me what course to take."

"If you can afford to give away a year's income in the shape of rent, and about as much more in the shape of a donation, of course you 're quite free to do it. I only wish that your generosity would begin at home, though; for I own to you I 'm very hard-up at this moment." This the Captain spoke with an attempted jocularity which decreased with every word, till it subsided into downright seriousness ere he finished.

"So far from being in a position to do an act of munificence, I am sorely pressed for money," said Martin.

The Captain started; the half-smile with which he had begun to receive this speech died away on his lips as he asked, "Is this really the case?"

"Most truly so," said Martin, solemnly.

"But how, in the name of everything absurd—how is this possible? By what stratagem could you have spent five thousand a year at Cro' Martin, and your estate was worth almost three times as much? Giving a very wide margin for waste and robbery, I 'd say five thousand could not be made away with there in a twelvemonth."

"Your question only shows me how carelessly you must have read my letters to you, in India," said Martin; "otherwise you could not have failed to see the vast improvements we have been carrying out on the property,—the roads, the harbors, the new quarries opened, the extent of ground covered by plantation,—all the plans, in fact, which Mary had matured—"

"Mary! Mary!" exclaimed the Captain. "And do you tell me that all these things were done at the instigation of a young girl of nineteen or twenty, without any knowledge, or even advice—"

"And who said she was deficient in knowledge?" cried Martin. "Take up the map of the estate; see the lands she has reclaimed; look at the swamps you used to shoot snipe over bearing corn crops; see the thriving village, where once the boatmen were starving, for they dared not venture out to sea without a harbor against bad weather."

"Tell me the cost of all this. What's the figure?" said the Captain; "that's the real test of all these matters, for if *your* income could only feed this outlay, I pronounce the whole scheme the maddest thing in Christendom. My mother's taste for carved oak cabinets and historical pictures is the quintessence of wisdom in comparison."

Martin was overwhelmed and silent, and the other went on,—"Half the fellows in 'ours' had the same story to tell,—of estates wasted, and fine fortunes squandered in what are called improvements. If the possession of a good property entails the necessity to spend it all in this fashion, one is very little better than a kind of land-steward to one's own estate; and, for my part, I'd rather call two thousand a year my own, to do what I pleased with, than have a nominal twenty, of which I must disburse nineteen."

"Am I again to remind you that this is not the question before us?" said Martin, with increased sternness.

"That is exactly the very question," rejoined the Captain. "Mary here coolly asks you, in the spirit of this same improvement-scheme, to relinquish a year's income, and make a present of I know not how much more, simply because things are going badly with them, just as if everybody has n't their turn of ill-fortune. Egad, I can answer for it, *mine* has n't been flourishing latterly, and yet I have heard of no benevolent plan on foot to aid or release me!"

To this heartless speech, uttered, however, in most perfect sincerity, Martin made no reply whatever, but sat with folded arms, deep in contemplation. At length, raising his head, he asked, "And have you, then, no counsel to give,—no suggestion to make me?"

"Well," said he, suddenly, "if Mary has not greatly overcharged all this story—"

"That she has not," cried Martin, interrupting him. "There's not a line, not a word of her letter, I'd not guarantee with all I'm worth in the world."

"In that case," resumed the Captain, in the same indolent tone, "they must be in a sorry plight, and *I* think ought to cut and run as fast as they can. I know that's what *we* do in India; when the cholera comes, we break up the encampment, and move off somewhere else. Tell Mary, then, to advise them to keep out of 'the jungle,' and make for the hill country.'"

Martin stared at the speaker for some seconds, and it was evident how difficult he found it to believe that the words he had just listened to were uttered in deliberate seriousness.

"If you have read that letter, you certainly have not understood it," said he at last, in a voice full of melancholy meaning.

"Egad, it's only too easy of comprehension," replied the Captain; "of all things in life, there's no mistaking a demand for money."

"Just take it with you to your own room, Harry," said Martin, with a manner of more affection than he had yet employed. "It is my firm persuasion that when you have re-read and thought over it, your impression will be a different one. Con it over in solitude, and then come back and give me your advice."

The Captain was not sorry to adopt a plan which relieved him so speedily from a very embarrassing situation, and, folding up the note, he turned and left the room.

There are a great number of excellent people in this world who believe that "Thought," like "Écarté," is a game which requires two people to play. The Captain was one of these; nor was it within his comprehension to imagine how any one individual could suffice to raise the doubts he was called on to canvass or decide. "Who should he now have recourse to?" was his first question; and he had scarcely proposed it to himself when a soft low voice said, "What is puzzling Captain Martin?—can I be of any service to him?" He turned and saw Kate Henderson.

"Only think how fortunate!" exclaimed he. "Just come in here to this drawing-room, and give me your advice."

"Willingly," said she, with a courtesy the more marked because his manner indicated a seriousness that betokened trouble.

"My father has just dismissed me to cogitate over this epistle; as if, after all, when one has read a letter, that any secret or mystical interpretation is to come by all the reconsideration and reflection in the world."

"Am I to read it?" asked Kate, as he placed it in her hand.

"Of course you are," said he.

"There is nothing confidential or private in it which I ought not to see?"

"Nothing; and if there were," added he, warmly, "*you* are one of ourselves, I trust,—at least *I* think you so."

Kate's lips closed with almost stern % impressiveness, but her color never changed at this speech, and she opened the letter in silence. For some minutes she continued to read with the same impassive expression; but gradually her cheek became paler, and a haughty, almost scornful, expression settled on her lips. "So patient are they in their trials," said she, reading aloud the expression of Mary's note. "Is it not possible, Captain Martin, that patience may be pushed a little beyond a virtue, and become something very like cowardice,—abject cowardice? And then," cried she impetuously, and not waiting for his reply, "to say that now is the time to show these poor people the saving care and protection that the rich owe them, as if the duty dated from the hour of their being struck down by famine, laid low by pestilence, or that the debt could ever be acquitted by the relief accorded to pauperism! Why not have taught these same famished creatures self-dependence, elevated them to the rank of civilized beings by the enjoyment of rights that give men self-esteem as well as liberty? What do you mean to do, sir?—or is that your difficulty?" cried she, hastily changing her tone to one of less energy.

"Exactly,—that is *my difficulty*. My father, I suspect, wishes me to concur in the pleasant project struck out by Mary, and that, by way of helping *them*, we should ruin *ourselves*."

"And *you* are for—" She stopped, as if to let him finish her question for her.

"Egad, I don't know well what I'm for, except it be self-preservation. I mean," said he, correcting himself, as a sudden glance of almost insolent scorn shot from Kate's eyes towards him,—"I mean that I 'm certain more than half of this account is sheer exaggeration. Mary is frightened,—as well she may be,—finding herself all alone, and hearing nothing but the high-colored stories the people brings her, and listening to calamities from morning to night."

"But still it *may* be all true," said Kate, solemnly. "It may be—as Miss Martin writes—that 'there is a blight on the land.'"

"What's to be done, then?" asked he, in deep embarrassment.

"The first step is to ascertain what is fact,—the real extent of the misfortune."

"And how is that to be accomplished?" asked he.

"Can you not think of some means?" said she, with a scarcely perceptible approach to a smile.

"No, by Jove! that I cannot, except by going over there one's self."

"And why not that?" asked she, more boldly, while she fixed her large full eyes directly upon him.

"If *you* thought that I ought to go,—if you advised it and would actually say 'Go'—"

"Well, if I should?"

"Then I'd set off to-night; though, to say truth, neither the journey nor the business are much to my fancy."

"Were they ten times less so, sir, I'd say, 'Go,'" said she, resolutely.

"Then go I will," cried the Captain; "and I'll start within two hours."

CHAPTER VI
MR. MERL'S DEPARTURE

Worthy reader, you are neither weak of purpose nor undecided in action; as little are you easily moved by soft influences, when aided by long eyelashes. But had you been so, it would have been no difficult effort for you to comprehend the state of mind in which Captain Martin repaired to his room to make preparation for his journey. There was a kind of half chivalry in his present purpose that nerved and supported him. It was like a knight-errant of old setting out to confront a peril at the behest of his lady-love; but against this animating conviction there arose that besetting sin of small minds,—a sense of distrust,—a lurking suspicion that he might be, all this while, nothing but the dupe of a very artful woman.

"Who can tell," said he to himself, "what plan she may have in all this, or what object she may propose to herself in getting *me* out of the way? I don't think she really cares one farthing about the distress of these people, supposing it all to be true; and as to the typhus fever and cholera, egad! if they be there, one ought to think twice before rushing into the midst of them. And then, again, what do I know about the country or its habits? I have no means of judging if it be poorer or sicklier or; more wretched than usual. To *my* eyes, it always seemed at the lowest depth of want and misery; every one went half starved and more than half naked. I 'm sure there is no necessity for my going some few hundred and odd miles to refresh my memory on this pleasant fact; and yet this is precisely what I 'm about to do. Is it by way of trying her power over me? By Jove, I 've hit it!" cried he, suddenly, as he stopped arranging a mass of letters which he was reducing to order before his departure. "That's her game; there's no doubt of it! She has said to herself, 'This will prove him. If he do this at my bidding, he'll do more.' Ay, but will he, mademoiselle? that's the question. A young hussar may turn out to be a very old soldier. What if I were just to tell her so. Girls of her stamp like a man all the better when he shows himself to be wide-awake. I 'd lay a fifty on it she 'll care more for me when she sees I 'm her own equal in shrewdness. And, after all, why should I go? I could send my valet, Fletcher,—just the kind of fellow for such a mission,—never knew the secret he could n't worm out; there never was a bit of barrack scandal he did n't get to the bottom of. He 'd be back here within a fortnight, with the whole state of the case, and I'll be bound there will be no humbugging *him*."

This bright idea was not, however, without its share of detracting reflections, for what became of all that personal heroism on which he reposed such hope, if the danger were to be encountered by deputy? This was a puzzle, not the less that he had not yet made up his mind whether he 'd really be in love with Kate Henderson, or only involve *her* in an unfortunate attachment for *him*. While he thus pondered and hesitated, strewing his room with the contents of drawers and cabinets, by way of aiding the labor of preparation, his door was suddenly opened, and Mr. Merl made his appearance. Although dressed with all his habitual regard to effect, and more than an ordinary display of chains and trinkets, that gentleman's aspect betokened trouble and anxiety; at least, there was a certain restlessness in his eye that Martin well understood as an evidence of something wrong within.

"Are you getting ready for a journey, Captain?" asked he, as he entered.

"I was thinking of it; but I believe I shall not go. I 'm undecided."

"Up the Rhine?"

"No; not in that direction."

"South,—towards Italy, perhaps?"

"Nor there, either. I was meditating a trip to England."

"We should be on the road together," said Merl. "I'm off by four o'clock."

"How so? What's the reason of this sudden start?"

"There's going to be a crash here," said Merl, speaking in a lower tone. "The Government have been doing the thing with too high a hand, and there's mischief brewing."

"Are you sure of this?" asked Martin.

"Only too sure, that's all. I bought in, on Tuesday last, at sixty-four and an eighth, and the same stock is now fifty-one and a quarter, and will be forty to-morrow. The day after—" Here Mr. Merl made a motion with his outstretched arm, to indicate utter extinction.

"You're a heavy loser, then?" asked Martin, eagerly.

"I shall be, to the tune of some thirteen thousand pounds. It was just on that account I came in here. I shall need money within the week, and must turn those Irish securities of yours into cash,—some of them at least,—and I want a hint from you as to which I ought to dispose of and which hold over.

You told me one day, I remember, that there was a portion of the property likely to rise greatly in value—"

"*You* told me, sir," said Captain Martin, breaking suddenly in, "when I gave you these same bonds, that they should remain in your own hands, and never leave them. That was the condition on which I gave them."

"I suppose, Captain, you gave them for something; you did not make a present of them," said the Jew, coloring slightly.

"If I did not make a present of them," rejoined Martin, "the transaction was about as profitable to me."

"You owed me the money, sir; that, at least, is the way I regard the matter."

"And when I paid it by these securities, you pledged yourself not to negotiate them. I explained to you how the entail was settled,—that the property must eventually be mine,—and you accepted the arrangement on these conditions."

"All true, Captain; but nobody told me, at that time, there was going to be a revolution in Paris,—which there will be within forty-eight hours."

"Confounded fool that I was to trust the fellow!" said Martin to himself, but quite loud enough to be heard; then turning to Merl, he said, "What do you mean by converting them into cash? Are you about to sell part of our estate?"

"Nothing of the kind, Captain," said Merl, smiling at the innocence of the question. "I am simply going to deposit these where I can obtain an advance upon them. I promise you, besides, it shall not be in any quarter by which the transaction can reach the ears of your family. This assurance will, I trust, satisfy *you*, and entitle *me* to the information I ask for."

"What information do you allude to?" asked Martin, who had totally forgotten what the Jew announced as the reason of his visit.

"I asked you, Captain," said Merl, resuming the mincing softness of his usual manner, "as to which of these securities might be the more eligible for immediate negotiation?"

"And how should I know, sir?" replied the other, rudely. "I am very little acquainted with the property itself; I know still less about the kind of dealings you speak of. It does not concern me in the least what you do, or how you do it. I believe I may have given you bonds for something very like double the amount of all you ever advanced to me. I hear of nothing from my father but the immense resources of this, and the great capabilities of that; but as these same eventualities are not destined to better *my* condition,

I have not troubled my head to remember anything about them. You have a claim of about twenty thousand against me."

"Thirty-two thousand four hundred and seventy-eight pounds," said the Jew, reading from a small note-book which he had just taken from his waistcoat pocket.

"That is some ten thousand more than ever I heard of," said Martin, with an hysterical sort of laugh. "Egad, Merl, the fellows were right that would not have you in the 'Cercle.' You 'd have 'cleared every man of them out,'—as well let a ferret into a rabbit warren."

"I was n't aware,—I had not heard that I was put up—"

"To be sure you were; in all form proposed, seconded, and duly blackballed. I own to you, I thought it very hard, very illiberal. There are plenty of fellows there that have no right to be particular; and so Jack Massingbred as much as told them. The fact is, Merl, you ought to have waited awhile, and by the time that Harlowe and Spencer Cavendish and a few more such were as deep in your books as I am, you 'd have had a walk over. Willoughby says the same. It might have cost you something smart, but you 'd have made it pay in the end,—eh, Merl?"

To this speech, uttered in a strain of jocular impertinence, Merl made no reply. He had just torn one of his gloves in pieces in the effort to draw it on, and he was busily exerting himself to get rid of the fragments.

"Lady Dorothea had given me a card for you for Saturday," resumed the Captain; "but as you 're going away—Besides, after this defeat at the Club, you could n't well come amongst all these people; so there's nothing for it but patience, Merl, patience—"

"A lesson that may be found profitable to others, perhaps," said the Jew, with one of his furtive looks at the Captain, who quailed under it at once.

"I was going to give you a piece of advice, Merl," said he, in a tone the very opposite to his late bantering one. "It was, that you should just take a run over to Ireland yourself, and see the property."

"I mean to do so, Captain Martin," said the other, calmly.

"I can't offer you letters, for they would defeat what you desire to accomplish; besides, there is no member of the family there at present but a young lady-cousin of mine."

"Just the kind of introduction I 'd like," said the Jew, with all the zest of a man glad to say what he knew would be deemed an impertinence.

Martin grew crimson with suppressed anger, but never spoke a word.

"Is this the Cousin Mary I have heard you speak of," said Merl,—"the great horsewoman, and she that ventures out alone on the Atlantic in a mere skiff?"

Martin nodded. His temper was almost an overmatch for him, and he dared not trust himself to speak.

"I should like to see her amazingly, Captain," resumed Merl.

"Remember, sir, you have no lien upon *her*," said Martin, sternly.

The Jew smirked and ran his fingers through his hair with the air of one who deemed such an eventuality by no means so very remote.

"Do you know, Master Merl," said Martin, staring at him from head to foot with an expression the reverse of complimentary, "I'm half disposed to give you a few lines to my cousin; and if you'll not take the thing as a *mauvais plaisanterie* on my part, I will do so.". "Quite the contrary, Captain. I'll deem it a great favor, indeed," said Merl, with an admirable affectation of unconsciousness.

"Here goes, then," said Martin, sitting down to a table, and preparing his writing materials, while in a hurried hand he began:—

"'Dear Cousin Mary,—This will introduce to you Mr. Herman Merl, who visits your remote regions on a tour of——What shall I say?"

"Pleasure,—amusement," interposed Merl.

"No, when I *am* telling a fib, I like a big one,—I'll say, philanthropy, Merl; and there's nothing so well adapted to cover those secret investigations you are bent upon,—a tour of philanthropy.

"'You will, I am sure, lend him all possible assistance in his benevolent object,—the same being to dispose of the family acres,—and at the same time direct his attention to whatever may be matter of interest,—whether mines, quarries, or other property easily convertible into cash,—treating him in all respects as one to whom I owe many obligations—and several thousand pounds.'

"Will that do, think you?"

"Perfectly; nothing better."

"In return, I shall ask one favor at your hands," said Martin, as he folded and addressed the epistle. "It is that you write me a full account of what you see in the West,—how the country looks, and the people. Of course it will all seem terribly poor and destitute, and all that sort of thing, to your eyes; but just try and find out if it be worse than usual. Paddy is such a shrewd fellow,

Merl, that it will require all your own sharpness not to be taken in by him. A long letter full of detail—a dash of figures in it—as to how many sheep have the rot, or how many people have caught the fever, will improve it,— you know the kind of thing I mean; and—I don't suppose you care about shooting, yourself, but you 'll get some one to tell you—are the birds plenty and in good condition. There's a certain Mr. Scanlan, if you chance upon him; he 's up to everything, and not a bad performer at dummy whist,— though I think *you* could teach him a thing or two." Merl smiled and tried to look flattered, while the other went on: "And there 's another, called Henderson,—the steward,—a very shrewd person,—but *you* don't need all these particulars; you may be trusted to your own good guidance,—eh, Merl?"

Merl again smiled in the same fashion as before; in fact, so completely had he resumed the bland expression habitual to him, that the Captain almost forgot the unpleasant cause of his visit, and all the disagreeable incidents of the interview.

"You could n't give me a few lines to this Mr. Scanlan?" asked Merl, with an air of easy indifference.

"Nothing easier," cried the Captain, reseating himself; then suddenly rising, with the expression of one to whom a sudden thought had just crossed the mind, "Wait one second for me here, Merl; I'll be back with you at once." And as he spoke he dashed out of the room, and hastened to his father.

"By a rare piece of luck," cried he, as he entered, "I 've just chanced upon the very fellow we want; an acquaintance I picked up at the Cape,— up to everything; he goes over to Ireland to-night, and he 'll take a run down to Cro' Martin, and send us his report of all he sees. Whatever he tells us may be relied upon; for, depend upon 't, no lady can humbug *him*. I 've just given him a note for Mary, and I 'll write a few lines also by way of introducing him to Scanlan."

Martin could barely follow the Captain, as with rapid utterance he poured forth this plan. "Do I know him? What's his name?" asked he at last.

"You never saw him. His name is Merl,—Herman Merl,—a fellow of considerable wealth; a great speculator,—one of those Stock Exchange worthies who never deal in less than tens of thousands. He has a crotchet in his head about buying up half the West of Ireland,—some scheme about flax and the deep-sea fishery. I don't understand it, but I suppose *he* does. At all events, he has plenty of money, and the head to make it fructify; and if he only take a liking to it, he 's the very fellow to buy up Kilkieran, and the islands, and the rest of that waste district you were telling me of t'other night. But I must n't detain him. He starts at four o'clock; and I only ran over here to tell you not to worry yourself any more about Mary's letter. He 'll look to it all."

And with this consolatory assurance the Captain hastened away, leaving Martin as much relieved in mind as an indolent nature and an easy conscience were sure to make him. To get anybody "to look to" anything had been his whole object in life; to know that, whatever happened, there was always somebody who misstated this, or neglected that, at whose door all the culpability—where there was such—could be laid and but for whom he had himself performed miracles of energy and devotedness, and endured all the tortures and trials of a martyr. He was, indeed, as are a great many others in this world, an excellent man to his own heart,—kind, charitable, and affectionate; a well-wisher to his kind, and hopeful of almost every one; but, all this while, his virtues, like a miser's gold, had no circulation; they remained locked up within him for his own use alone, and there he sat, counting them over and gazing at them, speculating upon all that this affluence could do, and—never doing it!

Life abounds with such men. They win respect while they live, and white marble records their virtues when they die! Nor are they all useless. Their outward bearing at least simulates whatever we revere in good men, and we accept them in the same spirit of compromise as we take stucco for stone; if they do no more, they show our appreciation of the "real article."

The Captain was not long in inditing a short note to Scanlan, to whom, "strictly confidential," Mr. Merl was introduced as a great capitalist and speculator, desirous to ascertain all the resources of the land. Scanlan was enjoined to show him every attention, making his visit in all respects as agreeable as possible.

"This fellow will treat you well, Merl," said the Captain, as he folded the letter; "will give you the best salmon you ever tasted, and a glass of Gordon's Madeira such as few could sport now-a-days. And if you have a fancy for a day with my Cousin Mary's hounds, he 'll mount you admirably, and show you the way besides." And with this speech Martin wished him good-bye; and closing the door after him, added, "And if he'll kindly assist you to a broken neck, it's about the greatest service he could render me!"

The laugh, silly and meaningless, that followed his utterance of this speech, showed that it was spoken in all the listlessness of one who had not really character enough to be even a "good hater."

CHAPTER VII
THE CLUB

So little impression had Merl's gloomy forebodings made upon Captain Martin, that he actually forgot everything that this shrewd gentleman predicted, and only partially recalled them when the conversation the next morning at the Club turned on the disturbed state of the capital. People in "society" find it excessively difficult to believe in anything like an organized opposition to the authorities of a government. They are so accustomed to hear of street assemblages being scattered by a few soldiers, mobs routed by a handful of mounted policemen, that they are slow to imagine how any formidable movement can take its rise in such a source. But the maladies of states, like those of the human frame, are often mere trifles in their origin; chance, and the concurrence of events swell their importance, till they assume an aspect of perhaps greater menace than they deserve. This is essentially the case in revolutionary struggles, where, at the outset, none ever contemplates the extent to which the mischief may reach. The proclamation of the "Ordinances," as they were called, had produced a great excitement in Paris. Groups of men in every street were gathered around some one reading aloud the violent commentaries of the public papers; thoughtful and stern faces were met at every corner; a look of expectancy — an expression that seemed to say, What next? — was perceptible on all sides. Many of the shops were half closed, and in some the objects of great value were withdrawn to places of greater security. It was clear to see that men apprehended some great crisis; but whence it should come, or by whose instrumentality promoted, none seemed able to guess. Now and then a mounted orderly would ride by at a smart trot, or a patrol party of dragoons dash past; and the significant glance that followed them indicated how full of meaning these signs appeared.

The day passed in this state of anxious uncertainty; and although the journals discussed the condition of the capital as full of danger and menace, an ostentatious announcement in the "Moniteur" proclaimed Paris to be tranquil. In society — at least in the world of fashion and high life — there were very few who would have disputed the official despatch. "Who and what were they who could dispute the King's Government? Who and where were there either leaders or followers? In what way should they attempt it? The troops in and around Paris numbered something over forty thousand, commanded by an old Marshal of the Empire, now the trustiest adherent of royalty. The days of Mirabeaus and Robespierres and Dantons had passed away; nor were these times in which men would like to recall the reigns of terror and the guillotine." So they reasoned—or, if the phrase be too strong, so they talked—who lounged on soft-cushioned ottomans, or moved listlessly over luxurious carpets; all agreeing that it would be treasonable in the Ministers to retreat or abate one jot of the high prerogative of the Crown. Powdered heads shook significantly, and gold-embroidered vests heaved indignantly at the bare thought that the old spirit of '95 should have survived amongst them; but not one dreamed that the event boded seriously, or that the destinies of a great nation were then in the balance.

It is but five-and-twenty years ago; and how much more have we learned of the manufacture of revolutions in the interval! Barricades and street warfare have become a science, and the amount of resistance a half-armed populace can offer to a regular force is as much a matter of certainty as a mathematical theorem. At that period, however, men were but in the infancy of this knowledge; the traditions of the Great Revolution scarcely were remembered, and, for the most part, they were inapplicable.

What wonder, then, if people in society smiled scornfully at the purposeless masses that occasionally moved past beneath their windows, shouting with discordant voices some fragments of the "Marseillaise," or, as they approached the residence of any in authority, venturing on the more daring cry of "Down with the Ordinances!" The same tone of haughty contempt pervaded the "Club." Young men of fashion, little given to the cares of political life, and really indifferent to the action of laws which never invaded the privileges of the play-table, or curtailed one prerogative of the "Coulisses," felt an angry impatience at all the turbulence and riot of the public streets.

In a magnificently furnished salon of the Club a number of these young men were now assembled. Gathered from every nation of Europe,—many of them bearing names of high historical interest,—they were, so far as dress, air, and appearance went, no ignoble representatives of the class they belonged to. The proud and haughty Spaniard, the fierce-eyed, daring-looking Pole, the pale, intellectual-faced Italian, the courteous Russian, and the fair-haired, stalwart Saxon were all there; and, however dissimilar in type, banded together by the magic influence of the "set" they moved in, to an almost perfect uniformity of sentiment and opinion.

"I vote that any man be fined ten Louis that alludes, however remotely, to this confounded question again," cried Count Gardoni, rising impatiently from his chair and approaching a card-table.

"And I second you!" exclaimed a Polish prince, with a Russian decoration at his button-hole.

"Carried *nem. con.*" said Captain Martin, seating himself at the play-table. "And now for the 'Lansquenet.'" And in a moment every seat was occupied, and purses of gold and pocket-books of bank-notes were strewed over the board. They were all men who played high; and the game soon assumed the grave character that so invariably accompanies large wagers. Wonderfully little passed, except the terms of the game itself. Gambling is a jealous passion, and never admits its votaries to wander in their attention. And now large sums passed from hand to hand, and all the passions of hope and fear racked heads and hearts around, while a decorous silence prevailed; or, when broken, some softly toned voice alone interrupted the stillness.

"Are you going, Martin?" whispered the young French Count de Nevers, as the other moved noiselessly back from the table.

"It is high time, I think," said Martin; "this is my seventeenth night of losing,—losing heavily, too. I'm sick of it!"

"Here's a chance for you, Martin," said a Russian prince, who had just assumed "the bank." "You shall have your choice of color, and your own stake."

"Thanks; but I'll not be tempted."

"I say red, and a thousand francs," cried a Neapolitan.

"There's heavier play outside, I suspect," said Martin, as a wild, hoarse shout from the streets re-echoed through the room.

"A fine,—a fine,—Martin is fined!" cried several around the table.

"You have n't left me wherewithal to pay it, gentlemen," said he, laughing. "I was just about to retire, a bankrupt, into private life."

"That's platoon fire," exclaimed the Pole, as the loud detonation of small arms seemed to shake the very room.

"Czernavitz also fined," cried two together.

"I bow in submission to the Court," said the Pole, throwing down the money on the table.

"Lend *me* as much more," said Martin; "it may change my luck." And with this gambler's philosophy, he again drew nigh the table.

This slight interruption over, the game proceeded as before. Martin, however, was now a winner, every wager succeeding, and every bet he made a gain.

"There's nothing like a dogged persistence," said the Russian. "Fortune never turns her back on him who shows constancy. See Martin, now; by that very resolution he has conquered, and here we are, all cleared out!"

"I am, for one," cried an Italian, flinging his empty purse on the table.

"There's my last Louis," said Nevers. "I reserve it to pay for my supper."

"Martin shall treat us all to supper!" exclaimed another.

"Where shall it be, then?" said Martin; "here, or at my own quarters?"

"Here, by all means," cried some.

"I 'm for the Place Vendôme," said the Pole, "for who knows but we shall catch a glimpse of that beautiful girl, Martin's 'Belle Irlandaise.'"

"I saw her to-night," said the Italian, "and I own she *is* all you say. She was speaking to Villemart, and I assure you the old Minister won't forget it in a hurry. Something or other he said about the noise in the street drew from him the word *canaille*. She turned round at once and attacked him. He replied, and the controversy grew warm; so much so, that many gathered around them to listen, amongst whom I saw the Duc de Guiche, Prince du Saulx, and the Austrian Minister. Nothing could be more perfect than her manner,—calm, without any effrontery; assured, and yet no sacrifice of delicacy. It was easy to see, too, that the theme was not one into which she stumbled by an accident; she knew every event of the Great Revolution, and used the knowledge with consummate skill, and, but for one slip, with consummate temper also.

"What was the slip you allude to?" cried the Russian.

"It was when Villemart, after a boastful enumeration of the superior merits of his order, called them the 'Enlighteners of the People.'

"'You played that part on one occasion,' said she; 'but I scarcely thought you 'd like to refer to it.'

"'How so? When do you mean?' asked he.

"'When they hung you to the lanterns,' said she, with the energy of a tigress in her look. Pardié! at that moment I never saw anything so beautiful or so terrible."

A loud uproar in the street without, in which the sound of troop-horses passaging to and fro could be distinguished, now interrupted the colloquy. As the noise increased, a low, deep roar, like the sound of distant thunder, could be heard, and the Pole cried out,—"Messieurs les Sans-culottes, I strongly advise you to turn homewards, for, if I be not much mistaken, here comes the artillery."

"The affair may turn out a serious one, after all," broke in the Italian.

"A serious one!" echoed the Pole, scornfully. "How can it? Forty battalions of infantry, ten thousand sabres, and eight batteries; are they not enough, think you, to rout this contemptible herd of street rioters?"

"There—listen! It has begun already!" exclaimed Martin, as the sharp report of fire-arms, quite close to the windows, was followed by a crash, and then a wild, mad shout, half rage, half defiance.

"There's nothing for it, in these things, but speedy action," said the Pole; "grape and cavalry charges to clear the streets, and rifle practice at anything that shows itself at the windows."

"It is so easy, so very easy, to crush a mob," said the Russian, "if you only direct your attention to the leader,—think of nothing but *him*. Once you show that, whatever may be the fate of others, death must be his, the whole assemblage becomes a disorganized, unwieldy mass, to be sabred or shot down at pleasure."

"Soldiers have no fancy for this kind of warfare," said De Nevers, haughtily; "victory is never glorious, defeat always humiliation."

"But who talks of defeat?" exclaimed the Pole, passionately. "The officer who could fail against such an enemy should be shot by a court-martial. We have, I believe, every man of us here, served; and I asked you, what disproportion of force could suggest a doubt of success?"

As he spoke, the door of the room was suddenly opened, and a young man, with dress all disordered, and the fragment of a hat in his hand, entered.

"What, Massingbred!" cried one, "how came you to be so roughly handled?"

"So much for popular politeness!" exclaimed the Russian, as he took up the tattered remains of a dress-coat, and exhibited it to the others.

"Pardon me, Prince," replied Massingbred, as he filled a glass of water and drank it off, "this courtesy I received at the hands of the military. I was turning my cab from the Boulevard to enter this street, when a hoarse challenge of a sentry, saying I know not what, attracted my attention. I drew up short to learn, and then suddenly came a rush of the people from behind, which terrified my horse, and set him off at speed; the uproar increasing, the affrighted animal dashed madly onward, the crowd flying on every side, when suddenly a bullet whizzed past my head, cutting my hat in two; a second, at the same instant, struck my horse, and killed him on the spot, cab and all rolling over as he fell. How I arose, gained my legs, and was swept away by the dense torrent of the populace, are events of which I am very far from clear. I only know that although the occurrence happened within half an hour ago, it seems to *me* an affair of days since."

"You were, doubtless, within some line of outposts when first challenged," said the Pole, "and the speed at which you drove was believed to be an arranged plan of attack, for you say the mob followed you."

"Very possibly your explanation is the correct one," said Massingbred, coolly; "but I looked for more steadiness and composure from the troops, while I certainly did not anticipate so much true courtesy and kindness as I met with from the people."

"Parbleu! here's Massingbred becoming Democrat," said one. "The next thing we shall hear is his defence of a barricade."

"You'll assuredly not hear that I attacked one in such company as inflicted all this upon me," rejoined he, with an easy smile.

"Here's the man to captivate your 'Belle Irlandaise,' Martin," cried one. "Already is he a hero and a martyr to Royal cruelty."

"Ah! you came too late to hear that," said the Pole, in a whisper to Massingbred; "but it seems La Henderson became quite a Charlotte Corday this evening, and talked more violent Republicanism than has been heard in a salon since the days of old Égalité."

"All lights must be extinguished, gentlemen," said the waiter, entering hastily. "The street is occupied by troops, and you must pass out by the Rue de Grenelle."

"Are the mobs not dispersing, then?" asked the Russian.

"No, your Highness. They have beaten back the troops from the Quai Voltaire, and are already advancing on the Louvre."

"What absurdity!" exclaimed the Pole. "If the troops permit this, there is treason amongst them."

"I can answer for it there is terror, at least," said Massingbred. "All the high daring and spirit is with what you would call the Sans-culottes."

"That a man should talk this way because he has lost a cab-horse!" cried the Pole, insolently.

"There are men who can bear the loss of a country with more equanimity,—I know that," whispered Massingbred in his ear, with all the calm sternness of an insult.

"You mean this for *me?*" said the Pole, in a low voice.

"Of course I do," was the answer.

"Where?—when?—how?" muttered the Pole, in suppressed passion.

"I leave all at your disposal," said Massingbred, smiling at the other's effort to control his rage.

"At Versailles,—to-morrow morning,—pistols."

Massingbred bowed, and turned away. At the same instant the waiter entered to say that the house must be cleared at once, or all within it consent to remain close prisoners.

"Come along, Martin," said Massingbred, taking his arm. "I shall want you to do me a favor. Let us make our escape by the Rue de Grenelle, and I 'll engage to pilot you safely to your own quarters."

"Has anything passed between you and Czernavitz?" asked Martin, as they gained the street.

"A slight exchange of civilities which requires an exchange of shots," said Jack, calmly.

"By George! I 'm sorry for it. He can hit a franc-piece at thirty paces."

"So can I, Martin; and, what's more, Anatole knows it. He's as brave as a lion, and it is my confounded skill has pushed him on to this provocation."

"He 'll shoot you," muttered Martin, in a half revery.

"Not impossible," said Massingbred. "He's a fellow who cannot conceal his emotions, and will show at once what he means to do."

"Well, what of that?"

"Simply, that if he intends mischief I shall know it, and send a bullet through his heart."

Little as Martin had seen of Massingbred,—they were but Club acquaintances of a few weeks back,—he believed that he was one of those smart, versatile men who, with abundance of social ability, acquire reputation for higher capacity than they possess; but, above all, he never gave him credit for anything like a settled purpose or a stern resolution. It was, then, with considerable astonishment that he now heard him avow this deadly determination with all the composure that could vouch for its sincerity. There was, however, little time to think of these things. The course they were driven to follow, by by-streets and alleys, necessitated a long and difficult way. The great thoroughfares which they crossed at intervals were entirely in the possession of the troops, who challenged them as they approached, and only suffered them to proceed when well satisfied with their account. The crowds had all dispersed, and to the late din and tumult there had succeeded the deep silence of a city sunk in sleep, only broken by the hoarse call of the sentinels, or the distant tramp of a patrol.

"It is all over, I suppose," said Martin. "The sight of the eight-pounders and the dark caissons has done the work."

"I don't think so," said Massingbred, "nor do the troops think so. These mobs are not like ours in England, who, with plenty of individual courage, are always poltroons in the mass. These fellows understand fighting as an art, know how to combine their movements, arrange the modes of attack or defence, can measure accurately the means of resistance opposed to them, and, above all, understand how to be led, — something far more difficult than it seems. In *my* good borough of Oughterard, — or yours, rather, Martin, for I have only a loan of it, — a few soldiers — the army, as they would call them — would sweep the whole population before them. Our countrymen can get up a row, these fellows can accomplish a revolt, — there's the difference."

"And have they any real, substantial grievance that demands such an expiation?"

"Who knows?" said he, laughingly. "There never was a Government too bad to live under, — there never was one exempt from great vices. Half the political disturbances the world has witnessed have arisen from causes remote from State Government; a deficient harvest, a dear loaf, the liberty of the Press invaded, — a tyranny always resented by those who can't read, — are common causes enough. But here we are now at the Place Vendôme, and certainly one should say the odds are against the people."

Massingbred said truly. Two battalions of infantry, with a battery of guns in position, were flanked by four squadrons of Cuirassiers, the formidable array filling the entire "Place," and showing by their air and attitude their readiness for any eventuality. A chance acquaintance with one of the staff enabled Massingbred and Martin to pass through their lines and arrive at their hotel.

"Remember," said the officer who accompanied them, "that you are close prisoners now. My orders are that nobody is to leave the Place under any pretext."

"Why, you can scarcely suspect that the Government has enemies in this aristocratic quarter?" said Massingbred, smiling.

"We have them everywhere," was the brief answer, as he bowed and turned away.

"I scarcely see how I'm to keep my appointment at Versailles to-morrow morning," said Massingbred, as he followed Martin up the spacious stairs. "Happily, Czernavitz knows me, and will not misinterpret my absence."

"Not to say that he may be unable himself to get there," said Martin. As he spoke, they had reached the door, opening which with his key, the Captain motioned to Massingbred to enter.

Massingbred stopped suddenly, and in a voice of deep meaning said, "Your father lives here?"

"Yes,—what then?" asked Martin.

"Only that I have no right to pass his threshold," said the other, in a low voice. "I was his guest once, and I'm not sure that I repaid the hospitality as became me. You were away at the time."

"You allude to that stupid election affair," said Martin. "I can only say that I never did, never could understand it. My only feeling was one of gratitude to you for saving me from being member for the borough. Come along," said he, taking his arm; "this is no time for your scruples, at all events."

"No, Martin, I cannot," said the other. "I'd rather walk up to one of those nine-pounders there than present myself to your lady-mother—"

"But you needn't. You are *my* guest; these are *my* quarters. You shall see nobody but myself till you leave this. Remember what the Captain told us; we are prisoners here." And without waiting for a reply, Martin pushed him before him into the room.

"Two o'clock," said Massingbred, looking at his watch; "and we are to be at Versailles by eight."

"Well, leave all the care of that to me," said Martin; "and do you throw yourself on the bed there, and take some rest. Without you prefer to sup first?"

"No, an hour's sleep is what I stand most in need of; and so I'll say good-night."

Massingbred said this less that he wanted repose than a brief interval to be alone with his own thoughts. And now, as he closed his eyes to affect sleep, it was really to commune with his own heart, and reflect over what had just occurred.

Independently that he liked Czernavitz personally, he was sorry for a quarrel at such a moment. There was a great game about to be played, and a mere personal altercation seemed something small and contemptible in the face of such events. "What will be said of us," thought he, "but that we were a pair of hot-headed fools, thinking more of a miserable interchange of weak sarcasms than of the high destinies of a whole nation? And it was *my* fault," added he to himself; "I had no right to reproach him with a calamity hard enough to bear, even without its being a reproach. What a strange thing is life, after all!" thought he; "everything of greatest moment that occurs in it the upshot of an accident,—my going to Ireland, my visit to the West, my election, my meeting with Kate Henderson, and now this duel." And, so ruminating, he dropped off into a sound sleep, undisturbed by sounds that might well have broken the heaviest slumber.

CHAPTER VIII
AN EVENING OF ONE OP THE "THREE DAYS"

On the evening which witnessed these events Lady Dorothea's "reception" had been more than usually brilliant. Numbers had come to show of how little moment they deemed this "street disturbance," as they were pleased to call it; others, again, were curious to pick up in society the opinions formed on what was passing, among whom were several high in the favor of the Court and the confidence of the Government. All, as they arrived, had some little anecdote or adventure to relate as to the difficulties which beset them on the way,—the distances which they were obliged to travel, the obstructions and passwords and explanations which met them at every turn. These were all narrated in the easy, jocular tone of passing trifles, the very inconvenience of which suggested its share of amusement.

As the evening wore on, even these became less frequent; the streets were already thinning, and, except in some remote, unimportant parts of the capital, the troops were in possession of all the thoroughfares. Of course, the great topic of conversation was the bold stroke of policy then enacting,—a measure which all pronounced wise and just, and eminently called for.

To have heard the sentiments then uttered, the disparaging opinions expressed of the middle and humbler classes, the hopelessness of ever seeing them sufficiently impressed with their own inferiority, the adulation bestowed on the monarch and all around him, one might really have fancied himself back again at the Tuileries in the time of Louis the Fourteenth. All agreed in deeming the occasion an excellent one to give the people a salutary lesson; and it was really pleasant to see the warm interest taken by these high and distinguished persons in the fortunes of their less happy countrymen.

To Lady Dorothea's ears no theme could be more grateful; and she moved from group to group, delighted to mingle her congratulations with those around, and exchange her hopes and aspirations and wishes with theirs. Kate Henderson, upon whom habitually devolved the chief part in these "receptions," was excited and flurried in manner; a more than ordinary effort to please being dashed, as it were, by some secret anxiety, and the expectation of some coming event. Had there been any one to watch her movements, he might have seen the eagerness with which she listened to each new account of the state of the capital, and how impatiently she drank in the last tidings from the streets; nor less marked was the expression of proud scorn upon her features, as she heard the insulting estimate of the populace, and the vainglorious confidence in the soldiery. But more than all these was her haughty indignation as she listened to the confused, mistaken opinions uttered on every side as to the policy of the Government and the benevolent intentions of the king. Once, and only once, did she forget the prudent resolve she wished to impose upon herself; but temper and caution and reserve gave way, as she heard a very distinguished person amusing a circle around him by an unfair and unfaithful portraiture of the great leaders of '92. It was then, when stung by the odious epithet of *canaille* applied to those for whose characters she entertained a deep devotion, that she forgot everything, and in a burst of indignant eloquence overwhelmed and refuted the speaker. This was the moment, too, in which she replied to Villemart by a word of terrible ferocity. Had the red cap of Liberty itself been suddenly hoisted in that brilliant assemblage, the dread and terror which arose could scarcely have been greater.

"Where are we?" cried the Marquise de Longueville. "I thought we were in the Place de Vendôme, and I find myself in the Faubourg St. Antoine!"

"Does my Lady know that her friend and confidante is a Girondist of the first water?" said an ex-Minister.

"Who could have suspected the spirit of Marat under the mask of Ninon de l'Enclos?" muttered Villemart.

"What is this I hear, dearest Kate?" cried the Duchesse de Mirecourt, as she drew the young girl's arm within her own. "They tell me you have terrified every one,—that Madame de Soissons has gone home ill, and the old Chevalier de Gardonnes has sent for his confessor."

"I have been very rash, very foolish," said Kate, as a deadly pallor came over her; "but I could bear it no longer. Besides, what does it matter? They 'll hear worse, and bear it too, before three days are over."

"Then it is all true?" cried the Duchess, eagerly. "You told Villemart that when the Government spoke with grape-shot, the people replied with the guillotine!"

"Not exactly," said Kate, with a faint smile. "But are they all going?"

"Of course they are. You have frightened them almost to death; and I know you only meant it for jest,—one of those little half-cruel jests you were ever fond of. Come with me and say so,—come, dearest." And she drew her, as she spoke, into the crowded salon, now already a scene of excited leave-taking. The brilliant company, however, fell back as they came forward, and an expression of mingled dismay and compassion was turned towards the young Duchess, who with a kind of heroic courage drew Kate's arm closer within her own.

"I am come to make an explanation, messieurs et mesdames," said the Duchess, with her most captivating smile; "pray vouchsafe me a hearing. My friend—my dearest, best friend here—has, in a moment of sportive pleasantry, suffered herself to jest—"

"It was a jest, then?" broke in Madame de Longueville, haughtily.

"Just as that is," replied Kate, lifting her hand and pointing in the direction whence came a terrible crash of artillery, followed by the rattle of musketry.

"Let us go,—let us away!" was now heard in affrighted accents on every side; and the splendid assemblage, with less of ceremony than might be expected, began to depart. Lady Dorothea alone was ignorant of what had occurred, and witnessed this sudden leave-taking with amazement. "You are surely not afraid?" said she to one; "there is nothing serious in all this."

"She has told us the reverse, my Lady," was the reply. "We should be compromised to remain longer in her company."

"Adieu, my Lady. I wish we left you in safer companionship."

"Farewell, Madame, and pray be warned of your danger," whispered another.

"Your Ladyship may be called upon to acquit debts contracted by another, if Mademoiselle continues a member of your family," said Villemart, as he bowed his departure.

"Believe me, Madame, none of us include *you* in the terrible sentiments we have listened to."

These, and a vast number of similar speeches attended the leave-taking of nearly each of her guests, till Lady Dorothea, confused, almost stunned by reiterated shocks, sat silently accepting these mysterious announcements, and almost imagining herself in all the bewilderment of a dream.

Twice she made an effort to ask some explanation, but failed; and it was only as the Duchesse de Mirecourt drew nigh to say farewell, that in a faint, weak voice she said,—"Can you tell me what all are hinting at, or am I only confusing myself with the terrible scenes without?"

"I 'd have prevented it had I been near. I only heard it when too late, my Lady," said the Duchess, sorrowfully.

"Prevented what?—heard what?" cried Lady Dorothea.

"Besides, she has often said as much amongst ourselves; we only laughed, as indeed every one would do now, did not events present so formidable an aspect."

"Who is she you speak of? Tell me, I beseech you. What does this mean?"

"I am the culprit, my Lady," said Kate, approaching with all the quiet stateliness of her peculiar manner. "I have routed this gorgeous assembly, shocked your most distinguished guests, and horrified all whose sentiments breathe loyalty! I am sincerely sorry for my offence; and it is a grave one."

"*You—you* have dared to do this?"

"Too true, madam," rejoined Kate.

"How and to whom have you had the insolence—"

She stopped, overcome by passion; and Kate replied,—"To all who pleased to listen, my Lady, I have said what doubtless is not often uttered in such choice company, but what, if I mistake not greatly, their ears will grow familiar with erelong."

"Nay, nay," said the Duchess, in a tone of apology, "the matter is not so serious as all this. Every one now is terrified. This disturbance, the soldiery, the vast crowds that beset the streets, have all produced so much excitement that even a few words spoken at random are enough to cause fear. It is one of Kate's fancies to terrorize thus over weak minds. She has the cruel triumph of not knowing what fear is. In a word, it is a mere trifling event, sure to be forgotten in the midst of such scenes as we are passing through."

This attempt at explanation, poured forth with rapid utterance, did not produce on Lady Dorothea the conviction it was intended to impose, and her Ladyship received the last adieus of the Duchess with a cold and stately formality; and then, as the door closed after her, turned to Kate Henderson, and said,—"I want *your* explanation of all this. Let me have it."

"It is easily given, my Lady," said Kate, calmly. And then, in a voice that never trembled nor varied, she narrated briefly the scene which had just occurred, not extenuating in the slightest her own share in the transaction, or offering a single syllable of excuse.

"And you, being who and what you are, dared thus to outrage the best blood of France!" exclaimed Lady Dorothea, trembling all over with passion.

"Perhaps, my Lady, if I sought for an apology, it would be in the fact of being who and what I am."

"And do you imagine that after conduct such as this, after exposing me to a partnership in the shame that attaches to yourself, that you are any longer to enjoy the shelter of my roof?"

"It never occurred to me to think of that, madam," said Kate, with an ill-repressed scorn.

"Then it is for *me* to remind you of it," said her Ladyship, sternly. "You shall, first of all, write me an humble apology for this vulgar tirade, this outrage upon my company, and then you shall leave the house. Sit down there, and write as I shall dictate to you."

Kate seated herself with an air of implicit obedience at a writing-table, and took up a pen.

"Write," cried Lady Dorothea, sternly. "Begin, 'My Lady.' No. 'I approach your Ladyship for the last time.' No, not that. 'If the sincere sorrow in which I pen these lines.' No. Do it yourself. You best can express the shame your heart should feel in such a moment. Let the words be your own!"

Kate leaned over the paper and wrote rapidly for a few seconds. Having finished, she read over the lines, and seemed to reflect on them.

"Show me that paper!" cried Lady Dorothea, impatiently. But, without obeying the command, Kate said, — "Your Ladyship will not be able to leave Paris for at least forty hours. By that time the Monarchy will have run its course in France. You will probably desire, however, to escape from the scenes of turbulence sure to ensue. This will secure you a free passage, whichever road you take."

"What raving is all this?" said Lady Dorothea, snatching the paper from her hand, and then reading aloud in French, — "'The authorities are required to aid and tender all assistance in their power to Lady Dorothea Martin and all who accompany her, neither giving nor suffering any opposition to be given to her or them in the prosecution of their journey.'

(Signed) "Jules Lagrange,

"'Minister of Police *ad interim*'

"And this in your own hand, too!" exclaimed Lady Dorothea, contemptuously.

"Yes, madam; but it will entitle it to the seal of the Prefecture, and entitle *you* to all that it professes."

"So that I have the honor to shelter within my walls a chief of this insurrection,—if it be worthy of such a name; one in the confidence of this stupid *canaille*, who fancy that the fall of a Monarchy is like a row in a *guinguette!*"

"Your Ladyship is no longer in a position to question me or arraign my actions. Before two days are over, the pageant of a king will have passed off the stage, and men of a different stamp take the direction of affairs. One of these will be he whose name I have affixed to that paper,—not without due warranty to do so. Your Ladyship may or may not choose to avail yourself of it."

"I spurn the imposition," said Lady Dorothea, tearing it in fragments. "So poor a cheat could not deceive *me*. As for yourself—"

"Oh, do not bestow a thought upon *me*, my Lady. I can suffice for my own guidance. I only wait for morning to leave this house."

"And it is to a city in such a state as this you would confide yourself. Truly, mademoiselle, Republicanism has a right to be proud of you. You are no half-convert to its principles."

"Am I again to say, my Lady, that your control over me has ceased?"

"It has not. It shall not cease till I have restored you to the humble roof from which I took you," said Lady Dorothea, passionately. "Your father is our creature; he has no other subsistence than what we condescend to bestow on him. He shall know, when you re-enter his doors, why and for what cause you are there. Till that time come, you are, as you have been, in my service."

"No, my Lady, the tie between us is snapped. Dependence is but a sad part at the best; but so long as it is coupled with a certain show of respect it is bearable. Destroy *that*, and it is mere slavery, abject and degrading. I cannot go back to your Ladyship's service." And she gave to the last word an emphasis of intense scorn.

"You must and you shall," said Lady Dorothea. "If *you* are forgetful of what it is your duty to remember, I am not. Here you shall remain; without," added she, in an accent of supreme contempt, "your counsel and direction shall be sought after by the high and mighty individuals who are so soon to administer the affairs of this nation."

The loud roll of a drum, followed by the louder clank of sabres and musketry, here startled the speakers; and Kate, hastening to the window, opened it, and stepped out upon the balcony. Day was just dawning; a gray half-light covered the sky, but the dark shadows of the tall houses still stretched over the Place. Here, now, the troops were all in motion; a sudden summons having roused them to form in rank. The hasty character of the movement showed that some emergency was imminent,—a fact confirmed by the frequent arrival and departure of orderlies at full speed.

After a brief interval of preparation the infantry formed in column, and, followed by the artillery and cavalry, moved out of the Place at a quick step. The measured tramp of the foot-soldiers, the clattering noise of the train and the dragoons could be heard long after they had passed out of sight; and Kate stood listening eagerly as to what would come next, when suddenly a man in plain clothes rode hastily from one of the side-streets into the centre of the Place. He looked around him for a moment or two, and then disappeared. Within a few seconds after, a dull, indistinct sound seemed to rise from the ground, which swelled gradually louder and louder, and at last grew into the regular footfall of a great multitude moving in measured time; and now a vast crowd poured into the Place, silent and wordless. On they came from the various quarters that opened into the square,—men, for the most part clad in blouses or in the coarse garb of laborers. They were armed either with musket or sword, and in many instances wore the cross-belt of the soldier. They proceeded at once to barricade the square at its opening into the Rue de la Paix,—a work which they accomplished with astonishing speed and regularity; for, while Kate still looked, a formidable rampart was thrown up across the entire street, along which a line of armed men was stationed, every one of whom, by his attitude and gesture, betrayed the old discipline of a soldier's life. Orders were given and obeyed, movements made, and dispositions effected, with all the regularity and precision of regular troops; and by the ready obedience of all, and the steady attitude observed, it was easy to see that these men were trained to arms and to habits of discipline. Not less evident was it that they who commanded them were not new to such duties. But, more important than all such signs was the fact that here and there through the mass might be seen the uniform of a soldier, or the epaulette of an officer, showing that desertion to the ranks of the people had already begun.

Kate was so occupied in attentive observation of the scene that she had not noticed the arrival of another person in the apartment, and whose voice now suddenly attracted her. It was Martin himself, hastily aroused from his bed by his servant, who in great alarm told him that the capital was in open revolt, the king's troops beaten back, and the people victorious everywhere. "There's not a moment to lose," cried he; "we must escape while we can. The road to Versailles is yet in possession of the troops, and we can take that way."

Lady Dorothea, partly overcome by the late scene, partly stunned by the repeated shocks she experienced, made no reply whatever; and Martin, judging from the expression of her features the anxiety she was suffering, hastily added, "Let me see Kate Henderson,—where is she?"

Lady Dorothea merely pointed towards the balcony, but did not utter a word.

"Oh, have I found you?" said Martin, stepping out upon the balcony. "You see what is doing,—I might say what is done," added he; "for I believe the game is well-nigh decided. Nothing but an overwhelming force will now crush this populace. We must get away, and at once. Will you give the orders? Send for post-horses; tell them to pack up whatever they can,—direct everything, in fact. My Lady is too ill,—too much overcome to act, or think of anything. Our whole reliance is upon you." While he was yet uttering these broken, disjointed sentences, he had drawn Kate by the arm within the room, and now stood beside Lady Dorothea's chair. Her Ladyship raised her head and fixed her eyes upon Kate, who sustained the gaze calmly and steadily, nor by the slightest movement displayed one touch of any emotion. The glance, at first haughty and defiant, seemed at length to grow weaker under the unmoved stare of the young girl, and finally she bent down her head and sat as though overcome.

"Come, Dora," said Martin, kindly, "rouse yourself; you are always equal to an effort when necessity presses. Tell Kate here what you wish, and she 'll do it."

"I want no aid,—no assistance, sir. Miss Henderson is her own mistress,—she may do what, or go where she pleases."

Martin made a sign to Kate not to mind what he believed to be the mere wandering of an over-excited brain; and then bending down over the chair, said, "Dear Dora, we must be active and stirring; the people will soon be masters of the capital,—for a while, at least,—and there is no saying what excesses they will commit."

"Do not offend Miss Henderson, sir," interposed Lady Dorothea; "she has equal confidence in their valor and their virtue."

"What does this mean?—when did she fall into this state?" asked he, eagerly. And although only spoken in a whisper, Lady Dorothea overheard them, and said,—"Let *her* tell you. She can give you the very fullest explanation."

"But, Dora, this is no time for trifling; we are here, in the midst of an enraged populace and a maddened soldiery. There, listen!—that was artillery; and now, hear!—the bells of the churches are sounding the alarm."

"They are ringing the knell of the Monarchy!" said Kate, solemnly.

A hoarse, wild shout—aery like that of enraged wild beasts—arose from the Place beneath, and all rushed to the window to see what had occurred. It was a charge of heavy cavalry endeavoring to force the barricade; and now, vigorously repulsed by the defenders, men and horses were rolling on the ground in terrible confusion, while on the barricade itself a hand-to-hand conflict was raging.

"Sharp work, by George!" said a voice behind Kate's shoulder. She turned and saw Captain Martin, who had just joined them unobserved.

"I thought you many a mile away," said Kate, in a whisper.

"So I should have been," replied he, in the same tone, "but I was n't going to lose this. I knew it was to come off to-day, and I thought it would have been a thousand pities to be absent."

"And are your wishes, then, with these gallant fellows?" said she, eagerly. "Do I hear you aright, that it was to aid them you remained? There! see how they bear down on the soldiery; they will not be restrained; they are crossing the barricade, and charging with the bayonet. It is only for liberty that men can fight thus. Oh that I were a man, to be amongst them!"

A stray shot from beneath here struck the architrave above their heads, and sent down a mass of plaster over them.

"Come, Dora, this is needless peril," said Martin, drawing her within the room. "If you will not leave this, at least do not expose yourself unnecessarily."

"But it is exactly to get away—to escape while there is time—that I came for," said the Captain. "They tell me that the mob are getting the best of it, and, worse again, that the troops are joining them; so, to make sure, I 've sent off Fenton to the post for horses, and I 'm expecting him every moment. But here he is. Well, have you got the horses?"

"No, sir: the horses have all been taken by the people to mount orderlies; the postmaster, too, has fled, and everything is in confusion. But if we had horses the streets are impassable; from here to the Boulevard there are no less than five barricades."

"Then what is to be done?" cried Martin.

"They say, sir," replied Fenton, "that by gaining the outer Boulevard on foot, carriages and horses are easily found there, to reach Belleville, St. Germain, or Versailles."

"He is right," said the Captain; "there is nothing else to be done. What do *you* think?" said he, addressing Kate, who stood intently watching the movements in the Place beneath.

"Yes; do you agree with this plan?" asked Martin, approaching her.

"Look!" cried she, eagerly, and not heeding the question; "the troops are rapidly joining the people,—they come in numbers now,—and yonder is an officer in his uniform."

"Shame on him!" exclaimed Lady Dorothea, indignantly.

"So say I too," said Kate. "He who wears a livery should not assume the port and bearing of a free man. This struggle is for liberty, and should only be maintained by the free!"

"How are we to pass these barricades?" cried Martin, anxiously.

"I will be your guide, sir, if that be all," said Kate. "You may trust me. I promise no more than I can perform."

"She speaks truly," said Lady Dorothea. "Alas that we should see the day when we cannot reject the aid!"

"There is a matter I want to speak to you about," said Martin, drawing his father aside, and speaking in a low, confidential tone. "Massingbred— Jack Massingbred—is now here, in my room. I know all about my mother's dislike to him, and *he* knows it; indeed, he has as much as owned to me that he deserved it all. But what is to be done? We cannot leave him here."

"How came he to be here?" asked Martin.

"He accompanied me from the Club, where, in an altercation of some sort, he had just involved himself in a serious quarrel. He came here to be ready to start this morning for Versailles, where the meeting was to take place; but indeed he had no thought of accepting shelter under our roof; and when he found where he was, it was with the greatest difficulty I could persuade him to enter. None of us anticipated such a serious turn of affairs as this; and now, of course, a meeting will be scarcely possible. What are we to do with him?"

"Ask him frankly to join us if we obtain the horses."

"But my mother?"

"I 'll speak to her,—but it were better you did it, Harry. These are not times to weigh scruples and balance difficulties. I don't myself think that Massingbred treated us fairly, but it is not now I 'd like to remember it. There, go; tell her what you have told me, and all will be well."

The Captain drew nigh Lady Dorothea, and, leaning over her chair, whispered to her for some minutes. At first, a slight gesture of impatience burst from her, but afterwards she seemed to hear him calmly and tranquilly.

"It would seem as though the humiliations of this night are never to have an end," said she, with a sigh. "But I'll bear my share of them."

"Remember," said the other, "that it was by no choice of *his* he came here. His foot was on the threshold before he suspected it."

"Miss Henderson sent me, my Lady," said a servant, entering hastily, "to say that there is not a minute to be lost. They are expecting an attack on the barricade in the Rue de la Paix, and we ought to pass through at once."

"By whose orders?" began she, haughtily; then, checking herself suddenly, and in a voice weak and broken, added: "I am ready. Give me your arm, Harry, and do not leave me. Where is Mr. Martin?" asked she.

"He is waiting for your Ladyship at the foot of the stairs with another gentleman," said the servant.

"That must be Massingbred, for I told them to call him," said the Captain.

When Lady Dorothea, supported by the arm of her son, had reached the gate, she found Martin and Massingbred standing to receive them, surrounded by a numerous escort of servants, each loaded with some portion of the family baggage.

"A hasty summons, sir," said she, addressing Massingbred, and thus abruptly avoiding the awkwardness of a more ceremonious meeting. "A few hours back none of us anticipated anything like this. Will it end seriously, think you?"

"There is every prospect of such, madam," said he, bowing respectfully to her salutation. "Every moment brings fresh tidings of defection among the troops, while the Marshal is paralyzed by contradictory orders."

"Is it always to be the fate of monarchy to be badly served in times of peril?" said she, bitterly.

"It is very difficult to awaken loyalty against one's convictions of right, madam. I mean," added he, as a gesture of impatience broke from her, "that these acts of the king, having no support from his real friends, are weak stimulants to evoke deeds of daring and courage."

"They are unworthy supporters of a Crown who only defend what they approve of. This is but Democracy at best, and smacks of the policy which has little to lose and everything to gain by times of trouble."

"And yet, madam, such cannot be the case here; at least, it is assuredly not so in the instance of him who is now speaking with Miss Henderson." And he pointed to a man who, holding the bridle of his horse on his arm, walked slowly at Kate's side in the street before the door.

"And who is he?" asked she, eagerly.

"The greatest banker in Paris, madam,—one of the richest capitalists of Europe,—ready to resign all his fortune in the struggle against a rule which he foresees intended to bring back the days of a worn-out, effete monarchy, rather than a system which shall invigorate the nation, and enrich it by the arts of commerce and trade."

"But his name—who is he?" asked she, more impatiently.

"Charles Lagrange, madam."

"I have heard the name before. I have seen it somewhere lately," said she, trying to remember where and how.

"You could scarcely have paid your respects at Neuilly, madam, without seeing him. He was, besides, the favored guest at Madame de Mirecourt's."

"You would not imply, sir, that the Duchess condescended to any sympathy with this party?"

"More than half the Court, madam, are against the Crown; I will not say, however, that they are, on that account, for the people."

"There! she is making a sign to us to follow her," said Martin, pointing towards Kate, who, still conversing with her companion, motioned to the others to come up.

"It is from that quarter we receive our orders," said Lady Dorothea, sneeringly, as she prepared to follow.

"What has she to do with it?" exclaimed the Captain. "To look at her, one would say she was deep in the whole business."

A second gesture, more urgent than before, now summoned the party to make haste.

Through the Place, crowded as it was by an armed and excited multitude, way was rapidly made for the little party who now issued from the door of the hotel. Kate Henderson walked in front, with Massingbred at her side talking eagerly, and by his gestures seeming as though endeavoring to extenuate or explain away something in his conduct; next came Lady Dorothea, supported between her husband and her son, and while walking slowly and with faltering steps, still carrying her head proudly erect, and gazing on the stern faces around her with looks of haughty contempt. After them were a numerous retinue of servants, with such effects as they had got hurriedly together,—a terror-struck set, scarcely able to crawl along from fear.

As they drew nigh the barricade, some men proceeded to remove a heavy wagon which adjoined a house, and by the speed and activity of their movements, urged on as they were by the orders of one in command, it might be seen that the operation demanded promptitude.

"We are scarcely safe in this," cried the officer. "See! they are making signs to us from the windows,—the troops are coming. If you pass out now, you will be between two fires."

"There is yet time," said Kate, eagerly. "Our presence in the street, too, will delay them, and give you some minutes to prepare. And as for ourselves, we shall gain one of the side-streets easily enough."

"Tie your handkerchief to your cane, sir," said the officer to Massingbred.

"My flag is ready," said Jack, gayly; "I only hope they may respect it."

"Now—now!" cried Kate, with eagerness, and beckoning to Lady Dorothea to hasten, "the passage is free, and not a second to be lost!"

"Are you not coming with us?" whispered Martin to her, as they passed out.

"Yes; I'll follow. But," added she, in a lower tone, "were the choice given me, it is here I'd take my stand."

She looked full at Massingbred as she spoke, and, bending down his head, he said, "Had it been your place, it were mine also!"

"Quick,—quick, my Lady," said Kate. "They must close up the passage at once. They are expecting an attack." And so saying, she motioned rapidly to Martin to move on.

"The woman is a fiend," said Lady Dorothea; "see how her eyes sparkle, and mark the wild exultation of her features."

"Adieu, sir,—adieu!" said Kate, waving her hand to one who seemed the chief of the party. "All my wishes are with you. Were I a man, my hand should guarantee my heart."

"Come—come back!" cried the officer. "You are too late. There comes the head of the column."

"No, never—never!" exclaimed Lady Dorothea, haughtily; "protection from such as these is worse than any death."

"Give me the flag, then," cried Kate, snatching it from Massingbred's hand, and hastening on before the others. And now the heavy wagon had fallen back to its place, and a serried file of muskets peeped over it.

"Where's Massingbred?" asked the Captain, eagerly.

"Yonder,—where he ought to be!" exclaimed Kate, proudly, pointing to the barricade, upon which, now, Jack was standing conspicuously, a musket on his arm.

The troops in front were not the head of a column, but the advanced guard of a force evidently at some distance off, and instead of advancing on the barricade, they drew up and halted in triple file across the street. Their attitude of silent, stern defiance—for it was such—evoked a wild burst of popular fury, and epithets of abuse and insult were heaped upon them from windows and parapets.

"They are the famous Twenty-Second of the Line," said the Captain, "who forced the Pont-Neuf yesterday and drove the mob before them."

"It is fortunate for us that we fall into such hands," said Lady Dorothea, waving her handkerchief as she advanced. But Kate had already approached the line, and now halted at a command from the officer. While she endeavored to explain how and why they were there, the cries and menaces of the populace grew louder and wilder. The officer, a very young subaltern, seemed confused and flurried; his eyes turned constantly towards the street from which they had advanced, and he seemed anxiously expecting the arrival of the regiment.

"I cannot give you a convoy, Mademoiselle," he said; "I. scarcely know if I have the right to let you pass. We may be attacked at any moment; for aught I can tell, *you* may be in the interests of the insurgents—"

"We are cut off, Lieutenant," cried a sergeant, running up at the moment. "They have thrown up a barrier behind us, and it is armed already."

"Lay down your arms, then," said Kate, "and do not sacrifice your brave fellows in a hopeless straggle."

"Listen not to her, young man, but give heed to your honor and your loyalty," cried Lady Dorothea. "Is it against such an enemy as this French soldiers fear to advance?"

"Forward!" cried the officer, waving his sword above his head. "Let us carry the barricade!" And a wild yell of defiance from the windows repeated the speech in derision.

"You are going to certain death!" cried Kate, throwing herself before him. "Let *me* make terms for you, and they shall not bring dishonor on you."

"Here comes the regiment!" called out the sergeant. "They have forced the barricade." And the quick tramp of a column, as they came at a run, now shook the street.

"Remember your cause and your King, sir," cried Lady Dorothea to the officer.

"Bethink you of your country,—of France,—and of Liberty!" said Kate, as she grasped his arm.

"Stand back!—back to the houses!" said he, waving his sword. "Voltigeurs, to the front!"

The command was scarcely issued, when a hail of balls rattled through the air. The defenders of the barricade had opened their fire, and with a deadly precision, too, for several fell at the very first discharge.

"Back to the houses!" exclaimed Martin, dragging Lady Dorothea along, who, in her eagerness, now forgot all personal danger, and only thought of the contest before her.

"Get under cover of the troops,—to the rear!" cried the Captain, as he endeavored to bear her away.

"Back—back—beneath the archway!" cried Kate, as, throwing her arms around Lady Dorothea, she lifted her fairly from the ground, and carried her within the deep recess of a *porte cochère*. Scarcely, however, had she deposited her in safety, than she fell tottering backwards and sank to the ground.

"Good Heavens! she is struck," exclaimed Martin, bending over her.

"It is nothing,—a spent shot, and no more," said Kate, as she showed the bullet which had perforated her dress beneath the arm.

"A good soldier, by Jove!" said the Captain, gazing with real admiration on the beautiful features before him; the faint smile she wore heightening their loveliness, and contrasting happily with their pallor.

"There they go! They are up the barricade already; they are over it,— through it!" cried the Captain. "Gallantly done!—gloriously done! No, by Jove! they are falling back; the fire is murderous. See how they bayonet them. The troops must win. They move together; they are like a wall! In vain, in vain; they cannot do it! They are beaten,—they are lost!"

"Who are lost?" said Kate, in a half-fainting voice.

"The soldiers. And there 's Massingbred on the top of the barricade, in the midst of it all. I see his hat They are driven back—beaten—beaten!"

"Come in quickly," cried a voice from behind; and a small portion of the door was opened to admit them. "The soldiers are retiring, and will kill all before them."

"Let *me* aid you; it is *my* turn now," said Lady Dorothea, assisting Kate to rise. "Good Heavens! her arm is broken,—it is smashed in two." And she caught the fainting girl in her arms.

Gathering around, they bore her within the gate, and had but time to bar and bolt it when the hurried tramp without, and the wild yell of popular triumph, told that the soldiers were retreating, beaten and defeated.

"And this to save me!" said Lady Dorothea, as she stooped over her. And the scalding tears dropped one by one on Kate's cheek.

"Tear this handkerchief, and bind it around my arm," said Kate, calmly; "the pain is not very great, and there will be no bleeding, the doctors say, from a gun-shot wound."

"I'll be the surgeon," said the Captain, addressing himself to the task with more of skill than might be expected. "I 've seen many a fellow struck down who did n't bear it as calmly," muttered he, as he bent over her. "Am I giving you any pain?"

"Not in the least; and if I were in torture, that glorious cheer outside would rally me. Hear!—listen!—the soldiers are in full retreat; the people, the noble-hearted people, are the conquerors!"

"Be calm, and think of yourself," said Lady Dorothea, mildly, to her; "such excitement may peril your very life."

"And it is worth a thousand lives to taste of it," said she, while her cheek flushed, and her dark eyes gleamed with added lustre.

"The street is clear now," said one of the servants to Martin, "and we might reach the Boulevard with ease."

"Let us go, then," said Lady Dorothea. "Let us look to *her* and think of nothing till she be cared for."

CHAPTER IX
SOME CONFESSIONS OF JACK MASSINGBRED

Upon two several occasions have we committed to Jack Massingbred the task of conducting this truthful history; for the third time do we now purpose to make his correspondence the link between the past and what is to follow. We are not quite sure that the course we thus adopt is free from its share of inconvenience, but we take it to avoid the evils of reiteration inseparable from following out the same events from merely different points of view. There is also another advantage to be gained. Jack is before our readers; we are not. Jack is an acquaintance; we cannot aspire to that honor. Jack's opinions, right or wrong as they may be, are part and parcel of a character already awaiting their verdict. What he thought and felt, hoped, feared, or wished, are the materials by which he is to be judged; and so we leave his cause in his own hands.

His letter is addressed to the same correspondent to whom he wrote before. It is written, too, at different intervals, and in different moods of mind. Like the letters of many men who practise concealment with the world at large, it is remarkable for great frankness and sincerity. He throws away his mask with such evident signs of enjoyment that we only wonder if he can ever resume it; but crafty men like to relax into candor, as royalty is said to indulge with pleasure in the chance moments of pretended equality. It is, at all events, a novel sensation; and even that much, in this routine life of ours, is something!

He writes from Spa, and after some replies to matters with which we have no concern, proceeds thus:—

"Of the Revolution, then, and the Three Glorious Days as they are called, I can tell you next to nothing, and for this simple reason, that I was there fighting, shouting, throwing up barricades, singing the 'Marseillaise,' smashing furniture, and shooting my 'Swiss,' like the rest. As to who beat the troops, forced the Tuileries, and drove Marmont back, you must consult the newspapers. Personal adventures I could give you to satiety, hairbreadth 'scapes and acts of heroism by the dozen; but these narratives are never new, and always tiresome. The serious reflectiveness sounds like humbug, and, if one treats them lightly, the flippancy is an offence. Jocular heroism is ever an insult to the reader.

"You say, '*Que diable allait-il faire dans cette galère?*' and I answer, it was all *her* doing. Yes, Harry, *she* was there. I was thinking of nothing less in the world than a great 'blow for freedom,' as the 'Globe' has it. I had troubled my head wonderfully little about the whole affair. Any little interest I took was in the notion that if our 'natural enemies,' the French, were to fall to and kill each other, there would be so much the fewer left to fight against us; but as to who was to get the upper hand, or what they were to do when they had it, I gave myself no imaginable concern. I had a vague, shadowy kind of impression that the government was a bad one, but I had a much stronger conviction that the people deserved no better. My leanings—my instincts, if you prefer it—were with the Crown. The mob and its sentiments are always repulsive. Popular enthusiasm is a great ocean, but it is an ocean of dirty water, and you cannot come out clean from the contact; and so I should have wished well to royalty, but for an accident,—a mere trifle in its way, but one quite sufficient, even on historic grounds, to account for a man's change of opinions. The troops shot my cab-horse, sent a bullet through poor 'Beverley,' and seriously damaged a new hat which I wore at the time, accompanying these acts with expressions the reverse of compliment or civility. I was pitched out into the gutter, and, most appropriately you will say, I got up a Radical, a Democrat, a Fourierist,—anything, in short, that shouts 'Down with Kings, and up with the Sovereign People!'

"My principles—don't smile at the word—led me into a stupid altercation with a very pleasant acquaintance, and we parted to meet the next morning in hostility,—at least, such was our understanding; but by the time that our difference should have been settled, *I* was carried away on a stretcher to the Hôtel Dieu, wounded, and he was flung, a corpse, into the Seine. I intended to have been a most accurate narrator of events, journalizing for you, hour by hour, with all the stirring excitement of the present tense, but I cannot; the crash and the hubbub are still in my brain, and the infernal chaos of the streets is yet over me. Not to speak of my wound,—a very ugly sabre-cut in the neck,—severing I don't know what amount of nerves, arteries, and such-like 'small deer,' every one of which, however, has its own peculiar perils in the shape of aneurisms, tetanus, and so forth, in case I am not a miracle of patience, calmness, and composure.

"The Martins are nursing and comforting and chicken-brothing me to my heart's content, and La Henderson, herself an invalid, with a terrible broken arm, comes and reads to me from time to time. What a girl it is! Wounded in a street encounter, she actually carried Lady Dorothea into a porte-cochère, and when they had lost their heads in terror, could neither issue an order to the servants nor know what way to turn, she took the guidance of the whole party, obtained horses and carriages and an escort, escaped from Paris, and reached Versailles in the midst of flying courtiers and dismayed ministers, and actually was the very first to bring the tidings that the game of monarchy was up,—that the king had nothing left for it but an inglorious flight. To the Duchesse de Mire-court she made this communication, which it seems none of the court-followers had the courage or honesty to do before. The Duchess, in her terror, actually dragged her into the presence of the king, and made her repeat what she had said. The scene, as told me, was quite dramatic; the king took her hand to lead her to a seat, but it was unfortunately of the wounded arm, and she fainted. The sight of the wounded limb so affected the nerves of monarchy that he gave immediate orders to depart, and was off within an hour.

"How they found me out a patient in a ward of the Hôtel Dieu, rescued and carried me away with them, I have heard full half a dozen times, but I 'm far from being clear enough to repeat the story; and, indeed, when I try to recall the period, the only images which rise up before me are long ranges of white coverlids, pale faces, and groans and cries of suffering, with the dark curly head of a great master of torture peeping at me, and whom, I am told, is the Baron Dupuytren, the Surgeon-in-Chief. After these comes a vision of litters and *charrettes,*—sore joltings and stoppages to drink water—But I shall rave if I go on. Better I should tell you of my pleasant little bedroom here, opening on a small garden, with a tiny fountain trying to sprinkle the wild myrtle and blush-roses around it, and sportively sending its little plash over me, as the wind wafts it into my chamber. My luxurious chair and easy-cushioned sofa, and my table littered with everything, from flowers to French romances; not to speak of the small rustic seat beside the window, where she has been sitting the last hour, and has only quitted to give me time to write this to you. I know it—I see it—all you can say, all that you are saying at this moment, is fifty times more forcibly echoing within my own heart, and repeating in fitful sentences: 'A ruined man—a broken fortune—a mad attachment—a life of struggle, difficulty, and failure!' But why should it be failure? Such a girl for a wife ought in itself to be an earnest of success. Are not her qualities exactly those that do battle with the difficulties of fortune? Self-denial—ambition—courage—an intense, an intuitive knowledge of the world—and then, a purpose-like devotion to whatever she undertakes, that throws an air of heroism over all her actions.

"Birth—blood—family connections—what have they done for me, except it be to entail upon me the necessity of selecting a career amidst the two or three that are supposed to suit the well-born? I may be a Life Guardsman, or an unpaid attaché, but I must not be a physician or a merchant. Nor is it alone that certain careers are closed against us, but certain opinions too. I must not think ill of the governing class,—I must never think well of the governed.

"Well, Harry, the colonies are the remedy for all this. There, at least, a man can fashion existence as arbitrarily as he can the shape and size of his house. None shall dictate his etiquette, no more than his architecture; and I am well weary of the slavery of this old-world life, with our worship of old notions and old china, both because they are cracked, damaged, and useless. I 'll marry her. I have made up my mind on 't. Spare me all your remonstrances, all your mock compassion. Nor is it like a fellow who has not seen the world in its best gala suit, affecting to despise rank, splendor, and high station. *I have* seen the thing. I have cantered my thoroughbred along Rotten Row, eaten my truffled dinners in Belgravia, whispered my nonsense over the white shoulders of the fairest and best-born of England's daughters. I know to a decimal fraction the value of all these; and, what 's more, I know what one pays for them,—the miserable vassalage, the poor slavery of mind, soul, and body they cost!

"It is the terror of exclusion here, the dread of coldness there—the possibility of offence to 'his Grace' on this side, or misconception by 'her Ladyship' on that—sway and rule a man so that he may neither eat, drink, nor sleep without a 'Court Guide' in his pocket. I 've done with it! now and forever,—I tell you frankly,—I return no more to this bondage.

"I have written a farewell address to my worthy constituents of Oughterard. I have told them that, 'feeling an instinct of independence within me, I can no longer remain their representative; that, as a man of honor, I shrink from the jobbery of the little borough politicians, and, as a gentleman, I beg to decline their intimacy.' They took me for want of a better—I leave them for the same reason.

"To my father I have said: 'Let us make a compromise. As your son I have a claim on the House. Now, what will you give for my share? I 'll neither importune you for place, nor embarrass you with solicitations for employment. Help me to stock my knapsack, and I 'll find my road myself.' *She* knows nothing of these steps on my part; nor shall she, till they have become irrevocable. She is too proud ever to consent to what would cost me thus heavily; but the expense once incurred,—the outlay made,— she cannot object to what has become the law of my future life.

"I send off these two documents to-night; this done, I shall write to her an offer of marriage. What a fever I 'm in! and all because I feel the necessity of defending myself to *you*,—to you of all men the most headstrong, reckless, and self-indulgent,—a fellow who never curbed a caprice nor restrained a passing fancy; and yet you are just the man to light your cigar, and while you puff away your blue cloud, mutter on about rashness, folly, insanity, and the rest of it, as if the state of your bank account should make that wisdom in *you*, which with *me* is but mere madness! But I tell you, Harry, it is your very thousands per annum that preclude you from doing what I can. It is your house in town, your stud at Tattersall's, your yacht at Cowes, your grouse-lodge in the Highlands, that tie and fetter you to live like some scores of others, with whom you have n't one solitary sympathy, save in income! You are bound up in all the recognizances of your wealth to dine stupidly, sup languidly, and sink down at last into a marriage of convenience, — to make a wife of her whom 'her Grace' has chosen for you without a single speculation in the contract save the thought of the earl you will be allied to, and the four noble families you 'll have the right to go in mourning for.

"And what worse than cant it is to talk of what they call an indiscreet match! What does — what can the world know as to the reasons that impel you, or me, or anybody else, to form a certain attachment? Are they acquainted with our secret and most hidden emotions? Do they understand the project of life we have planned to ourselves? Have they read our utter weariness and contempt for forms that *they* venerate, and social distinctions that *they* worship? I am aware that in some cases it requires courage to do this; and in doing it a man virtually throws down the glove to the whole world, and says, 'This woman's love is to me more than all of you' — and so say I at this moment. I must cry halt, I see, Harry. I have set these nerves at work in my wound, and the pain is agony. Tomorrow — to-night, if I 'm able — I shall continue.

"Midnight." They have just wished me good-night, after having spent the evening here reading out the newspapers for me, commenting upon them, and exerting themselves to amuse me in a hundred good-natured ways. You would like this same stately old Lady Dorothea. She is really 'Grande Dame' in every respect, — dress, air, carriage, gesture, even her slow and measured speech is imposing, and her prejudices, uttered as they are in such perfect sincerity of heart, have something touching about them, and her sorrowful pity for the mob sounded more gracefully than Kate's enthusiastic estimate of their high deservings. It does go terribly against the grain to fancy an alliance between coarse natures and noble sentiments, and to believe in the native nobility of those who never touch soap! I have had a kind of skirmish with La Henderson upon this theme to-night. She was cross and out of temper, and bore my bantering badly. The fact is, she is utterly disgusted at the turn things have taken in France; and not altogether without reason, since, after all their bluster and bloodshed and barricades, they have gone back to a monarchy again. They barred out the master to make 'the head usher' top of the school. Let us see if he won't be as fond of the birch as his predecessor. Like all mutineers, they found they could n't steer the ship when they had murdered the captain! How hopeless it makes one of humanity to see such a spectacle as this, Harry, and how low is one's estimate of the species after such experience! You meet some half-dozen semi-bald, spectacled old gentlemen in society, somewhat more reserved than the rest of the company, fond of talking to each other, and rather distrustful of strangers; you find them slow conversers at dinner, sorry whist-players in the drawing-room; you are told, however, that one is a President of the Council, another the Secretary for Foreign Affairs, and a third something equally important. You venerate them accordingly, while you mutter the old Swede's apothegm about the 'small intelligences' that rule mankind. Wait awhile! There is a row in the streets: a pickpocket has appealed to the public to rescue him from the ignoble hands of the police; an escaped felon has fired at the judge who sentenced him, in the name of Liberty and Fraternity. No matter what the cause, there *is* a row. The troops are called out; some are beaten, some join the insurgents. The government grows frightened—temporizes—offers terms—and sends for more soldiers. The people—I never clearly knew what the word meant—the people make extravagant demands, and will not even give time to have them granted,— in a word, the whole state is subverted, the king, if there be one, in flight, the royal family missing, the ministers nowhere! No great loss you 'll say, if the four or five smooth-faced imbecilities we have spoken of are not to the fore! But there is your error, Harry,—your great error. These men, used to conduct and carry on the government, cannot be replaced. The new capacities do nothing but blunder, and maybe issue contradictory orders and impede each other's actions. To improvise a Secretary of State is about as wise a proceeding as to take at hazard a third-class passenger and set him to guide the engine of a train. The only difference is that the machinery of state is ten thousand times more complex than that of a steam-engine, and the powers for mischief and misfortune in due proportion.

"But why talk of these things? I have had enough and too much of them already this evening; women, too, are unpleasant disputants in politics. They attach their faith to persons, not parties. Miss Henderson is, besides, a little spoiled by the notice of those maxim-mongers who write leaders in the 'Débats, and articles for the 'Deux Mondes.' They have, or affect to have, a kind of pitying estimate for our English constitutional forms, which is rather offensive. At least, she provoked me, and I am relapsing into bad temper, just by thinking of it.

"You tell me that you once served with Captain Martin, and I see you understand him; not that it requires much study to do so. You say he was reckoned a good officer; what a sneer is that on the art military!

"There are, however, many suitable qualities about him, and he certainly possesses the true and distinctive element of a gentleman,—he knows how to be idle. Ay, Harry, that is a privilege that your retired banker or enriched cotton-spinner never attains to. They must be up and doing,— where there is nothing to do. They carry the spirit of the counting-house and the loom into society with them, and having found a pleasure in business, they want to make a business of pleasure. Now, Martin understands idling to perfection. His tea and toast, his mutton cutlet, and his mustachios are abundant occupation for him. With luncheon about two o'clock, he saunters through the stables, sucking a lighted cigar, filing his nails, and admiring his boots, till it 's time to ride out. He comes to me about nine of an evening, and we play piquet till I get sleepy; after which he goes to 'the rooms,' and, I believe, plays high; at least, I suspect so; for he has, at times, the forced calm—that semi-jocular resignation—one sees in a heavy loser. He has been occasionally, too, probing me about Merl,—you remember the fellow who had the rooms near Knightsbridge,—so that I opine he has been dabbling in loans. What a sorry spectacle such a creature as this in the toils of the Israelite, for he is the 'softest of the soft.' I see it from the effect La Henderson has produced upon him. He is in love with her,—actually in love. He even wanted to make me his confidant—and I narrowly escaped the confession— only yesterday evening. Of course, he has no suspicion of my attachment in the same quarter, so that it would be downright treachery in me to listen to his avowal. Another feeling, too, sways me, Harry,—I don't think I could hear a man profess admiration for the woman that I mean to marry, without the self-same sense of resentment I should experience were I already her husband. I 'm certain I 'd shoot him for it.

"La belle Kate and I parted coldly—dryly, I should call it—this evening. I had fancied she was above coquetry, but she is not. Is any woman? She certainly gave the Captain what the world would call encouragement all the night; listened attentively to tiresome tiger-huntings and stories of the new country; questioned him about his Mahratta campaigns, and even hinted at how much she would like an Indian life. Perhaps the torment she was inflicting on Lady Dorothea amused her; perhaps it was the irritation she witnessed in me gave the zest to this pastime. It is seldom that she condescends to be either amused or amusing; and I own it is a part does not suit her. She is a thousand times more attractive sitting over her embroidery-frame, raising her head at times to say a few words,—ever apposite and well chosen,—always simple, too, and to the purpose; or even by a slight gesture bearing agreement with what is said around her; till, with a sudden impulse, she pours forth fast, rapidly, and fluently some glowing sentiment of praise or censure, some glorious eulogy of the good, or some withering depreciation of the wrong. Then it is that you see how dark those eyes can be, how deep-toned that voice, and with what delicacy of expression she can mould and fashion every mood of mind, and give utterance to sentiments that till then none have ever known how to embody.

"It is such a descent to her to play coquette! Cleopatra cannot—should not be an Abigail. I am low and depressed to-night; I scarcely know why: indeed, I have less reason than usual for heavy-heartedness. These people are singularly kind and attentive to me, and seem to have totally forgotten how ungratefully once before I repaid their civilities. What a stupid mistake do we commit in not separating our public life from our social one, so as to show that our opinions upon measures of state are disconnected with all the sentiments we maintain for our private friendships. I detect a hundred sympathies, inconceivable points of contact, between these people and myself. We pass hours praising the same things, and abusing the same people; and how could it possibly sever our relations that I would endow Maynooth when they would pull it down, or that I liked forty-shilling freeholders better than ten-pound householders? You 'll say that a certain earnestness accompanies strong convictions, and that when a man is deeply impressed with some supposed truths, he 'll not measure his reprobation of those who assail them. But a lawyer does all this, and forfeits nothing of the esteem of 'his learned brother on the opposite side.' Nay, they exchange very-ugly knocks at times, and inflict very unseemly marks even with the gloves on; still they go homeward, arm-in-arm, after, and laugh heartily at both plaintiff and defendant. By Jove! Harry, it may sound ill, but somehow it seems as though to secure even a moderate share of enjoyment in this life one must throne Expediency in the seat of Principle. I 'll add the conclusion to-morrow, and now say good-night.

"Three days have passed over since I wrote the last time to you, and it would require as many weeks were I to chronicle all that has passed through my mind in the interval. Events there have been few; but sensations— emotions, enough for a lifetime. Nor dare I recall them! Faintly endeavoring to trace a few broken memories, my pains of mind and body come back again, so that you must bear with me if I be incoherent, almost unintelligible.

"The day after I wrote to you, I never saw her. My Lady, who came as usual to visit me in the day, said something about Miss Henderson having a headache. Unpleasant letters from her family—obliged to give up the day to answering them; but all so confused and with such evident constraint as to show me that something disagreeable loomed in view.

"The Captain dropped in about four o'clock, and as the weather was unfavorable, we sat down to our party of piquet. By a little address, I continued to lose nearly every game, and so gradually led him into a conversation while we played; but I soon saw that he only knew something had occurred 'upstairs,' but knew not what.

"' I suspect, however,' added he, 'it is only the old question as to Kate's going away.' "'Going away! Going where?' cried I.

"'Home to her father; she is resolutely bent upon it,—has been so ever since we left Paris. My mother, who evidently—but on what score I know not—had some serious difference with her, is now most eager to make concessions, and would stoop to—what for her is no trifle—even solicitation to induce her to stay, has utterly failed; so, too, has my father. Persuasion and entreaty not succeeding, I suspect—but it is only suspicion—that they have had recourse to parental authority, and asked old Henderson to interfere. At least, a letter has come this morning from the West of Ireland, for Kate, which I surmise to be in his hand. She gave it, immediately on reading it, to my mother, and I could detect in her Ladyship's face, while she perused it, unmistakable signs of satisfaction. When she handed it back, too, she gave a certain condescending smile, which, in my mother, implies victory, and seems to say, "Let us be friends now,—I'm going to signal—cease firing."'

"'And Kate, did she make any remark—say anything?' "'Not a syllable. She folded up the document, carefully and steadily, and placed it in her work-box, and then resumed her embroidery in silence. I watched her narrowly, while I affected to read the paper, and saw that she had to rip out half she had done. After a while my mother said,—""'You'll not answer that letter to-day, probably?"

"""I mean to do so, my Lady," said she; "and, with your permission, will beg you to read my reply."

"""Very well," said my mother, and left the room. I was standing outside on the balcony at the time, so that Kate believed, after my mother's departure, she was quite alone. It was then she opened the letter, and re-read it carefully. I never took my eyes off her; and yet what was passing in her mind, whether joy, grief, disappointment, or pleasure, I defy any man to declare; nor when, having laid it down once more, she took up her work, not a line or a lineament betrayed her. It was plain enough the letter was no pleasant one, and I expected to have heard her sigh perhaps, or at least show some sign of depression; but no, she went on calmly, and at last began to sing, in a low, faint voice, barely audible where I stood, one of her little barcarole songs she is so fond of; and if there was no sorrow in her own heart, by Jove! she made mine throb heavily as I listened! I stood it as long as I was able, and then coughed to show that I was there, and entered the room. She never lifted her head, or noticed me, not even when I drew a chair close to her, and sat down at her side.

"'I suppose, Massingbred,' said he, after a pause, 'you 'll laugh at me, if I tell you I was in love with the Governess! Well, I should have laughed too, some six months ago, if any man had prophesied it; but the way I put the matter to myself is this: If I do succeed to a good estate, I have a right to indulge my own fancy in a wife; if I don't,—that is, if I be a ruined man,— where 's the harm in marrying beneath me?'

"'Quite right, admirably argued,' said I, impatiently; 'go on.'

"'I 'm glad you agree with me,' said he, with the stupid satisfaction of imbecility. 'I thought I had reduced the question to its very narrowest bounds.'

"'So you have; go on,' cried I.

"'"Miss Henderson," said I,—for I determined to show that I was speaking seriously, and so I did n't call her Kate,— "Miss Henderson, I want to speak to you. I have been long seeking this opportunity; and if you will vouchsafe me a few minutes now, and hear me, on a subject upon which all my happiness in life depends—"

"'When I got that far, she put her work down on her knee, and stared at me with those large, full eyes of hers so steadily—ay, so haughtily, too— that I half wished myself fifty miles away.

"'"Captain Martin," said she, in a low, distinct voice, "has it ever occurred to you in life to have, by a mere moment of reflection, a sudden flash of intelligence, saved yourself from some step, some act, which, if accomplished, had brought nothing but outrage to your feeling, and insult to your self-esteem? Let such now rescue you from resuming this theme."

"'"But you# don't understand me," said I. "What I wish to say—" Just at that instant my father came into the room in search of her, and I made my escape to hide the confusion that I felt ready to overwhelm me.'

"'And have you not seen her since?'

"'No. Indeed, I think it quite as well, too. She 'll have time to think over what I said, and see what a deuced good offer it is; for though I know she was going to make objections about inequality of station and all that at the time, reflection will bring better thoughts.'

"'And she 'll consent, you think?'

"'I wish I had a bet on it,' said he.

"'So you shall, then,' said I, endeavoring to seem thoroughly at my ease. 'It's a very unworthy occasion for a wager, Martin; but I'll lay five hundred to one she refuses you.'

"'Taken, and booked,' cried he, writing it down in his note-book. "I only regret it is not in thousands.'

"'So it should be, if I could honestly stake what I have n't got.'

"'You are so sanguine of winning? '

"' So certain, you ought to say.'

"' Of course you use no influence against me,—you take no step of any kind to affect her decision.'

"'Certainly not.'

"'Nor are you—But,' added he, laughing, 'I need n't make that proviso. I was going to say, you are not to ask her yourself.'

"'I 'll even promise you that, if you like,' said I.

"'Then what can you mean?' said he, with a puzzled look. 'But whatever it be, I can stand the loss. I 've won very close to double as much from you this evening.'

"'And as to the disappointment?'

"'Oh, *you* 'll not mention it, I 'm certain, neither will she, so none will be the wiser; and, after all, the real bore in all these cases is the gossip.' And with this consolatory reflection he left me to dress for dinner. How well bred a fellow seems who has no feeling, but just tact enough to detect the tone of the world and follow it! That's Martin's case, and his manners are perfect! After he was gone, I was miserable for not having quarrelled with him,—said something outrageous, insolent, and unbearable. That he should have dared to insult the young girl by such presumption as the offer of *his* hand is really too much. What difference of station—wide as the poles asunder—could compare with their real inequality? The fop, the idler, the incompetent, to aspire to *her!* Even his very narrative proclaimed his mean nature, wandering on, as it did, from a lounge on the balcony to an offer of marriage!

"Now, to conclude this wearisome story—and I fancy, Harry, that already you half deem me a fitting rival for the tiresome Captain,—but to finish, Martin came early into my room, and laying a bank-note for £100 on the bed, merely added, 'You were right; there's your money.' I'd have given double the sum to hear the details of this affair,—in what terms the refusal was conveyed,—on what grounds she based it; but he would not afford me the slightest satisfaction on any of these points. Indeed, he displayed more vigor of character than I suspected in him, in the way he arrested my inquiries. He left this for Paris immediately after, so that the mystery of that interview will doubtless remain impenetrable to me.

"We are all at sixes and sevens to-day. Old Martin, shocked by some tidings of Ireland that he chanced upon in the public papers, I believe, has had a stroke of paralysis, or a seizure resembling that malady. Lady Dorothea is quite helpless from terror, and but for Kate, the whole household would be in utter chaos and disorganization; but she goes about, with her arm in a sling, calm and tranquil, but with the energy and activity of one who feels that all depends upon her guidance and direction. The servants obey her with a promptitude that proclaims instinct; and even the doctor lays aside the mysterious jargon of his craft, and condescends to talk sense to her. I have not seen her; passing rumors only reach me in my solitude, and I sit here writing and brooding alternately.

"P. S. Martin is a little better; no immediate danger to life, but slight hopes of ultimate recovery. I was wrong as to the cause. It was a proclamation of outlawry against his son, the Captain, which he read in the 'Times.' Some implacable creditor or other had pushed his claim so far, as I believe is easy enough to do nowadays; and poor Martin, who connected this stigma with all the disgrace that once accompanied such a sentence, fell senseless to the ground, and was taken up palsied. He is perfectly collected and even tranquil now, and they wheeled me in to sit with him for an hour or so. Lady Dorothea behaves admirably; the first shock overwhelmed her, but that passed off, and she is now all that could be imagined of tenderness and zeal.

"Kate I saw but for a second. She asked me to write to Captain Martin, and request him to hasten home. It was no time to trifle with her; so I simply promised to do so, adding,—"'*You*, I trust, will not leave this at such a moment?'

"'Assuredly not,' said she, slightly coloring at what implied my knowledge of her plans.

"'Then all will go on well in that case,' said I.

"'I never knew that I was reckoned what people call lucky,' said she, smiling. 'Indeed, most of those with whom I have been associated in life might say the opposite.' And then, without waiting to hear me, she left the room.

"My brain is throbbing and my cheeks burning; some feverish access is upon me. So I send off this ere I grow worse.

"Your faithful friend,

"Jack Massingbred."

CHAPTER X
HOW ROGUES AGREE!

Leaving the Martins in their quiet retreat at Spa, nor dwelling any longer on a life whose daily monotony was unbroken by an incident, we once more turn our glance westward. Were we assured that our kind readers' sympathies were with us, the change would be a pleasure to us, since it is there, in that wild mountain tract, that pathless region of fern and wild furze, that we love to linger, rambling half listlessly through silent glens and shady gorges, or sitting pensively on the storm-lashed shore, till sea and sky melt into one, and naught lowers through the gloom save the tall crags above us.

We are once more back again at the little watering-place of Kilkieran, to which we introduced our readers in an early chapter of this narrative; but another change has come over that humble locality. The Osprey's Nest, the ornamented villa, on which her Ladyship had squandered so lavishly good money and bad taste, was now an inn! A vulgar sign-board, representing a small boat in a heavy sea, hung over the door, with the words "The Corragh" written underneath. The spacious saloon, whose bay-windows opened on the Atlantic, was now a coffee-room, and the small boudoir that adjoined it—desecration of desecrations—the bar!

It needs not to have been the friend or favored guest beneath a roof where elegance and refinement have prevailed to feel the shock at seeing them replaced by all that ministers to coarse pleasure and vulgar association. The merest stranger cannot but experience a sense of disgust at the contrast. Whichever way you turned, some object met the eye recalling past splendor and present degradation; indeed, Toby Shea, the landlord, seemed to feel as one of his brightest prerogatives the right of insulting the memory of his predecessors, and throwing into stronger antithesis the "former" and the "now."

"Here ye are now, sir, in my Lady's own parlor; and that's her bedroom, where I left your trunk," said he, as he ushered in a newly arrived traveller, whose wet and road-stained drapery bore traces of an Irish winter's day.

"Mr. Scanlan told me that your honor would be here at four o'clock, and he ordered dinner for two, at five, and a good dinner you 'll have."

"There; let them open my traps, and fetch me a pair of slippers and a dressing-gown," broke in the traveller; "and be sure to have a good fire in my bedroom. What an infernal climate! It has rained since the day I landed at Dublin; and now that I have come down here, it has blown a hurricane besides. And how cold this room is!" added he, shuddering.

"That's all by reason of them windows," said Toby, — "French windows they call them; but I'll get real Irish sashes put up next season, if I live. It was a fancy of that ould woman that built the place to have nothing that was n't foreign."

"They are not popular, then, — the Martins?" asked the stranger.

"Popular!" echoed Toby. "Begorra, they are not. Why would they be? Is it rack-renting, process sarving, extirminating, would make them popular? Sure we're all ruined on the estate. There isn't a mother's son of us might n't be in jail; and it's not Maurice's fault, either, — Mr. Scanlan's, I mean. Your honor's a friend of his, I believe," added he, stealthily. The stranger gave a short nod. "Sure he only does what he's ordered; and it's breaking his heart it is to do them cruel things they force him to."

"Was the management of the estate better when they lived at home?" asked the stranger.

"Some say yes, more says no. I never was their tenant myself, for I lived in Oughterard, and kept the 'Goose and Griddle' in John Street; but I believe, if the truth was told, it was always pretty much the same. They were azy and moderate when they did n't want money, but ready to take your skin off your back when they were hard up."

"And is that their present condition?"

"I think it is," said he, with a confident grin. "They 're spending thousands for hundreds since they went abroad; and that chap in the dragoons — the Captain they call him — sells a farm, or a plot of ground, just the way ye 'd tear a leaf out of a book. There 's Mr. Maurice now, — and I 'll go and hurry the dinner, for he 'll give us no peace if we 're a minute late."

The stranger — or, to give him his proper name, Mr. Merl — now approached the window, and watched, not without admiration, the skilful management by which Scanlan skimmed along the strand, zigzagging his smart nag through all the awkward impediments of the way, and wending his tandem through what appeared a labyrinth of confusion.

Men bred and born in great cities are somewhat prone to fancy that certain accomplishments, such as tandem-driving, steeple-chasing, and such like, are the exclusive acquirements of rank and station. They have only witnessed them as the gifts of guardsmen and "young squires of high degree," never suspecting that in the country a very inferior class is often endowed with these skilful arts. Mr. Merl felt, therefore, no ordinary reverence for Maurice Scanlan, a sentiment fully reciprocated by the attorney, as he beheld the gorgeous dressing-gown, rich tasselled cap, and Turkish trousers of the other.

"I thought I'd arrive before you, sir," said Scanlan, with a profound bow, as he entered the room; "but I'm glad you got in first. What a shower that was!"

"Shower!" said Merl; "a West India hurricane is a zephyr to it. I 'd not live in this climate if you 'd give me the whole Martin estate!"

"I 'm sure of it, sir; one must be bred in the place, and know no better, to stand it." And although the speech was uttered in all humility, Merl gave the speaker a searching glance, as though to say, "Don't lose your time trying to humbug me; I'm 'York,' too." Indeed, there was species of freemasonry in the looks that now passed between the two; each seemed instinctively to feel that he was in the presence of an equal, and that artifice and deceit might be laid aside for the nonce.

"I hope you agree with me," said Scanlan, in a lower and more confidential voice, "that this was the best place to come to. Here you can stay as long as you like, and nobody the wiser; but in the town of Oughterard they'd be at you morning, noon, and night, tracking your steps, questioning the waiter, ay, and maybe taking a peep at your letters. I 've known that same before now."

"Well, I suppose you 're right; only this place does look a little dull, I confess."

"It's not the season, to be sure," said Scanlan, apologetically.

"Oh! and there is a season here?"

"Isn't there, by George!" said Maurice, smacking his lips. "I 've seen two heifers killed here of a morning, and not so much as a beefsteak to be got before twelve o'clock. 'T is the height of fashion comes down here in July,— the Rams of Kiltimmon, and the Bodkins of Crossmaglin; and there was talk last year of a lord,—I forget his name; but he ran away from Newmarket, and the story went that he was making for this."

"Any play?" asked Merl.

"Play is it? That there is; whist every night, and backgammon."

Merl threw up his eyebrows with pretty much the same feeling with which the Great Napoleon repeated the words "Bows and Arrows!" as the weapons of a force that offered him alliance.

"If you'd allow me to dine in this trim, Mr. Scanlan," said he, "I'd ask you to order dinner."

"I was only waiting for you to give the word, sir," said Maurice, reverting to the habit of respect at any fresh display of the other's pretensions; and opening the door, he gave a shrill whistle.

The landlord himself answered the summons, and whispered a few words in Scanlan's ear.

"That's it, always," cried Maurice, angrily. "I never came into the house for the last ten days without hearing the same story. I 'd like to know who and what he is, that must always have the best that 's going?" Then turning to Merl, he added: "It's a lodger he has upstairs; an old fellow that came about a fortnight back; and if there's a fine fish or a fat turkey or a good saddle of mutton to be got, he 'll have it."

"Faix, he pays well," said Toby, "whoever he is."

"And he has secured our salmon, I find, and left us to dine on whiting," said Maurice.

"An eighteen-pound fish!" echoed Toby; "and it would be as much as my life is worth to cut it in two."

"And he's alone, too?"

"No, sir. Mr. Crow, the painter, is to dine with him. He's making drawings for him of all the wonderful places down the coast."

"Well, give us what we 're to have at once," said Maurice, angrily. "The basket of wine was taken out of the gig?"

"Yes, sir; all right and ready for you; and barrin' the fish you 'll have an elegant dinner."

This little annoyance over, the guests relished their fare like hungry men; nor, time and place considered, was it to be despised.

"Digestion is a great leveller." Mr. Merl and Mr. Scan-Ian felt far more on an equality when, the dinner over and the door closed, they drew the table close to the fire, and drank to each other in a glass of racy port.

"Well, I believe a man might live here, after all," said Merl, as he gazed admiringly on the bright hues of his variegated lower garments.

"I'm proud to hear you say so," said Scanlan; "for, of course, you've seen a deal of life; and when I say life, I mean fashion and high style,—nobs and swells."

"Yes; I believe I have," said Merl, lighting his cigar; "that was always my 'line.' I fancy there's few fellows going have more experience of the really great world than Herman Merl."

"And you like it?" asked Maurice, confidentially.

"I do, and I do not," said the Jew, hesitatingly. "To one like myself, who knows them all, always on terms of close intimacy,—friendship, I may say,—it's all very well; but take a new hand just launched into life, a fellow not of their own set,—why, sir, there's no name for the insults and outrage he'll meet with."

"But what could they do?" asked Scanlan, inquiringly.

"What?—anything, everything; laugh at him, live on him, win his last guinea,—and then, blackball him!"

"And couldn't he get a crack at them?"

"A what?"

"Couldn't he have a shot at some of them, at least?" asked Maurice.

"No, no," said Mr. Merl, half contemptuously; "they don't do *that*."

"Faix! and we'd do it down here," said Scanlan, "devil may care who or what he was that tried the game."

"But I'm speaking of London and Paris; I'm not alluding to the Sandwich Islands," said Merl, on whose brain the port and the strong fire were already producing their effects.

Scanlan's face flushed angrily; but a glance at the other checked the reply he was about to make, and he merely pushed the decanter across the table.

"You see, sir," said Merl, in the tone of a man laying down a great dictum, "there's worlds and worlds. There's Claude Willoughby's world, which is young Martin's and Stanhope's and mine. There, we are all young fellows of fortune, good family, good prospects, you understand,—no, thank you, no more wine;—I feel that what I've taken has got into my head; and this cigar, too, is none of the best. Would it be taking too great a liberty with you if I were to snatch a ten minutes' doze,—just ten minutes?"

"Treat me like an old friend; make yourself quite at home," said Maurice. "There's enough here"—and he pointed to the bottles on the table—"to keep me company; and I'll wake you up when I've finished them."

Mr. Merl made no reply; but drawing a chair for his legs, and disposing his drapery gracefully around him, he closed his eyes, and before Maurice had replenished his glass, gave audible evidence of a sound sleep.

Now, worthy reader, we practise no deceptions with you; nor so far as we are able, do we allow others to do so. It is but fair, therefore, to tell you that Mr. Merl was not asleep, nor had he any tendency whatever to slumber about him. That astute gentleman, however, had detected that the port was, with the addition of a great fire, too much for him; he recognized in himself certain indications of confusion that implied wandering and uncertain faculties, and he resolved to arrest the progress of such symptoms by a little repose. He felt, in short, that if he had been engaged in play, that he should have at once "cut out," and so he resolved to give himself the advantage of the prerogative which attaches to a tired traveller. There he lay, then, with closed eyes,—breathing heavily,—to all appearance sound asleep.

Maurice Scanlan, meanwhile, scanned the recumbent figure before him with the eye of a connoisseur. We have once before said that Mr. Scanlan's jockey experiences had marvellously aided his worldly craft, and that he scrutinized those with whom he came in contact through life, with all the shrewd acumen he would have bestowed upon a horse whose purchase he meditated. It was easy to see that the investigation puzzled him. Mr. Merl did not belong to any one category he had ever seen before. Maurice was acquainted with various ranks and conditions of men; but here was a new order, not referable to any known class. He opened Captain Martin's letter, which he carried in his pocket-book, and re-read it; but it was vague and uninstructive. He merely requested that "every attention might be paid to his friend Mr. Merl, who wanted to see something of the West, and know all about the condition of the people, and such like. He's up to everything, Master Maurice," continued the writer, "and so just the man for *you*." There was little to be gleaned from this source, and so he felt, as he folded and replaced the epistle in his pocket.

"What can he be," thought Scanlan, "and what brings him down here? Is he a member of Parliament, that wants to make himself up about Ireland and Irish grievances? Is he a money-lender, that wants to see the security before he makes a loan? Are they thinking of him for the agency?"—and Maurice flushed as the suspicion crossed him,—"or is it after Miss Mary he is?" And a sudden paleness covered his face at the thought. "I 'd give a cool hundred, this minute, if I could read you," said he to himself, "Ay, and I'd not ask any one's help how to deal with us afterwards," added he, as he drained off his glass. While he was thus ruminating, a gentle tap was heard at the door, and, anxious not to disturb the sleeper, Scanlan crossed the room with noiseless steps, and opened it.

"Oh, it's you, Simmy," said he, in a low voice. "Come in, and make no noise; he's asleep."

"And that's him!" said Crow, standing still to gaze on the recumbent figure before him, which he scrutinized with all an artist's appreciation.

"Ay, and what do you think of him?" whispered Scanlan.

"That chap is a Jew," said Sim, in the same cautious tone. "I know the features well; you see the very image of him in the old Venetian pictures. Whenever they wanted cunning and cruelty—but more cunning than cruelty—they always took that type."

"I would n't wonder if you were right, Simmy," said Scanlan, on whom a new light was breaking.

"I know I am; look at the spread of the nostrils, and the thick, full lips, and the coarse, projecting under-jaw. Faix!" said he to himself, "I 've seen the day I 'd like to have had a study of your face."

"Indeed!" said Scanlan.

"Just so; he'd make a great Judas!" said Crow, enthusiastically. "It is the miser all over. You know," added he, "if one took him in the historical way, you 'd get rid of the vulgarity, and make him grander and finer; for, looking at him now, he might be a dog-stealer."

Scanlan gave a low, cautious laugh as he placed a chair beside his own for the artist, and filled out for him a bumper of port.

"I was just dying for a glass of this," said Crow. "I dined with Mr. Barry upstairs; and though he's a fine-hearted old fellow in many respects, he's too abstemious; a pint of sherry for two at dinner, and a pint of port after, that's the allowance. Throw out as many hints as you like, suggest how and what you will, but devil a drop more you'll get."

"And who is he?" asked Scanlan.

"I wish you could tell me," said Crow.

"You haven't a notion; nor what he is?"

"Not the slightest. I think, indeed, he said he was in the army; but I'm not clear it wasn't a commissary or a surgeon; maybe he was, but he knows a little about everything. Take him on naval matters, and he understands them well; ask him about foreign countries,—egad, he was everywhere. Ireland seems the only place new to him, and it won't be so long; for he goes among the people, and talks to them, and hears all they have to say, with a patience that breaks my heart. Like all strangers, he's astonished with the acuteness he meets with, and never ceases saying, 'Ain't they a wonderful people? Who ever saw their equal for intelligence?'"

"Bother!" said Scanlan, contemptuously.

"But it is not bother! Maurice; he's right. They are just what he says."

"Arrah! don't be humbugging *me*, Mr. Crow," said the other. "They 're a set of scheming, plotting vagabonds, that are unmanageable by any one, except a fellow that has the key to them as I have."

"*You* know them, that's true," said Crow, half apologetically, for he liked the port, and did not feel he ought to push contradiction too far.

"And that's more than your friend Barry does, or ever will," said Scanlan. "I defy an Englishman—I don't care how shrewd he is—to understand Paddy."

A slight movement on Mr. Merl's part here admonished the speaker to speak lower.

"Ay," continued Maurice, "that fellow there—whoever he is or whatever he is—is no fool! he 's deep enough; and yet there 's not a bare-legged gossoon on the estate I won't back to take him in."

"But Barry's another kind of man entirely. You wouldn't call him cute or cunning; but he's a sensible, well-judging man, that has seen a deal of life."

"And what is it, he says, brings him here?" asked Scanlan.

"He never said a word about that yet," replied Crow, "further than his desire to visit a country he had heard much of, and, if I understand him aright, where some of his ancestors came from; for, you see, at times he's not so easy for one to follow, for he has a kind of a foreign twang in his tongue, and often mumbles to himself in a strange language."

"I mistrust all these fellows that go about the world, pretending they want to see this and observe that," said Scanlan, sententiously.

"It's mighty hard to mistrust a man that gives you the likes of that," said Crow, as he drew a neatly folded banknote from his pocket, and handed it to Scanlan. "Twenty pounds! And he gave you that?" "This very evening. 'It is a little more than our bargain, Mr. Crow,' said he, 'but not more than I can afford to give; and so I hope you 'll not refuse it.' These were his words, as he took my lot of drawings—poor daubs they were—and placed them in his portfolio."

"So that he is rich?" said Maurice, pensively, "There seems no end of his money; there's not a day goes over he does n't spend fifteen or sixteen pounds in meat, potatoes, barley, and the like. Sure, you may say he 's been feeding the two islands himself for the last fortnight; and what's more, one must n't as much as allude to it. He gets angry at the slightest word that can bring the subject forward. It was the other day he said to myself, 'If you can relieve destitution without too much parade of its sufferings, you are not only obviating the vulgar display of rich benevolence, but you are inculcating high sentiments and delicacy of feeling in those that are relieved. Take care how you pauperize the heart of a people, for you 'll have to make a workhouse of the nation.'"

"Sure, they're paupers already!" exclaimed Scanlan, contemptuously. "When I hear all these elegant sentiments uttered about Ireland, I know a man is an ass! This is a poor country,—the people is poor, the gentry is poor, the climate is n't the best, and bad as it is, you 're never sure of it. All that anybody can hope to do is to make his living out of it; but as to improving it,—raising the intellectual standard of the people, and all that balderdash we hear of,—you might just as well tell me that there was an Act of Parliament to make everybody in Connaught six feet high. Nature says one thing, and it signifies mighty little if the House of Commons says the other."

"And you 're telling me this in the very spot that contradicts every word you say!" cried Crow, half angrily; for the port had given him courage, and the decanter waxed low.

"How so?" exclaimed Scanlan.

"Here, where we sit—on this very estate of Cro' Martin—where a young girl—a child the other day—has done more to raise the condition of the people, to educate and civilize, than the last six generations together."

A long wailing whistle from Scanlan was the insulting reply to the assertion.

"What do you mean by that?" cried Crow, passionately.

"I mean that she has done more mischief to the property than five-and-forty years' good management will ever repair, Now don't be angry, Simmy; keep your temper, and draw your chair back again to the table. I 'm not going to say one word against her intentions; but when I see the waste of thousands of pounds on useless improvements, elegant roads that lead nowhere, bridges that nobody will ever pass, and harbors without boats, not to say the habits of dependence the people have got by finding everything done for them. I tell you again, ten years more of Miss Mary's rule will finish the estate."

"I don't believe a word of it!" blurted out Simmy, boldly. "I saw her yesterday coming out of a cabin, where she passed above an hour, nursing typhus fever and cholera. The cloak she took off the door—for she left it there to dry—was still soaked with rain; her wet hair hung down her shoulders, and as she stood bridling her own pony,—for there was not a living soul to help her—"

"She 'd have made an elegant picture," broke in Scanlan, with a laugh. "But that's exactly the fault of us in Ireland,—we are all picturesque; I wish we were prosperous! But come, Simmy, finish your wine; it's not worth disputing about. If all I hear about matters be true, there will be very little left of Cro' Martin when the debts are paid."

"What! do you mean to say that they 're in difficulty?"

"Far worse; the stories that reach me call it—ruin!"

Simmy drew his chair closer to the table, and in a whisper scarcely breathed, said, "That chap's not asleep, Maurice."

"I know it," whispered the other; and added, aloud, "Many a fellow that thinks he has the first charge on the property will soon discover his mistake; there are mortgages of more than eighty years' standing on the estate. You've had a great sleep, sir," said he, addressing Merl, who now yawned and opened his eyes; "I hope our talking did n't disturb you?"

"Not in the least," said Merl, rising and stretching his legs. "I'm all right now, and quite fresh for anything."

"Let me introduce Mr. Crow to you, sir,—a native artist that we 're all proud of."

"That's exactly what you are not then," said Crow; "nor would you be if I deserved it. You 'd rather gain a cause at the Quarter Sessions, or take in a friend about a horse, than be the man that painted the Madonna at Florence."

"He's cross this evening,—cross and ill-humored," said Scanlan, laughing. "Maybe he 'll be better tempered when we have tea."

"I was just going to ask for it," said Merl, as he arranged his whiskers, and performed a small impromptu toilet before the glass, while Simmy issued forth to give the necessary orders.

"We 'll have tea, and a rubber of dummy afterwards," said Scanlan, "if you've no objection."

"Whatever you like,—I 'm quite at your disposal," replied Merl, who now seated himself with an air of bland amiability, ready, according to the amount of the stake, to win pounds or lose sixpences.

CHAPTER XI
MR. MERL "AT FENCE"

All the projects which Mr. Scanlan had struck out for Merl's occupation on the following day were marred by the unfavorable weather. It blew fiercely from the westward, driving upon shore a tremendous sea, and sending white masses of drift and foam far inland. The rain, too, came down in torrents. The low-lying clouds, which scarcely reached more than half-way up the mountain sides, seemed as if rent asunder at times, and from them came a deluge, filling all the watercourses, and swelling rivulets to the size of mighty torrents. The unceasing roll of thunder, now near, now rumbling along in distant volleys, swelled the wild uproar, and helped to make up a scene of grand but desolate meaning.

What could well be drearier than that little line of cabins that formed the village of Kilkieran, as with strongly barricaded doors, and with roofs secured by ropes and spars, they stood exposed to the full violence of the wild Atlantic! Not a man, not a living thing was to be seen. The fishermen were all within doors, cowering in gloomy indolence over the scanty turf fires, and brooding darkly on the coming winter.

With a thorough conviction of all the dreariness of this scene, Mr. Merl stood at the window and looked out. He had been all his life too actively engaged in his pursuits of one kind or other to know much about what is called "being bored." Let rain fall ever so heavily, a cab could take him down to "'Change,"—the worst weather never marred a sale of stock, and Consols could rise even while the mercury was falling. The business-life of a great city seems to care little for weather, and possibly they whose intent faculties are bent on gain, scarcely remember whether the sun shines upon their labors.

Merl felt differently now; the scene before him was wilder and gloomier than anything he had ever beheld. Beyond and behind the village steep mountains rose on every side, of barren and rugged surface,—not a vestige of any culture to be seen; while on the road, which led along a narrow gorge, nothing moved. All was dreary and deserted.

"I suppose you'll keep the roof over you to-day, Mr. Merl?" said Scanlan, as he entered the room, buttoned up to the chin in a coarse frieze coat, while his head was protected by a genuine "sou'-wester" of oilskin.

"And are *you* going out in such weather?" asked Merl.

"'Needs must,' sir, as the proverb says. I have to be at the assizes at Oughterard this morning, to prosecute some scoundrels for cutting brambles in the wood; and I want to serve notices on a townland about eight miles from this; and then I 'll have to go round by Cro' Martin and see Miss Mary. That's not the worst of it," added he, with an impudent leer, "for she's a fine girl, and has the prettiest eyes in the kingdom."

"I have a letter for her," said Merl, — "a letter of introduction from Captain Martin. I suppose I might as well send it by you, and ask if I might pay my respects to-morrow or next day?"

"To be sure; I'll take it with pleasure. You'll like her when you see her. She's not a bit like the rest: no pride, no stand-off, — that is, when she takes a fancy; but she is full of life and courage for anything."

"Ah, yes, — the Captain said we should get on very well together," drawled out Merl.

"Did he, though!" cried Scanlan, eagerly. Then as suddenly checking his anxiety, he added: "But what does *he* know about Miss Mary? Surely they're as good as strangers to each other. And for the matter of that, even when he was here, they did n't take to each other, — she was always laughing at the way he rode."

"Wasn't he in the dragoons?" asked Merl, in a half-rebutting tone.

"So he was; but what does that signify? Sure it's not a cavalry seat, with your head down and your elbows squared, will teach you to cross country, — at least, with Mary Martin beside you. You'll see her one of these day yourself, Mr. Merl. May I never, if you don't see her now!" cried Scanlan, suddenly, as he pointed to the road along which a horse was seen coming at speed, the rider breasting the storm fearlessly, and only crouching to the saddle as the gusts swept past. "What in the name of all that's wonderful brings her here?" cried Maurice. "She wasn't down at Kilkieran for four months."

"She'll stop at this inn here, I suppose?" said Merl who was already performing an imaginary toilet for her visit.

"You may take your oath she'll not!" said Scanlan half roughly; "she 'd not cross the threshold of it! She 's going to some cabin or other. There she goes, — is n't that riding?" cried he, in animation. "Did you ever see a horse held neater? And see how she picks the road for him! Easy as she's sitting, she'd take a four-foot wall this minute, without stirring in her saddle."

"She hasn't got a nice day for pleasuring!" said the Jew, with a vulgar cackle.

"If ye call it pleasure," rejoined Scanlan, "what she's after; but I suspect there's somebody sick down at the end of the village. There, I'm right; she's pulling up at Mat Landy's,—I wonder if it's old Mat is bad."

"You know him?" asked Merl.

"To be sure I do. He's known down the coast for forty miles. He saved more men from shipwreck himself than everybody in the barony put together; but his heart is all but broke about a granddaughter that ran away. Sure enough, she's going in there."

"Did you see Miss Mary?" cried Crow, entering suddenly. "She's just gone down the beach. They say there's a case now down there."

"A case—of what?" said Merl.

"Cholera or typhus, as it may be," said Crow, not a little surprised at the unmistakable terror of the other's face.

"And she's gone to see it!" exclaimed the Jew.

"To do more than see it. She'll nurse the sick man, and bring him medicine and whatever he wants."

"And not afraid?"

"Afraid!" broke in Crow. "I'd like to know what she's afraid of. Ask Mr. Scanlan what would frighten her." But Mr. Scanlan had already slipped noiselessly from the room, and was already on his way down the shore.

"Well," said Merl, lighting his cigar, and drawing an arm-chair close to the fire, "I don't see the advantage of all that. She could send the doctor, I suppose, and make her servants take down to these people whatever she wanted to send them. What especial utility there is in going herself, I can't perceive."

"I'll tell you, then," said Crow. "It's more likely the doctor is busy this minute, ten or fifteen miles away,—for the whole country is down in sickness; but even if he wasn't, if it were not for her courage in going everywhere, braving danger and death every hour, there would be a general flight of all that could escape. They'd rush into the towns,—where already there's more sickness than they know how to deal with. She encourages some,—she shames more; and not a few are proud to be brave in such company, for she is an angel,—that's her name,—an angel."

"Well, I should like to see her," drawled out Merl, as he smoothed down his scrubby mustachios.

"Nothing easier, then," rejoined Crow. "Put on your coat and hat, and we 'll stroll down the beach till she comes out; it can't be very long, for she has enough on her hands elsewhere."

The proposition of a "stroll" in such weather was very little to Mr. Merl's taste; but his curiosity was stronger than even his fear of a drenching, and having muffled and shawled himself as if for an Arctic winter, they set out together from the inn.

"And you tell me," said he, "that the Martins used to live here,—actually pass their lives in this atrocious climate?"

"That they did,—and the worst mistake they ever made was to leave it," said Crow.

"I confess you puzzle me," said Merl.

"Very possibly I do, sir," was the calm reply; "but you'd have understood me at once had you known this country while they resided at Cro' Martin. It was n't only that the superfluities of their wealth ran over, and filled the cup of the poor man, but there was a sense of hope cherished, by seeing that however hard the times, however adverse the season, there was always 'his Honor,' as they called Mr. Martin, whom they could appeal to for aid or for lenient treatment."

"Very strange, very odd, all this," said Merl, musing. "But all that I hear of Ireland represents the people as if in a continual struggle for mere existence, and actually in a daily state of dependence on the will of somebody above them."

"And if that same condition were never to be exaggerated into downright want, or pushed to an actual slavery, we could be very happy with it," said Crow, "and not thank you, or any other Englishman that came here, to disturb it."

"I assure you I have no ambition to indulge in any such interference," said Merl, with a half-contemptuous laugh.

"And so you're not thinking of settling in Ireland?" asked Crow, in some surprise.

"Never dreamed of it!"

"Well, the story goes that you wanted to buy an estate, and came down to have a look at this property here."

"I'd not live on it if Martin were to make me a present of it to-morrow."

"I don't think he will," said Crow, gravely. "I am afraid he could n't, if he wished it."

"What, do you mean on account of the entail?" asked Merl.

"Not exactly." He paused, and after some silence said, "If the truth were told, there's a great deal of debt on this property,—more than any one suspects."

"The Captain's encumbrances?" asked Merl, eagerly.

"His grandfather's and his great-grandfather's! As for the present man, they say that he's tied up some way not to sell, except for the sake of redeeming some of the mortgages. But who knows what is true and what is false about all this?"

Merl was silent; grave fears were crossing his mind how far his claims were valid; and terrible misgivings shot across him lest the Captain might have been paying him with valueless securities.

"I gather from what you say," said he, at last, "that it would be rather difficult to make out a title for any purchaser of this estate."

"Don't be afraid of that, sir. They'll make you out a fair title."

"I tell you again, I'd not take it as a present," said Merl, half angrily.

"I see," said Crow, nodding his head sententiously. And then fixing his eyes steadily on him, he said, "You are a mortgagee."

Merl reddened,—partly anger, partly shame. Indeed, the feeling that such a capacity as Mr. Crow's should have pushed him hard, was anything but complimentary to his self-esteem.

"I don't want to pry into any man's affairs," said Crow, easily. "Heaven knows it's mighty little matter to Simmy Crow who lives in the big house there. I 'd rather, if I had my choice, be able to walk the wood with my sketch-book and brushes than be the richest man that ever was heartsore with the cares of wealth."

"And if a friend—a sincere, well-wishing friend—were to bind himself that you should enjoy this same happiness you speak of, Mr. Crow, what would you do in return?"

"Anything he asked me,—anything, at least, that a fair man could ask, and an honest one could do."

"There's my hand on it, then," said Merl. "It's a bargain."

"Ay, but let us hear the conditions," said Crow. "What could I possibly serve you in, that would be worth this price?"

"Simply this: that you'll answer all my inquiries, so far as you know about this estate; and where your knowledge fails, that you'll endeavor to obtain the information for me."

"Maybe I could tell you nothing at all—or next to nothing," said Crow. "Just ask me, now, what's the kind of question you 'd put; for, to tell truth, I 'm not over bright or clever,—the best of me is when I've a canvas before me."

Merl peered stealthily at the speaker over the great folds of the shawl that enveloped his throat; he was not without his misgivings that the artist was a "deep fellow," assuming a manner of simplicity to draw him into a confidence. "And yet," he thought, "had he really been shrewd and cunning, he 'd never have blurted out his suspicion as to my being a mortgagee. Besides," said he to himself, "there, and with that fact, must end all his knowledge of me." "You can dine with me to-day, Mr. Crow, can't you?"

"I 'm engaged to the stranger in No. 4,—the man I'm making the drawings for."

"But you could get off. You could ask him to excuse you by saying that something of importance required you elsewhere?"

"And dine in the room underneath?" asked Crow, with a comical look of distress at this suggestion.

"Well, let us go somewhere else. Is there no other inn in the neighborhood?"

"There's a small public-house near the gate of Cro' Martin, to be sure."

"Then we'll dine there. I'll order a chaise at four o'clock, and we 'll drive over together. And now, I 'll just return to the house, for this wading here is not much to my taste."

Mr. Merl returned gloomily to the house, his mind too deeply occupied with his own immediate interests to bestow any thought upon Mary Martin. The weather assuredly offered but little inducement to linger out of doors, for, as the morning wore on, the rain and wind increased in violence, while vast masses of mist swept over the sea and were carried on shore, leaving only, at intervals, little patches of the village to be seen,—dreary, storm-beaten, and desolate! Merl shuddered, as he cast one last look at this sad-colored picture, and entered the inn.

Has it ever been your ill-fortune, good reader, to find yourself alone in some dreary, unfrequented spot, the weather-bound denizen of a sorry inn, without books or newspapers, thrown upon the resources of your own thoughts, so sure to take their color from the dreary scene around them? It is a trying ordeal for the best of tempers. Your man of business chafes and frets against the inactivity; your man of leisure sorrows over monotony that makes idleness a penalty. He whose thoroughfare in life is the pursuit of wealth thinks of all those more fortunate than himself then hurrying on to gain, while he who is the mark of the world's flatteries and attentions laments over the dismal desolation of an uncompanionable existence.

If Mr. Merl did not exactly occupy any one of these categories, he fancied, at least, that he oscillated amidst them all. It was, indeed, his good pleasure to imagine himself a "man upon town," who played a little, discounted a little, dealt a little in old pictures, old china, old cabinets, and old plate, but all for mere pastime,—something, as he would say, "to give him an interest in it;" and there, certainly, he was right. Nothing so surely imparted an "interest" in Mr. Merl's eyes as having an investment. Objects of art, the greatest triumphs of genius, landscape the richest eye ever ranged over, political events that would have awakened a sense of patriotism in the dullest and coldest, all came before him as simple questions of profit and loss.

If he was not actually a philosopher, some of his views of life were characterized by great shrewdness. He had remarked, for instance, that the changeful fashions of the world are ever alternating; and that not only dress and costume and social customs undergo mutations, but that objects of positive sterling value are liable to the same wayward influences. We are all modern to-day, to-morrow we may be "Louis Quatorze," the next day "Cinque Centi" in our tastes. Now we are mad after Italian art, yesterday the Dutch school was in vogue. Our galleries, our libraries, our houses, our gardens, all feel the caprices of these passing moods. There was but one thing that Mr. Merl had perceived never changed, and that was the estimation men felt for money. Religions might decay, and states crumble, thrones totter, and kings be exiled, Cuyps might be depreciated and marquetry be held in mean esteem; but gold was always within a fraction at least of four pounds eleven shillings the ounce!

He remarked, too, that men gradually grow tired of almost everything; the pursuits of the young are not those of the middle-aged, still less of advanced life. The books which we once cried over are now thrown down with languor; the society we imagined perfection we now smile at for its very absurdities. We see vulgarity where we once beheld vigor; we detect exaggeration where we used to attribute power. There is only one theme of which our estimation never varies,—wealth! Mr. Merl had never yet met the man nor the woman who really despised it; nay, he had seen kings trafficking on 'Change. He had known great ministers deep speculators on the Bourse; valiant admirals, distinguished generals, learned judges, and even divines, had bought and sold with him, all eager in the pursuit of gain, and all employing, to the best of their ability, the high faculties of their intelligence to assist them in making crafty bargains.

If these experiences taught him the universal veneration men feel for wealth, they also conveyed another lesson, which was, the extreme gullibility of mankind. He met every day men who ruled cabinets and commanded fleets,—the reputed great of the earth,—and saw them easier victims in his hand than the commonest capacity in "Leadenhall Street." They had the earliest information, but could not profit by it; they never understood the temper on 'Change, knew nothing of the variations of the money-barometer, and invariably fell into snares that your city man never incurred. Hence Mr. Merl came to conceive a very low general opinion of what he himself called "the swells," and a very high one of Herman Merl.

If we have dwelt upon these traits of this interesting individual in this place, it is simply to place before our reader's mind the kind of lucubrations such a man might be disposed to indulge in. In fact, story-tellers like ourselves have very little pretension to go beyond the narrow limit; and having given to the reader the traits of a character, they must leave their secret working more or less to his ingenuity. So much, however, we are at liberty to declare, that Mr. Merl was terribly bored, and made no scruple of confessing it.

"What the deuce are you staring at? Is there anything really to be seen in that confounded dreary sea?" cried he, as Crow stood shading his eyes from the lightning flashes, and intently gazing on the scene without.

"That's one of the effects Backhuysen was so fond of!" exclaimed Crow, eagerly,—"a sullen sea, lead-colored and cold, with a white curl just crisping the top of the waves, over it a dreary expanse of dark sky, low-lying and black, till you come near the horizon, where there is a faint line of grayish white, just enough to show that you are on the wide, wide ocean, out of sight of land, and nothing living near, except that solitary sea-gull perched upon the breakers there. There's real poetry in a bit like that; it sets one a thinking over the desolation of those whose life is little better than a voyage on such a sea!"

"Better be drowned at once," broke in Merl, impatiently.

Crow started and looked at him; and had Merl but seen that glance, so scornful and contemptuous was it, even his self-esteem might have felt outraged. But he had not remarked it; and as little did he guess what was then passing in the poor artist's mind, as Crow muttered to himself, "I know one that will not be your guest to-day, if he dines on a cold potato, or does n't dine at all."

"Did I tell you," cried he, suddenly, "that there's no horses to be had?"

"No horses!" exclaimed Merl; "how so?"

"There's a great trial going on at the assizes to-day, and Mr. Barry is gone on to Oughterard to hear it, and he has the only pair of posters in the place."

"What a confounded hole!" burst out Merl, passionately. "That I ever should have set my foot in it! How are we to get through the day here? Have you thought of anything to be done?"

"I'll go down and find out how poor Landy is," said Crow; "for Miss Mary's horse is still at the door, and he must be very bad, indeed, or she wouldn't delay so long."

"And what if it should turn out the cholera, or typhus, or something as bad?"

"Well?" said Crow, interrogatively; for he could not guess the drift of the suggestion.

"Simply this, my worthy friend," resumed Merl, — "that I have no fancy for the pleasure of your company at dinner after such an excursion as you speak of."

"I was just going to say that myself," said Crow. "Good-bye!" And before Merl could interpose a word, he was gone.

CHAPTER XII
MR. MERL'S MEDITATIONS

Our last chapter left Mr. Herman Merl in bad company,—he was alone. Now, very few men's thoughts are companionable in the dreary solitude of a sorry inn. None of us, it is to be feared, are totally exempt from "this world's crosses;" and though the sorrows of life do fall very unequally, the light afflictions are accepted as very heavy burdens by those to whose lot they fall!

Just as it happens, then, on some gloomy day of winter, when we have "finished our book," and the newspapers are tiresome, we take the opportunity to look through our letters and papers,—to arrange our desk, and put a little order in our scattered and littered memoranda,—somewhat in the same spirit will Conscience grasp a similar moment to go over the past, glance at bygone events, and make, as it were, a clearance of whatever weighs upon our memory. I 'm not quite certain that the best of us come out of this Bankruptcy Court with a first-class certificate. Even the most merciful to his own errors will acknowledge that in many things he should do differently were they to be done over again; and he must, indeed, have fallen upon a happy lot in life who has not some self-reproach on the score of kindness unrequited,—slight injuries either unforgiven or unequally avenged,—friendships jeopardized, mayhap lost, by some mere indulgence of temper,—and enmities unreconciled, just for lack of the veriest sacrifice of self-love.

Were there any such court in morals as in law, what a sad spectacle would our schedule show, and how poor even the most solvent amongst us, if called on for a list of his liabilities!

Lest our moralizing should grow uncomfortable, dear reader, let us return to Mr. Merl, now occupied, as he was, in this same process of self-examination. He sat with a little note-book before him, recalling various incidents of the past. And if the lowering expression of his face might be trusted, his reveries were not rose-colored; and yet, as he turned over the pages, it might be seen that moments of gratulation alternated with the intervals of self-reproach.

"Wednesday, the 10th," muttered he to himself, "dined at Philippe's—supped with Arkright and Bailey—whist at double Nap. points—won four hundred and ten—might have made it a thousand, but B. flung the cards out of the window in a passion, and had to cease playing.

"Thursday—toothache—stayed at home, and played piquet with myself—discovered two new combinations, in taking in cards—Irving came to see me—won from him twenty pounds his mother had just sent him.

"Friday—a good day's work—walked into Martin for two thousand seven hundred, and took his bill at three months, with promise to renew—dined with Sitwell, and sold him my Perugino for six hundred—cost myself not as many francs—am to have the refusal of all Vanderbrett's cabinets for letting him off his match with Columbine, which, by the way, he was sure to win, as Mope is dead lame.

"Martin again—Saturday—came to have his revenge, but seemed quarrelsome; so I affected an engagement, and declined play.

"Sunday—gave him his revenge, to the tune of twelve hundred in my own favor—'Lansquenet' in the evening at his rooms—several swells present—thought it prudent to drop some tin, and so, lost one hundred and forty Naps.—Sir Giles Bruce the chief winner—rich, and within two months of being of age.

"Monday—the Perugino returned as a bad copy by Fava—took it at once, and said I was taken in myself—Sitwell so pleased that he sat down to écarté, and lost two hundred to me. I dine with him to-morrow.

"Tuesday—blank—dinner at Sitwell's—met Colonel Cardie, whom I saw at Hombourg, and so refused to play. It was, I suspect, a plan of Sitwell's to pit us against each other.

"Wednesday—sold out my African at seventy-one and an eighth—realized well, and bought in Poyais, which will rise for at least ten days to come—took Canchard's château at Ghent for his old debt at écarté—don't like it, as it may be talked about.

"Gave a dinner to Wilson, Morris, Leader, Whyte, and Martin—Lescour could n't come—played little whist afterwards—changed for hazard after supper—won a few Naps., and home to bed.

"Took Rigby's curricle and horses for the two hundred he owes me—glad to have done with him—he evidently wanted a row—and so play with him no more.

"Sent ten Naps, to the fund for the poor injured by the late inundations, as the police called to ask about my passport, &c.

"Saturday—the Curé of St. Rochette, to ask for alms—gave three hundred francs, and secured his services against the police—the curé mentions some curious drawings in the sacristy—promised to go and see them.

"Bought Walrond's library for a franc a volume—the Elzevirs alone worth double the amount paid—Bailey bolted, and so lose his last bills—Martin quarrelsome—said he never yet won at any sitting with me—lost seventy to him, and sent him home satisfied.

"Gave five hundred francs for the drawings at St. R— — —, abominable daubs; but the police grow more troublesome every day—besides, Crowthorpe is collecting early studies of Rembrandt—these sketches are marked R.

"A great evening—cleared Martin out—suspect that this night's work makes me an Irish estated gentleman—must obtain legal opinion as to these same Irish securities and post-obits, involving, as they do, a heavy sum."

Mr. Merl paused at this *entrée* in his diary, and began to reflect in no very gratulatory mood on the little progress he had as yet made in this same object of inquiry; in fact, he was just discovering what a vast number of more shrewd observers than himself have long since found out, that exploring in Ireland is rather tough work. Everything looks so easy and simple and plain upon the surface, and yet is so puzteling and complicated beneath; all seems so intelligible, where there is nothing in reality that is not a contradiction. It is true he was not harassing himself with problems of labor and wages, the condition of the people, the effects of emigration, and so forth. He wanted to ascertain some few facts as to the value of a certain estate, and what incumbrances it might be charged with; and to the questions he put on this head, every reply was an insinuated interrogatory to himself. "Why are *you* here, Mr. Merl?" "How does it concern *you?*" "What may be *your* interest in the same investigation?" This peculiar dialectic met him as he landed; it followed him to the West. Scanlan, the landlord, even that poor simpleton the painter—as he called Crow—had submitted him to its harsh rule, till Mr. Merl felt that, instead of pursuing an examination, he was himself everlastingly in the witness-box.

Wearied of these speculations, dissatisfied with himself and his fruitless journey, he summoned the landlord to ask if that "old gent" above stairs had not a book of some kind, or a newspaper, he could lend him. A ragged urchin speedily returned with a key in his hand, saying, "That's the key of No. 4. Joe says you may go up and search for yourself."

One more scrupulous might not exactly have fancied the office thus suggested to him. He, however, was rather pleased with the investigation, and having satisfied himself that the mission was safe, set forth to fulfil it. No. 4, as the stranger's room was called, was a large and lofty chamber, lighted by a single bay-window, the deep recess of which was occupied by a writing-table. Books, maps, letters, and drawings littered every part of the room. Costly weapons, too, such as richly chased daggers and inlaid pistols, lay carelessly about, with curiously shaped pipes and gold-embroidered tobacco-bags; a richly lined fur pelisse covered the sofa, and a skull-cap of the very finest sable lay beside it. All these were signs of affluence and comfort, and Mr. Merl pondered over them as he went from place to place, tossing over one thing after another, and losing himself in wild conjectures about the owner.

The writing-table, we have said, was thickly strewn with letters, and to these he now addressed himself in all form, taking his seat comfortably for the investigation. Many of the letters were in foreign languages, and from remote and far-away lands. Some he was enabled to spell out, but they referred to places and events he had never heard of, and were filled with allusions he could not fathom. At length, however, he came to documents which interested him more closely. They were notes, most probably in the stranger's own hand, of his late tour along the coast. Mournful records were they all,—sad stories of destitution and want, a whole people struck down by famine and sickness, and a land perishing in utter misery. No personal narrative broke the dreary monotony of these gloomy records, and Merl searched in vain for what might give a clew to the writer's station or his object. Carefully drawn-up statistics, tables of the varying results of emigration, notes upon the tenure of land and the price of labor were all there, interspersed with replies from different quarters to researches of the writer's making. Numerous appeals to charity, entreaties for small loans of money, were mingled with grateful acknowledgments for benefits already received. There was much, had he been so minded, that Mr. Merl might have learned in this same unauthorized inquiry. There were abundant traits of the people displayed, strange insight into customs and ways peculiar to them, accurate knowledge, too, of the evils of their social condition; and, above all, there were the evidences of that curious compound of credulity and distrust, hope and fatalism, energy and inertness, which make up the Irish nature.

He threw these aside, however, as themes that had no interest for him. What had he to do with the people? His care was with the soil, and less even with it than with its burdens and incumbrances. One conviction certainly did impress itself strongly upon him,—that he'd part with his claims on the estate for almost anything, in preference to himself assuming the cares and duties of an Irish landlord,—a position which he summed up by muttering to himself, "is simply to have so many acres of bad land, with the charge of feeding so many thousands of bad people." Here were suggestions, it is true, how to make them better, coupled with details that showed the writer to be one well acquainted with the difficulties of his task; here, also, were dark catalogues of crime, showing how destitution and vice went hand in hand, and that the seasons of suffering were those of lawlessness and violence. Various hands were detectable in these documents. Some evinced the easy style and graceful penmanship of education; others were written in the gnarled hand of the daily, laborer. Many of these were interlined in what Merl soon detected to be the stranger's own handwriting; and brief as such remarks were, they sufficed to show how carefully their contents had been studied by him.

"What could be the object of all this research? Was he some emissary of the Government, sent expressly to obtain this knowledge? Was he employed by some section of party politicians, or was he one of those literary philanthropists who trade upon the cheap luxury of pitying the poor and detailing their sorrows? At all events," thought Mr. Merl, "this same information seems to have cost him considerable research, and not a little money; and as I am under a pledge to give the Captain some account of his dear country, here is a capital opportunity to do so, not only with ease, but actually with honor." And having formed this resolve, he instantly proceeded to its execution. That wonderful little note-book, with its strong silver clasps, so full of strange and curious information, was now produced; but he soon saw that the various facts to be recorded demanded a wider space, and so he set himself to write down on a loose sheet of paper notices of the land in tillage or in pasture, the numerical condition of the people as compared with former years, their state, their prospects; but when he came to tell of the ravages made and still making by pestilence amongst them, he actually stopped to reread the records, so terrible and astounding were the facts narrated. A dreadful malady walked the land, and its victims lay in every house! The villages were depopulated, the little clusters of houses at cross roads were stricken, the lone shealing on the mountain side, the miserable cottage of the dreary moor, were each the scenes of desolation and death. It was as though the land were about to be devastated, and the race of man swept from its surface! As he read on, he came upon some strictures in the stranger's own hand upon these sad events, and perceived how terribly had the deserted, neglected state of the people aided the fatal course of the epidemic. No hospitals had been provided, no stores of any remedial kind, not a doctor for miles around, save an old physician who had been retained at Miss Martin's special charge, and who was himself nigh exhausted by the fatigue of his office.

Mr. Merl laid down his pen to think,—not, indeed, in any compassionate spirit of that suffering people; his sorrows were not for those who lay on beds of want and sickness; his whole anxiety was for a certain person very dear to his own heart, who had rashly accepted securities on a property which, to all seeming, was verging upon ruin; this conviction being strongly impressed by the lawless state of the country, and the hopelessness of expecting payment from a tenantry so circumstanced.

"Sympathy, indeed!" cried he; "I should like to hear of a little sympathy for the unlucky fellow who has accepted a mortgage on this confounded estate! These wretched creatures have little to lose,—and even death itself ought to be no unwelcome relief to a life like theirs,—but to a man such as I am, with abundance of projects for his spare cash, this is a pretty investment! It is not impossible that this philanthropic stranger, whoever he be, might buy up my bonds. He should have them a bargain,—ay, by Jove! I'd take off a jolly percentage to touch the 'ready;' and who knows, what with all his benevolence, his charity, and his Christian kindliness, if he 'd not come down handsomely to rescue this unhappy people from the hands of a Jew!"

And Mr. Merl laughed pleasantly, for the conceit amused him, and it sounded gratefully to his imagination that even his faith could be put out to interest, and the tabernacle be turned to good account. The noise of a chaise approaching at a sharp trot along the shingly beach startled him from his musings, and he had barely time to snatch up the paper on which he had scrawled his notes, and hasten downstairs, when the obsequious landlord, rushing to the door, ushered in Mr. Barry, and welcomed him back again.

Merl suffered his door to stand ajar, that he might take a look at the stranger as he passed. He was a very large, powerfully built man, somewhat stooped by age, but showing even in advanced years signs of a vigorous frame and stout constitution; his head was massive, and covered with snow-white hair, which descended on the back of his neck. His countenance must in youth have been handsome, and even yet bore the expression of a frank, generous, but somewhat impetuous nature,—so at least it struck him who now observed it; a character not improbably aided by his temper as he entered, for he had returned from scenes of misery and suffering, and was in a mood of indignation at the neglect he had just witnessed.

"You said truly," said he to the landlord. "You told me I shouldn't see a gentleman for twenty miles round; that all had fled and left the people to their fate, and I see now it is a fact."

"Faix, and no wonder," answered the host. "Wet potatoes and the shaking ague, not to speak of cholera morbus, is n't great inducements to stay and keep company with. I 'd be off, too, if I had the means."

"But I spoke of gentlemen, sir," said the stranger, with a strong emphasis on the word, — "men who should be the first to prove their birth and blood when a season of peril was near."

"Thrue for you, sir," chimed in Joe, who suddenly detected the blunder he had committed. "The Martins ought not to have run away in the middle of our distress."

"They left the ship in a storm; they 'll find a sorry wreck when they return to it," muttered the stranger, as he ascended the stairs.

"By Jacob! just what I suspected," said Merl to himself, while he closed the door; "this property won't be worth sixpence, and I am regularly 'done.'"

CHAPTER XIII
A NIGHT OF STORM

The curtains were closely drawn, and a cheerful turf fire blazed in the room where Mr. Merl sat at dinner. The fare was excellent, and even rustic cookery sufficed to make fresh salmon and mountain mutton and fat woodcocks delectable; while the remains of Mr. Scanlan's hamper set forth some choice Madeira and several bottles of Sneyd's claret. Nor was he for whose entertainment these good things were provided in any way incapable of enjoying them. With the peculiar sensuality of his race, he loved his dinner all to himself and alone. He delighted in the privileged selfishness that isolation conferred, and he revelled in a sort of complacent flattery at the thought of all the people who were dining worse than himself, and the stray thousands besides who were not destined on that day to dine at all.

The self-caressing shudder that came over him as the sound of a horse at speed on the shore outside was heard, spoke plainly as words themselves the pleasant comparison that crossed his mind between the condition of the rider and his own. He drew nearer the fire, he threw on a fresh log of pine, and, filling up a bumper, seemed to linger as he viewed it, as though wishing health and innumerable blessings to Mr. Herman Merl.

The noise of the clattering hoofs died away in distance and in the greater uproar of the storm, and Mr. Merl thought no more of them. How often happens it, dear reader, that some brief interruption flashes through our seasons of enjoyment; we are startled, perhaps; we even need a word or two to reassure us that all is well, and then the work of pleasure goes on, and we forget that it had ever been retarded; and yet, depend upon it, in that fleeting second of time some sad episode of human life has, like a spectre, crossed our path, and some deep sorrow gone wearily past us.

Let us follow that rider, then, who now, quitting the bleak shore, has entered a deep gorge between the mountain. The rain swept along in torrents; the wind in fitful gusts dashes the mountain stream in many a wayward shape, and snaps the stems of old trees in pieces; landslips and broken rocks impede the way; and yet that brave horse holds ever onward, now stretching to a fast gallop, now gathering himself to clear some foaming torrent, or some fragment of fallen timber.

The night is so dark that the rider cannot see the horse's length in advance; but every feature of the way is well known, and an instinctive sense of the peril to be apprehended at each particular spot guides that hand and nerves that heart. Mary Martin—for she it is—had ridden that same path at all seasons and all hours, but never on a wilder night, nor through a more terrible hurricane than this. At moments her speed relaxed, as if to breathe her horse; and twice she pulled up short, to listen and distinguish between the sound of thunder and the crashing noise of rocks rolling from the mountain. There was a sublimity in the scene, lit up at moments by the lightning; and a sense of peril, too, that exalted the adventurous spirit of the girl, and imparted to her heart a high heroic feeling. The glorious sentiment of confronting danger animated and excited her; and her courage rose with each new difficulty of the way, till her very brain seemed to reel with the wild transport of her emotions.

As she emerged from the gorge, she gained a high tableland, over which the wind swept unimpeded. Not a cliff, not a rock, not a tree, broke the force of the gale, which raged with all the violence of a storm at sea. Crouching low upon the saddle, stooping at times to the mane, she could barely make way against the hurricane; and more than once her noble charger was driven backward, and forced to turn his back to the storm. *Her* courage never failed. Taking advantage of every passing lull, she dashed forward, ready to wheel and halt when the wind shot past with violence.

Descending at last from this elevated plateau, she again entered a deep cleft between the mountain, the road littered with fallen earth and branches of trees, so as almost to defy a passage. After traversing upwards of a mile of this wearisome way, she arrived at the door of a small cabin, the first trace of habitation since she had quitted the village. It was a mere hovel, abutting against a rock, and in its dreary solitude seemed the last refuge of direst poverty.

She bent down from her saddle to look in at the window; but, except some faint embers on the hearth, all was dark within. She then knocked with her whip against the door, and called "Morris" two or three times; but no reply was given. Springing from her horse, Mary fastened the bridle to the hasp of the door-post, and entered. The heavy breathing of one in deep sleep at once caught her attention > and, approaching the fireplace, she lighted a piece of pine-wood to examine about her. On a low settle in one corner lay the figure of a young woman, whose pale, pinched features contrasted strongly with the bright ribbons of her cap floating loosely at either side. Mary tottered as she drew nigher; a terrible sense of fear was over her,—a terror of she knew not what. She held the flickering flame closer, and saw that she was dead! Poor Margaret, she had been one of Mary's chief favorites; the very cap that now decked her cold forehead was Mary's wedding-gift to her. But a few days before, her little child had been carried to the churchyard; and it was said that the mother never held up her head after. Sick almost to fainting, Mary Martin sank into a chair, and then saw, for the first time, the figure of a man, who, half kneeling, lay with his head on the foot of the bed, fast asleep! Weariness, utter exhaustion, were marked in his pale-worn features, while his attitude bespoke complete prostration. His hand still clasped a little rosary.

It seemed but the other day that she had wished them "joy" upon their wedding, and they had gone home to their little cabin in hopefulness and high-hearted spirit, and there she lay now a cold corpse, and he, bereaved and childless. What a deal of sad philosophy do these words reveal! What dark contrasts do we bring up when we say, "It was but the other day." It was but "the other day," and Cro' Martin was the home of one whose thriving tenantry reflected back all his efforts for their welfare, when movement and occupation bespoke a condition of activity and cheerful industry; when, even in their poverty, the people bore bravely up, and the cases of suffering but sufficed to call out traits of benevolence and kind feeling. It was but "the other day," and Mary herself rode out amidst the people, like some beloved sovereign in the middle of her subjects; happy faces beamed brighter when she came, and even misery half forgot itself in her presence. But "the other day" and the flag waved proudly from the great tower, to show that Cro'

Martin was the residence of its owner, and Mary the life and soul of all that household!

Such-like were her thoughts as she stood still gazing on the sad scene before her. She could not bring herself to awaken the poor fellow, who thus, perchance, stole a short respite from his sorrows; but leaving some money beside him on a chair, and taking one farewell look of poor Margaret, she stole silently away, and remounted her horse.

Again she is away through the storm and the tempest! Her pace is now urged to speed, for she knows every field and every fence,—where to press her horse to his gallop, where to spare and husband his strength. At one moment she steals carefully along amid fragments of fallen rocks and broken timber; at another, she flies, with racing speed, over the smooth sward. At length, through the gloom and darkness, the tall towers of Cro' Martin are seen over the deep woods; but her horse's head is not turned thitherward. No; she has taken another direction, and, skirting the wall of the demesne, she is off towards the wild, bleak country beyond. It is past midnight; not a light gleams from a cabin window as she dashes past; all is silent save the plashing rain, which, though the wind has abated, continues to fall in torrents. Crossing the bleak moor, whose yawning pits even in daylight suggest care and watchfulness, she gains the foot of the barren mountain on which Barnagheela stands, and descries in the distance the flickering of a light dimly traceable through the falling rain.

For the first time her horse shows signs of fatigue, and Mary caresses him with her hand, and speaks encouragingly to him as she slackens her pace, ascending the hill at a slow walk. After about half an hour of this toilsome progress, for the surface is stony and rock-covered, she reaches the little "boreen" road which forms the approach to the house. Mary has never been there before, and advances now slowly and carefully between two rude walls of dry masonry which lead to the hall-door. As she nears the house, the gleam of lights from between the ill-closed shutters attracts her, and suddenly through the swooping rain come the sounds of several voices in tones of riot and revelry. She listens; and it is now the rude burst of applause that breaks forth,—a din of voices loudly proclaiming the hearty approval of some sentiment or opinion.

While she halts to determine what course next to follow,—for these signs of revelry have disconcerted her,—she hears a rough, loud voice from within call out, "There's another toast you must drink now, and fill for it to the brim. Come, Peter Hayes, no skulking; the liquor is good, and the sentiment the same. Gentlemen, you came here to-night to honor my poor house—my ancestral house, I may call it—on the victory we 've gained over tyranny and oppression." Loud cheers here interrupted him, but he resumed: "They tried—by the aid of the law that they made themselves—to turn me out of my house and home. They did all that false swearing and forged writing could do, to drive me—me, Tom Magennis, the last of an ancient stock—out upon the highways." (Groans from the hearers.) "But they failed,—ay, gentlemen, they failed. Old Repton, with all his skill, and Scanlan, with all his treachery, could n't do it. Joe Nelligan, like Goliath—no, like David, I mean—put a stone between their two eyes, and laid them low." (Loud cheering, and cries of "Why is n't he here?" "Where is he to-night?") "Ay, gentlemen," resumed the speaker, "ye may well ask where is he this night? when we are celebrating not only our triumph, but his; for it was the first brief he ever held,—the first guinea he ever touched for a fee! I 'll tell you where he is. Skulking—ay, that's the word for it—skulking in Oughterard,—hiding himself for shame because he beat the Martins!" (Loud expressions of anger, and some of dissent, here broke forth; some inveighing against this cowardice, others defending him against the charge.) "Say what you like," roared Magennis; "I know, and he knows that I know it. What was it he said when Mahony went to him with my brief? 'I'll not refuse to undertake the case,' said he, 'but I 'll not lend myself to any scurrilous attack upon the family at Cro' Martin!'" (Groans.) "Ay, but listen," continued he: "'And if I find,' said he—'if I find that in the course of the case such an attempt should be made, I 'll throw down my brief though I never should hold another.' There's Joe Nelligan for you! There's the stuff you thought you 'd make a Patriot out of!"

"Say what you like, Tom Magennis, he's a credit to the town," said old Hayes, "and he won your cause this day against one of the 'cutest of the Dublin counsellors."

"He did so, sir," resumed Magennis, "and he got his pay, and there's nothing between us; and I told him so, and more besides; for I said, 'You may flatter them and crawl to them; you may be as servile as a serpent or a boa-constrictor to them; but take *my* word for it, Mister Joe,—or Counsellor Nelligan, if you like it better,—they'll never forget who and what you are,—the son of old Dan there, of the High Street,—and you 've a better chance to be the Chief Justice than the husband of Mary Martin!'"

"You told him that!" cried several together. "I did, sir; and I believe for a minute he meant to strike me; he got pale with passion, and then he got red—blood red; and, in that thick way he has when he 's angry, he said, 'Whatever may be my hopes of the Bench, I'll not win my way to it by ever again undertaking the cause of a ruffian!' 'Do you mean *me?*' said I,—'do you mean *me?*' But he turned away into the house, and I never saw him since. If it had n't been for Father Neal there, I 'd have had him out for it, sir!"

"We've other work before us than quarrelling amongst ourselves," said the bland voice of Father Rafferty; "and now for your toast, Tom, for I 'm dry waiting for it."

"Here it is, then," cried Magennis. "A speedy downfall to the Martins!"

"A speedy downfall to the Martins!" was repeated solemnly in chorus; while old Hayes interposed, "Barring the niece,—barring Miss Mary."

"I won't except one," cried Magennis. "My august leader remarked, 'It was false pity for individuals destroyed the great revolution of France.' It was—" Mary did not wait for more, but, turning her horse's head, moved slowly around towards the back of the house.

Through a wide space, of which the rickety broken gate hung by a single hinge, Mary entered a large yard, a court littered with disabled carts, harrows, and other field implements, all equally unserviceable. Beneath a low shed along one of the walls stood three or four horses, with harness on them, evidently belonging to the guests assembled within. All these details were plainly visible by the glare of an immense fire which blazed on the kitchen hearth, and threw its light more than half-way across the yard. Having disposed of her horse at one end of the shed, Mary stealthily drew nigh the kitchen window, and looked in. An old, very old woman, in the meanest attire, sat crouching beside the fire; and although she held a huge wooden ladle in her hand, seemed, by her drooped head and bent-down attitude, either moping or asleep. Various cooking utensils were on the fire, and two or three joints of meat hung roasting before it, while the hearth was strewn with dishes, awaiting the savory fare that was to fill them.

These, and many other indications of the festivity then going on within, Mary rapidly noticed; but it was evident, from the increasing eagerness of her gaze, that the object which she sought had not yet met her eye. Suddenly, however, the door of the kitchen opened and a figure entered, on which the young girl bent all her attention. It was Joan Landy, but how different from the half-timid, half-reckless peasant girl that last we saw her! Dressed in a heavy gown of white satin, looped up on either side with wreaths of flowers, and wearing a rich lace cap on her head, she rushed hurriedly in, her face deeply flushed, and her eyes sparkling with excitement. Hastily snatching up a check apron that lay on a chair, she fastened it about her, and drew near the fire. It was plain from her gesture, as she took the ladle from the old woman's hand, that she was angry, and by her manner seemed as if rebuking her. The old crone, however, only crouched lower, and spreading out her wasted fingers towards the blaze, appeared insensible to everything addressed to her. Meanwhile Joan busied herself about the fire with all the zealous activity of one accustomed to the task. Mary watched her intently; she scrutinized with piercing keenness every lineament of that face, now moved by its passing emotions, and she muttered to herself, "Alas, I have come in vain!" Nor was this depressing sentiment less felt as Joan, turning from the fire, approached a fragment of a broken looking-glass that stood against the wall. Drawing herself up to her full height, she stood gazing proudly, delightedly, at her own figure. The humble apron, too, was speedily discarded, and as she trampled it beneath her feet she seemed to spurn the mean condition of which it was the symbol. Mary Martin sighed deeply as she looked, and muttered once more, "In vain!"

Then suddenly starting, with one of those bursts of energy which so often had steeled her heart against peril, she walked to the kitchen-door, raised the latch, and entered. She had made but one step within the door when Joan turned and beheld her; and there they both stood, silently, each surveying the other. Mary felt too intensely the difficulty of the task before her to utter a word without well weighing the consequences. She knew how the merest accident might frustrate all she had in view, and stood hesitating and uncertain, when Joan, who now recognized her, vacillated between her instinctive sense of respect and a feeling of defiance in the consciousness of where she was. Happily for Mary the former sentiment prevailed, and in a tone of kindly anxiety Joan drew near her and said,—"Has anything happened? I trust in God no accident has befell you."

"Thank God, nothing worse than a wetting," said Mary,—"some little fatigue; and I'll think but little of either if they have brought me here to a good end. May I speak with you alone,—quite alone?"

"Come in here," said Joan, pushing open the door of a small room off the kitchen which served for a species of larder,—"come in here."

"I have come on a sad errand," said Mary, taking her hand between both her own, "and I would that it had fallen to any other than myself. It is for you to decide that! have not come in vain."

"What is it? tell me what it is?" cried Joan, as a sudden paleness spread over her features.

"These are days of sorrow and mourning everywhere," said Mary, gloomily. "Can you not guess what my tidings may be? No, no," cried she, as a sudden gesture of Joan interrupted her,—"no, not yet; he is still alive, and entreats to see you."

"To curse me again, is it?" cried the other, wildly; "to turn me from the door, and pray down curses on me,—is it for that he wants to see me?"

"Not for that, indeed," said Mary; "it is to see you—to give you his last kiss—his last blessing—to forgive you and be forgiven. Remember that he is alone, deserted by all that once were his. Your father and mother and sisters are all gone to America, and poor old Mat lingers on,—nay, the journey is nigh ended. Oh, do not delay, lest it be too late. Come now—now."

"And if I see him once, can I ever come back to this?" cried Joan, in bitter agony. "Will I ever be able to hear his words and live as I do now?"

"Let your own good heart guide you for that," cried Mary; "all I ask is that you should see him and be with him. I have pledged myself for your coming, and you will not dishonor my words to one on his death-bed."

"And I 'll be an outcast for it. Tom will drive me from the door and never see me again. I know it,—I know *him*!"

"You are wrong, Joan Landy."

"Joan!—who dares to call me Joan Landy when I'm Mrs. Magennis of Barnagheela? and if *I'm* not *your* equal, I 'm as good as any other in the barony. Was it to insult me you came here to-night, to bring up to me who I am and where I came from? That 's the errand that brought you through the storm! Ay," cried she, lashed to a wilder passion by her own words,—"ay! ay! and if you and yours had their will we 'd not have the roof to shelter us this night. It 's only to-day that we won the trial against you."

"Whatever my errand here this night," said Mary, with a calm dignity, "it was meant to serve and not insult you. I know, as well as your bitterest words can tell me, that this is not my place; but I know, too, if from yielding to my selfish pride I had refused your old grandfather this last request, it had been many a year of bitter reproach to me."

"Oh, you 'll break my heart, you will, you will!" cried Joan, bitterly. "You 'll turn the only one that's left against me, and I 'll be alone in the world."

"Come with me this night, and whatever happen I 'll befriend you," said Mary.

"And not desert me because I 'm what I am?"

"Never, Joan, never!"

"Oh, my blessings on you,—if the blessing of one like me is any good," cried she, kissing Mary's hand fervently. "Oh, they that praised you said the truth; you have goodness enough in your heart to make up for us all! I 'll go with you to the world's end."

"We'll pass Cro' Martin, and you shall have my horse—"

"No, no, Miss Mary, I 'll go on my feet; it best becomes me. I 'll go by Burnane—by the Gap—I know it well—too well!" added she, as the tears rushed to her eyes. As she was speaking, she took off the cap she wore and threw it from her; and then removing her dress, put on the coarse woollen gown of her daily wear. "Oh, God forgive me!" cried she, "if I curse the day that I ever wore better than this."

Mary assisted her with her dress, fastening the hood of her cloak over her head, and preparing her, as best she might, for the severe storm she was to encounter; and it was plain to see that Joan accepted these little services without a thought of by whom they were rendered, so intensely occupied was her mind by the enterprise before her. A feverish haste to be away marked all she did. It was partly terror lest her escape might be prevented; partly a sense of distrust in herself, and that she might abandon her own resolution.

"Oh, tell me," she cried, as the tears streamed from her eyes, and her lips quivered with agony,—"oh, tell me I'm doing right; tell me that God's blessing is going with me this night, or I can't do it."

"And so it is, dear Joan," said Mary; "be of good heart, and Heaven will support you. I 'm sure the trial is a sore one."

"Oh, is it not to leave this—to leave him—maybe forever? To be sure, it's forever," cried she, bitterly. "He 'll never forgive me!"

A wild burst of revelry now resounded from the parlor, and the discordant sounds of half-drunken voices burst upon their ears.

Joan started, and gazed wildly around her. The agonized look of her features bespoke her dread of detection; and then with a bound she sprung madly from the spot, and was away. Mary followed quickly; but before she had secured her horse and mounted, the other was already half-way down the mountain. Now catching, now losing sight of her again, Mary at last came up with her.

"Remember, dear Joan," said Mary, "there are nine weary miles of mountain before you."

"I know it well," was the brief reply.

"And if you go by Burnane the rocks are slippy with the rain, and the path to the shore is full of danger."

"If I was afeard of danger, would I be here?" cried she. "Oh, Miss Mary," added she, stopping and grasping her hand in both her own, "leave me to myself; don't come with me,—it's not one like you ought to keep me company."

"But Joan,—dear Joan,—I have promised to be your friend, and I am not one who forgets a pledge."

"My heart will break; it will break in two if you talk to me. Leave me, for the love of Heaven, and let me go my road all alone. There, at the two trees there, is the way to Cro' Martin; take it, and may the Saints guide you safe home!"

"And if I do, Joan, will you promise me to come straight back to Cro' Martin after you 've seen him? Will you do this?"

"I will,—I will," cried she, bathing Mary's hand with her tears as she kissed it.

"Then God bless and protect you, poor girl!" said Mary. "It is not for me to dictate to your own full heart. Goodbye,—good-bye."

Before Mary had dried the warm tears that rose to her eyes, Joan was gone.

CHAPTER XIV
THE END OF A BAR MESS

There are few things more puzzling to the uninitiated than the total separation lawyers are able to exercise between their private sentiments and the emotions they display in the wear and tear of their profession. So widely apart are these two characters, that it is actually difficult to understand how they ever can unite in one man. But so it is. He can pass his morning in the most virulent assaults upon his learned brother, ridiculing his law, laughing at his logic, arraigning his motives,—nay, sometimes ascribing to him some actually base and wicked. Altercations, heightened by all that passion stimulated by wit can produce, ensue. Nothing that can taunt, provoke, or irritate, is omitted. Personalities even are introduced to swell the acrimony of the contest; and yet, when the jury have given in their verdict and the court breaks up, the gladiators, who seemed only thirsting for each other's blood, are seen laughingly going homeward arm-in-arm, mayhap discoursing over the very cause which, but an hour back, seemed to have stamped them enemies for the rest of life.

Doubtless there is a great deal to be pleased at in all this, and, we ought to rejoice in the admirable temper by which men can discriminate between the faithful performance of a duty and the natural course of their affections. Still, small-minded folk—of which wide category we own ourselves to be a part—may have their misgivings that the excellence of this system is not without its alloy, and that even the least ingenious of men will ultimately discover how much principle is sapped, and how much truthfulness of character is sacrificed in this continual struggle between fiction and reality.

The Bar is the nursery of the Senate, and it would not be a very fanciful speculation were we to ascribe the laxity of purpose, the deficient earnestness, and the insincerity of principle we often deplore in our public men, to this same legal training.

The old lawyer, however, finds no difficulty in the double character. With his wig and gown he puts on his sarcasm, his insolence, and his incredulity. His brief bag opens to him a Pandora's box of noxious influences; and as he passes the precincts of the court, he leaves behind him all the amenities of life and all the charities of his nature. The young barrister does not find the transmutation so easy. He gives himself unreservedly to his client, and does not measure his ardor by the instructions in his brief. Let us ask pardon of our reader for what may seem *a mal à propos* digression; but we have been led to these remarks by the interests of our story.

It was in the large dining-room of the "Martin Arms" at Oughterard, that a party of lawyers spent the evening, some of whose events, elsewhere, our last chapter has recorded. It was the Bar mess of the Western Circuit, and the chair was filled by no less a person than "Father Repton." This able "leader" had determined not to visit the West of Ireland so long as his friend Martin remained abroad; but a very urgent entreaty from Scanlan, and a pressing request for his presence, had induced him to waive that resolve, and come down special to Oughterard for the Magennis case.

A simple case of ejectment could scarcely have called for that imposing array of learned counsel who had repaired to this unfrequented spot; so small a skirmish could never have called for the horse, foot, and dragoons of law,—the wily conveyancer, the clap-trap orator, the browbeater of witnesses, and the light sharpshooter at technicalities; and yet there they were all met, and—with all reverence be it spoken—very jolly companions they were.

An admirable rule precluded the introduction of, or even an allusion to, professional subjects, save when the burden of a joke, whose success might excuse the transgression; and thus these crafty, keen intelligences argued, disputed, jested, and disported together, in a vein which less practised talkers would find it hard to rival. To the practice of these social amenities is doubtless ascribable the absence of any rancor from the rough contests and collisions of public life, and thus men of every shade of politics and party, differing even in class and condition, formed admirable social elements, and cohered together to perfection.

As the evening wore on, the company insensibly thinned off. Some of the hard-workers retired early; a few, whose affectation it was to pretend engagements, followed. The "juniors" repaired in different groups to the chambers of their friends, where loo and brandy-and-water awaited them; and at last Repton was left, with only two others, sole occupants of that spacious apartment. His companions were, like himself, soldiers of the "Vieille Garde" veterans who remembered Curran and Lawrence Parsons, John Toler and Saurin, and a host of others, who only needed that the sphere should have been greater to be themselves among the great of the nation.

Rawlins was Repton's schoolfellow, and had been his rival at the Bar for nigh fifty years. Niel, a few years younger than either, was the greatest orator of his time. Both had been opposed to Repton in the present suit, and had held heavy retainers for their services.

"Well, Repton," said Rawlins, as soon as they were left thus to themselves, "are you pondering over it still? I see that you can't get it out of your head."

"It is quite true, I cannot," said Repton. "To summon us all down here,—to bring us some fifty miles away from our accustomed beat, for a trumpery affair like this, is totally beyond me. Had it been an election time, I should probably have understood it."

"How so?" cried Niel, in the shrill piercing voice peculiar to him, and which imparted to him, even in society, an air of querulous irritability.

"On the principle that Bob Mahon always puts a thoroughbred horse in his gig when he drives over to a country race. He's always ready for a match with what he jocularly calls 'the old screw I'm driving this minute;' so, Niel, I thought that the retainer for the ejectment might have turned out to be a special fee for the election."

"And he'd have given them a speech, and a rare good one, too, I promise you," said Rawlins; "and even if he had not time to speak it, the county paper would have had it all printed and corrected from his own hand, with all the appropriate interruption of 'vociferous cheering,' and the places where the orator was obliged to pause, from the wild tumult of acclamation that surrounded him."

"Which all resolves itself into this," screamed Niel,—"that some men's after-grass is better than other men's meadows."

"Mine has fallen to the scythe many a day ago," said Rawlins, plaintively; "but I remember glorious times and glorious fellows. It was, indeed, worth something to say, '*Vixissi cum illis.*'"

"There's another still better, Rawlins," cried Repton, joyously, "which is to have survived them!"

"Very true," cried Niel. "I'd always plead a demurrer to any notice to quit; for, take it all in all, this life has many enjoyments."

"Such as Attorney-Generalships, Masters of the Rolls, and such like," said Repton.

"By the way," said Rawlins, "who put that squib in the papers about your having refused the rolls,—eh, Niel?"

"Who but Niel himself?" chimed in Repton. "It was filing a bill of discovery. He wanted to know the intentions of the Government."

"I could have had but little doubt of them," broke in Niel. "It was my advice, man, cancelled your appointment as Crown Counsel, Repton. I told Massingbred, 'If you do keep a watch-dog, let it be, at least, one who 'll bite some one beside the family.'"

"He has muzzled you there, Repton," said Rawlins, laughing. "Eh, that was a bitter draught!"

"So it was," said Repton. "It was Curran wine run to the lees! and very unlike the racy flavor of the true liquor. And to speak in all seriousness, what has come over us all to be thus degenerate and fallen? It is not alone that we have not the equals of the first-rate men, but we really have nothing to compare with O'Grady, and Parsons, and a score of others."

"I 'll tell you why," cried Niel,—"the commodity is n't marketable. The stupid men, who will always be the majority everywhere, have got up the cry, that to be agreeable is to be vulgar. We know how large cravats came into fashion; tiresome people came in with high neckcloths."

"I wish they 'd go out with hempen ones, then," muttered Repton.

"I 'd not refuse them the benefit of the clergy," said Niel, with a malicious twinkle of the eye, that showed how gladly, when occasion offered, he flung a pebble at the Church.

"They were very brilliant,—they were very splendid, I own," said Rawlins; "but I have certain misgivings that they gave themselves too much to society."

"Expended too much of their powder in fireworks," cried Niel, sharply,—"so they did; but their rockets showed how high they could rise to."

"Ay, Niel, and we only burn our fingers with ours," said Repton, sarcastically.

"Depend upon it," resumed Rawlins, "as the world grows more practical, you will have less of great convivial display. Agreeability will cease to be the prerogative of first-rate men, but be left to the smart people of society, who earn their soup by their sayings."

"He's right," cried Niel, in his shrillest tone. "The age of alchemists is gone; the sleight-of-hand man and the juggler have succeeded him."

"And were they not alchemists?" exclaimed old Repton, enthusiastically. "Did they not transmute the veriest dross of the earth, and pour it forth from the crucible of their minds a stream of liquid gold?—glorious fellows, who, in the rich abundance of their minds, brought the learning of their early days to illustrate the wisdom of their age, and gave the fresh-heartedness of the schoolboy to the ripe intelligence of manhood."

"And yet how little have they bequeathed to us!" said Niel.

"Would it were even less," broke in Repton. "We read the witticism of brilliant conversera in some diary or journal, often ill recorded, imperfectly given, always unaccompanied by the accessories of the scene wherein they occurred. We have not the crash, the tumult, the headlong flow of social intercourse, where the impromptu fell like a thunderbolt, and the bon mots rattled like a fire of musketry. To attempt to convey an impression of these great talkers by a memoir, is like to picture a battle by reading out a list of the killed and wounded."

"Repton is right!" exclaimed Niel. "The recorded bon mot is the words of a song without the music."

"And often where it was the melody that inspired the verses," added Repton, always glad to follow up an illustration.

"After all," said Rawlins, "the fashion of the day is changed in other respects as well as in conversational excellence. Nothing is like what we remember it!—literature, dress, social habits, oratory. There, for instance, was that young fellow to-day; his speech to the jury,—a very good and sensible one, no doubt,—but how unlike what it would have been some five-and-thirty or forty years ago."

"It was first-rate," said Repton, with enthusiasm. "I say it frankly, and 'fas est ab hoste,' for he tripped me up in a point of law, and I have, therefore, a right to applaud him. To tell you the truth," he added slyly, "I knew I was making a revoke, but I thought none of the players were shrewd enough to detect me."

"Niel and I are doubtless much complimented by the remark," said Rawlins.

"Pooh, pooh!" cried Repton, "what did great guns like you and Niel care for such 'small deer.' You were only brought down here as a great *corps de réserve*. It was young Nelligan who fought the battle, and admirably he did it. While I was listening to him to-day, I could not help saying to myself, 'It's well for us that there were no fellows of this stamp in our day.' Ay, Rawlins, you know it well. We were speech-makers; these fellows are lawyers."

"Why didn't he dine with us to-day?" asked Niel, sharply.

"Heaven knows. I believe his father lives in the town here; perhaps, too, he had no fancy for a dress-parade before such drill-sergeants as you and Rawlins there."

"You are acquainted with him, I think?" asked Rawlins.

"Yes, slightly; we met strangely enough, at Cro' Martin last year. He was then on a visit there, a quiet, timid youth, who actually seemed to feel as though his college successes were embarrassing recollections in a society who knew nothing of deans or proctors. There was another young fellow also there at the time,—young Massingbred,—with about a tenth of this man's knowledge, and a fiftieth of his capacity, who took the lead of him on every subject, and by the bare force of an admirable manner and a most unabashed impudence, threw poor Nelligan completely into the background. It was the same kind of thing I 've often seen Niel there perform at the Four Courts, where he has actually picked up his law from a worsted opponent, as a highwayman arms himself with the pistols of the man he has robbed."

"I never pillaged *you*, Repton," said Niel, with a sarcastic smile. "*You* had always the privilege the poet ascribes to him who laughs 'before a robber.'"

"Vacuus sed non Inanis," replied Repton, laughing good-humoredly.

"But tell us more of this man, Nelligan," said Rawlins. "I 'm curious to hear about him."

"And so you are sure to do some of these days, Rawlins. That fellow is the man to attain high eminence."

"His religion will stop him!" cried Niel, sharply; for, being himself a Romanist, he was not sorry to have an opportunity of alluding to the disqualifying element.

"Say, rather, it will promote him," chimed in Repton. "Take my word for it, Niel, there is a spirit of mawkish reparation abroad which affects to feel that all your coreligionists have a long arrear due to them, and that all the places and emoluments so long withheld from their ancestors should be showered down upon the present generation;—pretty much upon the same principle that you 'd pension a man now because his grandfather had been hanged for rebellion!"

"And very justly, too, if you discovered that what you once called rebellion had been very good loyalty!" cried Niel.

"We have not, however, made the discovery you speak of," said Repton; "we have only commuted a sentence, in the sincere hope that you are wiser than your forefathers. But to come back. You may trust me when I say that a day is coming when you 'll not only bless yourself because you're a Papist, but that you *are* one! Ay, sir, it is in 'Liffey Street Chapel' we 'll seek for an attorney-general, and out of the Church of the Conception, if that be the name of it, we 'll cull our law advisers of the Crown. For the next five-and-twenty years, at least," said he, solemnly, "the fourth-rate Catholic will be preferred to the first-rate Protestant."

"I only hope you may be better at Prophecy than you are in Logic," cried Niel, as he tossed off his glass; "and so, I 'm sure, does Nelligan!"

"And Nelligan is exactly the man who will never need the preference, sir. His abilities will raise him, even if there were obstacles to be surmounted. It is men of a different stamp that the system will favor,—fellows without industry for the toils of a laborious profession, or talents for the subtleties of a difficult career; men who cherish ambition and are yet devoid of capacity, and will plead the old disabilities of their faith,—pretty much as a man might claim his right to be thought a good dancer because his father had a club foot."

"A most lame conclusion!" cried Niel. "Ah, Rawlins," added he, with much compassion, "our poor friend here is breaking terribly. Sad signs there are of decay about him. Even his utterance begins to fail him."

"No, no," said Repton, gayly. "I know what you allude to. It is an old imperfection of mine not to be able to enunciate the letter r correctly, and that was the reason today in court that I called you my ingenious Bother; but I meant Brother, I assure you."

They all laughed good-humoredly at the old man's sally; in good truth, so trained were they to these sort of combats, that they cared little for the wounds such warfare inflicted. And although the tilt was ever understood as with "reversed lances," none ever cherished an evil memory if an unlucky stroke smote too heavily.

"I have asked young Nelligan to breakfast with me tomorrow," said Repton; "will you both come and meet him?"

"We 're off at cock-crow!" cried Kiel. "Tell him, however, from me that I am delighted with his *débuts* and that all the best wishes of my friends and myself are with him."

And so they parted.

Repton, however, did not retire to bed at once; his mind was still intent upon the subject which had engaged him during the day, and as he walked to and fro in his room, he still dwelt upon it. Scanlan's instructions had led him to believe that the Martins were in this case to have been "put upon their title;" and the formidable array of counsel employed by Magennis seemed to favor the impression. Now it was true that a trifling informality in the service of the writ had quashed the proceedings for the present; but the question remained, "Was the great struggle only reserved for a future day?"

It was clear that a man embarrassed as was Magennis could never have retained that strong bar of eminent lawyers. From what fund, then, came these resources? Was there a combination at work? And if so, to what end, and with what object?

The crafty old lawyer pondered long and patiently over these things. His feelings might not inaptly be compared to those of a commandant of a garrison, who sees his stronghold menaced by an enemy he had never suspected. Confident as he is in the resources of his position, he yet cannot resist the impression that the very threat of attack has been prompted by some weakness of which he is unaware.

"To put us on our title," said he, "implies a great war. Let us try and find out who and what are they who presume to declare it!"

CHAPTER XV
A FIRST BRIEF

The reader has been already told that Joe Nelligan had achieved a great success in his first case. A disputed point of law had been raised, in itself insignificant, but involving in its train a vast variety of momentous interests. Repton, with an ingenuity all his own, had contrived to draw the discussion beyond its original limits, that he might entangle and embarrass the ambitious junior who had dared to confute him. Nelligan accepted the challenge at once, and after a stormy discussion of some hours came out the victor. For a while his timid manner, and an overpowering sense of the great odds against him, seemed to weigh oppressively on him. The very successes he had won elsewhere were really so many disparagements to him now, giving promise, as it were, of his ability. But, despite all these disadvantages, he entered the lists manfully and courageously.

What a many-sided virtue is this same courage, and how prone is the world to award its praises unequally for it! We are enthusiastic for the gallant soldier the earliest in the breach, or the glorious sailor who first jumps upon the enemy's quarter-deck, and yet we never dream of investing with heroism him who dares to combat with the most powerful intellects of debate, or enters the field of argument against minds stored with vast resources of knowledge, and practised in all the subtleties of disputation.

It is time, existence is not in the issue; but are there not things a thousand times dearer than life at peril? Think of him who has gone on from success to success; whose school triumphs have but heralded the riper glories of college life; who, rising with each new victory, is hailed by that dearest and best of all testimonies,—the prideful enthusiasm of his own age. Fancy him, the victor in every struggle, who has carried all before him,—the vaunted chief of his contemporaries,—fancy him beaten and worsted on his first real field of action. Imagine such a man, with all the prestige of his college fame, rudely encountered and overcome in the contest of public life, and say if any death ever equalled the suffering!

Happily, our task has not to record any such failure in the present case. Young Nelligan sat down amidst the buzzing sound of approving voices, and received a warm eulogy from the Court on the promise of so conspicuous an opening. And a proud man was Dan Nelligan on that day! At any other time how deeply honored had he felt by the distinguished notice of the great dignitaries who now congratulated him on his son's success! With what pride had he accepted the polite recognition of Chief Barons and silk-gowned "leaders"! Now, however, his heart had but room for one thought,—Joe himself,—his own boy,—the little child as it were of yesterday, now a man of mark and note, already stamped with the impress of success in what, to every Irishman's heart at least, is the first of all professions. The High Sheriff shook old Nelligan's hand in open court, and said, "It is an honor to our county, Nelligan, to claim him." The Judge sent a message that he wished to see him in his robing-room, and spoke his warm praises of the "admirable speech, as remarkable for its legal soundness as for its eloquence;" and Repton overtook him in the street, and, catching his hand, said, "Be proud of him, sir, for we are all proud of him."

Mayhap the hope is not a too ambitious one, that some one of those who may glance over these humble lines may himself have once stood in the position of Joe Nelligan, in so far as regards the hour of his triumph, and have felt in his heart the ecstasy of covering with his fame the "dear head" of a father.

If so, I ask him boldly,—whatever may have been the high rewards of his later fire, whatever honors may have been showered upon him, however great his career, and however brilliant its recognitions,—has he ever, in his proudest moments, tasted such a glorious thrill of delight as when he has fallen into his father's arms overcome by the happiness that he has made that father proud of him? Oh, ye who have experienced this thrill of joy within you, cherish and preserve it. The most glowing eulogies of eloquence, the most ornate paragraphs of a flattering press, are sorry things in comparison to it. For ourselves, we had rather have been Joe Nelligan when, with his father's warm tears dimming his eyes, he said, "God bless you, my boy!" than have gained all the honors that even talents like his can command!

He could not bear to absent himself from home that day; and although his father would gladly have celebrated his triumph by gathering his friends about him, Joe entreated that they might be alone. And they were so. The great excitement of the day over, a sense of weariness, almost sadness, stole over the young man; and while his father continued to relate for his mother's hearing various little incidents of the trial, he listened with a half-apathetic dreaminess, as though the theme oppressed him. The old man dwelt with delight on the flattering attention bestowed by the Court on Joseph's address, the signs of concurrence vouchsafed from time to time by the Bench, the approving murmur of the Bar while he spoke, and then the honest outburst of enthusiasm that shook the very walls as he concluded. "I tried," continued Dan Nelligan,—"I tried to force my way through the crowd, and come and tell you that he had gained the day, but I couldn't; they were all around me, shaking my hands, patting me on the shoulders, and saying, as if I did n't know it in my own heart, 'He 'll make you a proud man yet, Mr. Nelligan.'"

"I heard it all, five minutes after it was over," said Mrs. Nelligan; "and you 'd never guess who told me."

"Counsellor Walsh," cried Nelligan.

"No, indeed; I never seen him."

"It was Hosey Lynch, then, for I saw him running like mad through the town, spreading the news everywhere."

"It was not Hosey," said she, half contemptuously. "I wish, Joe, you'd give a guess yourself who told me."

"Guess, mother,—guess who told you what?" said he, suddenly starting from some deep meditation.

"Who told me that you won the cause, and beat all the great counsellors from Dublin."

"I'm sure, mother, it would be hard for me to say," said Joseph, smiling faintly; "some of our kind townsfolk, perhaps. Father Neal, old Peter Hayes, or—"

"I'll just tell you at once," broke she in, half irritated at the suggested source of her information. "It was Miss Mary herself, and no other."

"Miss Martin!" exclaimed old Nelligan.

"Miss Mary Martin!" echoed Joe; while a sickly paleness crept over his features, and his lips trembled as he spoke.

"How came you to see her? Where was she?" asked Nelligan, eagerly.

"I 'll tell you," replied she, with all the methodical preparation by which she heralded in the least important communications,—"I 'll tell you. I was sitting here, working at the window, and wondering when the trial would be over, for the goose that was for dinner was too near the fire, and I said to myself—"

"Never mind what you said to yourself,—confound the goose," broke in old Dan, fiercely.

"Faith, then, I 'd like to know if you 'd be pleased to eat your dinner on the cold loin of veal—"

"But Miss Martin, mother,—Miss Martin," urged Joe, impatiently.

"I'm coming to her, if you'll let me; but when you flurry me and frighten me, I 'm ready to faint. It was last Candlemas you gave me a start, Dan, about—what was it, now? Lucky Mason's dog, I believe. No, it was the chimney took fire—"

"Will you just go back to Miss Martin, if you please," said old Nelligan, sternly.

"I wish I knew where I was,—what I was saying last," said she, in a tone of deep sorrow and contrition.

"You were going to say how Miss Mary told you all about the trial, mother," said Joe, taking her hand kindly within his own.

"Yes, darling; now I remember it all. I was sitting here at the window hemming them handkerchiefs of yours, and I heard a sharp sound of a horse coming along quick, and, by the way he cantered, I said to myself, 'I know *you*,' and, sure enough, when I opened the window, there she was, Miss Mary herself, all dripping with wet, and her hat flattened on her face, at the door.

"'Don't ask me to get down, Mrs. Nelligan,' said she, 'for I'm in a great hurry. I have to ride out to Kilkieran with this'—and she showed me a bottle she had in the pocket of her saddle. 'I only called to tell you that your son has gained another—' What was it she called it?—a victory, or a battle,—no, it was something else—"

"Never mind—go on," cried Joe; "and then?"

"'But, my dear Miss Mary,' says I, 'you 're wet through and through. It's more than your life's worth to go off now another ten miles. I'll send our gossoon, Mickey Slater, with the medicine, if you 'll just come in and stay with us.' I did n't say to dinner, for I was ashamed to ask her to that.

"'I should be delighted, Mrs. Nelligan,' said she, 'but it is impossible to-day. I 'd have stayed and asked you for my dinner,'—her very words,— 'asked you for my dinner, but I have promised poor Mat Landy to go back to him. But perhaps it is as well as it is; and my aunt Dorothy might say, if she heard of it, that it was a strange choice I had made of a festive occasion,—the day on which we were beaten, and the society of him that worsted us.'

"'Oh, but, Miss Mary,' says I, 'sure you don't think the worse of poor Joe—'

"'I never thought more highly of him, my dear Mrs. Nelligan,' said she, 'than at this moment; and, whatever others may say or think, I'll maintain my opinion, that he is a credit to us all. Good-bye! good-bye!' and then she turned short round, and said, 'I can't answer for how my uncle may feel about what has occurred to-day, but you know *my* sentiments. Farewell!' And with that she was off; indeed, before I had time to shut down the window, she was out of sight and away."

"She ought to know, and she will know, that Joe never said one hard thing of her family. And though he had in his brief enough to tempt him to bring the Martins up for judgment, not a word, not a syllable did he utter." This old Nelligan spoke with a proud consciousness of his son's honorable conduct.

"Good heavens!" exclaimed Joe, "is it not enough that a man sells his intellect, pawns his capacity, and makes traffic of his brains, without being called on to market his very nature, and set up his very emotions for sale? If my calling demands this at my hands, I have done with it,—I renounce it."

"But I said you refrained, Joe. I remarked that you would not suffer the heat of discussion to draw you into an angry attack—"

"And you praise me for it!" broke in Joe, passionately. "You deem it an occasion to compliment me, that, in defending the cause of a worthless debauchee, I did not seize with avidity the happy moment to assail an honorable gentleman; and not alone you, but a dozen others, congratulated me on this reserve,—this constraint,—as though the lawyer were but a bravo, and, his stiletto once paid for, he must produce the body of his victim. I regard my profession in another and a higher light; but if even its practice were the noblest that could engage human faculties, and its rewards the highest that could crown them, I'd quit it tomorrow, were its price to be the sacrifice of an honorable self-esteem and the regard of—of those we care for." And in the difficult utterance of the last words his cheek became crimson, and his lip trembled.

"I 'll tell you what you 'll do, Joe," said his mother, whose kindness was not invariably distinguished by tact,—"just come over with *me* to-morrow to Cro' Martin. I 'm going to get slips of the oak-leaf geranium and the dwarf rose, and we 'll just go together in a friendly way, and when we 're there you 'll have some opportunity or other to tell Miss Mary that it wasn't your fault for being against them."

"He 'll do no such thing," broke in Nelligan, fiercely. "Miss Mary Martin wants no apologies,—her family have no right to any. Joe is a member of a high and powerful profession. If he does n't fill as great a place now, who knows where he 'll not be this day fifteen years, eh, my boy? Maybe I 'll not be here to see,—indeed, it's more than likely I 'll not,—but I know it now. I feel as sure of it as I do that my name 's Dan."

"And if you are not to see it, father," said Joe, as he pressed his father's hand between both his own,—"you and my dearest mother,—the prize will be nigh valueless. If I cannot, when my reward is won, come home,—to such a home as this,—the victory will be too late." And so saying he rose abruptly, and hurried from the room. The moment after he had locked his door, and, flinging himself upon his bed, buried his face between his hands.

With all the proud sensations of having achieved a great success, his heart was heavily oppressed. It seemed to him as though Destiny had decreed that his duty should ever place him in antagonism to his affections. Up to a short period before this trial came on he had frequently been in Miss Martin's company. Now, it was some trifling message for his mother; now, some book he had himself promised to fetch her; then visits to the sick— and Joe, latterly, had taken a most benevolent turn—had constantly brought them together; and often, when Mary was on foot, Joe had accompanied her to the gates of the demesne. In these meetings one subject usually occupied them,—the sad condition of the country, the destitution of the poor,—and on this theme their sympathies and hopes and fears all agreed. It was not only that they concurred in their views of the national character, but that they attributed its traits of good or evil to the very same causes; and while Nelligan was amazed at finding the daughter of a proud house deeply conversant with the daily life of the humblest peasant, she, too, was astonished how sincere in his respect for rank, how loyal in his devotion to the claims of blood, was one whose birth might have proclaimed him a democrat and a destroyer.

These daily discussions led them closer and closer to each other, till at length confidences grew up between them, and Mary owned to many of the difficulties that her lone and solitary station exposed her to. Many things were done on the property without—some in direct opposition to— her concurrence. As she once said herself, "We are so ready to satisfy our consciences by assuming that whatever we may do legally we have a right to do morally, and at the same time, in the actual condition of Ireland, what is just may be practically the very heaviest of all hardships." This observation was made with reference to some law proceedings of Scanlan's instituting, and the day after she chanced to make it Joe started for Dublin. It was there that Magennis's attorney had sent him the brief in that cause,—a charge which the etiquette of his profession precluded his declining.

In what way he discharged the trust we have seen,—what sorrow it cost him is more than we can describe. "Miss Martin," thought he, "would know nothing of the rules which prescribe our practice, and will look upon my conduct here as a treason. For weeks long she has conversed with me in candor over the state of the county and its people; we separate for a few days, and she finds me arrayed with others against the interests of her family, and actually paid to employ against her the very knowledge she has imparted to me! What a career have I chosen," cried he, in his agony, "if every success is to be purchased at such a price!" With such men as Magennis he had nothing in common; their society, their habits, their opinions were all distasteful to him, and yet it was for him and his he was to sacrifice the dearest hope of his heart,—to lose the good esteem of one whose praise he had accounted more costly than the highest distinction a sovereign could bestow on him. "And what a false position mine!" cried he again. "Associated by the very closest ties with a party not one of whose objects have my sympathies, I see myself separated by blood, birth, and station from all that I venerate and respect. I must either be a traitor to my own or to myself; declare my enmity to all I think most highly of, or suffer my motives to be impugned and my fame tarnished."

There was, indeed, one circumstance in this transaction which displeased him greatly, and of which he was only aware when too late. The Magennis defence had been "got up" by a subscription,—a fund to which Joseph's own father had contributed. Amongst the machinery of attack upon the landed gentry, Father Neal Rafferty had suggested the expediency of "putting them on their titles" in cases the most trivial and insignificant. Forfeiture and confiscation had followed each other so frequently in Irish history,—grants and revocations were so mixed up together,—some attested in all formality, others irregular and imperfect,—that it was currently believed there was scarcely one single estate of the whole province could establish a clear and indisputable title. The project was, therefore, a bold one which, while disturbing the rights of property, should also bring under discussion so many vexed questions of English rule and tyranny over the Irish. Libraries and cabinets were ransacked for ancient maps of the counties; and old records were consulted to ascertain how far the original conditions of service, and so forth, had been complied with on which these estates were held.

Joseph had frequently carried home books from the library of Cro' Martin, rare and curious volumes, which bore upon the ancient history of the country. And now there crossed him the horrible suspicion that the whole scheme of this attack might be laid to his charge, the information to substantiate which he had thus surreptitiously-obtained. It was clear enough, from what his mother had said, that such was not Miss Martin's present impression; but who could say what representations might be made to her, and what change effected in her sentiments? "And this," cried he, in indignation—"and this is the great career I used to long for!—this the broad highway I once fancied was to lead me to honor and distinction! Or is it, after all, my own fault, for endeavoring to reconcile two-things which never can have any agreement,—an humble origin and high aspirings? Were I an Englishman, the difficulty would not be impassable; but here, in Ireland, the brand of a lowly fortune and a despised race is upon me. Can I—dare I resist it?"

A long and arduous conflict was that in which he passed the night,—now inclining to abandon his profession forever, now to leave Ireland and join the English or some Colonial Bar; and at length, as day was breaking, and as though the fresh morning air which now blew upon him from his open window had given fresh energy to his nature, he determined he would persist in his career in his own country. "My fate shall be an example or a warning!" cried he. "They who come after me shall know whether there be rewards within reach of honest toil and steady industry without the contamination of a mock patriotism! If I do rise, it shall be from no aid derived from a party or a faction; and if I fail, I bring no discredit upon 'my order.'"

There are men who can so discipline their minds that they have but to establish a law to their actions to make their whole lives "a system." Such individuals the Germans not inaptly call "self-contained men," and of these was Joe Nelligan one.

A certain concentration of his faculties, and the fatigues of a whole night passed thus in thought, gave a careworn, exhausted look to his features as he entered the room where Repton sat awaiting him for breakfast.

"I see what's the matter with you," said the old lawyer, as he entered. "You have passed the night after a 'first brief.' This day ten years you'll speak five hours before the Lords 'in error,' and never lose a wink of sleep after it's over!"

CHAPTER XVI
MR. REPTON LOOKS IN

On the day after that some of whose events we have just recorded, and towards nightfall, Mary Martin slowly drove along the darkly wooded avenue of Cro' Martin. An unusual sadness overweighed her. She was just returning from the funeral of poor old Mat Landy, one of her oldest favorites as a child. He it was who first taught her to hold an oar; and, seated beside him, she first learned to steer a "corragh" through the wild waves of the Atlantic. His honest, simple nature, his fine manly contentedness with a very humble lot, and a cheerful gayety of heart that seemed never to desert him, were all traits likely to impress such a child as she had been and make his companionship a pleasure. With a heavy heart was it, therefore, now that she thought over these things, muttering to herself as she went along snatches of the old songs he used to sing, and repeating mournfully the little simple proverbs he would utter about the weather.

The last scene itself had been singularly mournful. Two fishermen of the coast alone accompanied the car which bore the coffin; death or sickness was in every house; few could be spared to minister to the dead, and even of those, the pale shrunk features and tottering limbs bespoke how dearly the duty cost them. Old Mat had chosen for his last resting-place a little churchyard that crowned a cliff over the sea, — a wild, solitary spot, — an old gable, a ruined wall, a few low gravestones, and no more. The cliff itself, rising abruptly from the sea to some four hundred feet, was perforated with the nests of sea-fowl, whose melancholy cries, as they circled overhead, seemed to ring out a last requiem. There it was they now laid him. Many a time from that bleak summit had he lighted a beacon fire to ships in distress.

Often and often, from that same spot, had he gazed out over the sea, to catch signs of those who needed succor, and now that bold heart was still and that strong arm stiffened, and the rough, deep voice that used to sound above the tempest, silent forever.

"Never mind, Patsey," said Mary, to one of the fishermen, who was endeavoring with some stray fragments of a wreck to raise a little monument over the spot, "I'll look to that hereafter." And so saying, she turned mournfully away to descend the cliff. A stranger, wrapped in a large boat-cloak, had been standing for some time near the place; and as Mary left it, he drew nigh and asked who she was.

"Who would she be?" said the fisherman, gruffly, and evidently in no humor to converse.

"A wife, or a daughter, perhaps?" asked the other again.

"Neither one nor the other," replied the fisherman.

"It is Miss Mary, sir,—Miss Martin,—God bless her!" broke in the other; "one that never deserts the poor, living or dead. Musha! but she's what keeps despair out of many a heart!"

"And has she come all this way alone?" asked he.

"What other way could she come, I wonder?" said the man he had first addressed. "Did n't they leave her there by herself, just as if she was n't belonging to them? They were kinder to old Henderson's daughter than to their own flesh and blood."

"Hush, Jerry, hush!—she 'll hear you," cried the other. And saluting the stranger respectfully, he began to follow down the cliff.

"Are there strangers stopping at the inn?" asked Mary, as she saw lights gleaming from some of the windows as she passed.

"Yes, miss, there's him that was up there at the churchyard—ye didn't remark him, maybe—and one or two more."

"I did not notice him," said Mary; and, wishing the men good-night, set out homeward. So frequent were the halts she made at different cabins as she drove along, so many times was she stopped to give a word of advice or counsel, that it was already duskish as she reached Cro' Martin, and found herself once more near home. "You're late with the post this evening, Billy," said she, overtaking the little fellow who carried the mail from Oughterard.

"Yes, miss, there was great work sortin' the letters that came in this morning, for I believe there's going to be another election; at least I heard Hosey Lynch say it was all about that made the bag so full."

"I 'm sorry for it, Billy," said she. "We have enough to think of, ay, and troubles enough, too, not to need the strife and bitterness of another contest amongst us."

"Thrue for ye, miss, indeed," rejoined Billy. "'Tis wishing them far enough I am, them same elections; the bag does be a stone heavier every day till it's over."

"Indeed!" said Mary, half smiling at the remark.

"Thrue as I 'm here, miss. I would n't wonder if it was the goold for bribin' the chaps makes it weigh so much."

"And is there any other news stirring in the town, Billy?"

"Next to none, miss. They were talkin' of putting up ould Nelligan's son for the mimber; and more says the Magennis of Barnagheela will stand."

"A most excellent choice that would be, certainly," said Mary, laughing.

"Faix! I heerd of another that wasn't much better, miss."

"And who could that be?" asked Mary, in astonishment.

"But sure you'd know better than me, if it was thrue, more by token it would be the master's own orders."

"I don't understand you, Billy."

"I mean, miss, that it's only his Honer, Mr. Martin, could have the power to make Maurice Scanlan a Parlimint man."

"And has any one hinted at such a possibility?" said she, in astonishment.

"Indeed, then, it was the talk of the market this mornin', and many a one said he's the very fellow would get in."

"Is he such a general favorite in Oughterard?"

"I'm not sure it's that, miss," said Billy, thoughtfully.

"Maybe some likes him, and more is afraid of him; but he himself knows everybody and everybody's business. He can raise the rent upon this man, take it off that; 'tis his word can make a barony-constable or one of the watch. They say he has the taxes, too, in his power, and can cess you just as he likes. Be my conscience, he 's all as one as the Prime Minister."

Just as Billy had delivered this sage reflection they had reached the hall door, where, having consigned the letter-bag to the hands of a servant, he turned his steps to the kitchen, to take an "air of the fire" before he set out homeward. Mary Martin had not advanced many steps within the hall when both her hands were cordially grasped, and a kind voice, which she at once recognized as Mr. Repton's, said, "Here I am, my dear Miss Martin; arrived in time, too, to welcome you home again. You paid me a visit yesterday—"

"Yes," broke she in; "but you were shaking your ambrosial curls at the time, browbeating the bench, or cajoling the jury, or something of that sort."

"That I was; but I must own with scant success. You 've heard how that young David of Oughterard slew the old Goliath of Dublin? Well, shall I confess it? I'm glad of it. I feel proud to think that the crop of clever fellows in Ireland is flourishing, and that when I, and a dozen like me, pass away, our places will be filled by others that will keep the repute of our great profession high in the public estimation."

"This is worthy of you, sir," cried Mary, pressing the arm ahe leaned on more closely.

"And now, my dear Miss Mary," said he, as they entered the drawing-room,—"now that I have light to look at you, let me make my compliments on your appearance. Handsomer than ever, I positively declare. They told me in the town that you half killed yourself with fatigue; that you frequently were days long on horseback, and nights watching by sick-beds; but if this be the result, benevolence is indeed its own reward."

"Ah, my dear Mr. Repton, I see you do not keep all your flatteries for the jury-box."

"My moments are too limited here to allow me time for an untruth. I must be off; to-night I have a special retainer for a great record at Roscommon, and at this very instant I should be poring over deeds and parchments, instead of gazing at 'orbs divinely blue;' not but, I believe, now that I look closer, yours are hazel."

"Let me order dinner, then, at once," said she, approaching the bell.

"I have done that already, my dear," said he, gayly; "and what is more, I have dictated the bill of fare. I guessed what a young lady's simple meal might be, and I have been down to the cook, and you shall see the result."

"Then it only remains for me to think of the cellar. What shall it be, sir? The Burgundy that you praised so highly last winter, or the Port that my uncle preferred to it?"

"I declare that I half suspect your uncle was right. Let us move for a new trial, and try both over again," said he, laughing, as she left the room.

"Just to think of such a girl in such a spot," cried he to himself, as he walked alone, up and down the room; "beauty, grace, fascination,—all that can charm and attract; and then, such a nature, childlike in gayety, and chivalrous,—ay, chivalrous as a chevalier!"

"I see, sir, you are rehearsing for Roscommon," said Mary, who entered the room while he was yet declaiming alone; "but I must interrupt you, for the soup is waiting."

"I obey the summons," said he tendering his arm. And they both entered the dinner-room.

So long as the meal lasted, Repton's conversation was entirely devoted to such topics as he might have discussed at a formal dinner-party. He talked of the world of society, its deaths, births, and marriages; its changes of place and amusement. He narrated the latest smart things that were going the round of the clubs, and hinted at the political events that were passing. But the servants gone, and the chairs drawn closer to the blazing hearth, his tone changed at once, and in a voice of tremulous kindness he said,—"I can't bear to think of the solitude of this life of yours!—nay, hear me out. I say this, not for *you*, since in the high devotion of a noble purpose you are above all its penalties; but I cannot endure to think that *we* should permit it."

"First of all," said Mary, rapidly, "what you deem solitude is scarcely such; each day is so filled with its duties, that when I come back here of an evening, it often happens that my greatest enjoyment is the very sense of isolation that awaits me. Do you know," added she, "that very often the letter-bag lies unopened by me till morning? And as to newspapers, there they lie in heaps, their covers unbroken to this hour. Such is actually the case to-day. I haven't read my letters yet."

"I read mine in my bed," cried Repton. "I have them brought to me by candlelight in winter, and I reflect over all the answers while I am dressing. Some of the sharpest things I have ever said have occurred to me while I was shaving; not," added he, hastily, "but one's really best things are always impromptu. Just as I said t' other day to the Viceroy,—a somewhat felicitous one. He was wishing that some historian would choose for his subject the lives of Irish Lord-Lieutenants; not, he remarked, in a mere spirit of party, or with the levity of partisanship, but in a spirit becoming the dignity of history,—such as Hume himself might have done. 'Yes, my Lord,' I replied, 'your observation is most just; it should be a continuation of Rapine.' Eh! it was a home-thrust, wasn't it?—'a continuation of Rapine.'" And the old man laughed till his eyes ran over.

"Do these great folk ever thoroughly forgive such things?" asked Mary.

"My dear child, their self-esteem is so powerful they never feel them; and even when they do, the chances are that they store them up in their memories, to retail afterwards as their own. I have detected my own stolen property more than once; but always so damaged by wear, and disfigured by ill-usage, that I never thought of reclaiming it."

"The affluent need never fret for a little robbery," said Mary, smiling.

"Ay, but they may like to be the dispensers of their own riches," rejoined Repton, who never was happier than when able to carry out another's illustration.

"Is Lord Reckington agreeable?" asked Mary, trying to lead him on to any other theme than that of herself.

"He is eminently so. Like all men of his class, he makes more of a small stock in trade than we with our heads full can ever pretend to. Such men talk well, for they think fluently. Their tact teaches them the popular tone on every subject, and they have the good sense never to rise above it."

"And Massingbred, the secretary, what of him?"

"A very well-bred gentleman, strongly cased in the triple armor of official dulness. Such men converse as stupid whist-players play cards; they are always asking to 'let them see the last trick;' and the consequence is they are ever half an hour behind the rest of the world. Ay, Miss Mary, and this is an age where one must never be half a second in arrear. This is really delicious Port; and now that the Burgundy is finished, I think I prefer it. Tell Martin I said so when you write to him. I hope the cellar is well stocked with it."

"It was so when my uncle went away, but I fear I have made great inroads upon it. It was my chief remedy with the poor."

"With the poor! such wine as this,—the richest grape that ever purpled over the Douro! Do you tell me that you gave this to these—Heaven forgive me, what am I saying? Of course you gave it; you gave them what was fifty times more precious,—the kind ministerings of your own angelic nature, the soft words and soft looks and smiles that a prince might have knelt for. I 'm not worthy to drink another glass of it," added he, as he pushed the decanter from him towards the centre of the table.

"But you shall, though," said Mary, filling his glass, "and it shall be a bumper to my health."

"A toast I'd stake my life for," said he, reverently, as he lifted her hand to his lips and kissed it with all the deference of a courtier. "And now," added he, refilling his glass, "I drink this to the worthy fellow whose portrait is before me; and may he soon come back again." He arose as he spoke, and giving his hand to Mary, led her into the drawing-room. "Ay, my dear Miss Mary," said he, following up the theme in his own thoughts, "it is here your uncle ought to be. When the army is in rout and dismay, the general's presence is the talisman that restores discipline. Everything around us at this moment is full of threatening danger. The catalogue of the assizes is a dark record; I never saw its equal, no more have I ever witnessed anything to compare with the dogged indifference of the men arraigned. The Irishman is half a fatalist by nature; it will be an evil hour that makes him wholly one!"

"But still," said Mary, "you 'd scarcely counsel his return here at this time. The changes that have taken place would fret him deeply, not to speak of even worse!"

She delivered the last few words in a voice broken and trembling; and Repton, turning quickly towards her, said, — "I know what you point at: the irritated feeling of the people, and that insolent menace they dared to affix to his own door."

"You heard of that, then?" cried she, eagerly.

"To be sure, I heard of it; and I heard how your own hands tore it down, and riding with it into the midst of them at Kiltimmon market, you said, 'I 'll give five hundred pounds to him who shows me who did this, and I 'll forfeit five hundred more if I do not horsewhip the coward from the county.'"

Mary hid her face within her hands; but closely as she pressed them there, the warm tears would force their way through, and fall, dropping on her bosom.

"You are a noble girl," cried he, in ecstasy; "and in all your great trials there is nothing finer than this, that the work of your benevolence has never been stayed by the sense of ill-requital, and you have never involved the character of a people in the foul crime of a miscreant."

"How could I so wrong them, sir?" broke she out. "Who better than myself can speak of their glorious courage, their patient resignation, their noble self-devotion? Has not the man, sinking under fever, crawled from his bed to lead me to the house of another deeper in misery than himself? Have I not seen the very poorest sharing the little alms bestowed upon their wretchedness? Have I not heard the most touching words of gratitude from lips growing cold in death? You may easily show me lands of greater comfort, where the blessings of wealth and civilization are more widely spread; but I defy you to point to any where the trials of a whole people have been so great and so splendidly sustained."

"I'll not ask the privilege of reply," said Repton; "perhaps I 'd rather be convinced by you than attempt to gainsay one word of your argument."

"At your peril, sir," said she, menacing him with her finger, while a bright smile lit up her features.

"The chaise is at the door, sir," said a servant, entering and addressing Repton.

"Already!" exclaimed he. "Why, my dear Miss Mary, it can't surely be eight o'clock. No; but," added he, looking at his watch, "it only wants a quarter of ten, and I have not said one half of what I had to say, nor heard a fourth of what you had to tell me."

"Let the postboy put up his horses, William," said Miss Martin, "and bring tea."

"A most excellent suggestion," chimed in Repton. "Do you know, my dear, that we old bachelors never thoroughly appreciate all that we have missed in domesticity till we approach a tea-table. We surround ourselves with fifty mockeries of home-life; we can manage soft carpets, warm curtains, snug dinners, but somehow our cup of tea is a rude imitation that only depicts the inaccuracy of the copy. Without the priestess the tea-urn sings forth no incantation."

"How came it that Mr. Repton remained a Benedict?" asked she, gayly.

"By the old accident, that he would n't take what he might have, and could n't get what he wished. Add to that," continued he, after a pause, "when a man comes to a certain time of life without marrying, the world has given to him a certain place, assigned to him, as it were, a certain part which would be utterly marred by a wife. The familiarity of one's female acquaintance—the pleasantest spot in old bachelorhood—could n't stand such an ordeal; and the hundred-and-one eccentricities pardonable and pardoned in the single man would be condemned in the married one. You shake your head. Well, now, I 'll put it to the test. Would you, or could you, make me your confidant so unreservedly if there were such a person as Mrs. Repton in the world? Not a bit of it, my dear child. We old bachelors are the lay priests of society, and many come to us with confessions they 'd scruple about making to the regular authorities."

"Perhaps you are right," said she, thoughtfully; "at all events, I should have no objection to you as my confessor."

"I may have to claim that promise one of these day yet," said he, significantly. "Eh, here comes William again. Well, the postboy won't wait, or something has gone wrong. Eh, William, what is it?"

"The boy's afraid, sir, if you don't go soon, that there will be no passing the river at Barnagheela,—the flood is rising every minute."

"And already the water is too deep," cried Mary. "Give the lad his supper, William. Let him make up his cattle, and say that Mr. Repton remains here for the night."

"And Mr. Repton obeys," said he, bowing; "though what is to become of 'Kelly *versus* Lenaham and another,' is more than I can say."

"They 'll have so many great guns, sir," said Mary, laughing; "won't they be able to spare a twenty-four pounder?"

"But I ought, at least, to appear in the battery, my dear. They 'll say that I stayed away on account of that young fellow Nelligan; he has a brief in that cause, and I know he 'd like another tussle with me. By the way, Miss Mary, that reminds me that I promised him to make his—no, not his excuses, he was too manly for that; but his—his explanations to you about yesterday's business. He was sorely grieved at the part assigned him; he spoke feelingly of all the attentions he once met at your uncle's hands, but far more so of certain kindnesses shown to his mother by yourself; and surmising that you might be unaware of the exacting nature of our bar etiquette, that leaves no man at liberty to decline a cause, he tortured himself inventing means to set himself right with you."

"But I know your etiquette, sir, and I respect it; and Mr. Nelligan never stood higher in my estimation than by his conduct of yesterday. You can tell him, therefore, that you saw there was no necessity to touch on the topic; it will leave less unpleasantness if we should meet again."

"What a diplomatist it is!" said Repton, smiling affectionately at her. "How successful must all this tact be when engaged with the people! Nay, no denial; you know in your heart what subtle devices it supplies you with."

"And yet, I 'm not so certain that what you call my diplomacy may not have involved me in some trouble,—at least, there is the chance of it."

"As how, my dear child?"

"You shall hear, sir. You know the story of that poor girl at Barnagheela, whom they call Mrs. Magennis? Well, her old grandfather—as noble a heart as ever beat—had never ceased to pine after her fall. She had been the very light of his life, and he loved her on, through her sorrow, if not her shame, till, as death drew nigh him, unable to restrain his craving desire, he asked me to go and fetch her, to give her his last kiss and receive his last blessing. It was a task I had fain have declined, were such an escape open to me, but I could not. In a word, I went and did his bidding. She stayed with him till he breathed his last breath, and then—in virtue of some pledge I hear that she made him—she fled, no one knows whither. All trace of her is lost; and though I have sent messengers on every side, none have yet discovered her."

"Suicide is not the vice of our people," said Repton, gravely.

"I know that well, and the knowledge makes me hopeful. But what sufferings are yet before her, what fearful trials has she to meet!"

"By Jove!" cried Repton, rising and pacing the room, "you have courage, young lady, that would do honor to a man. You brave the greatest perils with a stout-heartedness that the best of us could scarcely summon."

"But, in this case, the peril is not mine, sir."

"I am not so sure of that, Miss Mary," said Repton, doubtingly,—"I 'm not so sure of that." And, with crossed arms and bent-down head, he paced the room slowly back and forwards. "Ay," muttered he to himself, "Thursday night—Friday, at all events—will close the record. I can speak to evidence on the morning, and be back here again some time in the night. Of course it is a duty,—it is more than a duty." Then he added, aloud, "There 's the moon breaking out, and a fine breezy sky. I 'll take the road, Miss Mary, and, with your good leave, I 'll drink tea with you on Friday evening. Nay, my dear, the rule is made absolute."

"I agree," said she, "if it secures me a longer visit on your return."

A few moments afterwards saw Repton seated in the corner of his chaise, and hurrying onward at speed. His eyes soon closed in slumber, and as he sank off to rest, his lips murmured gently, "My Lord, in rising to address the Court, under circumstances of no ordinary difficulty, and in a case where vast interest, considerable influence, and, I may add—may add—" The words died away, and he was asleep.

CHAPTER XVII
LADY DOROTHEA'S LETTER

Though it was late when Repton took his departure, Mary Martin felt no inclination for sleep, but addressed herself at once to examine the letter bag, whose contents seemed more than usually bulky. Amid a mass of correspondence about the estate, she came at length upon the foreign letters, of which there were several from the servants to their friends or relations at Cro' Martin,—all, as usual, under cover to Miss Martin; and at last she found one in Lady Dorothea's own hand, for herself,—a very rare occurrence; nay, indeed, it was the first epistle her Ladyship had favored her with since her departure.

It was not, then, without curiosity as to the cause that Mary broke the large seal and read as follows:—

"Carlsruhe, Saturday Evening, Cour de Bade.

"My dear Niece,—It was only yesterday, when looking over your uncle's papers, I chanced upon a letter of yours, dated some five or six weeks back, and which, to my great astonishment, I discovered had never been communicated to me,—though this mark of deficient confidence will doubtless seem less surprising to *you*.

"To bring your letter to your mind, *I* may observe it is one in which you describe the condition of the people on the estate, and the fatal inroads then making upon them by famine and pestilence. It is not my intention here to advert to what may possibly be a very natural error in your account,— the exaggerated picture you draw of their sufferings; your sympathy with them, and your presence to witness much of what they are enduring, will explain and excuse the highly colored statement of their sorrows. It were to be wished that an equally valid apology could be made for what I am forced to call the importunity of your demands in their favor. Five of your six last letters now before me are filled with appeals for abatements of rent, loans to carry out improvements, stipends for schoolmasters, doctors, scripture-readers, and a tribe of other hangers-on, that really seem to augment in number as the pauperism of the people increases. However ungracious the task of disparaging the accuracy of your view, I have no other alternative but to accept it, and hence I am forced to pen these lines myself in preference to committing the office to another.

"It really seems to me that you regard our position as landed proprietors in the light of a mere stewardship, and that it is our bounden duty to expend upon the tenantry the proceeds of the estate, reserving a scanty percentage, perhaps, for ourselves to live upon. How you came to this opinion, and whence you acquired it, I have no means of knowing. If, however, it has been the suggestion of your own genius, it is right you should know that you hold doctrines in common with the most distinguished communists of modern times, and are quite worthy of a seat of honor beside those who are now convulsing society throughout Europe.

"I am unwilling to utter anything like severity towards errors, many of which take their rise in a mistaken and ill-directed benevolence, because the original fault of committing the management of this property to your hands was the work of another. Let me hope that sincere sorrow for so fatal a mistake may not be the primary cause of his present attack—"

When Mary read so far, she started with a sudden fear; and turning over the pages of the long letter, she sought for some allusion to her uncle. At length she found the following lines:—"Your cousin would have left this for Ireland, but for the sudden seizure your poor uncle has suffered from, and which came upon him after breakfast, in apparently his ordinary health. The entire of the left side is attacked,—the face particularly,—and his utterance quite inarticulate."

For some minutes she could read no more; the warm tears rolled down her cheeks and dropped heavily on the paper, and she could only mutter to herself, "My poor, dear uncle,—my last, my only friend in the world!" Drying her eyes, with a great effort she read on:—

"The remedies have been so far successful as to arrest the progress of the malady, and his appetite is good, and his spirits, everything considered, are excellent. Of course, all details of business are strictly excluded from his presence; and your cousin has assumed whatever authority is necessary to the management of the property. We thought at one time your presence here might have been desirable, but, considering the distance, the difficulty of travelling without suitable companionship, and other circumstances, it would, on the whole, be a step we should not recommend; and, indeed, your uncle himself has not expressed any wishes on the subject."

She dropped the letter at these words, and, covering her face with her hands, sobbed bitterly and long; at length, and with an effort which taxed her strength to the utmost, she read on:—

"Although, however, you are to remain at Cro' Martin, it will be more than ever imperative you should reduce the establishment there within the very strictest possible limits; and to begin this-reform, I 'm fully assured it is necessary you should depose old Mrs. Broon, who is really incapable of her duties, while her long-acquired habits of expense render her incompatible with any new regulations to enforce economy. A moderate pension—something, however, in accordance with her real wants and requirements, rather than what might be called her expectations—should be settled upon her, and there are several farmers on the estate, any one of whom would gladly take charge of her. The gardens still figure largely in the account, and considering the very little probability of our makings the place a residence again, might be turned to more profitable use. You will confer with Henderson on the subject, and inquire how far it might be advisable to cultivate vegetables for market, or convert them into paddocks for calves, or, in short, anything which, if less remunerative, should still save the enormous outlay we now hear of I scarcely like to allude to the stable, knowing how much you lean to the enjoyment of riding and driving; but really these are times when retrenchment is called for at every hand; and I am persuaded that for purposes of health walking is infinitely better than carriage exercise. I know myself, that since I have taken to the habit of getting out of the carriage at the wells, and walking twice round the parterre, I feel myself braced and better for the day.

"It is not improbable but when the changes I thus suggest, and others similar to them, are enacted, that you will see to what little purpose a large house is maintained for the mere accommodation of a single individual, without suitable means, or indeed any reason whatever, to dispense them. If then, I say, you should come to this conviction,—at which I have already arrived,—a very great saving might be effected by obtaining a tenant for Cro' Martin, while you, if still desirous of remaining in the county, might be most comfortably accommodated at the Hendersons'."

Three times did Mary Martin read over this passage before she could bring herself to believe in its meaning; and hot tears of sorrow coursed down her cheeks as she became assured of its import.

"It is not," went on the epistle—"it is not in your uncle's present most critical state that I could confer with him on this project, nor strengthen my advice by what most probably would be *his* also. I therefore make the appeal simply to your own sense of what you may think in accordance with our greatly increased outlay and your own requirements. Should you receive this suggestion in the spirit in which it is offered, I think that both for your uncle's satisfaction and your own dignity, the proposal ought to come from yourself. You could make it to me in a letter, stating all the reasons in its favor, and of course not omitting to lay suitable stress upon the isolation of your present life, and the comfort and security you would derive from the protection of a family. Mrs. H. is really a very nice person, and her tastes and habits would render her most companionable; and she would, of course, make you an object of especial attention and respect. It is, besides, not impossible that the daughter may soon return—though this is a point I have not leisure to enter upon at present. A hundred a year would he a very handsome allowance for Henderson, and indeed for that sum he ought to keep your pony, if you still continue your taste for equipage. You would thus be more comfortable, and really richer,—that is, have more disposable means—than you have hitherto had. I forbear to insist further upon what—till it has your own approval—may be a vain advocacy on my part. I can only say, in conclusion, that in adopting this plan you would equally consult what is due to your own dignity, as what is required by your uncle's interests. Your cousin, I am forced to avow it, has been very silly, very inconsiderate, not alone in contracting heavy debts, but in raising large sums to meet them at fabulous rates of interest. The involvements threaten, from what I can gather, to imperil a considerable part of the estate, and we are obliged to send for Scanlan to come out here, and confer with him as to the means of extrication. I feel there is much to be said in palliation of errors which have their origin in high and generous qualities. Plantagenet was thrown at a very early age into the society of a most expensive regiment, and naturally contracted the tastes and habits around him. Poor fellow, he is suffering severely from the memory of these early indiscretions, and I see that nothing but a speedy settlement of his difficulties will ever restore him to his wonted spirits. You will thus perceive, that if my suggested change of life to you should not conform entirely to your wishes, that you are in reality only accepting your share of the sacrifices called for from each of us.

"There are a great number of other matters on which I wished to touch,— some, indeed, are not exactly within your province, such as the political fortunes of the borough, whose seat Mr. Massingbred has determined to vacate. Although not admitting the reason for his conduct, I am strongly convinced that the step is a mere acknowledgment of an error on his part, and an effort, however late, at the *amende honorable*. The restitution, for so I am forced to regard it, comes most inopportunely, since it would be a most ill-chosen moment in which to incur the expense of a contested election; besides that, really your cousin has no desire whatever for Parliamentary honors. Plantagenet, however, would seem to have some especial intentions on the subject which he keeps secret, and has asked of Massingbred not to send off his farewell address to the constituency for some days. But I will not continue a theme so little attractive to you.

"Dr. Schubart has just called to see your uncle. He is not altogether so satisfied with his state as I could have hoped; he advises change of scene, and a little more intercourse with the world, and we have some thought of Nice, if we cannot get on to Naples. Dr. S., to whom I spoke on the subject of your Irish miseries, tells me that cholera is now the most manageable of all maladies, if only taken early; that you must enjoin the persons attacked to a more liberal diet, no vegetables, and a sparing use of French wines, excepting, he says, the generous 'Vins du Midi.' There is also a mixture to be taken—of which he promised me the prescription—and a pill every night of arnica or aconite—I 'm not quite certain which—but it is a perfect specific. He also adds, what must be felt as most reassuring, that the disease never attacks but the very poorest of the population. As to typhus, he smiled when I spoke of it. It is, he says, a mere 'Gastrite,' a malady which modern science actually despises. In fact, my dear niece, these would seem, like all other Irish misfortunes, the mere offshoots of her own dark ignorance and barbarism. If it were not for the great expense—and of course that consideration decides the question—I should have requested you to send over your doctor here to confer with Dr. Schubart. Indeed, I think it might be a very reasonable demand to make of the Government, but unhappily my present 'relations' with my relative Lord Reckington preclude any advances of mine in that quarter.

"I was forgetting to add that, with respect to cholera, and indeed fever generally, that Dr. S. lays great stress upon what he calls the moral treatment of the people, amusing their minds by easily learned games and simple pleasures. I fear me, however, that the coarser natures of our population may not derive adequate amusement from the resources which would have such eminent success with the enlightened peasant of the Rhine land. Dr. S., I may remark, is a very distinguished writer on politics, and daily amazes us with the astounding speculations he is forming as to the future condition of Europe. His conviction is that our great peril is Turkey, and that Mohammedanism will be the religion of Europe before the end of the present century. Those new baths established at Brighton by a certain Hamet are a mere political agency, a secret propaganda, which his acuteness has alone penetrated. Miss Henderson has ventured to oppose these views with something not very far from impertinent ridicule, and for some time back, Dr. S. only discusses them with myself alone.

"I had left the remainder of the sheet for any intelligence that might occur before post hour, but I am suddenly called away, and shall close it at once. When I was sitting with your uncle awhile ago, I *half* broached the project I was suggesting to you, and he seemed highly to approve of so much as I ventured to tell him. Nothing then is wanting but your own concurrence to make it as practicable as it is deemed advisable by your affectionate aunt,

"Dorothea Martin."

The eccentricities of her aunt's character had always served as extenuating circumstances with Mary Martin. She knew the violence of her prejudices, the enormous amount of her self-esteem, and the facility with which she was ever able to persuade herself that whatever she wished to do assumed at once all the importance and gravity of a duty! This thorough appreciation of her peculiarities enabled Mary to bear up patiently under many sore trials and some actual wrongs. Where the occasion was a light one, she could afford to smile at such trials, and, even in serious cases, they palliated the injustice; but here was an instance wherein all her forgiveness was in vain. To take the moment of her poor uncle's illness—that terrible seizure, which left him without self-guidance, if even a will—to dictate these hard and humiliating terms, was a downright cruelty. Nor did it diminish the suffering which that letter cost her that its harsh conditions seemed dictated by a spirit of contempt for Ireland and its people. As Mary re-read the letter, she felt that every line breathed this tone of depreciation. It was to her Ladyship a matter of less than indifference what became of the demesne, who inhabited the house,—the home of "the Martins" for centuries! She was as little concerned for the prestige of "the old family," as she was interested for the sorrows of the people. If Mary endeavored to treat these things dispassionately to her own heart, by dwelling upon all the points which affected others, still, her own individual wrong would work to the surface, and the bitter and insulting suggestion made to her rose up before her in all its enormity.

She did her very best to turn her thoughts into some other channel,—to fix them upon her poor uncle, on his sick-bed, and sorrowing as he was sure to be; to think of her cousin Harry, struggling against the embarrassments of his own imprudence; of the old housekeeper, Catty Broon, to whom she could not summon courage to speak the cruel tidings of her changed lot,—but all, all in vain; back she would come to the humiliation that foreshadowed her own fortune, and threatened to depose her from her station forever.

An indignant appeal to her uncle—her own father's brother—was her first resolve. "Let me learn," said she to herself, "from his own lips, that such is the destiny he assigns me; that in return for my tried affection, my devotion, he has no other recompense than to lower me in self-esteem and condition together. Time enough, when assured of this, to decide upon what I shall do. But to whom shall I address this demand?" thought she again. "That dear, kind uncle is now struck down by illness. It were worse than cruelty to add to his own sorrows any thought of *mine*. If he have concurred in Lady Dorothea's suggestion, who knows in what light it may have been presented to him, by what arguments strengthened, with what perils contrasted? Is it impossible, too, that the sacrifice may be imperative? The sale of part of the property, the pressure of heavy claims,—all show that it may be necessary to dispose of Cro' Martin. Oh," exclaimed she, in agony, "it is but a year ago, that when Mr. Repton hinted vaguely at such a casualty, how stoutly and indignantly did I reject it!

"'Your uncle may choose to live abroad,' said he; 'to sell the estate, perhaps.' And I heard him with almost scornful defiance; and now the hour is come! and even yet I cannot bring myself to believe it. When Repton drew the picture of the tenantry, forsaken and neglected, the poor unnoticed, and the sick uncared for, he still forgot to assign me my place in the sad 'tableau,' and show that in destitution my lot was equal to their own; the very poorest and meanest had yet some spot, poor and mean though it were, they called a home, that Mary Martin was the only one an outcast!"

These gloomy thoughts were darkened as she bethought her that of her little fortune—on which, by Scanlan's aid, she had raised a loan—a mere fragment remained,—a few hundred pounds at most. The outlay on hospitals and medical assistance for the sick had more than quadrupled what she had estimated. The expense once begun, she had persevered with almost reckless determination. She had despatched to Dublin, one by one, the few articles of jewelry and value she possessed for sale; she had limited her own expenditure to the very narrowest bounds, nor was it till driven by the utmost urgency that she wrote the appeal to her uncle of which the reader already knows.

"How I once envied Kate Henderson," cried she, aloud, "the brilliant accomplishments she possessed, the graceful charm that her cultivation threw over society, and the fascination she wielded, by acquirements of which I knew nothing; but how much more now do I envy her, that in those same gifts her independence was secured,—that, high above the chances of the world, she could build upon her own efforts, and never descend to a condition of dependence!"

Her diminished power amongst the people had been fully compensated by the sincere love and affection she had won from them by acts of charity and devotion. Even these, however, owed much of their efficacy to the prestige of her station. No peasant in Europe puts so high a value on the intercourse with a rank above his own as does the Irish. The most pleasant flattery to his nature is the notice of "the gentleman," and it was more than half the boon Mary bestowed upon the poor, that she who sat down beside the bed, who heated the little drink, who raised the head to swallow it, was the daughter of the Great House! Would not her altered fortune destroy this charm? was now her bitter reflection. Up to this hour, greatly reduced as were the means she dispensed, and the influence she wielded, she still lived in the proud home of her family, and all regarded her as the representative of her honored name. But now—No, she could not endure the thought! "If I must descend to further privations," said she to herself, "let me seek out some new scene,—some spot where I am unknown, have never been heard of; there, at least, I shall be spared the contrast of the past with the present, nor see in every incident the cruel mockery of my former life.

"And yet," thought she, "how narrow-minded and selfish is all this, how mean-spirited, to limit the question to my own feelings! Is there no duty involved in this sacrifice? Shall I not still—reduced though I be in fortune—shall I not still be a source of comfort to many here? Will not the very fact of my presence assure them that they are not deserted? They have seen me under some trials, and the lesson has not been fruitless. Let them then behold me, under heavier ones, not dismayed nor cast down. What I lose in the prestige of station I shall more than gain in sympathy; and so I remain!" No sooner was the resolve formed than all her wonted courage came back. Rallying with the stimulus of action before her, she began to plan out a new life, in which her relation to the people should be closer and nearer than ever. There was a small ornamental cottage on the demesne, known as the Chalet, built by Lady Dorothea after one she had seen in the Oberland; this Mary now determined on for her home, and there, with Catty Broon alone, she resolved to live.

"My aunt," thought she, "can scarcely be so wedded to the Henderson scheme but that this will equally satisfy her wishes; and while it secures a home and a resting-place for-poor Catty, it rescues *me* from what I should feel as a humiliation."

The day was already beginning to dawn as Mary sat down to answer Lady Dorothea's letter. Most of her reply referred to her uncle, to whose affection she clung all the more as her fortunes darkened. She saw all the embarrassment of proffering her services to nurse and tend him, living, as he was, amidst his own; but still, she said that of the journey or its difficulties she should never waste a thought, if her presence at his sick-bed could afford him the slightest satisfaction. "He knows me as a nurse already," said she. "But tell him that I have grown, if not wiser, calmer and quieter than he knew me formerly; that I should not disturb him by foolish stories, but sit patiently save when he would have me to talk. Tell him, too, that if changed in many things, in my love to *him* I am unaltered." She tried to add more, but could not. The thought that these lines were to be read to her uncle by Lady

Dorothea chilled her, and the very tones of that supercilious voice seemed to ring in her ears, and she imagined some haughty or insolent comment to follow them as they were uttered.

With regard to her own future, she, in a few words, remarked upon the unnecessary expense of maintaining a large house for the accommodation of a single person, and said that, if her Ladyship concurred in the plan, she would prefer taking up her home at the Chalet with old Catty for companion and housekeeper.

She pointed out the advantages of a change which, while securing a comfortable home to them, would equally suggest to their dependants lessons of thrift and self-sacrifice, and added, half sportively, "As for me, when I find myself *en Suisse*, I 'm sure I shall less regret horses and dogs, and such-like vanities, and take to the delights of a dairy and cream cheeses with a good grace. Indeed, I 'm not quite certain but that Fortune, instead of displacing, will in reality be only installing me in the position best suited to me. Do not, then, be surprised, if at your return you find me in sabots and an embroidered bodice, deep in the mystery of all cottage economics, and well content to be so.

"You are quite right, my dear aunt," she continued, "not to entertain me with politics. The theme is as much above as it is distasteful to me; and so grovelling are my sentiments, that I 'd rather hear of the arrival of a cargo of oatmeal at Kilkieran than learn that the profoundest statesman of Great Britain had condescended to stand for our dear borough of Oughterard. At the same time, if Cousin Harry should change his mind, and turn his ambition towards the Senate, tell him I 'm quite ready to turn out and canvass for him to-morrow, and that the hospitalities of the Chalet shall do honor to the cause. As you speak of sending for Mr. Scanlan, I leave to him to tell you all the events of our late assizes here,—a task I escape from the more willingly, since I have no successes to record. Mr. Repton, however,—he paid me a visit yesterday, and stopped here to dinner,—says that he has no fears for the result at the next trial, and honestly confesses that our present defeat was entirely owing to the skill and ability of the counsel opposed to us. By some delay or mistake, I don't exactly know which, Scanlan omitted to send a retainer to young Mr. Nelligan, and who, being employed for the other side, was the chief cause of our failure. My uncle will be pleased to learn that Mr. N.'s address to the jury was scrupulously free from any of that invective or attack so frequently levelled at landlords when defending the rights of property. Repton called it 'a model of legal argument, delivered with the eloquence of a first-rate speaker, and the taste and temper of a gentleman.' Indeed, I understand that the tone of the speech has rendered all the ribaldry usual on such occasions in local journals impossible, and that the young barrister has acquired anything but popularity in consequence. Even in this much, is there a dawn of better things; and under such circumstances a defeat may be more profitable than a victory."

With a few kind messages to her uncle, and an earnest entreaty for early tidings of his state, Mary concluded a letter in which her great difficulty lay in saying far less than her thoughts dictated, and conveying as much as she dare trust to Lady Dorothea's interpretation. The letter concluded and sealed, she lay down, dressed as she was, on her bed, and fell a-thinking over the future.

There are natures to whom the opening of any new vista in life suggests fully as much of pleasure as anxiety. The prospect of the unknown and the untried has something of the adventurous about it which more than counterbalances the casualties of a future. Such a temperament was hers; and the first sense of sorrowful indignation over, she really began to speculate upon her cottage life with a certain vague and dreamy enjoyment. She foresaw, that when Cro' Martin Castle fell into other hands, that her own career ceased, her occupation was gone, and that she should at once fashion out some new road, and conform herself to new habits. The cares of her little household would probably not suffice to engage one whose active mind had hitherto embraced so wide a field of action, and Mary then bethought her how this leisure might be devoted to study and improvement. It was only in the eager enthusiasm of her many pursuits that she buried her sorrows over her neglected and imperfect education; and now a time was approaching when that reflection could no longer be resisted. She pondered long and deeply over these thoughts, when suddenly they were interrupted; but in what way, deserves a chapter of its own,—albeit a very brief one.

CHAPTER XVIII
MR. MERL'S EXPERIENCES IN THE WEST

"What card is this?—who left it?" said Mary, as she took up one from her breakfast-table.

"It is a gentleman that came to the inn late last night, miss, and sent a boy over to ask when he could pay his respects at the castle."

"'Mr. Herman Merl,'—a name I never heard of," muttered Mary to herself. "Doubtless some stranger wishing to see the house. Say, whenever he pleases, George; and order Sorrel to be ready, saddled and at the door, within an hour. This must be a busy day," said she, still speaking to herself, as the servant left the room. "At Oughterard before one; a meeting of the Loan Fund—I shall need some aid for my hospital; the Government order for the meal to be countersigned by a justice—Mr. Nelligan will do it. Then there 's Taite's little boy to be balloted for in the Orphan House; and Cassidy's son to be sent up to Dublin. Poor fellow, he has a terrible operation to go through. And I shall need Priest Rafferty's name to this memorial from the widows; the castle authorities seem to require it. After that, a visit to Kyle-a-Noe, to see all my poor sick folk: that will be a long business. I hope I may be able to get down to the shore and learn some tidings of poor Joan. She never leaves my thoughts, and yet I feel that no ill has befallen her."

"The gentleman that sent the card, miss, is below stairs. He is with Mr. Crow, at the hall-door," said George.

"Show him into the drawing-room, George, and tell Mr. Crow to come here, I wish to speak to him." And before Mary had put away the papers and letters which littered the table, the artist entered.

"Good morning, Mr. Crow," said Mary, in return for a number of most courteous salutations, which he was performing in a small semicircle in front of her. "Who is your friend Mr.—'Mr. Herman Merl '?" read she, taking up the card.

"A friend of your cousin's, Miss Mary,—of the Captain's. He brought a letter from him; but he gave it to Scanlan, and somehow Mr. Maurice, I believe, forgot to deliver it."

"I have no recollection of it," said she, still assorting the papers before her. "What is this visit meant for,—curiosity, pleasure, business? Does he wish to see the house?"

"I think it's Miss Martin herself he'd like to see," said Crow, half slyly.

"But why so? It's quite clear that I cannot show him any attentions. A young girl, living as I do here, cannot be expected to receive guests. Besides, I have other things to attend to. You must do the honors of Cro' Martin, Mr. Crow. You must entertain this gentleman for me. I 'll order luncheon before I go out, and I 'm sure you 'll not refuse me this service."

"I wish I knew a real service to render you, Miss Mary," said he, with unfeigned devotedness in his look as he spoke.

"I think I could promise myself as much," said Mary, smiling kindly on him. "Do you happen to know anything of this stranger, Mr. Crow?"

"Nothing, miss, beyond seeing him this week back at Kilkieran."

"Oh, I have heard of him, then," broke in Mary. "It is of him the people tell me such stories of benevolence and goodness. It was he that sent the yawl out to Murran Island with oatmeal and potatoes for the poor. But I thought they called him Mr. Barry?"

"To be sure they do; and he's another guess man from him below stairs. This one here"—Mr. Crow now spoke in a whisper—"this one here is a Jew, I 'd take the Testament on it, and I 'd not be surprised if he was one of them thieving villains that they say robbed the Captain! All the questions he does be asking about the property, and the rents, if they 're well paid, and what arrears there are, shows me that he isn't here for nothing."

"I know nothing of what you allude to, Mr. Crow," said she, half proudly; "it would ill become *me* to pry into my cousin's affairs. At the same time, if the gentleman has no actual business with me, I shall decline to receive him."

"He says he has, miss," replied Crow. "He says that he wants to speak to you about a letter he got by yesterday's post from the Captain."

Mary heard this announcement with evident impatience; her head was, indeed, too full of other cares to wish to occupy her attention with a ceremonial visit. She was in no mood to accept the unmeaning compliments of a new acquaintance. Shall we dare to insinuate, what after all is a mere suspicion on our part, that a casual glance at her pale cheeks, sunken eyes, and careworn features had some share in the obstinacy of her refusal? She was not, indeed, "in looks," and she knew it. "Must I repeat it, Mr. Crow," said she, peevishly, "that you can do all this for me, and save me a world of trouble and inconvenience besides? If there should be—a very unlikely circumstance—anything confidential to communicate, this gentleman may write it." And with this she left the room, leaving poor Mr. Crow in a state of considerable embarrassment. Resolving to make the best of his difficulty, he returned to the drawing-room, and apologizing to Merl for Miss Martin's absence on matters of great necessity, he conveyed her request that he would stop for luncheon.

"She ain't afraid of me, I hope?" said Merl.

"I trust not. I rather suspect she is little subject to fear upon any score," replied Crow.

"Well, I must say it's not exactly what I expected. The letter I hold here from the Captain gives me to understand that his cousin will not only receive me, but confer with and counsel me, too, in a somewhat important affair."

"Oh, I forgot," broke in Crow; "you are to write to her, she said,—that is, if there really were anything of consequence, which you deemed confidential, you know,—you were to write to her."

"I never put my hand to paper, Mr. Crow, without well knowing why. When Herman Merl signs anything, he takes time to consider what's in it," said the Jew, knowingly.

"Well, shall I show you the house,—there are some clever specimens of the Dutch masters here?" asked Crow, anxious to change the topic.

"Ay, with all my heart. I suppose I must accept this privilege as my experience of the much-boasted Irish hospitality," said he with a sneer, which required all Crow's self-control to resist answering. To master the temptation, and give himself a few moments' repose, he went about opening windows and drawing back curtains, so as to admit a fuller and stronger light upon the pictures along the walls.

"There now," said he, pointing to a large landscape, "there's a Both, and a fine one too; as mellow in color and as soft in distance as ever he painted."

"That's a copy," said the other. "That picture was painted by Woeffel, and I 'll show you his initials, too, A. W., before we leave it."

"It came from the Dordrecht gallery, and is an undoubted Both!" exclaimed Crow, angrily.

"I saw it there myself, and in very suitable company, too, with a Snyders on one side and a Rubens on t' other, the Snyders being a Faltk, and the Rubens a Metziger; the whole three being positively dear at twenty pounds. Ay, here it is," continued he, pointing to the hollow trunk of a decayed tree: "there's the initials. So much for your original by Both."

"I hope you'll allow that to be a Mieris?" said Crow, passing on to another.

"If you hadn't opened the shutters, perhaps I might," said Merl; "but with a good dash of light I see it is by Jansens,—and a clever copy, too."

"A copy!" exclaimed the other.

"A good copy," I said. "The King of Bavaria has the original. It is in the small collection at Hohen Schwangau."

"There, that's good!" cried he, turning to a small unfinished sketch in oils.

"I often wondered who did it," cried Crow.

"That! Why, can you doubt, sir? That's a bit of Vandyke's own. It was one of the hundred and fifty rough things he threw off as studies for his great picture of St. Martin parting his cloak."

"I'm glad to hear you say so," said Crow, in delight. "I felt, when I looked at it, that it was a great hand threw in them colors."

"You call this a Salvator Rosa, don't you?" said Merl, as he stood before a large piece representing a bandit's bivouac in a forest, with a pale moonlight stealing through the trees.

"Yes, that we do," said Crow, stoutly.

"Of course, it's quite sufficient to have blended lights, rugged foregrounds, and plenty of action to make a Salvator; but let me tell you, sir, that it's not even a copy of him. It is a bad—ay, and a very bad—Haemlens,— an Antwerp fellow that lived by poor facsimiles."

"Oh dear, oh dear!" cried Crow, despairingly. "Did I ever hear the like of this!"

"Are these your best things, Mr. Crow?" said Merl, surveying the room with an air of consummate depreciation.

"There are others. There are some portraits and a number of small cabinet pictures."

"Gerard Dows, and Jansens, and such like?" resumed Merl; "I understand: a mellow brown tint makes them, just as a glossy white satin petticoat makes a Terburg. Mr. Crow, you 've caught a Tartar," said he, with a grin. "There's not a man in Europe can detect a copy from the original sooner than him before you. Now seven out of every eight of these here are veritable 'croûtes,'—what we call 'croûtes,' sir,—things sold at Christie's, and sent off to the Continent to be hung up in old châteaux in Flanders, or dilapidated villas in Italy, where your exploring Englishman discovers them by rare good luck, and brings them home with him as Cuyps or Claudes or Vandykes. I'll undertake," said he, looking around him,—"I'll undertake to furnish you with a gallery, in every respect the duplicate of this, for—let me see—say three hundred pounds. Now, Mr. Crow," said Merl, taking a chair, and spreading out his legs before the fire, "will you candidly answer me one question?"

"Tell me what it is," said Crow, cautiously.

"I suppose by this time," said Merl, "you are tolerably well satisfied that Herman Merl is not very easily duped? I mean to say that at least there are *softer* fellows to be found than the humble individual who addresses you."

"I trust there are, indeed," said the other, sighing, "or it would be a mighty poor world for Simmy Crow and the likes of him."

"Well, I think so too," said Merl, chuckling to himself. "The wide-awake ones have rather the best of it. But, to come back to my question, I was simply going to ask you if the whole of the Martin estate—house, demesne, woods, gardens, quarries, farms, and fisheries—was not pretty much of the same sort of thing as this here gallery?"

"How? What do you mean?" asked Crow, whose temper was barely, and with some difficulty, restrainable.

"I mean, in plain words, a regular humbug,—that's all! and no more the representative of real value than these daubs here are the works of the great masters whose names they counterfeit."

"Look here, sir," said Crow, rising, and approaching the other with a face of angry indignation, "for aught I know, you may be right about these pictures. The chances are you are a dealer in such wares,—at least you talk like one,—but of the family that lived under this roof, and whose bread

I have eaten for many a day, if you utter one word that even borders on disrespect,—if you as much as hint at—"

What was to be the conclusion of Mr. Crow's menace we have no means of recording, for a servant, rushing in at the instant, summoned the artist with all speed to Miss Martin's presence. He found her, as he entered, with flushed cheeks and eyes flashing angrily, in one of the deep recesses of a window that looked out upon the lawn.

"Come here, sir," cried she, hurriedly,—"come here, and behold a sight such as you scarcely ever thought to look upon from these windows. Look here!" And she pointed to an assemblage of about a hundred people, many of whom were rudely armed with stakes, gathered around the chief entrance of the castle. In the midst was a tall man, mounted upon a wretched horse, who seemed from his gestures to be haranguing the mob, and whom Crow speedily recognized to be Magennis of Barnagheela.

"What does all this mean?" asked he, in astonishment.

"It means this, sir," said she, grasping his arm and speaking in a voice thick from passionate eagerness. "That these people whom you see there have demanded the right to enter the house and search it from basement to roof. They are in quest of one that is missing; and although I have given my word of honor that none such is concealed here, they have dared to disbelieve me, and declare they will see for themselves. They might know me better," added she, with a bitter smile,—"they might know me better, and that I no more utter a falsehood than I yield to a menace. See!" exclaimed she, "they are passing through the flower-garden,—they are approaching the lower windows. Take a horse, Mr. Crow, and ride for Kiltimmon; there is a police-station there,—bring up the force with you,—lose no time, I entreat you."

"But how—leave you here all alone?"

"Have no fears on that score, sir," said she, proudly; "they may insult the roof that shelters me, to myself they will offer no outrage. But be quick; away at once, and with speed!"

Had Mr. Crow been, what it must be owned had been difficult, a worse horseman than he was, he would never have hesitated to obey this behest. Ere many minutes, therefore, he was in the saddle and flying across country at a pace such as he never imagined any energy could have exacted from him.

"They have got a ladder up to the windows of the large drawing-room, Miss Mary," said a servant; "they'll be in before many minutes."

Taking down two splendidly ornamented pistols from above the chimney-piece, Mary examined the priming, and ordering the servant away, she descended by a small private stair to the drawing-room beneath. Scarcely, however, had she crossed the threshold than she was met by a man eagerly hurrying away. Stepping back in astonishment, and with a face pale as death, he exclaimed, "Is it Miss Martin?"

"Yes, sir," replied she, firmly; "and your name?"

"Mr. Merl—Herman Merl," said he, with a stealthy glance towards the windows, on the outside of which two fellows were now seated, communicating with those below.

"This is not a moment for much ceremony, sir," said she, promptly; "but you are here opportunely. These people will have it that I am harboring here one that they are in pursuit of. I have assured them of their error, I have pledged my word of honor upon it, but they are not satisfied. They declare that they will search the house, and I as firmly declare they-shall not."

"But the person is really not here?" broke in Merl.

"I have said so, sir," rejoined she, haughtily.

"Then why not let them search? Egad, I'd say, look away to your heart's content, pry into every hole and corner you please, only don't do any mischief to the furniture—don't let any—"

"I was about to ask your assistance, sir, but your counsel saves me from the false step. To one who proffers such wise advice, arguments like these"—and she pointed to the pistols—"arguments like these would be most distasteful; and yet let us see if others may not be of your mind too." And steadily aiming her weapon for a second or two, she sent a ball through the window, about a foot above the head of one of the fellows without. Scarcely had the report rung out and the splintering glass fallen, than the two men leaped to the ground, while a wild cheer, half derision, half anger, burst from the mob beneath. "Now, sir," continued she, with a smile of a very peculiar meaning, as she turned towards Merl,—"now, sir, you will perceive that you have got into very indiscreet company, such as I 'm sure Captain Martin's letter never prepared you for; and although it is not exactly in accordance with the usual notions of Irish hospitality to point to the door, perhaps you will be grateful to me when I say that you can escape by that corridor. It leads to a stair which will conduct you to the stable-yard. I'll order a saddle-horse for you. I suppose you ride?" And really the glance which accompanied these words was not a flattery.

However the proposition might have met Mr.' Merl's wishes there is no means of knowing, for a tremendous crash now interrupted the colloquy, and the same instant the door of the drawing-room was burst open, and Magennis, followed by a number of country people, entered.

"I told you," cried he, rudely, "that I'd not be denied. It's your own fault if you would drive me to enter here by force."

"Well, sir, force has done it," said she, taking a seat as she spoke. "I am here alone, and you may be proud of the achievement!" The glance she directed towards Merl made that gentleman shrink back, and eventually slide noiselessly from the room, and escape from the scene altogether.

"If you'll send any one with me through the house, Miss Martin," began Magennis, in a tone of much subdued meaning—"No, sir," broke she in—"no, sir, I'll give no such order. You have already had my solemn word of honor, assuring you that there was not any one concealed here. The same incredulous disrespect you have shown to my word would accompany whatever direction I gave to my servants. Go wherever you please; for the time you are the master here. Mark me, sir," said she, as, half crestfallen and in evident shame, he was about to move from the room—"mark me, sir, if I feel sorry that one who calls himself a gentleman should dishonor his station by discrediting the word, the plighted word, of a lady, yet I can forgive much to him whose feelings are under the impulse of passion. But how shall I speak my contempt for *you*," —and she turned a withering look of scorn on the men who followed him, —"for you, who have dared to come here to insult me, —I, that if you had the least spark of honest manhood in your natures, you had died rather than have offended? Is this your requital for the part I have borne amongst you? Is it thus that you repay the devotion by which I have squandered all that I possessed, and would have given my life, too, for you and yours? Is it thus, think you, that your mothers and wives and sisters would requite me? Or will they welcome you back from your day's work, and say, Bravely done? You have insulted a lone girl in her home, outraged the roof whence she never issued save to serve you, and taught her to believe that the taunts your enemies cast upon you, and which she once took as personal affronts to herself, that they are just and true, and as less than you merited. Go back, men," added she, in a voice trembling with emotion, —"go back, while it is time. Go back in shame, and let me never know who has dared to offer me this insult!" And she hid her face between her hands, and bent down her head upon her lap. For several minutes she remained thus, overwhelmed and absorbed by intensely painful emotion, and when she lifted up her head, and looked around, they were gone! A solemn silence reigned on every side; not a word, nor a footfall, could be heard. She rushed to the window just in time to see a number of men slowly entering the wood, amidst whom she recognized Magennis, leading his horse by the bridle, and following the others, with bent-down head and sorrowful mien.

"Oh, thank Heaven for this!" cried she, passionately, as the tears gushed out and coursed down her face. "Thank Heaven that they are not as others call them—cold-hearted and treacherous, craven in their hour of trial, and cruel in the day of their vengeance! I knew them better!" It was long before she could sufficiently subdue her emotion to think calmly of what had occurred. At last she bethought her of Mr. Merl, and despatched a servant in his pursuit, with a polite request that he would return. The man came up with Merl as he had reached the small gate of the park, but no persuasions, no entreaties, could prevail on that gentleman to retrace his steps; nay, he was frank enough to say, "He had seen quite enough of the West," and to invoke something very unlike benediction on his head if he ever passed another day in Galway.

CHAPTER XIX
MR. MERL'S "LAST" IRISH IMPRESSION

Never once turning his head towards Cro' Martin, Mr. Merl set out for Oughterard, where, weary and footsore, he arrived that same evening. His first care was to take some refreshment; his next to order horses for Dublin early for the following morning. This done, he sat down to write to Captain Martin, to convey to him what Merl designated as a "piece of his mind," a phrase which, in popular currency, is always understood to imply the very reverse of any flattery. The truth was, Mr. Merl began to suspect that his Irish liens were a very bad investment, that property in that country was held under something like a double title, the one conferred by law, the other maintained by a resolute spirit and a stout heart; that parchments required to be seconded by pistols, and that he who owned an estate must always hold himself in readiness to fight for it.

Now, these were all very unpalatable considerations. They rendered possession perilous, they made sale almost impossible. In the cant phrase of Ceylon, the Captain had sold him a wild elephant; or, to speak less figuratively, disposed of what he well knew the purchaser could never avail himself of. If Mr. Merl was an emblem of blandness and good temper at the play-table, courteous and conceding at every incident of the game, it was upon the very wise calculation that the politeness was profitable. The little irregularities that he pardoned all gave him an insight into the character of his antagonists; and where he appeared to have lost a battle, he had gained more than a victory in knowledge of the enemy.

These blandishments were, however, no real part of the man's natural temperament, which was eminently distrustful and suspicious, wary to detect a blot, prompt and sharp to hit it. A vague, undefined impression had now come over him that the Captain had overreached him; that even if unincumbered,—which was far from the case,—this same estate was like a forfeited territory, which to own a man must assert his mastery with the strong hand of force. "I should like to see myself settling down amongst those savages," thought he, "collecting my rents with dragoons, or levying a fine with artillery. Property, indeed! You might as well convey to me by bill of sale the right over a drove of wild buffaloes in South America, or give me a title to a given number of tigers in Bengal. He'd be a bold man that would even venture to come and have a look at 'his own.'"

It was in this spirit, therefore, that he composed his epistle, which assuredly lacked nothing on the score of frankness and candor. All his "Irish impressions" had been unfavorable. He had eaten badly, he had slept worse; the travelling was rude, the climate detestable; and lastly, where he had expected to have been charmed with the ready wit, and amused with the racy humor of the people, he had only been terrified—terrified almost to death—by their wild demeanor, and a ferocity that made his heart quake. "Your cousin," said he,—"your cousin, whom, by the way, I only saw for a few minutes, seemed admirably adapted to the exigencies of the social state around her; and although ball practice has not been included amongst the ordinary items of young ladies' acquirements, I am satisfied that it might advantageously form part of an Irish education.

"As to your offer of a seat in Parliament, I can only say," continued he, "that as the Member of Oughterard I should always feel as though I were seated over a barrel of gunpowder; while the very idea of meeting my constituency makes me shudder. I am, however, quite sensible of the honor intended me, both upon that score and in your proposal of my taking up my residence at Cro' Martin. The social elevation, and so forth, to ensue from such a course of proceeding would have this disadvantage,—it would not pay! No, Captain Martin, the settlement between us must stand upon another basis,—the very simple and matter-of-fact one called £ s. d. I shall leave this to-morrow, and be in town, I hope, by Wednesday; you can, therefore, give your man of business, Mr. Saunders, his instructions to meet me at Wimpole's, and state what terms of liquidation he is prepared to offer. Suffice it for the present to say that I decline any arrangement which should transfer to me any portion of the estate. I declare to you, frankly, I'd not accept the whole of it on the condition of retaining the proprietorship."

When Mr. Merl had just penned the last sentence, the door slowly and cautiously was opened behind him, and a very much carbuncled face protruded into the room. "Yes, that's himself," muttered a voice; and ere Merl had been able to detect the speaker, the door was closed. These casual interruptions to his privacy had so frequently occurred since the commencement of his tour, that he only included them amongst his other Irish "disagreeables;" and so he was preparing to enter on another paragraph, when a very decisive knock at the door startled him, and before he could say "Come in," a tall, red-faced, vulgar-looking man, somewhat stooped in the shoulders, and with that blear-eyed watery expression so distinctive in hard drinkers, slowly entered, and shutting the door behind him, advanced to the fire.

"My name, sir, is Brierley," said he, with a full, rich brogue.

"Brierley—Brierley—never heard of Brierley before," said Mr. Merl, affecting a flippant ease that was very remote from his heart.

"Better late than never, sir," rejoined the other, coolly seating himself, and crossing his arms on his breast. "I have come here on the part of my friend Tom,—Mr. Magennis, I mean,—of Barnagheela, who told me to track you out."

"Much obliged, I'm sure, for the attention," said Merl, with an assumed smartness.

"That 's all right; so you should," continued Brierley. "Tom told me that you were present at Cro' Martin when he was outraged and insulted,—by a female of course, or he wouldn't be making a complaint of it now,—and as he is not the man that ever lay under a thing of the kind, or ever will, he sent me here to you, to arrange where you 'd like to have it, and when."

"To have what?" asked Merl, with a look of unfeigned terror.

"Baythershin! how dull we are!" said Mr. Brierley, with a finger to his very red nose. "Sure it's not thinking of the King's Bench you are, that you want me to speak clearer."

"I want to know your meaning, sir,—if you have a meaning."

"Be cool, honey; keep yourself cool. Without you happen to find that warmth raises your heart, I 'd say again, be cool. I've one simple question to ask you,"—here he dropped his voice to a low, cautious whisper,—"Will ye blaze?"

"Will I what?" cried Merl.

Mr. Brierley arose, and drawing himself up to his full height, extended his arm in the attitude of one taking aim with a pistol. "Eh!" cried he, "you comprehend me now, don't you?"

"Fight—fight a duel!" exclaimed Merl, aloud.

"Whisht! whisht! speak lower," said Brierley; "there's maybe a chap listening at the door this minute!"

Accepting the intimation in a very different spirit from that in which it was offered, Merl rushed to the door, and threw it wide open. "Waiter!—landlord!—house!—waiter!" screamed he, at the top of his voice. And in an instant three or four slovenly-looking fellows, with dirty napkins in dirtier hands, surrounded him.

"What is it, your honer?—what is it?" asked they, in a breath.

"Don't you hear what the gentleman's asking for?" said Brierley, with a half-serious face. "He wants a chaise-to the door as quick as lightning. He 's off this minute."

"Yes, by Jupiter! that I am," said Merl, wiping the perspiration from his forehead.

"Take your last look at the West, dear, as you pass the Shannon, for I don't think you 'll ever come so far again," said Brierley, with a grin, as he moved by him to descend the stairs.

"If I do, may—" But the slam of his room-door, and the rattle of the key as he locked it, cut short Mr. Merl's denunciation.

In less than half an hour afterwards a yellow post-chaise left the "Martin Arms" at full speed, a wild yell of insult and derision greeting it as it swept by, showing how the Oughterard public appreciated its inmate!

CHAPTER XX
SOMETHING NOT EXACTLY FLIRTATION

Most travelled reader, have you ever stood upon the plateau at the foot of the Alten-Schloss in Baden, just before sunset, and seen the golden glory spread out like a sheen over the vast plain beneath you, with waving forests, the meandering Rhine, and the blue Vosges mountains beyond all? It is a noble landscape, where every feature is bold, and throughout which light and shade alternate in broad, effective masses, showing that you are gazing on a scene of great extent, and taking in miles of country with your eye. It is essentially German, too, in its characteristics. The swelling undulations of the soil, the deep, dark forests, the picturesque homesteads, with shadowy eaves and carved quaint balconies, the great gigantic wagons slowly toiling through the narrow lanes, over which the "Lindens" spread a leafy canopy,—all are of the Vaterland.

Some fancied resemblance—it was in reality no more—to a view from a window at Cro' Martin had especially endeared this spot to Martin, who regularly was carried up each evening to pass an hour or so, dreaming away in that half-unconsciousness to which his malady had reduced him. There he sat, scarcely a remnant of his former self, a leaden dulness in his eye, and a massive immobility in the features which once were plastic with every passing mood that stirred him. The clasped hands and slightly bent-down head gave a character of patient, unresisting meaning to his figure, which the few words he dropped from time to time seemed to confirm.

At a little distance off, and on the very verge of the cliff, Kate Henderson was seated sketching; and behind her, occasionally turning to walk up and down the terraced space, was Massingbred, once more in full health, and bearing in appearance the signs of his old, impatient humor. Throwing away his half-smoked cigar, and with a face whose expression betokened the very opposite of all calm and ease of mind, he drew nigh to where she sat, and watched her over her shoulder. For a while she worked away without noticing his presence. At last she turned slightly about, and looking up at him, said, "You see, it's very nearly finished."

"Well, and what then?" asked he, bluntly.

"Do you forget that I gave you until that time to change your opinion? that when I was shadowing in this foreground I said, 'Wait 'till I have done this sketch, and see if you be of the same mind,' and you agreed?"

"This might be very pleasant trifling if nothing were at stake, Miss Henderson," said he; "but remember that I cannot hold all my worldly chances as cheaply as *you* seem to do them."

"Light another cigar, and sit down here beside me,—I don't dislike smoke, and it may, perchance, be a peace calumet between us; and let us talk, if possible, reasonably and calmly."

He obeyed like one who seemed to feel that her word was a command, and sat down on the cliff at her side.

"There, now," said she, "be useful; hold that color-case for me, and give me your most critical counsel. Do you like my sketch?"

"Very much indeed."

"Where do you find fault with it? There must be a fault, or your criticism is worth nothing."

"Its greatest blemish in my eyes is the time it has occupied you. Since you began it you have very rarely condescended to speak of anything else."

"A most unjust speech, and an ungrateful one. It was when throwing in those trees yonder, I persuaded you to recall your farewell address to your borough friends; it was the same day that I sketched that figure there, that I showed you the great mistake of your present life. There is no greater error, believe me, than supposing that a Parliamentary success, like a social one, can be achieved by mere brilliancy. Party is an army, and you must serve in the ranks before you can wear your epaulets."

"I have told you already,—I tell you again,—I 'm tired of the theme that has myself alone for its object."

"Of whom would you speak, then?" said she, still intently busied with her drawing.

"You ask me when you know well of whom," said he, hurriedly. "Nay, no menaces; I could not if I would be silent. It is impossible for me any longer to continue this struggle with myself. Here now, before I leave this spot, you shall answer me—" He stopped suddenly, as though he had said more than he intended, or more than he well knew how to continue.

"Go on," said she, calmly. And her fingers never trembled as they held the brush.

"I confess I do envy that tranquil spirit of yours," said he, bitterly. "It is such a triumph to be calm, cold, and impassive at a moment when others feel their reason tottering and their brain a chaos."

"There is nothing so easy, sir," said she, proudly. "All that I can boast of is not to have indulged in illusions which seem to have a charm for *you*. You say you want explicit-ness. You shall have it. There was one condition on which I offered you my friendship and my advice. You accepted the bargain, and we were friends. After a while you came and said that you rued your compact; that you discovered your feelings for me went further; that mere friendship, as you phrased it, would not suffice—"

"I told you, rather," broke he in, "that I wished to put that feeling to the last test, by linking your fortune with my own forever."

"Very well, I accept that version. You offered to make me your wife, and in return, I asked you to retract your words,—to suffer our relations to continue on their old footing, nor subject me to the necessity of an explanation painful to both of us. For a while you consented; now you seem impatient at your concession, and ask me to resume the subject. Be it so, but for the last time."

Massingbred's cheeks grew deadly pale, but he never uttered a word.

After a second's pause, she resumed: "Your affections are less engaged in this case than you think. You would make me your wife just as you would do anything else that gave a bold defiance to the world, to show a consciousness of your own power, to break down any obstacle, and make the prejudices or opinions of society give way before you. You have energy and self-esteem enough to make this succeed. Your wife—albeit the steward's daughter—

the governess! would be received, invited, visited, and the rest of it; and so far as *you* were concerned the triumph would be complete. Now, however, turn a little attention to the other side of the medal. What is to requite *me* for all this courtesy on sufferance, all this mockery of consideration? Where am I to find my friendships, where even discover my duties? You only know of one kind of pride, that of station and social eminence. I can tell you there is another, loftier far,—the consciousness that no inequality of position can obliterate, what I feel and know in myself of superiority to those fine ladies whose favorable notice you would entreat for me. Smile at the vanity of this declaration if you like, sir, but, at least, own that I am consistent; for I am prouder in the independence of my present dependence than I should be in all the state of Mr. Massingbred's wife. You can see, therefore, that I could not accept this change as the great elevation you would deem it. You would be stooping to raise one who could never persuade herself that she was exalted. I am well aware that inequality of one sort or another is the condition of most marriages. The rank of one compensates for the wealth of the other. Here it is affluence and age, there it is beauty and poverty. People treat the question in a good commercial spirit, and balance the profit and loss like tradesfolk; but even in this sense our compact would be impossible, since *you* would endow me with what has no value in my eyes, and *I*, worse off still, have absolutely nothing to give in return."

"Give me your love, dearest Kate," cried he, "and, supported by that, you shall see that I deserve it. Believe me, it is your own proud spirit that exaggerates the difficulties that would await us in society."

"I should scorn myself if I thought of them," broke she in, haughtily; "and remember, sir, these are not the words of one who speaks in ignorance. I, too, have seen that great world, on which your affections are so fixed. I have mixed with it, and know it. Notwithstanding all the cant of moralists, I do not believe it to be more hollow or more heartless than other classes. Its great besetting sin is not of self-growth, for it comes of the slavish adulation offered by those beneath it,—the grovelling worship of the would-be fine folk, who would leave friends and home and hearth to be admitted even to the antechambers of the great. They who offer up this incense are in my eyes far more despicable than they who accept the sacrifice; but I would not cast my lot with either. Do not smile, sir, as if these were high-flown sentiments; they are the veriest commonplaces of one who loves commonplace, who neither seeks affections with coronets nor friendships in gold coaches, but who would still less be of that herd—mute, astonished, and awe-struck— who worship them!"

"You deem me, then, deficient in this same independence of spirit?" cried Massingbred, half indignantly.

"I certainly do not accept your intention of marrying beneath you as a proof of it. Must I again tell you, sir, that in such cases it is the poor, weak, patient, forgotten woman pays all the penalty, and that, in the very conflict with the world the man has his reward?"

"If you loved me, Kate," said he, in a tone of deep sorrow, "it is not thus you would discuss this question."

She made no reply, but bending down lower over her drawing, worked away with increased rapidity.

"Still," cried he, passionately, "I am not to be deterred by a defeat. Tell me, at least, how I can win that love, which is to me the great prize of life. You read my faults, you see my shortcomings clearly enough; be equally just, then, to anything there is of good or hopeful about me. Do this, Kate, and I will put my fate upon the issue."

"In plain words," said she, calmly, "you ask me what manner of man I would consent to marry. I 'll tell you. One who with ability enough to attain any station, and talents to gain any eminence, has lived satisfied with that in which he was born; one who has made the independence of his character so felt by the world that his actions have been regarded as standards, a man of honor and of his word; employing his knowledge of life, not for the purposes of overreaching, but for self-correction and improvement; well bred enough to be a peer, simple as a peasant; such a man, in fact, as could afford to marry a governess, and, while elevating her to his station, never compromise his own with his equals. I don't flatter myself," said she, smiling, "that I 'm likely to draw this prize; but I console myself by thinking that I could not accept aught beneath it as great fortune. I see, sir, the humility of my pretensions amuses you, and it is all the better for both of us if we can treat these things jestingly."

"Nay, Kate, you are unfair—unjust," broke in Mas-singbred.

"Mr. Martin begins to feel it chilly, Miss Henderson," said a servant at this moment. "Shall we return to the hotel?"

"Yes, by all means," said she, rising hastily. The next instant she was busily engaged shawling and muffling the sick man, who accepted her attentions with the submissive-ness of a child.

"That will do, Molly, thank you, darling," said he, in a feeble voice; "you are so kind, so good to me."

"The evening is fresh, sir, almost cold," said she.

"Yes, dear, the climate is not what it used to be. We have cut down too many of those trees, Molly, yonder." And he pointed with his thin fingers towards the Rhine. "We have thinned the wood overmuch, but they'll grow again, dear, though I shall not be here to see them."

"He thinks I am his niece," whispered Kate, "and fancies himself at Cro' Martin."

"I suppose they'll advise my trying a warm country, Molly, a milder air," muttered he, as they slowly carried him along. "But home, after all, is home; one likes to see the old faces and the old objects around them,—all the more when about to leave them forever!" And as the last words came, two heavy tears stole slowly along his cheeks, and his pale lips quivered with emotion. Now speaking in a low, weak voice to himself, now sighing heavily, as though in deep depression, he was borne along towards the hotel. Nor did the gay and noisy groups which thronged the thoroughfares arouse him. He saw them, but seemed not to heed them. His dreary gaze wandered over the brilliant panorama without interest or speculation. Some painful and difficult thoughts, perhaps, did all these unaccustomed sights and sounds bring across his mind, embarrassing him to reconcile their presence with the scene he fancied himself beholding; but even these impressions were faint and fleeting.

As they turned to cross the little rustic bridge in front of the hotel, a knot of persons moved off the path to make way for them, one of whom fixed his eyes steadily on the sick man, gazing with the keen scrutiny of intense interest; then suddenly recalling himself to recollection, he hastily retreated within the group.

"You are right," muttered he to one near him, "he is 'booked;' my bond will come due before the month ends."

"And you'll be an estated gent, Herman, eh?" said a very dark-eyed, hook-nosed man at his side.

"Well, I hope I shall act the part as well as my neighbors," said Mr. Merl, with that mingled assurance and humility that made up his manner.

"Was n't that Massingbred that followed them,—he that made the famous speech the other day in Parliament?"

"Yes," said Merl. "I 've got a bit of 'stiff' with his endorsement in my pocket this minute for one hundred and fifty."

"What's it worth, Merl?"

"Perhaps ten shillings; but I 'd not part with it quite so cheaply. He'll not always be an M.P., and we shall see if he can afford to swagger by an old acquaintance without so much as a 'How d' ye do?'"

"There, he is coming back again," said the other. And at the same moment Massingbred walked slowly up to the spot, his easy smile upon his face, and his whole expression that of a careless, unburdened nature.

"I just caught a glimpse of you as I passed, Merl," said he, with a familiar nod; "and you were exactly the man I wanted to see."

"Too much honor, sir," said Merl, affecting a degree of haughty distance at the familiarity of this address.

Massingbred smiled at the mock dignity, and went on; "I have something to say to you. Will you give me a call this evening at the Cour de Bade, say about nine or half-past?"

"I have an engagement this evening."

"Put it off, then, that's all, Master Merl, for mine is an important matter, and very nearly concerns yourself."

Merl was silent. He would have liked much to display before his friends a little of the easy dash and swagger that he had just been exhibiting, to have shown them how cavalierly he could treat a rising statesman and a young Parliamentary star of the first order; but the question crossed him, Was it safe? what might the luxury cost him? "Am I to bring that little acceptance of yours along with me?" said he, in a half whisper, while a malicious sparkle twinkled in his eye.

"Why not, man? Certainly, if it gives you the least pleasure in life; only don't be later than half-past nine." And with one of his sauciest laughs Massingbred moved away, leaving the Jew very far from content with "the situation."

Merl, however, soon rallied. He had been amusing his friends, just before this interruption, with a narrative of his Irish journey: he now resumed the theme. All that he found faulty, all even that he deemed new or strange or unintelligible in that unhappy country, he had dressed up in the charming colors of his cockney vocabulary, and his hearers were worthy of him! There is but little temptation, however, to linger in their company, and so we leave them.

CHAPTER XXI
LADY DOROTHEA

The Cour de Bade, at which excellent hotel the Martins were installed, received on the day we have just chronicled a new arrival. He had come by the diligence, one of that undistinguishable ten thousand England sends off every week from her shores to represent her virtues or her vices, her oddities, vulgarities, and pretensions, to the critical eyes of continental Europe.

Perfectly innocent of any foreign language, and with a delightful ambiguity as to the precise geography of where he stood, he succeeded, after some few failures, in finding out where the Martins stopped, and had now sent up his name to Lady Dorothea, that name being "Mr. Maurice Scanlan."

Lady Dorothea Martin had given positive orders that except in the particular case of this individual she was not to be interrupted by any visitor. She glanced her eye at the card, and then handed it across the table to her son, who coolly read it, and threw it from him with the air of one saying to himself, "Here's more of it! more complication, more investigation, deeper research into my miserable difficulties, and consequently more unhappiness." The table at which they were seated was thickly covered with parchments, papers, documents, and letters of every shape and size. There were deeds, and bonds, and leases, rent-rolls, and valuations, and powers of attorney, and all the other imposing accessories of estated property. There were also voluminous bills of costs, formidable long columns of figures, "carried over" and "carried over" till the very eye of the reader wearied of the dread numerals and turned recklessly to meet the awful total at the bottom! Terrified by the menacing applications addressed to Mr. Martin on his son's account, and which arrived by every post, Lady Dorothea had resolved upon herself entering upon the whole state of the Captain's liabilities, as well as the complicated questions of the property generally.

Distrust of her own powers was not in the number of her Ladyship's defects. Sufficiently affluent to be always able to surround herself with competent subordinates, she fancied—a not very uncommon error, by the way—that she individually accomplished all that she had obtained through another. Her taste in the fine arts, her skill in music, her excellence as a letter-writer, were all accomplishments in this wise; and it is not improbable that, had she been satisfied to accept her success in finance through a similar channel, the result might have proved just as fortunate. A shrinking dislike, however, to expose the moneyed circumstances of the family, and a feeling of dread as to the possible disclosures which should come out, prevented her from accepting such co-operation. She had, therefore, addressed herself to the task with no other aid than that of her son,—a partnership, it must be owned, which relieved her very little of her burden.

Had the Captain been called away from the pleasures and amusements of life to investigate the dry records of some far-away cousin's embarrassments,—to dive into the wearisome narrative of money-borrowing, bill-renewing, and the rest of it, by one whom he had scarcely known or seen,—his manner and bearing could not possibly have betrayed stronger signs of utter weariness and apathy than he now exhibited. Smoking his cigar, and trimming his nails with a very magnificent penknife, he gave short and listless replies to her Ladyship's queries, and did but glance at the papers which from time to time she handed to him for explanation or inquiry.

"So he is come at last!" exclaimed she, as the Captain threw down the visiting-card. "Shall we see him at once?"

"By Jove! I think we've had enough of 'business,' as they call it, for one morning," cried he. "Here have we been since a little after eleven, and it is now four, and I am as sick of accounts and figures as though I were a Treasury clerk."

"We have done next to nothing, after all!" said she, peevishly.

"And I told you as much when you began," said he, lighting a fresh cigar. "There's no seeing one's way through these kind of things after the lapse of a year or two. Fordyce gets hold of the bills you gave Mossop, and Rawkins buys up some of the things you had given renewals for, and then all that trash you took in part payment of your acceptances turns up, some day or other, to be paid for; and what between the bills that never were to be negotiated—but somehow do get abroad—and the sums sent to meet others applied in quite a different direction, I'll lay eighty to fifty in tens or ponies there's no gentleman living ever mastered one of these embarrassments. One must be bred to it, my Lady, take my word for it. It's like being a crack rider or a poet,—it's born with a man. 'The Henderson,'" added he, after a pause, "she can do it, and I should like to see what she couldn't!"

"I am curious to learn how you became acquainted with these financial abilities of Miss Henderson?" said Lady Dorothea, haughtily.

"Simply enough. I was poring over these confounded accounts one day at Manheim, and I chanced to ask her a question,—something about compound interest, I think it was,—and so she came and looked over what I was doing, or rather endeavoring to do. It was that affair with Throgmorton, where I was to meet one third of the bills, and Merl and he were to look to the remainder; but there was a reservation that if Comus won the Oaks, I was to stand free—no, that's not it—if Comus won the double event—"

"Never mind your stupid contract. What of Miss Henderson?" broke in Lady Dorothea.

"Well, she came over, as I told you, and took up a pencil and began working away with all sorts of signs and crosses,—regular algebra, by Jove!—and in about five minutes out came the whole thing, all square, showing that I stood to win on either event, and came off splendidly if the double should turn up. 'I wish,' said I to her, 'you'd just run your eye over my book and see how I stand.' She took it over to the fire, and before I could well believe she had glanced at it, she said: 'This is all full of blunders. You have left yourself open to three casualties, any one of which will sweep away all your winnings. Take the odds on Roehampton, and lay on Slingsby a couple of hundred more,—three, if you can get it,—and you 'll be safe enough. And when you 've done that,' said she, 'I have another piece of counsel to give; but first say will you take it?' 'I give you my word upon it,' said I. 'Then it is this,' said she: 'make no more wagers on the turf. You haven't skill to make what is called a "good book," and you 'll always be a sufferer.'"

"Did n't she vouchsafe to offer you her admirable assistance?" asked her Ladyship, with a sneer.

"No, by Jove!" said he, not noticing the tone of sarcasm; "and when I asked her, 'Would not she afford me a little aid?' she quickly said, 'Not on any account. You are now in a difficulty, and I willingly come forward to extricate you. Far different were the case should I conspire with you to place others in a similar predicament. Besides, I have your pledge that you have now done with these transactions, and forever.'"

"What an admirable monitor! One only wonders how so much morality coexists with such very intimate knowledge of ignoble pursuits."

"By Jove! she knows everything," broke in the Captain. "Such a canter as she gave me t' other morning about idleness and the rest of it, saying how I ought to study Hindostanee, and get a staff appointment, and so on,—that every one ought to place himself above the accidents of fortune; and when I said something about having no opportunity at hand, she replied, 'Never complain of that; begin with *me*. I know quite enough to initiate you; and as to Sanscrit, I 'm rather "up" in it.'"

"I trust you accepted the offer?" said her Ladyship, with an ambiguous smile.

"Well, I can't say I did. I hate work, — at least that kind of work. Besides, one doesn't like to come out 'stupid' in these kind of things, and so I merely said, 'I 'd think of it — very kind of her,' and so on."

"Did it never occur to you all this while," began her Ladyship; and then suddenly correcting herself, she stopped short, and said, "By the way, Mr. Scanlan is waiting for his answer. Ring the bell, and let him come in."

Perhaps it was the imperfect recollection of that eminent individual, — perhaps the altered circumstances in which she now saw him, and possibly some actual changes in the man himself, — but really Lady Dorothea almost started with surprise as he entered the room, dressed in a dark pelisse, richly braided and frogged, an embroidered travelling-cap in his hand, and an incipient moustache on his upper lip, — all evidencing how rapidly he had turned his foreign experiences to advantage. There was, too, in his address a certain confident assurance that told how quickly the habits of the "Table d'hôte" had impressed him, and how instantaneously his nature had imbibed the vulgar ease of the "Continent."

"You have just arrived, Mr. Scanlan?" said her Ladyship, haughtily, and not a little provoked at the shake-hand salutation her son had accorded him.

"Yes, my Lady, this instant, and such a journey as we 've had! No water on the Rhine for the steamers; and then, when we took to the land, a perfect deluge of rain, that nearly swept us away. At Eisleben, or some such name, we had an upset."

"What day did you leave Ireland?" asked she, in utter indifference as to the casualty.

"Tuesday fortnight last, my Lady. I was detained two days in Dublin making searches —"

"Have you brought us any letters, sir?"

"One from Miss Mary, my Lady, and another from Mr. Repton — very pressing he said it was. I hope Mr. Martin is better? Your Ladyship's last —"

"Not much improvement," said she, stiffly, while her thin lips were compressed with an expression that might mean pride or sorrow, or both.

"And the country, sir? How did you leave it looking?"

"Pretty well, my Lady. More frightened than hurt, as a body might say. They 've had a severe winter, and a great deal of sickness; the rains, too, have done a deal of mischief; but on the whole matters are looking up again."

"Will the rents be paid, sir?" asked she, sharply.

"Indeed, I hope so, my Lady. Some, of course, will be backward, and beg for time, and a few more will take advantage of Magennis's success, and strive to fight us off."

"There must have been some gross mismanagement in that business, sir," broke in her Ladyship. "Had I been at home, I promise you the matter would have ended differently."

"Mr. Repton directed all the proceedings himself, my Lady. He conferred with Miss Mary."

"What could a young lady know about such matters?" said she, angrily. "Any prospect of a tenant for the house, sir?"

"If your Ladyship really decides on not going back—"

"Not the slightest intention of doing so, sir. If it depended upon me, I'd rather pull it down and sell the materials than return to live there. You know yourself, sir, the utter barbarism we were obliged to submit to. No intercourse with the world—no society—very frequently no communication by post. Surrounded by a set of ragged creatures, all importunity and idleness, at one moment all defiance and insolence, at the next crawling and abject. But it is really a theme I cannot dwell upon. Give me your letters, sir, and let me see you this evening." And taking the papers from his hand, she swept out of the room in a haughty state.

The Captain and Mr. Scanlan exchanged looks, and were silent, but their glances were far more intelligible than aught either of them would have ventured to say aloud; and when the attorney's eyes, having followed her Ladyship to the door, turned and rested on the Captain, the other gave a brief short nod of assent, as though to say, "Yes, you are right; she's just the same as ever."

"And *you*, Captain," said Scanlan, in his tone of natural familiarity,— "how is the world treating *you*?"

"Devilish badly, Master Scanlan."

"Why, what is it doing, then?"

"I'll tell you what it's doing! It's charging me fifty—ay, sixty per cent; it's protesting my bills, stimulating my blessed creditors to proceed against me, worrying my very life out of me with letters. Letters to the governor, letters to the Horse Guards, and, last of all, it has just lamed Bonesetter, the horse 'I stood to win' on for the Chester Cup, I would n't have taken four thousand for my book yesterday morning!"

"Bad news all this."

"I believe you," said he, lighting a cigar, and throwing another across the table to Scanlan. "It's just bad news, and I have nothing else for many a long day past. A fellow of your sort, Master Maurice, punting away at county races and small sweepstakes, has a precious deal better time of it than a captain of the King's Hussars with his head and shoulders in the Fleet."

"Come, come, who knows but luck will turn, Captain? Make a book on the Oaks."

"I've done it; and I'm in for it, too," said the other, savagely.

"Raise a few thousands, you can always sell a reversion."

"I have done that also," said he, still more angrily.

"With your position and advantages you could always marry well. If you'd just beat up the manufacturing districts, you'd get your eighty thousand as sure as I'm here! And then matrimony admits of a man's changing all his habits. He can sell off hunters, get rid of a racing stable, and twenty other little embarrassments, and only gain character by the economy."

"I don't care a brass farthing for that part of the matter, Scanlan. No man shall dictate to me how I 'm to spend my money. Do you just find me the tin, and I 'll find the talent to scatter it."

"If it can't be done by a post-obit—"

"I tell you, sir," cried Martin, peevishly, "as I have told you before, that has been done. There is such a thing as pumping a well dry, is n't there?"

Scanlan made a sudden exclamation of horror; and after a pause, said, "Already!"

"Ay, sir, already!"

"I had my suspicions about it," muttered Scanlan, gloomily.

"You had? And how so, may I beg to ask?" said Martin, angrily.

"I saw him down there, myself."

"Saw whom? Whom are you talking of?"

"Of that Jew, of course. Mr. Merl, he calls himself."

A faint groan was all Martin's reply, as he turned away to hide his face.

Scanlan watched him for a minute or so, and then resumed: "I guessed at once what he was at; *he* never deceived me, talking about snipe and woodcocks, and pretending to care about hare-hunting. I saw my man at a glance. 'It's not sporting ever brought you down to these parts,' said I. '*Your* game is young fellows, hard up for cash, willing to give up their birthright for a few thousands down, and never giving a second thought whether they paid twenty per cent, or a hundred and twenty.' Well, well, Captain, you ought to have told me all about it. There wasn't a man in Ireland could have putted you through like myself."

"How do you mean?" cried Martin, hurriedly.

"Sure, when he was down in the West, what was easier? Faix, if I had only had the wind of a word that matters were so bad, I 'd have had the papers out of him long ago. You shake your head as if you did n't believe me; but take my word for it, I 'm right, sir. I 'd put a quarrel on him."

"*He'd* not fight you!" said Martin, turning away in disappointment.

"Maybe he wouldn't; but mightn't he be robbed? Couldn't he be waylaid, and carried off to the Islands? There was no need to kill him. Intimidation would do it all! I'd lay my head upon a block this minute if I would n't send him back to London without the back of a letter in his company; and what's more, a pledge that he 'd never tell what's happened to him!"

"These cockney gents are more 'wide awake' than you suspect, Master Maurice, and the chances are that he never carried a single paper or parchment along with him."

"Worse for him, then," said Scanlan. "He'd have to pass the rest of his days in the Arran Islands. But I'm not so sure he's as 'cute as you think him," added Maurice, after a pause. "He left a little note-book once behind him that told some strange stories, by all accounts."

"What was that you speak of?" cried Martin, eagerly.

"I did n't see it myself, but Simmy Crow told me of it; and that it was full of all the fellows he ruined,—how much he won from this man, what he carried off from that; and, moreover, there was your own name, and the date of the very evening that he finished you off! It was something in this wise: 'This night's work makes me an estated gentleman, *vice* Harry Martin, Esquire, retired upon less than half-pay!'"

A terrible oath, uttered in all the vehemence of a malediction, burst from Martin, and seizing Scanlan's wrist, he shook his arm in an agony of passion.

"I wish I had given you a hint about him, Master Scanlan," said he, savagely.

"It's too late to think of it now, Captain," said the other; "the fellow is in Baden."

"Here?" asked Martin.

"Ay. He came up the Rhine along with me; but he never recognized me,—on account of my moustaches perhaps,—he took me for a Frenchman or a German, I think. We parted at Mayence, and I saw no more of him."

"I would that I was to see no more of him!" said Martin, gloomily, as he walked into another room, banging the door heavily behind him.

CHAPTER XXII
HOW PRIDE MEETS PRIDE

Kate Henderson sat alone in her room reading a letter from her father, her thoughtful brow a shade more serious perhaps than its wont, and at times a faint, half-sickly smile moving her dimpled cheek. The interests of our story have no concern with that letter, save passingly, nor do we regret it. Enough, if we say it was in reply to one of her own, requesting permission to return home, until, as she phrased it, she could "obtain another service." That the request had met scant favor was easy to see, as, folding up the letter, she laid it down beside her with a sigh and a muttered "I thought as much!—'So long as her Ladyship is pleased to accept of your services,'" said she, repeating aloud an expression of the writer. "Well, I suppose he's right; such is the true reading of the compact, as it is of every compact where there is wealth on one side, dependence on the other! Nor should I complain," said she, still more resolutely, "if these same services could be rendered toilfully, but costing nothing of self-sacrifice in honorable feeling. I could be a drudge—a slave—to-morrow; I could stoop to any labor; but I cannot—no, I cannot—descend to companionship! They who hire us," cried she, rising, and pacing the room in slow and measured tread, "have a right to our capacity. We are here to do their bidding; but they can lay no claim to that over which we ourselves have no control—our sympathies, our affections—we cannot sell these; we cannot always give them, even as a gift." She paused, and opening the letter, read it for some seconds, and then flinging it down with a haughty gesture, said, "'Nothing menial—nothing to complain of in my station!' Can he not see that there is no such servitude as that which drags out existence, by subjecting, not head and hands, but heart and soul, to the dictates of another? The menial—the menial has the best of it. Some stipulate that they are not to wear a livery; but what livery exacts such degradation as this?" And she shook the rich folds of her heavy silk dress as she spoke. The tears rose up and dimmed her eyes, but they were tears of offended pride, and as they stole slowly along her cheeks, her features acquired an expression of intense haughtiness. "They who train their children to this career are but sorry calculators!—educating them but to feel the bitter smart of their station, to see more clearly the wide gulf that separates them from what they live amongst!" said she, in a voice of deep emotion.

"Her Ladyship, Miss Henderson," said a servant, throwing wide the door, and closing it after the entrance of Lady Dorothea, who swept into the room in her haughtiest of moods, and seated herself with all that preparation that betokened a visit of importance.

"Take a seat, Miss Henderson," said she. And Kate obeyed in silence. "If in the course of what I shall have to say to you," resumed her Ladyship, — "if in what I shall feel it my *duty* to say to you, I may be betrayed into any expression stronger than in a calmer moment would occur to me, — stronger in fact, than strict justice might warrant — "

"I beg your Ladyship's pardon if I interrupt, but I would beg to remark — "

"What?" said Lady Dorothea, proudly.

"That simply your Ladyship's present caution is the best security for future propriety. I ask no other."

"You presume too far, young lady. I cannot answer that *my* temper may not reveal sentiments that my judgment or my breeding might prefer to keep in abeyance."

"If the sentiments be there, my Lady, I should certainly say, better to avow them," said Kate, with an air of most impassive coldness.

"I 'm not aware that I have asked your advice on that head, Miss Henderson," said she, almost insolently. "At the same time, your habits of late in this family may have suggested the delusion."

"Will your Ladyship pardon me if I confess I do not understand you?"

"You shall have little to complain of on that score, Miss Henderson; I shall not speak in riddles, depend upon it. Nor should that be an obstacle if your intelligence were only the equal of your ambition."

"Now, indeed, is your Ladyship completely beyond me."

"Had you felt that I was as much 'above' you, Miss Henderson, it were more to the purpose."

"I sincerely hope that I have never forgotten all the deference I owe your Ladyship," said Kate. Nor could humble words have taken a more humble accent; and yet they availed little to conciliate her to whom they were addressed; nay, this very humility seemed to irritate and provoke her to a greater show of temper, as with an insolent laugh she said, — "This mockery of respect never imposed on we, young lady. I have been bred and born in a rank where real deference is so invariable that the fictitious article is soon detected, had there been any hardy enough to attempt it."

Kate made no other answer to this speech than a deep inclination of her head. It might mean assent, submission, anything.

"You may remember, Miss Henderson," said her Ladyship, with all the formality of a charge in her manner, — "you may remember that on the day I engaged your services you were obliging enough to furnish me with a brief summary of your acquirements." She paused, as if expecting some intimation of assent, and after an interval of a few seconds, Kate smiled, and said, — "It must have been a very meagre catalogue, my Lady."

"Quite the reverse. It was a perfect marvel to me how you ever found time to store your mind with such varied information; and yet, notwithstanding that imposing array of accomplishments, I now find that your modesty — perhaps out of deference to my ignorance — withheld fully as many more."

Kate's look of bewilderment at this speech was the only reply she made.

"Oh, of course you do not understand me," said Lady Dorothea, sneeringly; "but I mean to be most explicit. Have you any recollection of the circumstance I allude to?"

"I remember perfectly the day, madam, I waited on you for the first time."

"That's exactly what I mean. Now, pray, has any portion of our discourse dwelt upon your mind?"

"Yes, my Lady; a remark of your Ladyship's made a considerable impression upon me at the moment, and has continued frequently to rise to my recollection since that."

"May I ask what it was?"

"It was with reference to the treatment I had been so long accustomed to in the family of the Duchesse de Luygnes, and which your Ladyship characterized by an epithet I have never forgotten. At the time I thought it severe; I have learned to see it just. You called it an 'irreparable mischief.' Your Ladyship said most truly."

"I was never more convinced of the fact than at this very moment," said Lady Dorothea, as a flush of anger covered her cheek. "The ill-judging condescension of your first protectors has left a very troublesome legacy for their successors. Your youth and inexperience — I do not desire to attribute it to anything more reprehensible — led you, probably, into an error regarding the privileges you thus enjoyed, and you fancied that you owed to your own claims what you were entirely indebted to from the favor of others."

"I have no doubt that the observation of your Ladyship is quite correct," said Kate, calmly.

"I sincerely wish that the conviction had impressed itself upon your conduct then," said Lady Dorothea, whose temper was never so outraged as by the other's self-possession. "Had such been the case, I might have spared myself the unpleasantness of my present task." Her passion was now fully roused, and with redoubled energy she continued: "Your ambition has taken a high flight, young lady, and, from the condescension by which I accorded you a certain degree of influence in this family, you have aspired to become its head. Do not affect any misconception of my meaning. My son has told me everything—everything—from your invaluable aid to him in his pecuniary difficulties, to your sage counsels on his betting-book; from the admirable advice you gave him as to his studies, to the disinterested offer of your own tuition. Be assured if *he* has not understood all the advantages so generously presented to him, I, at least, appreciate them fully. I must acknowledge you have played your game cleverly, and you have made the mock independence of your character the mask of your designs. With another than myself you might have succeeded, too," said her Ladyship, with a smile of bitter irony; "but *I* have few self-delusions, Miss Henderson, nor is there amongst the number that of believing that any one serves me, in any capacity, from any devotion to my own person. I natter myself, at least, that I have so much of humility."

"If I understand your Ladyship aright, I am charged with some designs on Captain Martin?" said Kate, calmly.

"Yes; precisely so," said Lady Dorothea, haughtily.

"I can only protest that I am innocent of all such, my Lady," said she, with an expression of great deference. "It is a charge that does not admit of any other refutation, since, if I appeal to my conduct, your Ladyship's suspicions would not exculpate me."

"Certainly not."

"I thought so. What, then, can I adduce? I'm sure your Ladyship's own delicacy will see that this is not a case where testimony can be invoked. I cannot—you would not ask me to—require an acquittal from the lips of Captain Martin himself; humble as I stand here, my Lady, you never could mean to expose me to this humiliation." For the first time did her voice falter, and a sickly paleness came over her as she uttered the last words.

"The humiliation which you had intended for this family, Miss Henderson, is alone what demands consideration from *me*. If what you call your exculpation requires Captain Martin's presence, I confess I see no objection to it."

"It is only, then, because your Ladyship is angry with me that you could bring yourself to think so, especially since another and much easier solution of the difficulty offers itself."

"How so? What do you mean?"

"To send me home, madam."

"I understand you, young lady. I am to send you back to your father's house as one whose presence here was too dangerous, whose attractions could only be resisted by means of absence and distance. A very interesting martyrdom might have been made of it, I 've no doubt, and even some speculation as to the conduct of a young gentleman so suddenly bereaved of the object of his affections. But all this is much too dignified for me. *My* son shall be taught to respect himself without the intervention of any contrivance."

As she uttered the last words, she arose and approached the bell.

"Your Ladyship surely is not going—"

"I am going to send for Captain Martin, Miss Henderson."

"Do not, I entreat of you,—I implore your Ladyship," cried Kate, with her clasped hands trembling as she spoke.

"This agitation is not without a cause, and would alone decide me to call for my son."

"If I have ever deserved well at your hands, my Lady,—if I have served you faithfully in anything,—if my devotion has lightened you of one care, or aided you through one difficulty,—spare me, oh, spare me, I beseech you, this—degradation!"

"I have a higher consideration to consult here, Miss Henderson, than any which can have reference to you." She pulled the bell violently, and while her hand still held the cord, the servant entered. "Tell Captain Martin to come here," said she, and sat down.

Kate leaned her arm upon the chimney-piece, and, resting her head on it, never uttered a word.

For several minutes the silence was unbroken on either side. At last Lady Dorothea started suddenly, and said,—"We cannot receive Captain Martin here."

"Your Ladyship is full of consideration," said Kate, bitterly. "For a moment I had thought it was only an additional humiliation to which you had destined me."

"Follow me into the drawing-room, Miss Henderson," said Lady Dorothea, proudly, as she left the room. And with slow, submissive mien Kate quitted the chamber, and walked after her.

Scarcely had the door of the drawing-room been closed upon them than it was re-opened to admit Captain Martin. He was booted and spurred for his afternoon canter, and seemed in no wise pleased at the sudden interruption to his project.

"They said you wanted me," cried he; "and here have I been searching for you in your dressing-room, and all over the house."

"I desire to speak with you," said she, proudly; and she motioned to a chair.

"I trust the *séance* is to be a brief one, otherwise I'll beg a postponement," said he, half laughingly. Then turning his glance towards Kate, he remarked for the first time the deathlike color of her face, and an expression of repressed suffering that all her self-control could not conceal. "Has anything happened? What is it?" said he, in a half-whisper.

But she never replied, nor even seemed to heed his question.

"Tell me, I beseech you," cried he, turning to Lady Dorothea,—"tell me, has anything gone wrong?"

"It is precisely on that account I have sent for you, Captain Martin," said her Ladyship, as she assigned to him a seat with a motion of her hand. "It is because a great deal has gone wrong here—and were it not for my vigilance, much more still likely to follow it—I have sent for you, sir, that you should hear from this young lady's lips a denial which, I own, has not satisfied *me*; nor shall it, till it be made in your presence and meet with your corroboration. Your looks, Miss Henderson," said she, addressing her, "would imply that all the suffering of the present moment falls to *your* share; but I would beg you to bear in mind what a person in *my* sphere must endure at the bare possibility of the event which now demands investigation."

"Good heavens! will not you tell me what it is?" exclaimed Martin, in the last extremity of impatience.

"I have sent for you, sir," resumed she, "that you should hear Miss Henderson declare that no attentions on your part—no assiduities, I should perhaps call them—have ever been addressed to her; that, in fact"—here her Ladyship became embarrassed in her explanation,—"that, in fact, those counsels—those very admirable aids to your conduct which she on so many occasions has vouchsafed to afford you—have had no object—no ulterior object, I should perhaps call it—and that your—your intercourse has ever been such as beseems the heir of Cro' Martin, and the daughter of the steward on that property!"

"By Jove, I can make nothing of all this!" cried the Captain, whose bewildered looks fully corroborated the assertion.

"Lady Dorothea, sir, requires you to assure her that I have never made love to you," said Kate Henderson, with a look of scorn that her Ladyship did not dare to reply to. "*I*," added she, "have already given my pledge on this subject. I trust that your testimony will not gainsay me."

"Confound me if I can fathom it at all!" said he, more distracted than ever. "If you are alluding to the offer I made you—"

"The offer you made," cried Lady Dorothea. "When?—how?—in what wise?"

"No, no, I will speak out," said he, addressing Kate. "I am certain *you* never divulged it; but I cannot accept that all the honorable dealing should be on one side only. Yes, my Lady, however you learned it, I cannot guess, but it is perfectly true; I asked Miss Henderson to be my wife, and she refused me."

A low, faint sigh broke from Lady Dorothea, and she fell back into her chair.

"She would have it,—it's not my fault,—you are witness it's not," muttered he to Kate. But she motioned him in silence to the door, and then opening the window, that the fresh air might enter, stood silently beside the chair.

A slight shivering shook her; and Lady Dorothea—her cheeks almost lividly pale—raised her eyes and fixed them on Kate Henderson.

"You have had your triumph!" said she, in a low but firm voice.

"I do not feel it such, madam," said Kate, calmly. "Nor is it in a moment of humiliation like this that a thought of triumph can enter."

"Hear me,—stoop down lower. You can leave this—tomorrow, if you wish it."

Kate bowed slowly in acquiescence.

"I have no need to ask you that what has occurred here should never be mentioned."

"You may trust me, madam."

"I feel that I may. There—I am better—quite well, now! You may leave me." Kate courtesied deeply, and moved towards the door. "One word before you go. Will you answer me one question? I'll ask but one; but your answer must be full, or not at all."

"So it shall be, madam. What is it?"

"I want to know the reason—on what grounds—you declined the proposal of my son?"

"For the same good reason, madam, that should have prevented his ever making it."

"Disparity—inequality of station, you mean?"

"Something like it, madam. Our union would have been both a blunder and a paradox. Each would have married beneath him!" And once more courtesying, and with an air of haughty dignity, Kate withdrew, and left her Ladyship to her own thoughts.

Strange and conflicting were the same thoughts; at one moment stimulating her to projects of passionate vengeance, at the next suggesting the warmest measures of reconciliation and affection. These indeed predominated, for in her heart pride seemed the emblem of all that was great, noble, or exalted; and when she saw that sentiment, not fostered by the accidents of fortune, not associated with birth, lineage, and high station, but actually rising superior to the absence of all these, she almost felt a species of worship for one so gloriously endowed.

"She might be a duchess!" was the only speech she uttered, and the words revealed a whole volume of her meditations. It was curious enough how completely all recollection of her son was merged and lost in the greater interest Kate's character supplied. But so is it frequently in life. The traits which most resemble our own are those we alone attach importance to, and what we fancy admiration of another is very often nothing more than the gratified contemplation of ourselves.

CHAPTER XXIII
MAURICE SCANLAN ADVISES WITH "HIS COUNSEL"

Jack Massingbred sat in expectation of Mr. Merl's arrival till nigh ten o'clock; and if not manifesting any great degree of impatience at the delay, still showing unmistakable signs of uneasiness, as though the event were not destitute of some cause for anxiety. At last a note arrived to say that a sudden and imperative necessity to start at once for England would prevent Mr. Merl from keeping his appointment. "I shall be in town by Tuesday," continued the writer, "and if Captain Martin has any communication to make to me respecting his affairs, let it be addressed to Messrs. Twining and Scape's, solicitors, Furnival's Inn. I hope that with regard to your own matter, you will make suitable provision for the acceptance due on the ninth of next month. Any further renewal would prove a great inconvenience to yours

"Very sincerely and to command,

"Herman Merl."

"Negotiations have ended ere they were opened, and war is proclaimed at once," said Massingbred, as he read over this brief epistle. "You may come forth, Master Scanlan," added he, opening the door of his bedroom, and admitting that gentleman. "Our Hebrew is an overmatch for us. He declines to appear."

"Why so? How is that?" asked Scanlan.

"There 's his note," said the other; "read and digest it."

"This smacks of suspicion," said Scanlan. "He evidently suspects that we have concerted some scheme to entangle him, and he is resolved not to be caught."

"Precisely; he 'll do nothing without advice. Well, well, if he but knew how unprepared we are, how utterly deficient not only in resources, but actually in the commonest information of our subject, he might have ventured here in all safety."

"Has Captain Martin not put you in possession of the whole case, then?"

"Why, my good Scanlan, the Captain knows nothing, actually nothing, of his difficulties. He has, it is true, a perfect conviction that he is out of his depth; but whether he be in five fathom water or fifty, he doesn't know; and, what's stranger, he does n't care!"

"After all, if it be over his head, I suppose it's pretty much the same thing," said Scanlan, with a bitter laugh.

"I beg to offer my dissent to that doctrine," said Mas-singbred, gently. "Where the water is only just out of a man's depth, the shore is usually not very distant. Now, if we were quite certain such were the case here, we might hope to save him. If, on the contrary, he has gone down out of all sight of land—" He stopped, gazed steadily at Scanlan for a few seconds, and then in a lower tone, not devoid of a touch of anxiety, said, "Eh, do you really know this to be so?"

"I'll tell you all I know, Mr. Massingbred," said he, as having turned the key in the door, he took his seat at the table. "And I 'll tell you, besides, how I came by the knowledge, and I 'll leave it to your own judgment to say what his chance is worth. When Merl was stopping at Kilkieran, he left there a little pocket-book, with memorandums of all his secret transactions. Mighty nice doings they were,—and profitable, too,—as you 'll perceive when you look over it."

"You have it, then," cried Jack, eagerly.

"Here it is," said he, producing the precious volume, and laying his hand firmly on it. "Here it is now. I got it under a pledge to hand it to himself, which I need n't tell you I never had the slightest intention of performing. It's not every day in the week one has the good luck to get a peep into the enemy's brief, and this is exactly what you 'll find here."

Massingbred stretched out his hand to take the book, but Scanlan quietly replaced it in his pocket, and, with a dry and very peculiar smile, said,—"Have a little patience, sir. We must go regularly to work here. You shall see this book—you shall examine it—and even retain it—but it must be on conditions." "Oh, you may confide in me, Scanlan. Even if Mr. Merl were my friend,—which I assure you he is not,—I could not venture to betray *you*."

"That's not exactly what I 'm thinking of, Mr. Massingbred. I 'm certain you 'd say nothing to Merl of what you saw here. My mind is easy enough upon that score."

"Well, then, in what direction do your suspicions point?"

"They 're not suspicions, sir," was the dry response.

"Fears,—hesitations,—whatever you like to call them."

"Are we on honor here, Mr. Massingbred?" said Scanlan, after a pause.

"For myself, I say decidedly so," was the firm reply.

"That will do, sir. I ask only one pledge, and I 'm sure you 'll not refuse it: if you should think, on reflection, that what I propose to you this evening is neither practicable nor advisable,—that, in fact, you could neither concur in it nor aid it,—that you'll never, so long as you live, divulge it to any one,—man, woman, or child. Have I that promise?"

"I think I may safely say that."

"Ay, but do you say it?"

"I do; here is my promise."

"That will do. I don't ask a word more. Now, Mr. Massingbred," said he, replacing the book on the table, "I 'll tell you in the fewest words I can how the case stands,—and brevity is essential, for we have not an hour to lose. Merl is gone to London about this business, and we 'll have to follow him. He 'd be very glad to be rid of the affair to-morrow, and he 'll not waste many days till he is so. Read that bit there, sir," said he, pointing to a few closely written lines in the note-book.

"Good heavens!" cried Jack, "this is downright impossible. This is a vile falsehood, devised for some infernal scheme of roguery. Who 'd believe such a trumpery piece of imposition? Ah, Scanlan, you are not the wily fellow I took you for. This same precious note-book was dropped as a decoy, as I once knew a certain noble lord to have left his betting-book behind him. An artful device, that can only succeed once, however. And you really believed all this?"

"I did, and I do believe it," said Scanlan, firmly.

"If you really say so, we must put the matter to the test. Captain Martin is here,—we 'll send for him, and ask him the question; but I must say I don't think your position will be a pleasant one after that reply is given."

"I must remind you of your promise already, it seems," said Scanlan. "You are pledged to say nothing of this, if you cannot persuade yourself to act along with me in it."

"Very true," said Massingbred, slowly; "but I never pledged myself to credit an impossibility."

"I ask nothing of the kind. I only claim that you should adhere to what you have said already. If this statement be untrue, all my speculations about it fall to the ground at once. I am the dupe of a stale trick, and there's an end of it."

"Ay, so far all well, Master Scanlan; but I have no fancy to be associated in the deception. Can't you see that?"

"I can, sir, and I do. But perhaps there may be a readier way of satisfying your doubts than calling for the Captain's evidence. There is a little page in this same volume devoted to one Mr. Massingbred. *You* surely may have some knowledge about *his* affairs. Throw your eye over that, sir, and say what you think of it."

Massingbred took the book in his hand and perused the place pointed out to him.

"By Jove! this *is* very strange," said he, after a pause. "Here is my betting-book on the St. Hubert all transcribed in full,—however the Jew boy got hold of it; and here's mention of a blessed hundred-pound note, which, in less than five years, has grown to upwards of a thousand!"

"And all true? All fact?"

"Perfectly true,—most lamentable fact, Master Scanlan! How precise the scoundrel is in recording this loan as 'after supper at Dubos'! Ay, and here again is my unlucky wager about Martingale for the 'Chester,' and the handicap with Armytage. Scanlan, I recant my rash impression. This is a real work of its great author! *Aut Merl—aut Diabolus.*"

"I could have sworn it," said Scanlan.

"To be sure you could, man, and have done, ere this time o' day, fifty other things on fainter evidence. But let me tell you it requires strong testimony to make one believe that there should live such a consummate fool in the world as would sell his whole reversionary right to a splendid state of some twelve thousand—"

"Fifteen at the lowest," broke in Scanlan.

"Worse again. Fifteen thousand a year for twenty-two thousand seven hundred and sixty-four pounds sterling."

"And he has done it."

"No, no; the thing is utterly incredible, man. Any one must see that if he did want to make away with his inheritance, that he could have obtained ten, twenty times that sum amongst the tribe of Merl."

"No doubt, if he were free to negotiate the transaction. But you 'll see, on looking over these pages, in what a network of debt he was involved,— how, as early as four years ago, at the Cape, he owed Merl large sums, lost at play, and borrowed at heavy interest. So that, at length, this same twenty-two thousand, assumed as paid for the reversion, was in reality but the balance of an immense demand for money lost, bills renewed, sums lent, debts discharged, and so on. But to avoid the legal difficulty of an 'immoral obligation,' the bale of the reversion is limited to this simple payment of twenty-two thousand—"

"Seven hundred and sixty-four pounds, sir. Don't let us diminish the price by a fraction," said Massingbred. "Wonderful people ye are, to be sure; and whether in your talent for savings, or dislike for sausages, alike admirable and praiseworthy! What a strange circle do events observe, and how irrevocable is the law of the material, the stern rule of the moral world, decay, decomposition, and regeneration following on each other; and as great men's ashes beget grubs, so do illustrious houses generate in their rottenness the race of Herman Merls."

Scanlan tried to smile at the rhapsodical conceit, but for some private reason of his own he did not relish nor enjoy it.

"So, then, according to the record," said Massingbred, holding up the book, "there is an end of the 'Martins of Cro' Martin'?"

"That's it, sir, in one word."

"It is too shocking—too horrible to believe," said Mas-singbred, with more of sincerity than his manner usually displayed. "Eh, Scanlan,—is it not so?" added he, as waiting in vain for some show of concurrence.

"I believe, however," said the other, "it's the history of every great family's downfall: small liabilities growing in secrecy to become heavy charges, severe pressure exerted by those out of whose pockets came eventually the loans to meet the difficulties,—shrewdness and rapacity on one side, folly and wastefulness on the other."

"Ay, ay; but who ever heard of a whole estate disposed of for less than two years of its rental?"

"That's exactly the case, sir," said he, in the same calm tone as before; "and what makes matters worse, we have little time to look out for expedients. Magennis will put us on our title at the new trial next assizes. Merl will take fright at the insecurity of his claim, and dispose of it,—Heaven knows to whom,—perhaps to that very league now formed to raise litigation against all the old tenures."

"Stop, stop, Scanlan! There is quite enough difficulty before us, without conjuring up new complications," cried Massingbred. "Have you anything to suggest? What ought to be done here?"

Scanlan was silent, and leaning his head on his hand seemed lost in thought.

"Come, Scanlan, you 've thought over all this ere now. Tell me, man, what do you advise?"

Scanlan was silent.

"Out with it, Scanlan. I know, I feel that you have a resource in store against all these perils! Out with it, man."

"Have I any need to remind you of your promise, Mr. Massingbred?" asked the other, stealthily.

"Not the slightest, Scanlan. I never forget a pledge."

"Very well, sir; that's enough," said Scanlan, speaking rapidly, and like one anxious to overcome his confusion by an effort. "We have just one thing to do. We must buy out Merl. Of course as reasonably as we can, but buy him out we must. What between his own short experiences of Ireland, and the exposure that any litigation is sure to bring with it, he's not likely to be hard to deal with, particularly when we are in possession, as I suppose we may be, through *your* intimacy with the Captain, of all the secret history of these transactions. I take it for granted that he 'll be as glad of a settlement that keeps all 'snug,' as ourselves. Less than the twenty-two thousand we can't expect he'll take."

"And how are we to raise that sum without Mr. Martin's concurrence?"

"I wish that was the only difficulty," said Scanlan.

"What do you mean?"

"Just this: that in his present state no act of his would stand. Sure his mind is gone. There isn't a servant about him could n't swear to his fancies and imaginations. No, sir, the whole thing must be done amongst ourselves. I have eight thousand some hundred pounds of my own available at a moment; old Nelligan would readily—for an assignment of the Brewery and the Market Square—advance us ten thousand more;—the money, in short, could be had—more if we wanted it—the question—"

"As to the dealing with Merl?" broke in Jack.

"No, sir, not that, though of course it is a most important consideration."

"Well, what then?"

"As to the dealing with Maurice Scanlan, sir," said he, making a great effort. "There's the whole question in one word."

"I don't see that there can be any grave obstacle against that. You know the property."

"Every acre of it."

"You know how you'd like your advance to be secured to you—on what part of the estate. The conditions, I am certain, might be fairly left in your own hands; I feel assured you'd not ask nor expect anything beyond what was equitable and just."

"Mr. Massingbred, we might talk this way a twelvemonth, and never be a bit nearer our object than when we began," said Scanlan, resolutely. "I want two things, and I won't take less than the two together. One is to be secured in the agency of the estate, under nobody's control whatever but the Martins themselves. No Mister Repton to say 'Do this, sign that, seal the other.' I 'll have nobody over me but him that owns the property."

"Well, and the other condition?"

"The other—the other—" said Scanlan, growing very red—"the other, I suppose, will be made the great difficulty—at least, on my Lady's side. She 'll be bristling up about her uncle the Marquis, and her half-cousin the Duke, and she'll be throwing in my teeth who I am, and what I was, and all the rest of it, forgetting all the while where they 'll be if they reject my terms, and how much the most noble Viceroy will do for her when she has n't a roof over her head, and how many letters his Grace will write when she has n't a place to address them to,—not to say that the way they're treating the girl at this very moment shows how much they think of her as one of themselves, living with old Catty Broon, and cantering over the country without as much as a boy after her. Sure, if they were n't Pride itself, it's glad they might be that a—a—a respectable man, that is sure to be devoted to their own interests forever, and one that knows the estate well, and, moreover than that, that doesn't want to be going over to London,— no, nor even to Dublin,—that doesn't care a brass farthing for the castle and the lodge in the park,—that, in short, Mr. Massingbred, asks nothing for anybody, but is willing to trust to his industry and what he knows of life— There it is now,—there's my whole case," said he, stammering, and growing more and more embarrassed. "I haven't a word to add to it, except this: that if they'd rather be ruined entirely, left without stick or stone, roof or rafter in the world, than take my offer, they 've nothing to blame but themselves and their own infernal pride!" And with this peroration, to deliver which cost him an effort like a small apoplexy, Maurice Scanlan sat down at the table, and crossed his arms on his breast like one prepared to await his verdict with a stout heart.

At last, and with the start of one who "suddenly bethought him of a precaution that ought not to be neglected," he said, — "Of course, this is so far all between ourselves, for if I was to go up straight to my Lady, and say, 'I want to marry your niece,' I think I know what the answer would be."

Although Massingbred had followed this rambling and incoherent effort at explanation with considerable attention, it was only by the very concluding words that he was quite certain of having comprehended its meaning. If we acknowledge that he felt almost astounded by the pretension, it is but fair to add that nothing in his manner or air betokened this feeling. Nay, he even by a slight gesture of the head invited the other to continue; and when the very abrupt conclusion did ensue, he sat patiently, as it were revolving the question in his own mind.

Had Scanlan been waiting for the few words which from a jury-box determine a man's fate forever, he could not have suffered more acute anxiety than he felt while contemplating the other's calm and unmoved countenance. A bold, open rejection of his plan, a defiant repudiation of his presumption, would not probably have pained him more, if as much as the impassive quietness of Jack's demeanor.

"If you think that this is a piece of impudence on my part, Mr. Massingbred, — if it's your opinion that in aspiring to be connected with the Martins I'm forgetting my place and my station, just say so at once. Tell it to me frankly, and I'll know how to bear it," said he, at last, when all further endurance had become impossible.

"Nothing of the kind, my dear Scanlan," said Jack, smiling blandly. "Whatever snobbery once used to prevail on these subjects, we have come to live in a more generous age. The man of character, the man who unites an untarnished reputation to very considerable abilities, with talent to win any station, and virtues to adorn it, such a man wants no blazonry to illustrate his name, and it is mainly by such accessions that our English aristocracy, refreshed and invigorated as it is, preserves its great acknowledged superiority."

It would have required a more acute critic than Maurice Scanlan to have detected the spirit in which this rhapsody was uttered. The apparent earnestness of the manner did not exactly consort with a certain pomposity of enunciation and an over-exactness in the tone of the declamation. On the whole Maurice did not like it. It smacked to his ears very like what he had often listened to in the Four Courts at the close of a "junior's" address; and there was a Nisi Prius jingle in it that sounded marvellously unlike conviction.

"If, then," resumed Massingbred, "they who by the accidents of fortune, or the meritorious services of their forefathers, represent rather in their elevation the gratitude of their country than—"

"I 'm sorry to interrupt you, sir,—indeed, I'm ashamed of myself for doing it,—for your remarks are beautiful, downright eloquent; but the truth is, this is a case touches me too closely to make me care for a grand speech about it. I 'd rather have just a few words—to the evidence, as one might say,—or a simple answer to a plain question, Can this thing be done?"

"There's where you beat us, Scanlan. There's where we cannot approach you. You are practical. You reduce a matter at once to the simple dimension of efficacy first, then possibility, and with these two conditions before you you reject the fifty extraneous considerations, outlying contingencies, that distract and embarrass such fellows as me."

"I have no pretension to abilities like yours, Mr. Massingbred," said Scanlan, with unassumed modesty.

"Ah, Scanlan, yours are the true gifts, take my word for it!—the recognized currency by which a man obtains what he seeks for; and there never was an era in which such qualities bore a higher value. Our statesmen, our diplomatists, our essay-writers,—nay, our very poets, addressing themselves as they do to the correction of social wrongs and class inequalities,—they are all 'practical'! That is the type of our time, and future historians will talk of this as the 'Age of Fact'!"

If one were to judge from Maurice Scanlan's face during the delivery of this peroration, it might be possibly inferred that he scarcely accepted the speech as an illustration in point, since anything less practical he had never listened to.

"When I think," resumed he, "what a different effect I should have produced in the 'House' had I possessed this requisite! You, possibly, may be under the impression that I achieved a great success?"

"Well, I did hear as much," said Scanlan, half doggedly.

"Perhaps it was so. A first speech, you are aware, is always listened to indulgently; not so a second, especially if a man rises soon after his first effort. They begin to suspect they have got a talkative fellow, eager and ready to speak on every question; they dread that, and even if he be clever, they 'll vote him a bore!"

"Faith! I don't wonder at it!" said Maurice, with a hearty sincerity in the tone.

"Yet, after all, Scanlan, let us be just! How in Heaven's name, are men to become debaters, except by this same training? You require men not alone to be strong upon the mass of questions that come up in debate, but you expect them to be prompt with their explanations, always prepared with their replies. Not ransacking history, or searching through 'Hansard,' you want a man who, at the spur of the moment, can rise to defend, to explain, to simplify, or mayhap to assail, to denounce, to annihilate. Is n't that true?"

"I don't want any such thing, sir!" said Scanlan, with a sulky determination that there was no misunderstanding.

"You don't. Well, what *do* you ask for?"

"I'll tell you, sir, and in very few words, too, what I do *not* ask for! I don't ask to be humbugged, listening to this, that, and the other, that I have nothing to say to; to hear how you failed or why you succeeded; what you did or what you could n't do. I put a plain case to you, and I wanted as plain an answer. And as to your flattering me about being practical, or whatever you call it, it's a clean waste of time, neither less nor more!"

"The agency and the niece!" said Massingbred, with a calm solemnity that this speech had never disconcerted.

"Them 's the conditions!" said Scanlan, reddening over face and forehead.

"You 're a plucky fellow, Scanlan, and by Jove I like you for it!" said Massingbred. And for once there was a hearty sincerity in the way he spoke. "If a man *is* to have a fall, let it be at least over a 'rasper,' not be thrown over a furrow in a ploughed field! You fly at high game, but I'm far from saying you'll not succeed." And with a jocular laugh he turned away and left him.

CHAPTER XXIV
A CONSULTATION

Jack Massingbred was one of those who, in questions of difficulty, resort to the pen in preference to personal interference. It was a fancy of his that he wrote better than he talked. Very probably he thought so because the contrary was the fact. On the present occasion another motive had also its influence. It was Lady Dorothea that he addressed, and he had no especial desire to commit himself to a direct interview.

His object was to convey Mr. Scanlan's propositions,—to place them fully and intelligibly before her Ladyship without a syllable of comment on his own part, or one word which could be construed into advocacy or reprobation of them. In truth, had he been called upon for an opinion, it would have sorely puzzled him what to say. To rescue a large estate from ruin was, to be sure, a very considerable service, but to accept Maurice Scanlan as a near member of one's family seemed a very heavy price even for that. Still, if the young lady liked him, singular as the choice might appear, other objections need not be insurmountable. The Martins were very unlikely ever to make Ireland their residence again, they would see little or nothing of this same Scanlan connection, "and, after all," thought Jack, "if we can only keep the disagreeables of this life away from daily intercourse, only knowing them through the post-office and at rare intervals, the compact is not a bad one."

Massingbred would have liked much to consult Miss Henderson upon the question itself, and also upon his manner of treating it; but to touch upon the point of a marriage of inequality with her, would have been dangerous ground. It was scarcely possible he could introduce the topic without dropping a word, or letting fall a remark she could not seize hold of. It was the theme, of all others, in which her sensitiveness was extreme; nor could he exactly say whether she sneered at a *mésalliance,* or at the insolent tone of society regarding it.

Again he bethought him of the ungraciousness of the task he had assumed, if, as was most probable, Lady Dorothea should feel Mr. Scanlan's pretensions an actual outrage. "She'll never forgive me for stating them, that's certain," said he; "but will she do so if I decline to declare them, or worse still, leave them to the vulgar interpretation Scanlan himself is sure to impart to them?" While he thus hesitated and debated with himself, now altering a phrase here, now changing a word there, Captain Martin entered the room, and threw himself into a chair with a more than ordinary amount of weariness and exhaustion.

"The governor's worse to-day, Massingbred," said he, with a sigh.

"No serious change, I hope?" said Jack.

"I suspect there is, though," replied the other. "They sent for me from Lescour's last night, where I was winning smartly. Just like *my* luck always, to be called away when I was 'in vein,' and when I got here, I found Schubart, and a French fellow whom I don't know, had just bled him. It must have been touch and go, for when I saw him he was very ill—very ill indeed—and they call him better."

"It was a distinct attack, then,—a seizure of some sort?" asked Massingbred.

"Yes, I think they said so," said he, lighting his cigar.

"But he has rallied, has n't he?"

"Well, I don't fancy he has. He lifts his eyes at times, and seems to look about for some one, and moves his lips a little, but you could scarcely say that he was conscious, though my mother insists he is."

"What does Schubart think?"

"Who minds these fellows?" said he, impatiently. "They're only speculating on what will be said of themselves, and so they go on: 'If this does not occur, and the other does not happen, we shall see him better this evening.'"

"This is all very bad," said Massingbred, gloomily—"It's a deuced deal worse than you know of, old fellow," said Martin, bitterly.

"Perhaps not worse than I suspect," said Massingbred.

"What do you mean by that?"

Massingbred did not reply, but sat deep in thought for some time. "Come, Martin," said he, at last, "let us be frank; in a few hours it may be, perhaps, too late for frankness. Is this true?" And he handed to him Merl's pocket-book, open at a particular page.

Martin took it, and as his eyes traced the lines a sickly paleness covered his features, and in a voice scarcely stronger than an infant's, he said, "It is so."

"The whole reversionary right?"

"Every acre—every stick and stone of it—except," added he, with a sickly attempt at a smile, "a beggarly tract, near Kiltimmon, Mary has a charge upon."

"Read that, now," said Jack, handing him his recently written letter. "I was about to send it without showing it to you; but it is as well you saw it."

While Martin was reading, Massingbred never took his eyes from him. He watched with all his own practised keenness the varying emotions the letter cost; but he saw that, as he finished, selfishness had triumphed, and that the prospect of safety had blunted every sentiment as to the price.

"Well," said Jack, "what say you to that?"

"I say it's a right good offer, and on no account to be refused. There is some hitch or other—I can't say what, but it exists, I know—which ties us up against selling. Old Repton and the governor, and I think my mother, too, are in the secret; but I never was, so that Scanlan's proposal is exactly what meets the difficulty."

"But do you like his conditions?" asked Jack.

"I can't say I do. But what 's that to the purpose? One must play the hand that is dealt to them; there 's no choice! I know that, as agent over the property, he 'll make a deuced good thing of it for himself. It will not be five nor ten per cent will satisfy Master Maurice."

"Yes; but there is another condition, also," said Jack, quietly.

"About Mary? Well, of course it's not the kind of thing one likes. The fellow is the lowest of the low; but even that's better, in some respects, than a species of half gentility, for he actually has n't one in the world belonging to him. No one ever heard of his father or mother, and he's not the fellow to go in search of them."

"I confess that *is* a consideration," said Massingbred, with a tone that might mean equally raillery or the reverse, "so that you see no great objection on that score?"

"I won't say I 'd choose the connection; but 'with a bad book it's at least a hedge,'—eh, Massy, is n't it?"

"Perhaps so," said the other, dryly.

"It does n't strike me," said Martin, as he glanced his eye again over the letter, "that you have advocated Scanlan's plan. You have left it without, apparently, one word of comment. Does that mean that you don't approve of it?"

"I never promised him I would advocate it," said Jack.

"I have no doubt, Massingbred, you think me a deuced selfish fellow for treating the question in this fashion; but just reflect a little, and see how innocently, as I may say, I was led into all these embarrassments. I never suspected how deep I was getting. Merl used to laugh at me if I asked him how we stood; he always induced me to regard our dealings as trifles, to be arranged to-day, to-morrow, or ten years hence."

"I am not unversed in that sort of thing, unluckily," said Massingbred, interrupting him. "There is another consideration, however, in the present case, to which I do not think you have given sufficient weight."

"As to Mary, my dear fellow, the matter is simple enough. Our consent is a mere form. If she liked Scanlan, she 'd marry him against all the Martins that ever were born; and if she did n't, she 'd not swerve an inch if the whole family were to go to the stake for it. She 's not one for half measures, I promise you; and then, remember, that though she is one 'of us,' and well born, she has never mingled with the society of her equals; she has always lived that kind of life you saw yourself,—taking a cast with the hounds one day, nursing some old hag with the rheumatism the next. I 've seen her hearing a class in the village school, and half an hour after, breaking in a young horse to harness. And what between her habits and her tastes, she is really not fit for what you and I would call the world." As Massingbred made no reply, Martin ascribed his silence to a part conviction, and went on: "Mind, I 'm not going to say that she is not a deuced deal too good for Maurice Scanlan, who is as vulgar a hound as walks on two legs; but, as I said before, Massy, we haven't much choice."

"Will Lady Dorothea be likely to view the matter in this light?" asked Jack, calmly.

"That is a mere matter of chance. She 's equally likely to embrace the proposal with ardor, or tell a footman to kick Scanlan out of the house for his impertinence; and I own the latter is the more probable of the two,—not, mark you, from any exaggerated regard for Mary, but out of consideration to the insult offered to herself."

"Will she not weigh well all the perils that menace the estate?"

"She'll take a short method with them,—she'll not believe them."

"Egad! I must say the whole negotiation is in a very promising state!" exclaimed Jack, as he arose and walked the room. "There is only one amongst us has much head for a case of difficulty."

"You mean Kate Henderson?" broke in Martin.

"Yes."

"Well, we 've lost *her* just when we most needed her."

"Lost her! How—what do you mean?"

"Why, that she is gone—gone home. She started this morning before daybreak. She had a tiff with my mother last night. I will say the girl was shamefully treated,—shamefully! My Lady completely forgot herself. She was in one of those blessed paroxysms in which, had she been born a Pasha, heads would have been rolling about like shot in a dockyard, and she consequently said all manner of atrocities; and instead of giving her time to make the *amende*, Kate beat a retreat at once, and by this time she is some twenty miles on her journey."

Massingbred walked to the window to hide the emotion these tidings produced; for, with all his self-command, the suddenness of the intelligence had unmanned him, and a cold and sickly feeling came over him. There was far more of outraged and insulted pride than love in the emotions which then moved him. The bitter thought of the moment was, how indifferent she felt about *him*,—how little *he* weighed in any resolve she determined to follow. She had gone without a word of farewell,—perhaps without a thought of him. "Be it so," said he to himself; "there has been more than enough of humiliation to me in our intercourse. It is time to end it! The whole was a dream, from which the awaking was sure to be painful. Better meet it at once, and have done with it." There was that much of passion in this resolve that proved how far more it came from wounded pride than calm conviction; and so deeply was his mind engrossed with this feeling, that Martin had twice spoken to him ere he noticed his question.

"Do you mean, then, to show that letter to my mother?"

"Ay; I have written it with that object Scanlan asked me to be his interpreter, and I have kept my pledge.—And did she go alone,—unaccompanied?"

"I fancy so; but, in truth, I never asked. The doctors were here, and all that fuss and confusion going on, so that I had really little head for anything. After all, I suspect she's a girl might be able to take care of herself,—should n't you say so?"

Massingbred was silent for a while, and then said: "You 'll have to be on the alert about this business of yours, Martin; and if I can be of service to you, command me. I mean to start for London immediately."

"I 'll see my mother at once, then," said he, taking up Massingbred's letter.

"Shall I meet you in about an hour, in the Lichtenthal Avenue?"

"Agreed," said he; and they parted.

We have no need, nor have we any right, to follow Massingbred as he strolled out to walk alone in an alley of the wood. Irresolution is an intense suffering to men of action; and such was the present condition of his mind. Week after week, month after month, had he lingered on in companionship with the Martins, till such had become the intimacy between them that they scrupled not to discuss before him the most confidential circumstances, and ask his counsel on the most private concerns. He fancied that he was "of them;" he grew to think that he was, somehow, part and parcel of the family, little suspecting the while that Kate Henderson was the link that bound him to them, and that without her presence they resolved themselves into three individuals for whom he felt wonderfully little of interest or affection. "She is gone, and what have I to stay for?" was the question he put to himself; and for answer he could only repeat it.

CHAPTER XXV
A COMPROMISE

There are many who think that our law of primogeniture is a sad hardener of the heart,—estranging the father from the son, widening petty misunderstandings to the breadth of grievances, engendering suspicions where there should be trustfulness, and opening two roads in life to those who should rightfully have trod one path together. If one half of this be the price we pay for our "great houses," the bargain is a bad one! But even taking a wide margin for exaggeration,—allowing much for the prejudices of those who assail this institution,—there is that which revolts against one's better nature, in the ever-present question of money, between the father and his heir. The very fact that separate rights suggest separate interests is a source of discord; while the inevitable law of succession is a stern defiance to that sense of protection on one side, and dependence on the other, that should mark their relations to each other.

Captain Martin was not devoid of affection for his family. He had, it is true, been very little at home, but he did not dislike it, beyond the "boredom" of a rather monotonous kind of life. He was naturally of a plastic temperament, however, and he lived amongst a set whose good pleasure it is to criticise all who belong to them with the very frankest of candor. One told how his governor, though rolling in wealth, kept him on a most beggarly allowance, illustrating, with many an amusing story, traits of avarice that set the table in a roar. Another exhibited his as such a reckless spendthrift that the family estate would never cover the debts. There was a species of rivalry on seeing who should lay most open to public view details and incidents purely belonging to a family. It was even a principle of this new school to discuss, and suffer others to discuss before them, the class and condition of life of their parents in a tone of mockery and derision, whenever the occasion might admit it; and the son of the manufacturer or the trader listened to allusions to his birth and parentage, and even jested upon them himself, in a spirit more flattering to his philosophy than to his pride.

Martin had lived amidst all this for years. He had been often complimented upon the "jolly good thing he was to have one of these days;"

he had been bantered out of many a wise and prudent economy, by being reminded of that "deuced fine property nobody could keep him out of." "What can it signify to *you* old fellow, a few hundreds more or less. You must have fifteen thousand a year yet. The governor can't live forever, I take it." Others, too, as self-invited guests, speculated on all the pleasures of a visit to Cro' Martin; and if at first the young man heard such projects with shame and repugnance, he learned at last to listen to them with indifference, perhaps with something less!

Was it some self-accusing on this score that now overwhelmed him as he sat alone in his room, trying to think, endeavoring to arouse himself to action, but so overcome that he sat there only half conscious, and but dimly discerning the course of events about him? At such moments external objects mingle their influences with our thoughts, and the sound of voices, the tread of footsteps, the mere shutting of a door, seem to blend themselves with our reveries, and give somewhat of reality to our dreamy fancies. A large clock upon the mantelpiece had thus fixed his attention, and he watched the minute-hand as though its course was meting out the last moments of existence. "Ere it reach that hour," thought he, fixing his gaze upon the dial, "what a change may have come over all my fortunes!" Years—long years—seemed to pass over as he waited thus; scenes of childhood, of infancy itself, mingled with the gay dissipations of his after-life; school days and nights at mess, wild orgies of the play-table and sad wakings on the morrow, all moved through his distracted brain, till at length it was only by an effort that he could shake off these flitting fancies and remember where he was.

He at once bethought him that there was much to be done. He had given Massingbred's letter to his mother, entreating a prompt answer, but two hours had now elapsed and she had not sent her reply. There was a struggle between his better nature and his selfishness whether to seek her. The thought of that sick-room, dark and silent, appalled him. "Is it at such a time I dare ask her to address her mind to this? and yet hours are now stealing over which may decide my whole fate in life." While he thus hesitated, Lady Dorothea entered the room. Nights of anxiety and watching, the workings of a spirit that fought inch by inch with fortune, were deeply marked upon her features. Weariness and fatigue had not brought depression on her, but rather imparted a feverish lustre to her eyes, and an expression of haughty energy to her face.

"Am I to take this for true," said she, as, seating herself in front of him, she held out Massingbred's letter,—"I mean, of course, what relates to yourself?"

He nodded sorrowfully, but did not speak.

"All literally the fact?" said she, speaking slowly, and dwelling on every word. "You have actually sold the reversion of the estate?"

"And am beggared!" said he, sternly.

Lady Dorothea tried to speak. She coughed, cleared her throat, made another effort, but without succeeding; and then, in a slightly broken voice, said, "Fetch me a glass of water. No, sit down; I don't want it." The blood again mounted to her pale cheeks, and she was herself again.

"These are hard terms of Scanlan's," said she, in a dry, stern tone. "He has waited, too, till we have little choice remaining. Your father is worse."

"Worse than when I saw him this morning?"

"Weaker, and less able to bear treatment. He is irritable, too, at that girl's absence. He asks for her constantly, and confuses her in his mind with Mary."

"And what does Schubart think?"

"I'll tell you what he *says*," replied she, with a marked emphasis on the last word. "He says the case is hopeless; he has seen such linger for weeks, but even a day—a day—" She tried to go on; but her voice faltered, her lip trembled, and she was silent.

"I had begun to believe it so," muttered Martin, gloomily. "He scarcely recognized me yesterday."

"He is perfectly collected and sensible now," said Lady Dorothea, in her former calm tone. "He spoke of business matters clearly and well, and wished to see Scanlan."

"Which I trust you did not permit?" asked Martin, hurriedly.

"I told him he should see him this evening, but there is no necessity for it. Scanlan may have left this before evening."

"You suspect that Scanlan would say something,—would mention to him something of this affair?"

"Discretion is not the quality of the low-born and the vulgar," said she, haughtily; "self-importance alone would render him unsafe. Besides,"— and this she said rapidly,—"there is nothing to detain the man here, when he knows that we accept his conditions."

"And are we to accept them?" said Martin, anxiously.

"Dare we refuse them? What is the alternative? I suppose what you have done with your Jew friend has been executed legally—formally?"

"Trust *him* for that; he has left no flaw there!" said Martin, bitterly.

"I was certain of it," said she, with a scarcely perceptible sneer. "Everything, therefore, has been effected according to law?"

"Yes, I believe so," replied he, doggedly.

"Then really there is nothing left to us but Scanlan. He objects to Repton; so do I. I always deemed him obtrusive and familiar. In the management of an Irish estate such qualities may be reckoned essential. I know what we should think of them in England, and I know where we should place their possessor."

"I believe the main question that presses now is, are we to have an estate at all?" said the Captain, bitterly.

"Yes, sir, you have really brought it to that," rejoined she, with equal asperity.

"Do you consent to his having the agency?" asked Martin, with an immense effort to suppress passion.

"Yes."

"And you agree, also, to his proposal for Mary?"

"It is matter of complete indifference to me who Miss Martin marries, if she only continue to reside where she does at present. I 'm certain she 'd not consult *me* on the subject; I'm sure I'd never control *her*. It is a *mésalliance*, to be sure; but it would be equally so, if she, with her rustic habits and uneducated mind, were to marry what would be called her equal. In the present case, she 'll be a little better than her station; in the other, she 'd be vastly beneath it!"

"Poor Molly!" said he, half aloud; and, for the first time, there was a touch of his father's tone and manner in the words.

Lady Dorothea looked at him, and with a slight shrug of the shoulders seemed to sneer at his low-priced compassion.

"Scoff away!" said he, sternly; "but if I thought that any consent we gave to this scheme could take the shape of a coercion, I 'd send the estate to the—"

"You have, sir; you have done all that already," broke in Lady Dorothea. "When the troubled breathing that we hear from yonder room ceases, there is no longer a Martin of Cro' Martin!"

"Then what are we losing time for?" cried he, eagerly. "Are moments so precious to be spent in attack and recrimination? There's Scanlan sitting on a bench before the door. Call him up—tell him you accept his terms—let him start for London, post haste. With every speed he can master he 'll not be a minute too soon. Shall I call him? Shall I beckon to him?"

"Send a servant for him," said Lady Dorothea, calmly, while she folded up the letter, and laid it on the table at her side.

Martin rang the bell and gave the order, and then, assuming an air of composure he was very far from feeling, sat silently awaiting Scanlan's entrance. That gentleman did not long detain them. He had been sitting, watch in hand, for above an hour, looking occasionally up at the windows, and wondering why he had not been summoned. It was, then, with an almost abrupt haste that he at last presented himself.

"Read over that letter, sir," said Lady Dorothea, "and please to inform me if it rightly conveys your propositions."

Scanlan perused Massingbred's letter carefully, and folding it up, returned it. "Yes, my Lady," said he, "I think it embraces the chief points. Of course there is nothing specified as to the mode of carrying them out,—I mean, as to the security I should naturally look for. I believe your Ladyship does not comprehend me?"

"Not in the least, sir."

"Well, if I must speak plainer, I want to be sure that your concurrence is no mere barren concession, my Lady; that, in admitting my pretensions, your Ladyship favors them. This is, of course," said he, in a tone of deference, "if your Ladyship condescends to accept the terms at all; for, as yet, you have not said so."

"If I had not been so minded, sir, this interview would not have taken place."

"Well, indeed, I thought as much myself," said he; "and so I at once entered upon what one might call the working details of the measure."

"How long will it take you to reach London, sir?" asked she, coldly.

"Four days, my Lady, travelling night and day."

"How soon after your arrival there can you make such arrangements as will put this affair out of all danger, using every endeavor in your power?"

"I hope I could answer for that within a week,—maybe, less."

"You'll have to effect it in half that time, sir," said she, solemnly.

"Well, I don't despair of that same, if I have only your Ladyship's promise to all that is set down there. I 'll neither eat nor sleep till the matter is in good train."

"I repeat, sir, that if this settlement be not accomplished in less than a week from the present moment, it may prove utterly valueless."

"I can only say I'll do my best, my Lady. I'd be on the road this minute, if your Ladyship would dismiss me."

"Very well, sir,—you are free. I pledge myself to the full conditions of this letter. Captain Martin binds himself equally to observe them."

"I 'd like it in writing under your Ladyship's hand," said Scanlan, in a half whisper, as though afraid to speak such doubts aloud. "It is not that I have the least suspicion or misgiving in life about your Ladyship's word,— I'd take it for a million of money,—but when I come to make my proposals in person to Miss Mary—"

"There, sir, that will do!" said she, with a disdainful look, as if to repress an explanation so disagreeable. "You need not enter further upon the question. If you address me by letter, I will reply to it."

"There it is, my Lady," said he, producing a sealed epistle, and placing it on the table before her. "I had it ready, just not to be losing time. My London address is inside; and if you'll write to me by to-morrow's post,— or the day after," added he, remarking a movement of impatience in her face—"You shall have your bond, sir,—you shall have your bond," broke she in, haughtily.

"That ought to be enough, I think," said the Captain, with a degree of irritation that bespoke a long internal conflict.

"I want nothing beyond what I shall earn, Captain Martin," said Scanlan, as a flash of angry meaning covered his features.

"And we have agreed to the terms, Mr. Scanlan," said her Ladyship, with a great effort to conciliate. "It only remains for us to say, a good journey, and every success attend you."

"Thank you, my Lady; I'm your most obedient. Captain, I wish you good-bye, and hope soon to send you happy tidings. I trust, if Mr. Martin asks after me, that you 'll give him my respectful duty; and if—"

"We'll forget nothing, sir," said Lady Dorothea, rising; and Scanlan, after a moment's hesitation as to whether he should venture to offer his hand,—a measure for which, happily, he could not muster the courage,— bowed himself out of the room, and closed the door.

"Not a very cordial leave-taking for one that's to be her nephew," muttered he, with a bitter laugh, as he descended the stairs. "And, indeed, my first cousin, the Captain, is n't the model of family affection. Never mind, Maurice, your day is coming!" And with this assuring reflection he issued forth to give orders for his journey.

A weary sigh—the outpouring of an oppressed and jaded spirit—broke from Lady Dorothea as the door closed after him. "Insufferable creature!" muttered she to herself? and then, turning to the Captain, said aloud, "Is that man capable of playing us false?—or, rather, has he the power of doing so?"

"It is just what I have been turning over in my own mind," replied he. "I don't quite trust him; and, in fact, I'd follow him over to London, if I were free at this moment."

"Perhaps you ought to do so; it might be the wisest course," said she, hesitatingly.

"Do you think I could leave this with safety?" asked he. But she did not seem to have heard the question. He repeated it, and she was still silent. "If the doctors could be relied on, they should be able to tell us."

"To tell us what?" asked she, abruptly, almost sternly.

"I meant that they'd know—that they'd perhaps be in a position to judge—that they at least could warn us—" Here he stopped, confused and embarrassed, and quite unable to continue. That sense of embarrassment, however, came less of his own reflections than of the cold, steady, and searching look which his mother never ceased to bend on him. It was a gaze that seemed to imply, "Say on, and let me hear how destitute of all feeling you will avow yourself." It was, indeed, the meaning of her stare, and so he felt it, as the color came and went in his cheek, and a sense of faintish sickness crept over him.

"The post has arrived, my Lady, and I have left your Ladyship's letters on the dressing-table," said a servant. And Lady Dorothea, who had been impatiently awaiting the mall, hastened at once to her room.

CHAPTER XXVI
A LETTER THAT NEVER
REACHES ITS ADDRESS

It was not without a very painful emotion that Lady Dorothea turned over a mass of letters addressed to her husband. They came from various quarters, written in all the moods of many minds. Some were the mere gossip of clubs and dinnerparties,—some were kindly and affectionate inquiries, gentle reproachings on his silence, and banterings about his pretended low spirits. A somewhat favorite tone is that same raillery towards those whose lot in life seems elevated above the casualties of fortune, forgetting the while that the sunniest path has its shadows, and they whom we deem exempt from the sore trials of the world have their share of its sorrows. These read strangely now, as he to whom they were addressed lay breathing the heavy and labored breath, and muttering the low broken murmurs that prelude the one still deeper sleep!

With a tremulous hand, and a gesture of fretful impatience, she threw them from her one after the other. The topics and the tone alike jarred upon her nerves. They seemed so unfeeling, too, and so heartless at such a moment. Oh, if we wanted to moralize over the uncertainty of life, what a theme might we have in the simple fact that, quicker than the lines we are writing fall from our pen, are oftentimes changing the whole fate and fortune of him for whom we destine them! We are telling of hope where despair has already entered,—we are speaking joy to a house of mourning! But one letter alone remained unopened. It was in Repton's hand, and she broke the seal, wondering how he, who of all men hated writing, should have turned a correspondent.

The "strictly confidential" of the cover was repeated within; but the hour had come when she could violate the caution, and she read on. The first few lines were a half-jesting allusion to Martin's croakings about his health; but even these had a forced, constrained air, and none of the jocular ease of the old man's manner. "And yet," continued he, "it is exactly about your health I am most anxious. I want you to be strong and stout, body and mind, ready for action, and resolute. I know the tone and style that an absentee loves and even requires to be addressed in. He wants to be told that, however he may be personally regretted, matters go on wonderfully well in his absence, that rent is paid, farms improved, good markets abound, and the county a pattern of quietness. I could tell you all this, Martin, and not a syllable of it be true. The rents are not paid, partly from a season of great pressure, but, more still, from an expectancy on the side of the people that something—they know not what—is coming. The Relief Bill only relieved those who wanted to job in politics and make market of their opinions; the masses it has scarcely touched. They are told they are emancipated, but I am at a loss to know in what way they realize to their minds the new privilege. Their leaders have seen this. Shrewd fellows as they are, they have guessed what disappointment must inevitably ensue when the long-promised boon can show nothing as its results but certain noisy mob-orators made Parliament men; and so they have slyly hinted,—as yet it is only a hint,—'this is but the first step—an instalment they call it—of a large debt, every fraction of which must yet be paid!'

"Now there is not in all Europe a more cunning or a deeper fellow than Paddy. He has an Italian's subtlety and a Celt's suspicion; but enlist his self-love, his vanity, and his acquisitiveness in any scheme, and all his shrewdness deserts him. The old hackney coach-horses never followed the hay on the end of the pole more hopefully than will he travel after some promised future of 'fine times,' with plenty to eat and drink, and nothing to do for it! They have booked themselves now for this journey, and the delusion must run its course. Meanwhile rents will not be paid, farms not improved, bad prices and poverty will abound, and the usual crop of discontent and its consequent crime. I 'm not going to inflict you with my own opinions on this theme. You know well enough already that I never regarded these 'Agrarian disturbances,' as they are called, in the light of passing infractions of the peace, but traced in them the continuous working of a long preconcerted plan,—the scheme of very different heads from those who worked it,—by which the law should ever be assailed and the right of property everlastingly put in dispute. In plain words, the system was a standing protest against the sway of the Saxons in Ireland! 'The agitators' understood thoroughly how to profit by this, and they worked these alternate moods of outrage and peace pretty much as the priests of old guided their auguries. They brought the game to that perfection that a murder could shake a ministry, or a blank calendar become the triumph of an Administration!

"Such is, at the moment I am writing, the actual condition of Ireland! Come home, then, at once,—but come alone. Come back resolved to see and act for yourself. There is a lingering spark of the old feudalism yet left in the people. Try and kindle it up once more into the old healthful glow of love to the landlord. Some would say it is too late for all this; but I will not think so. Magennis has given us an open defiance; we are to be put on our title. Now, you are well aware there is a complication here, and I shall want to consult you personally; besides, we must have a search through those registries that are locked up in the strong-room. Mary tells me you carried away the key of it. I tell you frankly, I wish we could hit upon some means of stopping Magennis. The suit is a small war, that demands grand preparation,—always a considerable evil! The fellow, I am told, is also concocting another attack,—an action against your niece and others for the forcible abduction of his wife. It would read fabulously enough, such a charge, but as old Casey said, 'There never yet was anything you could n't impute at law, if you only employed the word "conspiracy;"' and I believe it! The woman certainly has deserted him, and her whereabouts cannot be ascertained. The scandal of such a cause would of course be very great; but if you were here we might chance upon some mode of averting it,—at all events, your niece shouldn't be deserted at such a moment. What a noble girl it is, Martin, and how gloriously she comprehends her station! Give me a dozen like her, and I 'll bid defiance to all the machinations of all the agitators; and they know it!

"If your estate has resisted longer than those of your neighbors the demoralizing influences that are now at work here, you owe it to Mary. If crime has not left its track of blood along your avenue or on your door-sill, it is she who has saved you. If the midnight hour has not been scared by the flame of your burning house or haggard, thank *her* for it,—ay, Martin, *her* courage, *her* devotion, *her* watchful charity, *her* unceasing benevolence, the glorious guarantee her daily life gives, that *she*, at least, is with the people in all their sufferings and their trials! You or I had abandoned with impatience the cause that she had succored against every disappointment. Her woman's nature has endowed her with a higher and a nobler energy than ever a man possessed. She *will not* be defeated.

"Henderson may bewail, and Maurice Scanlan deride, the shortcomings of the people. But through evil and good report she is there to hear from their own lips, to see with her own eyes, the story of their sorrows. Is this nothing? Is there no lesson in the fact that she, nurtured in every luxury, braves the wildest day of winter in her mission of charity?—that the most squalid misery, the most pestilent disease never deterred her? I saw her a few days back coming home at daybreak; she had passed the night in a hovel where neither you nor I would have taken shelter in a storm. The hectic flush of fatigue and anxiety was on her cheek; her eyes, deep sunk, showed weariness; and her very voice, as she spoke to me, was tremulous and weak; and of what, think you, was her mind full? Of the noble calm, the glorious, patient endurance of those she had just quitted. 'What lessons might we not learn,' said she, 'beneath the wet thatch of poverty! There are three struck down with fever in that cabin; she who remains to nurse them is a little girl of scarcely thirteen. There is all that can render sickness wretched around them. They are in pain and in want; cold winds and rain sweep across their beds, if we could call them such. If they cherish the love of life, it must be through some instinct above all reason; and there they lie, uncomplaining. The little remnant of their strength exhausts itself in a look of thankfulness,—a faint effort to say their gratitude. Oh, if querulous hypochondriacism could but see them, what teaching it might learn! Sufferings that call forth from us not alone peevishness and impatience, but actually traits of rude and ungenerous meaning, develop in them an almost refined courtesy, and a trustfulness that supplies all that is most choice in words of gratitude.'

"And this is the girl whose life every day, every hour is imperilling,—who encounters all the hazards of our treacherous climate, and all the more fatal dangers of a season of pestilence, without friends, without a home! Now, Martin, apart from all higher and better considerations on the subject, this was not your compact,—such was not the text of your bargain with poor Barry. The pledge you gave him at your last parting was that she should be your daughter. That you made her feel all the affection of one, none can tell more surely than myself. That your own heart responds to her love I am as fully convinced of. But this is not enough, my dear Martin. She has rights—actual rights—that no special pleading on the score of intentions or good wishes can satisfy. I should but unworthily discharge my office, as your oldest friend in the world, if I did not place this before you broadly and plainly. The country is dull and wearisome, devoid of society, and without resources, and you leave it; but you leave behind you, to endure all its monotony, all its weariness, one who possesses every charm and every attention that are valued in the great world! There is fever and plague abroad, insurrection threatens, and midnight disturbances are rife, and she who is to confront these perils is a girl of twenty. The spirit of an invading party threatens to break down all the prestige of old family name and property,—a cunningly devised scheme menaces the existence of an influence that has endured for centuries; and to oppose its working, or fall victim to its onslaught, you leave a young lady, whose very impulses of generous meaning may be made snares to entrap her. In a word, you neglect duty, desert danger, shun the path of honorable exertion, and retreat before the menace of an encounter, to place, where you should stand yourself, the frail figure and gentle nature of one who was a child, as it were, but yesterday. Neither your health nor your happiness can be purchased at such a price,—your conscience is too sound for that,—nor can your ease! No, Martin, your thoughts will stray over here, and linger amongst these lonely glens that she is treading. Your fancy will follow her through the dark nights of winter, as alone she goes forth on her mission of mercy. You will think of her, stooping to teach the young—bending over the sick-bed of age. And then, tracing her footsteps homeward, you will see her sit down by a solitary hearth,—none of her own around her,—not one to advise, to counsel, to encourage her! I will say no more on this theme; your own true heart has already anticipated all that I could *speak*,—all that *you* should *do*.

"Now for one more question, and I shall have finished the most painful letter I ever wrote in my life. There are rumors—I cannot trace them, nor fully understand them, but they imply that Captain Martin has been raising very considerable sums by reversionary bonds and post-obits. Without being able to give even a guess, as to the truth of this, I draw your attention to the bare possibility, as of a case full of very serious complications. Speak to your son at once on the subject, and learn the truth,—the whole truth. My own fears upon the matter have been considerably strengthened by hearing of a person who has been for several weeks back making inquiries on the estate. He has resided usually at Kilkieran, and spends his time traversing the property in all directions, investigating questions of rent, wages, and tenure of land. They tell marvellous stories of his charity and so forth,— blinds, doubtless, to cover his own immediate objects. Mary, however, I ought to say, takes a very different view of his character, and is so anxious to know him personally that I promised her to visit him, and bring him to visit her at the cottage. And, by the way, Martin, why should she be at the cottage,—why not at Cro' Martin? What miserable economy has dictated a change that must reflect upon her influence, not to speak of what is justly due to her own station? I could swear that you never gave a willing consent to this arrangement. No, no, Martin, the plan was never yours.

"I 'm not going to bore you with borough politics. To tell truth, I can't comprehend them. They want to get rid of Massingbred, but they don't see who is to succeed him. Young Nelligan ought to be the man, but he will not. He despises his party,—or at least what would call itself his party,—and is resolved never to concern himself with public affairs. Meanwhile he is carrying all before him at the Bar, and is as sure of the Bench as though he were on it.

"When he heard of Magennis's intention of bringing this action against Mary, he came up to town to ask me to engage him on our side, 'since,' said he, 'if they send me a brief I cannot refuse it, and if I accept it, I promise you it shall be my last cause, for I have resolved to abandon the Bar the day after.' This, of course, was in strictest secrecy, and so you must regard it. He is a cold, calm fellow, and yet on this occasion he seemed full of impulsive action.

"I had something to tell you about Henderson, but I actually forget what it was. I can only remember it was disagreeable; and as this epistle has its due share of bitters, my want of memory is perhaps a benefit; and so to release you at once, I 'll write myself, as I have never ceased to be for forty years,

"Your attached friend,

"Val. Repton."

"I believe I was wrong about Henderson; at least the disagreeable went no further than that he is supposed to be the channel through which Lady Dorothea occasionally issues directions, not always in agreement with Mary's notions. And as your niece never liked the man, the measures are not more palatable when they come through his intervention."

Lady Dorothea was still pondering over this letter, in which there were so many things to consider, when a hurried message called her to the sick-room. As she approached the room, she could hear Martin's voice calling imperiously and angrily to the servants, and ordering them to dress him. The difficulty of utterance seemed to increase his irritation, and gave to his words a harsh, discordant tone, very unlike his natural voice.

"So," cried he, as she entered, "you have come at last. I am nigh exhausted with telling them what I want. I must get up, Dora. They must help me to dress."

As he was thus speaking, the servants, at a gesture from her Ladyship, quietly stole from the chamber, leaving her alone at his bedside.

"You are too weak for this exertion, Godfrey," said she, calmly. "Any effort like this is certain to injure you."

"You think so?" asked he, with the tone of deference that he generally used towards her. "Perhaps you are right, Dora; but how can it be helped?—there is so much to do, such a long way to travel. What a strange confusion is over me! Do you know, Dolly,"—here his voice fell to a mere whisper,—"you'll scarcely credit it; but all the time I have been fancying myself at Cro' Martin, and here we are in—in—what do you call the place?"

"Baden."

"Yes—yes—but the country?"

"Germany."

"Ay, to be sure, Germany; hundreds of miles away from home!" Here he raised himself on one arm, and cast a look of searching eagerness through the room. "Is he gone?" whispered he, timidly.

"Of whom are you speaking?" said she.

"Hush, Dolly, hush!" whispered he, still lower. "I promised I'd not tell any one, even you, of his being here. But I must speak of it—I must—or my brain will turn. He was here—he sat in that very chair—he held my hand within both his own. Poor, poor fellow! how his eyes filled when he saw me! He little knew how changed he himself was!—his hair white as snow, and his eyes so dimmed!"

"This was a dream, Godfrey,—only a dream!"

"I thought you'd say so,—I knew it," said he, sorrowfully; "but I know better. The dear old voice rang in my heart as I used to hear it when a child, as he said, 'Do you remember me?' To be sure I remembered him, and told him to go and fetch Molly; and his brow darkened when I said this, and he drew back his hand and said, 'You have deserted her,—she is not here!'"

"All this is mere fancy, Godfrey; you have been dreaming of home."

"Ay," muttered he, gloomily, "it was but too true; we did desert her, and that was not our bargain, Dolly. It was all the poor fellow asked at our hands,—his last, his only condition. What's that letter you have there?" cried he, impatiently, as Lady Dorothea, in the agitation of the moment, continued to crumple Repton's letter between her fingers.

"A letter I have been reading," said she, sternly.

"From whom—from whom?" asked he, still more eagerly.

"A letter from Mr. Repton. You shall read it when you are better. You are too weak for all this exertion, God-frey; you must submit—"

"Submit!" broke he in; "the very word he said. You submit yourself to anything, if it only purchase your selfish ease. No, Dolly, no, I am wrong. It was I that said so. I owned to him how unworthily I had acted. Give me that letter, madam. Let me see it," said he, imperiously.

"When you are more tranquil, Godfrey,—in a fitting state."

"I tell you, madam," cried he, fiercely, "this, is no time for trifling or deception. Repton knows all our affairs. If he has written now, it is because matters are imminent. My head is clear now. I can think—I can speak. It is full time Harry should hear the truth. Let him come here."

"Take a little rest, Godfrey, be it only half an hour, and you shall have everything as you wish it."

"Half an hour! you speak of half an hour to one whose years are minutes now!" said he, in a broken voice. "This poor brain, Dora, is already wandering. The strange things I have seen so lately—that poor fellow come back after so many years—so changed, so sadly changed—but I knew him through all the mist and vapor of this feverish state; I saw him clearly, my own dear Barry!" The word, as it were the last barrier to his emotion, brought forth a gush of tears; and burying his face within the bedclothes, he sobbed himself to sleep. As he slept, however, he continued to mutter about home and long passed years,—of boyish sports with his brother; childish joys and sorrows were all mingled there, with now and then some gloomier reveries of later days.

"He has been wandering in his mind!" whispered Lady Dorothea to her son, as he joined her in the darkened room. "He woke up, believing that he had seen his brother, and the effect was very painful."

"Has he asked for *me?*" inquired the other.

"No; he rambled on about Mary, and having deserted her, and all that; and just as ill-luck would have it, here is a letter from Repton, exactly filled with the very same theme. He insists on seeing it; but of course he will have forgotten it when he awakes."

"You have written to Scanlan?" asked he.

"Yes; my letter has been sent off."

"Minutes are precious now. If anything should occur here,"—his eyes turned towards the sick-bed as he spoke,—"Merl will refuse to treat. His people—I know they are his—are hovering about the hotel all the morning. I heard the waiter whispering as I passed, and caught the words, 'No better; worse, if anything.' The tidings would be in London before the post."

Lady Dorothea made no reply, and all was now silent, save the unequal but heavy breathings of the sick man, and the faint, low mutterings of his dream. "In the arras—between the window and the wall—there it is, Barry," cried he, in a clear, distinct voice. "Repton has a copy of it, too, with Catty's signature,—old Catty Broon."

"What is he dreaming of?" asked the young man.

But, instead of replying to the question, Lady Dorothea bent down her head to catch the now muttered words of the sleeper.

"He says something of a key. What key does he mean?" asked he.

"Fetch me that writing-desk," said Lady Dorothea, as she took several keys from her pockets; and noiselessly unlocking the box, she began to search amidst its contents. As she continued, her gestures grew more and more hurried; she threw papers recklessly here and there, and at last emptied the entire contents upon the table before her. "See, search if there be a key here," cried she, in a broken voice; "I saw it here three days ago."

"There is none here," said he, wondering at her eagerness.

"Look carefully,—look well for it," said she, her voice trembling at every word.

"Is it of such consequence—"

"It is of such consequence," broke she in, "that he into whose hands it falls can leave you and me beggars on the world!" An effort at awaking by the sick man here made her hastily restore the papers to the desk, which she locked, and replaced upon the table.

"Was it the Henderson did this?" said she aloud, as if asking the question of herself. "Could she have known this secret?"

"Did what? What secret?" asked he, anxiously.

A low, long sigh announced that the sick man was awaking; and in a faint voice he said, "I feel better, Dora. I have had a sleep, and been dreaming of home and long ago. To-morrow, or next day, perhaps, I may be strong enough to leave this. I want to be back there again. Nay, don't refuse me," said he, timidly.

"When you are equal to the journey—"

"I have a still longer one before me, Dora, and even less preparation for it. Harry, I have something to say to you, if I were strong enough to say it,—this evening, perhaps." Wearied by the efforts he had made, he lay back again with a heavy sigh, and was silent.

"Is he worse—is he weaker?" asked his son.

A mournful nod of the head was her reply.

Young Martin arose and stole noiselessly from the room, he scarcely knew whither; he indeed cared not which way he turned. The future threw its darkest shadows before him. He had little to hope for, as little to love. His servant gave him a letter which Massingbred had left on his departure, but he never opened it; and in a listless vacuity he wandered out into the wood.

It was evening as he turned homeward. His first glance was towards the windows of his father's room. They were wont to be closely shuttered and fastened; now one of them lay partly open, and a slight breeze stirred the curtain within. A faint, sickly fear of he knew not what crept over him. He walked on quicker; but as he drew nigh the door, his servant met him. "Well!" cried he, as though expecting a message.

"Yes, sir, it is all over; he went off about an hour since." The man added something; but Martin heard no more, but hurried to his room, and locked the door.

CHAPTER XXVII
A VERY BRIEF INTERVIEW

When Jack Massingbred found himself once more "in town," and saw that the tide of the mighty world there rolled on the same full, boiling flood he had remembered it of yore, he began to wonder where and how he had latterly been spending his life. There were questions of politics—mighty interests of which every one was talking—of which he knew nothing; party changes and new social combinations had arisen of which he was utterly ignorant. But what he still more acutely deplored was that he himself had, so to say, dropped out of the memory of his friends, who accosted him with that half-embarrassed air that says, "Have you been ill?—or in India?—or how is it that we have n't met you about?" It was last session he had made a flash speech,—an effort that his own party extolled to the skies, and even the Opposition could only criticise the hardihood and presumption of so very young a member of the House,—and now already people had ceased to bear him in mind.

The least egotistical of men—and Massingbred did not enter into this category—find it occasionally very hard to bear the cool "go-by" the world gives them whenever a chance interval has withdrawn them from public view. The stern truth of how little each atom of the social scheme affects the working of the whole machinery is far from palatable in its personal application. Massingbred was probably sensitive enough on this score, but too consummate a tactician to let any one guess his feelings; and so he lounged down to the "House," and lolled at his Club, and took his airings in the Park with all the seeming routine of one who had never abdicated these enjoyments for a day.

He had promised, and really meant, to have looked after Martin's affairs on his reaching London; but it was almost a week after his return that he bethought him of his pledge, his attention being then called to the subject by finding on his table the visiting-card of Mr. Maurice Scanlan. Perhaps he was not sorry to have something to do; perhaps he had some compunctions of conscience for his forgetfulness; at all events, he sent his servant at once to Scanlan's hotel, with a request that he would call upon him as early as might be. An answer was speedily returned that Mr. Scanlan was about to start for

Ireland that same afternoon, but would wait upon him immediately. The message was scarcely delivered when Scanlan himself appeared.

Dressed in deep mourning, but with an easy complacency of manner that indicated very little of real grief, he threw himself into a chair, saying, "I pledge you my word of honor, it is only to yourself I 'd have come this morning, Mr. Massingbred, for I 'm actually killed with business. No man would believe the letters I've had to read and answer, the documents to examine, the deeds to compare, the papers to investigate—"

"Is the business settled, then—or in train of settlement?" broke in Jack.

"I suppose it *is* settled," replied Scanlan, with a slight laugh. "Of course you know Mr. Martin is dead?"

"Dead! Good heavens! When did this occur?"

"We got the news—that is, Merl did—the day before yesterday. A friend of his who had remained at Baden to watch events started the moment he breathed his last, and reached town thirty hours before the mail; not, indeed, that the Captain has yet written a line on the subject to any one."

"And what of the arrangement? Had you come to terms previously with Merl?"

"No; he kept negotiating and fencing with us from day to day, now asking for this, now insisting on that, till the evening of his friend's arrival, when, by special appointment, I had called to confer with him. Then, indeed, he showed no disposition for further delay, but frankly told me the news, and said, 'The Conferences are over, Scanlan. I 'm the Lord of Cro' Martin.'"

"And is this actually the case,—has he really established his claim in such a manner as will stand the test of law and the courts?"

"He owns every acre of it; there's not a flaw in his title; he has managed to make all Martin's debts assume the shape of advances in hard cash. There is no trace of play transactions throughout the whole. I must be off, Mr. Massing-bred; there 's the chaise now at the door."

"Wait one moment, I entreat of you. Can nothing be done? Is it too late to attempt any compromise?"

"To be sure it is. He has sent off instructions already to serve the notice for ejectment. I 've got orders myself to warn the tenants not to pay the last half-year, except into court."

"Why, are *you* in Mr. Merl's service, then?" asked Jack, with one of his quiet laughs.

"I am, and I am not," said Scanlan, reddening. "You know the compact I made with Lady Dorothea at Baden. Well, of course there is no longer any question about that. Still, if Miss Mary agrees to accept me, I'll stand by the old family! There's no end of trouble and annoyance we could n't give Merl before he got possession. I know the estate well, and where the worst fellows on it are to be found! It's one thing to have the parchments of a property, and it is another to be able to go live on it, and draw the rents. But I can't stay another minute. Good-bye, air. Any chance of seeing you in the West soon?"

"I'm not sure I'll not go over to-morrow," said Jack, musing.

"I suppose you are going to blarney the constituency?" said Maurice, laughing heartily at his coarse conceit. Then suddenly seeing that Massingbred did not seem to relish the freedom, he hurriedly repeated his leave-takings, and departed.

CHAPTER XXVIII
THE DARK SIDE OF A CHARACTER

"Ye might ken the style of these epistles by this time, Dinah," said Mr. Henderson, as he walked leisurely up and down a long low-ceilinged room, and addressed himself to a piece of very faded gentility, who sat at a writing-table. "She wants to hear naething but what she likes, and, as near as may be, in her ain words too."

"I always feel as if I was copying out the same letter every time I write," whined out a weak, sickly voice.

"The safest thing ye could do," replied he, gravely. "She never tires o' reading that everybody on the estate is a fule or a scoundrel, and ye canna be far wrang when ye say the worst o' them all. Hae ye told her aboot the burnin' at Kyle-a-Noe?"

"Yes, I have said that you have little doubt it was malicious."

"And hae ye said that there's not a sixpence to be had out of the whole townland of Kiltimmon?"

"I have. I have told her that, except Miss Mary herself, nobody would venture into the barony."

"The greater fule yerself, then," said he, angrily. "Couldna ye see that she'll score this as a praise o' the young leddy's courage? Ye maun just strike it out, ma'am, and say that the place is in open rebellion—"

"I thought you bade me say that Miss Mary had gone down there and spoken to the people—"

"I bade ye say," broke he angrily in, "that Miss Mary declared no rent should be demanded o' them in their present distress; that she threw the warrants into the fire, and vowed that if we called a sale o' their chattels, she 'd do the same at the castle, and give the people the proceeds."

"You only said that she was in such a passion that she declared she 'd be right in doing so."

"I hae nae time for hair-splitting, ma'am. I suppose if she had a right she 'd exercise it! Put down the words as I gie them to ye! Ye hae no forgotten the conspeeracy?"

"I gave it exactly as you told me, and I copied out the two paragraphs in the papers about it, beginning, 'Great scandal,' and 'If our landed gentry expect—'"

"That's right; and ye hae added the private history of Joan? They 'll make a fine thing o' that on the trial, showing the chosen associate o' a young leddy to hae been naething better than—Ech! what are ye blubberin' aboot,—is it yer feelin's agen? Ech! ma'am, ye are too sentimental for a plain man like me!"

This rude speech was called up by a smothering effort to conceal emotion, which would not be repressed, but burst forth in a violent fit of sobbing.

"I know you didn't mean it. I know you were not thinking—"

"If ye canna keep your ain counsel, ye must just pay the cost o' it," said he, savagely. "Finish the letter there, and let me send it to the post. I wanted ye to say a' about the Nelligans comin' up to visit Miss Mary, and she goin' ower the grounds wi' them, and sendin' them pineapples and grapes, and how that the doctor's girls are a'ways wi' her, and that she takes old Catty out to drive along wi' herself in the pony phaeton, which is condescendin' in a way her Leddyship will no approve o'. There was mony a thing beside I had in my head, but ye hae driven them a' clean awa' wi' your feelin's!" And he gave the last word with an almost savage severity.

"Bide a wee!" cried he, as she was folding up the letter. "Ye may add that Mister Scanlan has taken to shootin' over the preserves we were keepin' for the Captain, and if her Leddyship does not wish to banish the woodcocks a'the-gither, she 'd better gie an order to stop him. Young Nelli-gan had a special permission from Miss Mary hersel' and if it was na that he canna hit a haystack at twenty yards, there 'd no be a cock pheasant in the demesne! I think I 'm looking at her as she reads this," said he, with a malicious grin. "Ech, sirs, won't her great black eyebrows meet on her forehead, and her mouth be drawn in till never a bit of a red lip be seen! Is na that a chaise I see comin' up the road?" cried he, suddenly. "Look yonder!"

"I thought I saw something pass," said she, trying to strain her eyes through the tears that now rose to them.

"It's a post-chaise wi' twa trunks on the top. I wonder who's comin' in it?" said Henderson, as he opened the sash-door, and stood awaiting the arrival. The chaise swept rapidly round the beech copse, and drew up before the door; the postilion, dismounting, lowered the steps, and assisted a lady to alight. She threw back her veil as she stood on the ground, and Kate Henderson, somewhat jaded-looking and pale from her journey, was before her father. A slight flush—very slight—rose to his face as he beheld her, and without uttering a word he turned and re-entered the house.

"Ye are aboot to see a visitor, ma'am," said he to his wife; and, taking his hat, passed out of the room. Meanwhile Kate watched the postboy as he untied the luggage and deposited it at her side.

"Did n't I rowl you along well, my Lady?—ten miles in little more than an hour," said he, pointing to his smoking cattle.

"More speed than we needed," said she, with a melancholy smile, while she placed some silver in his hand.

"What's this here, my Lady? It's like one of the owld tenpenny bits," said he, turning over and over a coin as he spoke.

"It's French money," said she, "and unfortunately I have got none other left me."

"Sure they'll give you what you want inside," said he, pointing towards the house.

"No, no; take this. It is a crown piece, and they'll surely change it for you in the town." And so saying, she turned towards the door. When she made one step towards it, however, she stopped. A painful irresolution seemed to possess her; but, recovering it, she turned the handle and entered.

"We did not know you were coming; at least, he never told me," said her stepmother, in a weak, broken voice, as she arose from her seat.

"There was no time to apprise you," said Kate, as she walked towards the fire and leaned her arm on the chimney-piece.

"You came away suddenly, then? Had anything unpleasant—was there any reason—"

"I had been desirous of leaving for some time back. Lady Dorothea only gave her consent on Tuesday last,—I think it was Tuesday; but my head is not very clear, for I am somewhat tired." There was an indescribable sadness in the way these simple words were uttered and in the sigh which followed them.

"I 'm afraid he 'll not be pleased at it!" said the other, timidly.

Another sigh, but still weaker than the former, was Kate's only reply.

"And how did you leave Mr. Martin? They tell us here that his case is hopeless," said Mrs. Henderson.

"He is very ill, indeed; the doctors give no hope of saving him. Is Miss Martin fully aware of his state?"

"Who can tell? We scarcely ever see her. You know that she never was very partial to your father, and latterly there has been a greater distance than ever between them. They differ about everything; and with that independent way he has—"

A wide stare from Kate's full dark eyes, an expression of astonishment, mingled with raillery, in her features, here arrested the speaker, who blushed deeply in her embarrassment.

"Go on," said Kate, gently. "Pray continue, and let me hear what it is that his independence accomplishes."

"Oh, dear!" sighed the other. "I see well you are not changed, Kate. You have come back with your old haughty spirit, and sure you know well, dear, that he 'll not bear it."

"I 'll not impose any burden on his forbearance. A few days' shelter—a week or two at furthest—will not be, perhaps, too much to ask."

"So, then, you have a situation in view, Kate?" asked she, more eagerly.

"The world is a tolerably wide one, and I 'm sure there is room for me somewhere, even without displacing another. But let us talk of anything else. How are the Nelligans? and Joe, what is he doing?"

"The old people are just as you left them; but Mr. Joseph is a great man now,—dines with the Lord-Lieutenant, and goes into all the grand society of Dublin."

"Is he spoiled by his elevation?"

"Your father thinks him haughtier than he used to be; but many say that he is exactly what he always was. Mrs. Nelligan comes up frequently to the cottage now, and dines with Miss Martin. I 'm sure I don't know how my Lady would like to see her there."

"She is not very likely," said Kate, dryly.

"Why not?"

"I mean, that nothing is less probable than Lady Dorothea's return here."

"I suppose not!" half sighed Mrs. Henderson, for hers was one of those sorrowful temperaments that extract only the bitter from the cup of life. In reality, she had little reason to wish for Lady Dorothea's presence, but still she could make a "very good grievance" out of her absence, and find it a fitting theme for regret. "What reason do you mean to give for your coming home, Kate, if he should ask you?" inquired she, after a pause.

"That I felt dissatisfied with my place," replied Kate, coldly.

"And we were always saying what a piece of good luck it was for you to be there! Miss Mary told Mrs. Nelligan—it was only the other day—that her uncle could n't live without you,—that you nursed him, and read to him, and what not; and as to her Ladyship, that she never took a drive in the carriage, or answered a note, without asking your advice first."

"What a profound impression Miss Martin must have received of my talents for intrigue!" said Kate, sneeringly.

"I believe not. I think she said something very kind and good-natured, just as if it was only people who had really very great gifts that could condescend to make themselves subservient without humiliation. I know she said 'without humiliation,' because your father laughed when he heard of it, and remarked, 'If it's Kate's humility they like, they are assuredly thankful for small mercies!'"

"I should like to go over and see Miss Martin. What distance is it from this to the cottage?"

"It's full three miles; but it's all through the demesne."

"I'm a good walker, and I'll go," said she, rising. "But first, might I ask for a little refreshment,—a cup of tea? Oh, I forgot," added she, smiling, "tea is one of the forbidden luxuries here."

"No; but your father doesn't like to see it in the daytime. If you'd take it in your own room—"

"Of course, and be most thankful. Am I to have the little room with the green paper, where I used to be, long ago?"

"Well, indeed, I can scarcely tell. The bed was taken down last autumn; and as we never thought of your coming home—"

"Home!" sighed Kate, involuntarily.

"But come into my room, and I 'll fetch you a cup of tea directly."

"No, no; it is better not to risk offending him," said Kate, calmly. "I remember, now, that this was one of his antipathies. Give me anything else, for I have not eaten to-day."

While her stepmother went in search of something to offer her, Kate sat down beside the fire, deep in thought. She had removed her bonnet, and her long silky hair fell in rich masses over her neck and shoulders, giving a more fixed expression to her features, which were of deathlike paleness.

And so she sat, gazing intently on the fire, as though she were reading her very destiny in the red embers before her. Her preoccupation of mind was such that she never noticed the opening of the door, nor remarked that her father had entered. The noise of a chair being moved suddenly startled her. She looked up, and there he stood, his hat on his head and his arms closely folded on his breast, at the opposite side of the fire.

"Well, lassie," said he, after a long and steady stare at her, "ye hae left your place, or been turned oot o' it,—whilk is the case?"

"I came away of my own accord," said she, calmly.

"And against my Leddy's wish?"

"No, with her full consent."

"And how did ye do it? for in her last letter to my sel', she says, 'I desire ye, therefore, to bear in mind that any step she takes on this head'— meaning about going away—'shall have been adopted in direct opposition to my wishes.' What has ye done since that?"

"I have succeeded in convincing her Ladyship that I was right in leaving her!" said Kate.

"Was it the force of your poleetical convictions that impelled ye to this course?" said he, with a bitter grin, "for they tell me ye are a rare champion o' the rights o' the people, and scruple not to denounce the upper classes, while ye eat their bread."

"I denounce no one; nor, so far as I know myself, is ingratitude amongst my faults."

"Maybe, if one were to tak' your ain narrative for it, ye hae nae faults worse than mere failings! But this is na telling me why ye left my Leddy."

Kate made no answer, but sat steadily watching the fire.

"Ye wad rayther, mayhap, that I asked hersel' aboot it! Well, be it so. And noo comes anither point. Do ye think that if your conduct has in any way given displeasure to your mistress, or offended those in whose service ye were,—do ye think, I say, that ye hae the right to involve *me* in your shame and disgrace?"

"Do you mean," said she, calmly, "that I had no right to come here?"

"It 's just exactly what I mean; that if ye canna mak' friends for yoursel', ye ought not to turn away those whilk befriend your family."

"But what was I to have done, then?" said she, gently. "There were circumstances that required—imperatively required me—to leave Lady Dorothea—"

"Let me hear them," said he, breaking in, "It would lead me to speak of others than myself,—of events which are purely family matters,—were I to enter upon this theme. Besides," said she, rising, "I am not, so far as I know, on my trial. There is not anything laid to my charge. I have no apologies to render."

At this moment her stepmother appeared with a tray at the door, and seeing Henderson, endeavored to retire unobserved, but his quick eye had already detected her, and he cried out, "Come here,—ye canna do too much honor to a young leddy who has such a vara profound esteem for hersel'! Cake and wine! my faith! No but ye 'll deem it vara vulgar fare, after the dainties ye hae been used to! And yet, lassie, these are nae the habits here!"

"She has eaten nothing to-day!" meekly observed her stepmother.

"My fayther wad hae askit her hoo much has she earned the day?" said Henderson, severely.

"You are quite right, sir," broke in Kate,—"I have earned nothing. Not just yet," added she, as her stepmother pressed a glass of wine on her acceptance; "a little later, perhaps. I have no appetite now."

"Are ye sae stupid, ma'am, that ye canna see ye are dealin' wi' a fine leddy, wha is no obleeged to hae the same mind twa minutes thegither? Ye 'll hae to train wee Janet to be a' ready for whate'er caprice is uppermost. But mine me, lassie,"—here he turned a look of stern meaning towards her,—"ye hae tried for mony a lang day to subdue *me* to your whims and fancies, as they tell me ye hae done wi' sae mony others, and ye are just as far fra it noo as the first time ye tried it. Ye canna cheat nor cajole *me! I* know ye!" And with these words, uttered in a tone of intense passion, he slowly walked out of the room.

"Had he been angry with you?—had anything occurred before I came in?" asked her stepmother.

"Very little," sighed Kate, wearily. "He was asking me why I came here, I believe. I could scarcely tell him; perhaps I don't very well know, myself."

"He can't get it out of his head," said the other, in a low, stealthy whisper, "that, if you should leave Lady Dorothea, he will be turned away out of the stewardship. He is always saying it,—he repeats it even in his dreams. But for that, he 'd not have met you so—so—unkindly."

Kate pressed her hand affectionately, and smiled a thankful acknowledgment of this speech. "And the cottage," said she, rallying suddenly, "is about three miles off?"

"Not more. But you could scarcely walk there and back again. Besides, it is already growing late, and you have no chance of seeing Miss Mary if you 're not there by breakfast-time, since, when she comes home of an evening, she admits no one. She reads or studies, I believe, all the evening."

"I think she'd see me," said Kate; "I should have so much to tell her about her friends. I 'm sure she 'd see *me*,—at least, I'll try."

"But you'll eat something,—you 'll at least drink a glass of wine before you set out?"

"I do not like to refuse you," said Kate, smiling good-naturedly, "but I could n't swallow now. I have a choking feeling here in my throat, like a heavy cold, that seems as though it would suffocate me. Good-bye, for a while. I shall be quite well, once I 'm in the open air. Good-bye!" And, so saying, she wrapped her shawl around her, and motioning a farewell with her hand, set out on her errand.

CHAPTER XXIX
THE COTTAGE

It was one of those fresh and breezy days where brilliant flashes of sunlight alternate with deep shadow, making of every landscape a succession of pictures, that Kate Henderson set out on her way to the cottage. Her path led through the demesne, but it was as wild as any forest scene in Germany, now wending through dark woods, now issuing forth over swelling lawns, from which the view extended many a mile away,—at one moment displaying the great rugged mountains of Connemara, and at another, the broad blue sea, heaving heavily, and thundering in sullen roar against the rocks.

The fast-flitting clouds, the breezy grass, the wind-shaken foliage, and the white-crested waves, all were emblems of life; there was motion and sound and conflict! and yet to her heart, as she walked along, these influences imparted no sense of pleasure or relief. For a few seconds, perhaps, would she suddenly awake to the consciousness of the fair scene before her, and murmur to herself, perchance, the lines of some favorite poet; but in another moment her gloomy thoughtfulness was back again, and with bent-down head was she again moving onward. At times she walked rapidly forward, and then, relaxing her pace, she would stroll listlessly along, as though no object engaged her. And so was it in reality,—her main desire being to be free, in the open air; to be from beneath that roof whose shadow seemed to darken her very heart! Could that haughty spirit have humbled itself in sorrow, she might have found relief; but her proud nature had no such resource, and in her full heart injury and wrong had alone their place.

"And this," burst she forth at length,—"and this is Home! this the dreamland of those far away over the seas,—the cherished spot of all affections,—the quiet nook wherein we breathe an atmosphere of love, blending our lives with all dearest to us. Is it, then, that all is hollow, false, and untrue; or is it that I alone have no part in the happiness that is diffused around me? I know not which would be the sadder!"

Thus, reasoning sadly, she went along, when suddenly, on the slope of a gentle hill in front of her, gracefully encircled with a young wood of larch and copper-beech, she caught sight of the cottage. It was a tasteful imitation of those seen in the Oberland, and with its wild background of lofty mountain, an appropriate ornament to the landscape.

A small stream running over a rocky, broken bed formed the boundary of the little grounds, and over this a bridge of a single plank conducted the way to the cottage. The whole was simple and unpretending; there was none of that smart trimness which gives to such scenes the air of an imitation. The lawn, it is true, was neatly shaven, and the flower-plots, which broke its uniformity, clean from weeds; but the flowers were of the simplest kind, — the crocus and the daffodil had to stand no dangerous rivalry, and the hyacinth had nothing to vie with.

Kate loitered for some time here, now gazing at the wild, stern landscape, now listening to the brawling rivulet, whose sounds were the only ones in the stillness. As she drew nigh the cottage, she found the windows of a little drawing-room open. She looked in: all was comfortable and neat-looking, but of the strictest simplicity. She next turned to the little porch, and pulled the bell; in a few seconds the sounds of feet were heard approaching, and a very old woman, whose appearance and dress were the perfection of neatness, appeared.

"Don't you know me, Mrs. Broon?" said Kate, gently.

"I do not, then, my Lady," said she, respectfully, "for my eyes is gettin' dimmer every day."

"I 'm Kate Henderson, Mrs. Broon. Do you forget me?"

"Indeed I do not," said Catty, gravely. "You were here with the master and my Lady?"

"Yes. I went away with them to Germany; but I have come home for a while, and wish to pay my respects to Miss Mary."

"She isn't at home to-day," was the dry response.

"But she will return soon, I conclude. She'll be back some time in the evening, won't she?"

"If she plazes it, she will. There's nobody to control or make her do but what she likes herself," said Catty.

"I ask," said Kate, "because I'm a little tired. I've come off a long journey, and if you'd allow me to rest myself, and wait awhile in the hope of seeing Miss Martin, I'd be very thankful."

"Come in, then," said Catty; but the faint sigh with which the words were uttered, gave but a scant significance of welcome.

Kate followed her into the little drawing-room, and at a sign from the old woman, took a seat.

"Miss Mary is quite well, I'm glad to hear," said Kate, endeavoring to introduce some conversation.

"Will they ever come back?" asked the old woman, in a stern, harsh voice, while she paid no attention whatever to Kate's remark.

"It is very unlikely," said Kate. "Your poor master had not long to live when I came away. He was sinking rapidly."

"So I heard," muttered the other, dryly; "the last letter from Mr. Repton said 'he was n't expected.'"

"I fear it will be a great shock to Miss Mary," said Kate.

The old woman nodded her head slowly several times without speaking.

"And, perhaps, cause great changes here?" continued Kate.

"There's changes enough, and too many already," muttered Catty. "I remember the place upwards of eighty years. I was born in the little house to the right of the road as you come up from Kelly's mills. There was no mill there then, nor a school-house, no, nor a dispensary either! Musha, but the people was better off, and happier, when they had none of them."

Kate smiled at the energy with which these words were uttered, surmising, rightfully, that Catty's condemnation of progress had a direct application to herself.

"Now it's all readin' and writin', teachin' honest people to be rogues, and givin' them new contrivances to cheat their masters. When I knew Cro' Martin first," added she, almost fiercely, "there was n't a Scotch steward on the estate; but there was nobody turned out of his houldin', and there was n't a cabin unroofed to make the people seek shelter under a ditch."

"The world would then seem growing worse every day," remarked Kate, quietly.

"To be sure it is. Why would n't it? Money is in every one's heart. Nobody cares for his own flesh and blood. 'T is all money! What will I get if I take that farm over another man's head, or marry that girl that likes somebody better than me? 'Tis to be rich they're all strivin', and the devil never made people his own children so completely as by teachin' them to love goold!"

"Your young mistress has but little of this spirit in her heart?" said Kate.

"Signs on it! look at the life she leads: up before daybreak, and away many times before I'm awake. She makes a cup of coffee herself, and saddles the pony, too, if Patsey is n't there to do it; and she's off to Glentocher, or Knock-mullen, twelve, fourteen miles down the coast, with barley for one, and a bottle of wine for the other. Sometimes she has a basket with her, just a load to carry, with tay and shugar; ay, and—for she forgets nothing—toys for the children, too, and clothes, and even books. And then to see herself, she's not as well dressed as her own maid used to be. There's not a night she does n't sit up patchin' and piecin' her clothes. 'T is Billy at the cross-roads made her shoes last time for her, just because he was starvin' with nothing' to do. She ordered them, and she wears them, too; it makes him so proud, she says, to see them. And this is the niece of the Martins of Cro' Martin! without one of her kith or kin to welcome her home at nightfall,— without father or mother, brother or sister,—without a kind voice to say 'God bless her,' as she falls off to sleep many a time in that big chair there; and I take off her shoes without her knowin' it, she does be so weary and tired; and in her dhrames it's always talking to the people, givin' them courage, and cheerin' them up, tellin' them there's good times for every one; and once, the other evenin', she sang a bit of a song, thinkin' she was in Mat Leahy's cabin amusin' the children, and she woke up laughin', and said, 'Catty, I've had such a pleasant dhrame. I thought I had little Nora, my godchild, on my knee, and was teachin' her "Why are the daisies in the grass?" I can't tell you how happy I felt!' There it was: the only thing like company to her poor heart was a dhrame!"

"I do not wonder that you love her, Catty," said Kate; and the words fell tremulously from her lips.

"Love her! what's the use of such as me lovin' her?" cried the old woman, querulously. "Sure, it's not one of my kind knows how good she is! If you only seen her comin' in here, after dark, maybe, wet and weary and footsore, half famished with cold and hunger,—out the whole livelong day, over the mountains, where there was fever and shakin' ague, and starvin' people, ravin' mad between disease and destitution; and the first word out of her mouth will be, 'Oh, Catty, how grateful you and I ought to be with our warm roof over us, and our snug fire to sit at,' never thinkin' of who she is and what she has the right to, but just makin' herself the same as *me*. And then she'd tell me where she was, and what she seen, and how well the people was bearin' up under their trials,—all the things they said to her, for they'd tell her things they would n't tell the priest. 'Catty,' said she, t' other night, 'it looks like heartlessness in me to be in such high spirits in the midst of all this misery here; but I feel as if my courage was a well that others were drinking out of; and when I go into a cabin, the sick man, as he turns his head round, looks happier, and I feel as if it was my spirit that was warmin' and cheerin' him; and when a poor sick sufferin' child looks up at me and smiles, I 'm ready to drop on my knees and thank God in gratitude.'"

Kate covered her face with her hands, and never spoke; and now the old woman, warming with the theme she loved best, went on to tell various incidents and events of Mary's life,—the perilous accidents which befell her, the dangers she braved, the fatigues she encountered. Even recounted by *her*, there was a strange adventurous character that ran through these recitals, showing that Mary Martin, in all she thought and said and acted, was buoyed and sustained by a sort of native chivalry that made her actually court the incidents where she incurred the greatest hazard. It was plain to see what charm such traits possessed for her who recorded them, and how in her old Celtic blood ran the strong current of delight in all that pertained to the adventurous and the wild.

"'Tis her own father's nature is strong in her," said Catty, with enthusiasm. "Show him the horse that nobody could back, tell him of a storm where no fisherman would launch his boat, point out a cliff that no man could climb, and let me see who 'd hould him! She 's so like him, that when there 's anything daring to be done you would n't know her voice from his own. There, now, I hear her without," cried the old woman, as, rising suddenly, she approached the window. "Don't you hear something?"

"Nothing but the wind through the trees," said Kate.

"Ay, but *I* did, and my ears are older than yours. She's riding through the river now; I hear the water splashin'."

Kate tried to catch the sounds, but could not; she walked out upon the lawn to listen, but except the brawling of the stream among the rocks, there was nothing to be heard.

"D' ye see her comin'?" asked Catty, eagerly.

"No. Your ears must have deceived you. There is no one coming."

"I heard her voice, as I hear yours now. I heard her spake to the mare, as she always does when she 's plungin' into the river. There, now, don't you hear that?"

"I hear nothing, I assure you, my dear Mrs. Broon. It is your own anxiety that is misleading you; but if you like, I'll go down towards the river and see." And without waiting for a reply Kate hastened down the slope. As she went, she could not help reflecting over the superstition which attaches so much importance to these delusions, giving them the character of actual warnings. It was doubtless from the mind dwelling so forcibly on Miss Martin's perilous life that the old woman's apprehensions had assumed this palpable form, and thus invented the very images which should react upon her with terror.

"Just as I thought," cried Kate, as she stood on the bank of the stream; "all silent and deserted, no one within sight." And slowly she retraced her steps towards the cottage. The old woman stood at the door, pale and trembling; an attempt to smile was on her features, but her heart denied the courage of the effort.

"Where is she now?" cried Catty, wildly. "She rang the bell this minute, and I heerd the mare trottin' round to the stable by herself, as she always does. But where's Miss Mary?"

"My dear Mrs. Broon," said Kate, in her kindest accents, "it is just as I told you. Your mind is anxious and uneasy about Miss Martin; you are unhappy at her absence, and you think at every stir you hear her coming; but I have been to the river-side, and there is no one there. I'll go round to the stables, if you wish it."

"There's no tracks of a hoof on the gravel," muttered the old woman, in a broken voice; "there was nobody here!"

"So I said," replied Kate. "It was a mere delusion,—a fancy."

"A delusion,—a fancy!" cried Catty, scornfully; "that's the way they always spake of whatever they don't understand. It's easier to say that than confess you don't see how to explain a thing; but I heerd the same sounds before you came to-day; ay, and I went down to see why she wasn't comin', and at the pool there was bubbles and froth on the water, just as if a baste had passed through, but no livin' thing to be seen. Wasn't that a delusion, too?"

"An accident, perchance. Only think, what lives of misery we should lead were we ever tracing our own fears, and connecting them with all the changes that go on around us!"

"It's two days she's away, now," muttered the old woman, who only heeded her own thoughts; "she was to be back last night, or early this mornin'."

"Where had she gone to?" asked Kate, who now saw that the other had lapsed into confidence.

"She's gone to the islands!—to Innishmore, and maybe, on to Brannock!"

"That's a long way out to sea," said Kate, thoughtfully; "but still, the weather is fine, and the day favorable. Had she any other object than pleasure in this excursion?"

"Pleasure is it?" croaked Catty. "'Tis much pleasure she does be given herself! Her pleasure is to be where there 's fever and want,—in the lonely cabin, where the sick is lyin'! It 's to find a poor crayture that run away from home she 's gone now,—one Joan Landy. She's missin' this two months, and nobody knows where she 's gone to! and Miss Mary got so uneasy at last that she could n't sleep by night nor rest by day,—always talkin' about her, and say in' as much as it was all her fault; as if *she* could know why she went, or where?"

"Did she go alone on this errand, then?"

"To be sure she did. Who could she have with her? She towld Loony she 'd want the boat with four men in it, and maybe to stay out three days, for she 'd go to all the islands before she came back."

"Loony 's the best sailor on the coast, I 've heard; and with such weather as this there is no cause for alarm."

Catty did not seem to heed the remark; she felt that within her against which the words of consolation availed but little, and she sat brooding sorrowfully and in silence.

"The night will soon be fallin' now," said she, at last. "I hope she's not at sea!"

In spite of herself, Kate Henderson caught the contagion of the old woman's terrors, and felt a dreamy, undefined dread of coming evil. As she looked out, however, at the calm and fair landscape, which, as day declined, grew each moment more still, she rallied from the gloomy thoughts, and said,—"I wish I knew how to be of any service to you, Mrs. Broon. If you could think of anything I could do—anywhere I could go—" She stopped suddenly at a gesture from the old woman, who, lifting her hand to impress silence, stood a perfect picture of eager anxiety to hear. Bending down her head, old Catty stood for several seconds motionless.

"Don't ye hear it now?" broke she in. "Listen! I thought I heerd something like a wailin' sound far off, but it is the wind. See how the tree-tops are bendin'!—That's three times I heerd it now," said Catty. "If ye live to be as old as me, you 'll not think light of a warnin'. You think your hearin' better because you're younger; but I tell you that there 's sounds that only reach ears that are goin' to where the voices came from. When eyes grow dim to sights of this world, they are strainin' to catch a glimpse of them that's beyond it." Although no tears rose to her eyes, the withered face trembled in her agony, and her clasped hands shook in the suffering of her sorrow.

Against impressions of this sort, Kate knew well enough how little reasoning availed, and she forbore to press arguments which she was aware would be unsuccessful. She tried, however, to turn the current of the old woman's thoughts, by leading her to speak of the condition of the country and the state of the people. Catty gave short, abrupt, and unwilling answers to all she asked, and Kate at length arose to take her leave.

"You're goin' away, are ye?" said Catty, half angrily.

"I have only just remembered that I have a long way to walk, and it is already growing late."

"Ay, and ye 're impatient to be back again, at home, beside your own fire, with your own people. But *she* has no home, and her own has deserted her!"

"Mine has not many charms for me!" muttered Kate to herself.

"It's happy for you that has father and mother," went on the old woman. "Them 's the only ones, after all!—the only ones that never loves the less, the less we desarve it! I don't wonder ye came back again!" And in a sort of envious bitterness Catty wished her a good-night.

If the distance she had to walk was not shortened by the tenor of her thoughts, as little did she feel impatient to press onward. Dreary and sad enough were her reveries. Of the wild visionary ambitions which once had stirred her heart, there remained nothing but disappointments. She had but passed the threshold of life to find all dreary and desolate; but perhaps the most painful feeling of the moment was the fact that now pressed conviction on her, and told that in the humble career of such a one as Mary Martin there lay a nobler heroism and a higher devotion than in the most soaring path of political ambition, and that all the theorizing as to popular rights made but a sorry figure beside the actual benefits conferred by one true-hearted lover of her kind. "She is right, and I am wrong!" muttered she to herself. "In declining to entertain questions of statecraft she showed herself above, and not beneath, the proud position she had taken. The very lowliness of this task is its glory. Oh, if I could but win her confidence and be associated in such a labor! and yet my very birth denies me the prestige that hers confers." And then she thought of home, and all the coldness of that cheerless greeting smote upon her heart.

The moon was up ere Kate arrived at her father's door. She tapped at it gently, almost timidly. Her stepmother, as if expecting her, came quickly, and in a low, cautious whisper told her that she would find her supper ready in her bedroom.

"To-morrow, perhaps, he may be in better humor or better spirits. Good-night." And so Kate silently stole along to her room, her proud heart swelling painfully, and her tearless eye burning with all the heat of a burning brain.

CHAPTER XXX
"A TEA-PARTY" AT MRS. CRONAN'S

Once more, but for the last time, we are at Kilkieran. To a dreary day of incessant rain succeeded an evening still drearier. Wild gusts swept along the little shore, and shook the frail windows and ill-fitting doors of the cottages, while foam and sea-drift were wafted over the roofs, settling like snow-flakes on the tall cliffs above them. And yet it was midsummer! By the almanac the time was vouched to be the opening of the season; a fact amply corroborated by the fashionable assemblage then enjoying the hospitalities of Mrs. Cronan's tea-table. There they were, with a single exception, the same goodly company already presented to the reader in an early chapter of our story. We have already mentioned the great changes which time had worked in the appearance of the little watering-place. The fostering care of proprietorship withdrawn, the ornamental villa of the Martins converted into a miserable village inn, the works of the pier and harbor suspended, and presenting in their unfinished aspect the dreary semblance of ruin and decay,—all conspired with the falling fortunes of the people to make the scene a sad one. Little evidence of this decline, however, could be traced in the aspect of that pleasant gathering, animated with all its ancient taste for whist, scandal, and shrimps; their appetite for such luxuries seeming rather to have increased than diminished by years. Not that we presume to say they could claim any immunity against the irrevocable decrees of age. Unhappily, the confession may be deemed not exactly in accordance with gallantry; but it is strictly true, time had no more forgotten the living than the inanimate accessories of the picture. Miss Busk, of the Emporium, had grown more sour and more stately. The vinegar of her temperament was verging upon verjuice, and the ill opinion of mankind experience enforced had written itself very legibly on her features. The world had not improved upon her by acquaintance. Not so Captain Bodkin; fatter and more wheezy than ever, he seemed to relish life rather more than when younger. He had given up, too, that long struggle with himself about bathing, and making up his mind to suffer no "sea-change;" he was, therefore, more cheerful than before.

As for Mrs. Cronan, "the little comforts she was used to" had sorely diminished by the pressure of the times, and, in consequence, she drew unlimited drafts upon the past to fill up the deficiencies of the present. Strange enough is it, that the faults and follies of society are just as adhesive ingredients as its higher qualities! These people had grown so used to each other in all their eccentric ways and oddities, that they had become fond of them; like a pilot long accustomed to rocks and sandbanks, they could only steer their course where there was something to avoid!

The remainder of the goodly company had grown stouter or thinner, jollier or more peevish, as temperament inclined; for it is with human nature as with wine: if the liquor does not get racier with years, it degenerates sadly.

The first act of the whist and backgammon playing was over, and the party now sat, stood, crouched, lounged, or lay, as chance and the state of the furniture permitted, at supper. At the grand table, of course, were the higher dignitaries, such as Father Maher, the Captain, Miss Busk, and Mrs. Clinch; but cockles were eaten, and punch discussed in various very odd quarters; bursts of joyous laughter, too, came from dark pantries, and sounds of merriment mingled with the jangling crash of kitchen utensils. Reputations were roasted and pancakes fried, characters and chickens alike mangled, and all the hubbub of a festival prevailed in a scene where the efforts of the fair hostess were directed to produce an air of unblemished elegance and gentility.

Poor Clinch, the revenue officer, who invariably eat what he called "his bit" in some obscure quarter, alone and companionless, was twice "had up" before the authorities for the row and uproar that prevailed, and underwent a severe cross-examination, "as to where he was when Miss Cullenane was making the salad," and, indeed, cut a very sorry figure at the conclusion of the inquiry. All the gayeties and gravities of the scene, however, gradually toned down as the serious debate of the evening came on; which was no other than the lamentable condition of the prospects of Kilkieran, and the unanimous opinion of the ruinous consequences that must ensue from the absence of the proprietor.

"We 've little chance of getting up the news-room now," said the Captain. "The Martins won't give a sixpence for anything."

"It is something to give trade an impulse we want, sir," broke in Miss Busk, — "balls and assemblies; evening reunions of the *élite* of society, where the elegance of the toilet should rival the *distingué* air of the company."

"That's word for word out of the 'Intelligence,'" cried the Captain. "It's unparliamentary to quote the newspapers."

"I detest the newspapers," broke in Miss Busk, angrily; "after advertising the Emporium for two seasons in the 'Galway Celt,' they gave me a leading article beginning, 'As the hot weather is now commencing, and the season for fashion approaches, we cannot better serve the interests of our readers than by directing attention to the elegant "Symposium!"' 'Symposium!'—I give you my word of honor that's what they put it."

"On my conscience! it might have been worse," chuckled out the Captain.

"It was young Nelligan explained to me what it was," resumed Miss Busk; "and Scanlan said, 'I'd have an action against them for damages.'"

"Keep out of law, my dear!—keep out of law!" sighed Mrs. Cronan. "See to what it has reduced me! I, that used to go out in my own coach, with two men in green and gold; that had my house in town, and my house in the country; that had gems and ornaments such as a queen might wear! And there's all that's left me now!" And she pointed to a brooch about the size of a cheese-plate, where a melancholy gentleman in uniform was represented, with a border of mock pearls around him. "The last pledge of affection!" sobbed she.

"Of course you wouldn't pledge it, my dear," muttered the deaf old Mrs. Few; "and they'd give you next to nothing on it, besides."

"We 'll have law enough here soon, it seems," said Mrs. Cronan, angrily; for the laugh this blunder excited was by no means flattering and pleasant. "There 's Magennis's action first for trial at the Assizes."

"That will be worth hearing," said Mrs. Clinch. "They 'll have the first lawyers from Dublin on each side."

"Did you hear the trick they played off on Joe Nelligan about it?" asked the Captain. "It was cleverly done. Magennis found out, some way or other, that Joe wanted to be engaged against him; and so what does he do but gets a servant dressed up in the Martin livery, and sends him to Joe's house on the box of a coach, inside of which was a gentleman that begged a word with the Counsellor. 'You 're not engaged, I hope, Counsellor Nelligan,' says he, 'in Magennis against Martin?' 'No,' says Joe, for he caught a glimpse of the livery. 'You're quite free?' says the other. 'Quite free,' says he. 'That's all I want, then,' says he; 'here's your brief, and here's your retainer;' and he put both down on the table, and when Joe looked down he saw he was booked for Magennis. You may imagine how he felt; but he never uttered a word, for there was no help for it."

"And do you mean to tell me," cried Mrs. Clinch, "that the lawyers can't help themselves, but must just talk and rant and swear for any one that asks them first?"

"It's exactly what I mean, ma'am," responded the Captain. "They 've no more choice in the matter than the hangman has as to who be 'll hang."

"Then I'd as soon be a gauger!" exclaimed the lady, with a contemptuous glance at poor Clinch, who winced under the observation.

"But I don't see what they wanted young Nelligan for," said Miss Busk; "what experience or knowledge has *he?*"

"He's just the first man of the day," said Bodkin. "They tell me that whether it be to crook out a flaw in the enemy's case, to pick a hole in a statement, to crush a witness, or cajole the jury, old Repton himself is n't his equal."

"I suppose, from the airs he gives himself, he must be something wonderful," said Mrs. Cronan.

"Well, now, I differ from you there, ma'am," replied Bodkin. "I think Joe is just what he always was. He was cold, silent, and distant as a boy, and he 's the same as a man. Look at him when he comes down here at the Assizes, down to the town where his father is selling glue and hides and tenpenny-nails, and he 's just as easy and unconstrained as if the old man was Lord of Cro' Martin Castle."

"That's the height of impertinence," broke in Miss Busk; "it's only real blood has any right to rise above the depreciating accidents of condition. I know it by myself."

"Well, I wonder what he 'll make of this case, anyhow," said feodkin, to escape a controversy he had no fancy for. "They tell me that no action can lie on it. It's not abduction—"

"For shame, Captain; you forget there are ladies here," said Mrs. Clinch.

"Indeed I don't," sighed he, with a half-comic melancholy in his look.

"I'll tell you how they do it, sir," chimed in Father Maher. "Whenever there 's anything in law that never was foreseen or provided for, against which there is neither act nor statute, they 've one grand and unfailing resource,—they charge it as a conspiracy. I 've a brother an attorney, and he tells me that there is n't a man, woman, or child in the kingdom but could be indicted for doing something by a conspiracy."

"It's a great comfort to know that," said Bodkin, gravely.

"And what can they do to her if she's found guilty?" asked Mrs. Cronan.

"Make her smart for the damages, ma'am; leave her something less to expend on perversion and interference with the people," said the priest. "The parish isn't the same since she began visiting this one and reading to that. Instead of respect and confidence in their spiritual guides, the people are running after a young girl with a head full of wild schemes and contrivances. We all know by this time how these things end, and the best receipt to make a Protestant begins, 'First starve your Papist.'"

"I rise to order," called out Bodkin. "We agreed we'd have no polemics nor party discussions."

"Why am I appealed to, then, for explanations that involve them?" cried the priest, angrily. "I'm supported, too, in my observations by a witness none will dispute,—that Scotchman, Henderson—"

"By the way, isn't his daughter come home to him?" asked Bodkin, eager for a diversion.

"Indeed she is, sir; and a pretty story there is about it, too. Miss Busk knows it all," said Mrs. Cronan.

"I have it in confidence, ma'am, from Jemima Davis,—Lady Dorothea's second maid; but I don't think it a fit subject for public conversation."

"And ain't we in committee here?" chimed in Bodkin; "have we any secrets from each other?" The racy laugh of the old fellow, as he threw a knowing glance around the table, rather disconcerted the company. "Let's hear about Henderson's daughter."

"The story is soon told, sir. Lady Dorothea detected her endeavoring to draw young Martin into a private marriage. The artful creature, by some means or other, had obtained such an insight into the young man's difficulties that she actually terrorized over his weak mind. She discovered, too, it is suspected, something rather more than indiscretions on his part."

A long low whistle from the priest seemed to impart a kind of gratified surprise at this announcement.

"He had got into a habit of signing his name, they say; and whether he signed it to something he had no right to, or signed another name by mistake—"

"Oh, for shame," broke in Bodkin; "that wouldn't be one bit like a Martin."

"Perhaps you are acquainted with all the circumstances better than myself, sir?" said Miss Busk, bristling up with anger. "Maybe you 've heard how the Henderson girl was turned away out of the French duke's family,— how she was found in correspondence with the leaders of the mob in Paris? Maybe, sir, you are aware that she has some mysterious hold over her father, and he dares not gainsay one word she says?"

"I don't know one word of it; and if it wasn't thought rude, I'd say I don't believe it, either," said Bodkin, stoutly.

"I believe the worst that could be said of her," said Mrs. Clinch.

"Well, well, make her as bad as you like; but how does that prove anything against young Martin? and if you can find nothing heavier to say of him than that he wanted to marry a very handsome girl—"

"A low creature!" broke in Miss Busk.

"The lowest of the low!" chimed in Mrs. Cronan.

"An impudent, upsetting minx!" added Mrs. Clinch. "Nothing would serve her but a post-chaise the morning she arrived by the mail for Dublin; and, signs on it, when she got home she had n't money to pay for it."

"It was n't that she left her place empty-handed, then," said Miss Busk. "Jemima tells me that she managed the whole house,—paid for everything; and we all know what comes of that."

Miss Busk, in delivering this sentiment, was seated with her back to the door, towards which suddenly every eye was now turned in mingled astonishment and confusion; she moved round to see the cause, and there beheld the very object of her commentary standing close behind her chair. Closely wrapped in a large cloak, the hood of which she wore over her head, her tall figure looked taller and more imposing in its motionless attitude.

"I have to ask pardon for this intrusion, ladies," said she, calmly; "but you will forgive me when I tell the reason of it. I have just received very sad tidings, which ought to be conveyed to Miss Martin; she is at the islands, and I have no means of following her, unless Mr. Clinch will kindly lend me the revenue boat—"

"And accompany you, I hope," broke in Mrs. Clinch, with a sneer.

Kate did not notice the taunting remark, but went on, "You will be grieved to hear that Mr. Martin is no more."

"Martin dead!" muttered the Captain.

"Dead! When did he die?" "Where did it happen?" "How?" "Of what malady?" "Are his remains coming home?" were asked in quick succession by several voices.

"This letter will tell you all that I know myself," said she, laying it on the table. "May I venture to hope Mr. Clinch will so far oblige me? The fishermen say the sea is too rough for their craft."

"It's not exactly on the King's service, I opine, ma'am," broke in Mrs. Clinch; "but of course he is too gallant to oppose your wishes."

"Faith! if you wanted any one with you, and would accept of myself," broke in Bodkin, "I'm ready this minute; not that exactly salt water is my element."

"The young lady is accustomed to travel alone, or she is much belied," said Miss Busk, with a sneer.

"I suppose you'd better let her have the boat, Clinch," said his wife, in a whisper. "There's no knowing what might come of it if you refused."

"I 'll go down and muster the crew for you, Miss Henderson," said Clinch, not sorry to escape, although the exchange was from a warm cabin to the beating rain without.

"Poor Martin!" sighed Bodkin; "he was the first of the family for many a long year that did n't breathe his last under his own roof. I 'm sure it weighed heavily on him."

"I trust his son will follow his example, nevertheless," said the priest. "I don't want to see one of the name amongst us."

"You might have worse, Father Maher," said Bodkin, angrily.

And now a lively discussion ensued as to the merits of him they had lost, for the most part with more of charity than many of their dissertations; from this they branched off into speculations about the future. Would the "present man" reside at home? would her Ladyship come back? what would be Mary's position? how would Scanlan fare? what of Henderson, too? In fact, casualties of every kind were debated, and difficulties started, that they might be as readily reconciled. Meanwhile Kate was hastening down to the shore, followed, rather than escorted, by little Clinch, who even in the darkness felt that the conjugal eye was upon him.

CHAPTER XXXI
THE BRANNOCK ISLANDS

A little to the northwest of the island of Innishmore are scattered a number of small islets, some scarcely more than barren rocks, called the Brannocks. One of these alone was inhabited, and that by a single family. No isolation could be more complete than that of these poor people, who thus dwelt amid the wide waste of waters, never seeing the face of a stranger, and only at long intervals visiting the mainland. Indeed the only intercourse they could be said to maintain with their fellow-men was when by chance they fell in with some homeward-bound ship at sea, and sold the little produce of their nets; for they lived by fishing, and had no other subsistence.

The largest of these islands was called "Brannock-buoy," or the Yellow Brannock, from the flower of a kind of crocus which grew profusely over it. It was a wild, desolate spot, scarcely rising above the waves around it, save in one quarter, where a massive column of rock rose to the height of several hundred feet, and formed the only shelter against the swooping wind, which came without break or hindrance from the far-away shores of Labrador. At the foot of this strong barrier—so small and insignificant as to escape notice from the sea—stood the little cabin of Owen Joyce. Built in a circular form, the chimney in the middle, the rude structure resembled some wigwam of the prairies rather than the home of civilized beings.

Certain low partitions within subdivided the space into different chambers, making the centre the common apartment of the family, where they cooked and ate and chatted; for, with all their poverty and privation, theirs was a life not devoid of its own happiness, nor did they believe that their lot was one to repine at.

Seasons of unprofitable labor, years of more or less pressure, they had indeed experienced, but actual want had never visited them; sickness, too, was almost as rare. Owen Joyce was, at the time we speak of, upwards of eighty; and although his hair was white as snow, his cheek was ruddy, his white teeth were perfect, and his eye—like that of Moses—"was not dim." Surrounded by his children and grandchildren, the old man lived happy and contented, his daily teaching being to impress upon them the blessings they derived from a life so sheltered from all the accidents of fortune; to have, as he called the island, "the little craft all their own."

The traits of race and family, the limited range of their intercourse with the world, served to make them all wonderfully alike, not only in feature but expression; so that even the youngest child had something of the calm, steadfast look which characterized the old man. The jet-black hair and eyes and the swarthy skin seemed to indicate a Spanish origin, and gave them a type perfectly distinctive and peculiar.

In the midst of them moved one who, though dressed in the light-blue woollen kirtle, the favorite costume of the islands, bore in her fresh bright features the traces of a different blood; her deep blue eye, soft and almost sleepy, her full, well-curved lips, were strong contrasts to the traits around her. The most passing glance would have detected that she was not "one of them," nor had she been long an inmate of this dwelling.

It chanced that some short time before, one of Joyce's sons, in boarding an outward-bound American ship, had heard of a young countrywoman who, having taken her passage for New York, no sooner found herself at sea—parted, as she deemed it, forever from home and country—than she gave way to the most violent grief; so poignant, indeed, was her sorrow that the captain compassionately offered to relinquish her passage-money if Joyce would take charge of her, and re-land her on the shores of Ireland. The offer was accepted, and the same evening saw her safely deposited on the rocky island of Brannock. Partly in gratitude to her deliverer, partly in the indulgence of a secret wish, she asked leave to remain with them and be their servant; the compact was agreed to, and thus was she there.

Theirs was not a life to engender the suspicions and distrusts which are current in the busier walks of men. None asked her a reason for her self-banishment, none inquired whether the cause of her exile was crime or misfortune. They had grown to feel attachment to her for the qualities of her gentle, quiet nature, a mild submissive temper, and a disposition to oblige, that forgot nothing save herself. Her habits had taught her resources and ways which their isolated existence had denied them, and she made herself useful by various arts, which, simple as they were, seemed marvellous to the apprehension of her hosts; and thus, day by day, gaining on their love and esteem, they came at length to regard her with an affection mingled with a sort of homage.

Poor Joan Landy—for we have not to explain that it was she—was happy,—happier than ever she had been before. The one great sorrow of her life was, it is true, treasured in her heart; her lost home, her blighted hope, her severed affection—for she actually loved Magennis—were griefs over which she wept many an hour in secret; but there was a sense of duty, a conscious feeling of rectitude, that supported her in her sacrifice, and as she thought of her old grandfather's death-bed, she could say to her heart, "I have been true to my word with him."

The unbroken quiet, the unchanging character of the life she led,—its very duties following a routine that nothing ever disturbed,—gave her ample time for thought; and thought, though tinged with melancholy, has its own store of consolation; and if poor Joan sorrowed, she sorrowed like one who rather deplored the past than desired to re-live it! As time wore on, a dreamy indistinctness seemed to spread itself over the memory of her former life: it appeared little other than a mind-drawn picture. Nothing actual or tangible remained to convince her of its reality. It was only at rare intervals, and in the very clearest weather, the outline of the mountains of the mainland could be seen; and when she did behold them, they brought only some vague recollection to her; and so, too, the memories of her once home came through the haze of distance, dim and indistinct.

It was at the close of a day in June that the Joyces sat in front of the little cabin, repairing their nets, and getting their tackle in readiness for the sea. For some time previous the weather had been broken and unfavorable. Strong west winds and heavy seas—far from infrequent in these regions, even in midsummer—had rendered fishing impracticable; but now the aspect of a new moon, rising full an hour before sunset, gave promise of better, and old Joyce had got the launch drawn up on shore to refit, and sails were spread out upon the rocks to dry, and coils of rope, and anchors, and loose spars littered the little space before the door. The scene was a busy and not an unpicturesque one. There was every age, from the oldest to very infancy, all active, all employed. Some were calking the seams of the boat, others overhauled sails and cordage; some were preparing the nets, attaching cork floats or sinkers; and two chubby urchins, mere infants, laughing, fed the fire that blazed beneath a large pitch-pot, the light blue smoke rising calmly into the air, and telling those far away that the lone rock was not without inhabitants. To all seeming, these signs of life and habitation bad attracted notice; for a small boat which had quitted Innishmore for the mainland some time before, now altered her course, and was seen slowly bearing up towards the Brannocks. Though the sea was calm and waveless, the wind was only sufficient to waft her along at the slowest rate; a twinkling flash of the sea at intervals showed, however, that her crew were rowing, and at length the measured beat of the oars could be distinctly heard.

Many were the speculations of those who watched her course. They knew she was not a fishing-craft; her light spars and white sails were sufficient to refute that opinion. Neither was she one of the revenue-boats. What could she be, then, since no large ship was in sight to which she could have belonged? It is only to those who have at some one period or other of life sojourned in some lone spot of earth, away from human intercourse, that the anxiety of these poor people could be intelligible. If, good reader,—for to you we now appeal,—it has not been your lot to have once on a time lived remote from the world and its ways, you cannot imagine how intensely interesting can become the commonest of those incidents which mark ordinary existence. They assume, indeed, very different proportions from the real, and come charged with innumerable imaginings about that wondrous life, far, far away, where there are thoughts and passions and deeds and events which never enter into the dreamland of exile! It was a little after sunset that the boat glided into the small creek which formed the only harbor of the island; and the moment after, a young girl sprang on the shore, and hastened towards them.

Before the Joyces had recovered from their first surprise, they saw Joan burst from the spot, and, rushing down the slope, throw herself at the stranger's feet.

"And have I found you at last, dear Joan?" cried a soft, low voice, while the speaker raised her tenderly from the ground, and took her hand kindly within both her own.

"Oh, Miss Mary, to think you 'd come after me this far! over the say!" burst out Joan, sobbing through her joy; for joy it was that now lit up her features, and made her eyes sparkle even through the fresh tears that filled them.

"They told me you had sailed from Galway," resumed Mary, "and I wrote to the ship-agent and found it was correct: your name was in the list of passengers, and the date of the day you sailed; but, I know not how it was, Joan, I still clung to the notion that you had contrived this plan to escape being discovered, and that you were concealed somewhere along the coast or in the islands. I believe I used to dream of this at first, but at last I thought of it all day long."

"Thought of *me* all day long?" broke in Joan, sobbing.

"And why not, poor child? Was I not the cause of your leaving your home? Was it not my persuasion that induced you to leave the roof that sheltered you? I have often wondered whether I had right and reason on my side. I know at the time I believed I had such. At all events, but for me you had never quitted that home; but see, Joan, how what we are led to do with an honest purpose, if it fail to effect what we had in view, often leads to better and happier ends than we ever dreamed of. I only thought of conveying to you the last message of your poor grandfather. I little imagined how so simple an act could influence all your future fortune in life; and such it has done. Mr. Magennis, suspecting or discovering what share I had in your flight, has begun a law proceeding against me, and to give him a rightful claim for redress, has declared you to be—all that you wish, dear Joan—his lawful, wedded wife."

It was some time before the poor girl could stifle the sobbing which burst from her very heart. She kissed Mary's hands over and over with rapture, and cried out at length, in broken, faltering accents, "Did n't they say well that called you a saint from heaven? Didn't they tell truth that said, God gave you as a blessing to us?"

"My poor Joan, you are grateful to me for what I have no share in. I am nothing but the bearer of good tidings. But tell me, how have you fared since we parted? Let me hear all that has happened to you."

Joan told her simple story in a few words, never deviating from the narrative, save to speak her heartfelt gratitude to the poor people who had sheltered and befriended her.

"There they are!" cried she, pointing to the group, who, with a delicacy of sentiment that might have graced the most refined class, sat apart, never venturing by a look to obtrude upon the confidence of the others,—"there they are; and if the world was like them, life would n't have many crosses!"

Mary rose, and drew nigh the old man, who stood up respectfully to receive her.

"He does n't know much English, Miss Mary," whispered Joan in her ear.

"Nor am I well skilled in Irish," said Mary, smiling; "but I 'll do my best to thank him."

However imperfectly she spoke the native tongue, the words seemed to act like a charm on those who heard them; and as, young and old, they gathered around her, their eager looks and delighted faces beamed with a triumphant joy. They had learned from the boatmen that it was the young princess—as in the language of the people she was called—was before them, and their pride and happiness knew no bounds.

Oh, if courtiers could feel one tithe of the personal devotion to the sovereign that did these poor peasants to her they regarded as their chief, what an atmosphere of chivalry would breathe within the palace of royalty! There was nothing they would not have done or dared at her bidding; and as she crossed their threshold, and sat down beside their hearth, the tears of joy that rose to every eye showed that this was an event to be treasured till memory could retain no more!

If Mary did not speak the native dialect fluently, there was a grace and a charm about the turn of the expressions she used that never failed to delight those who heard her. That imaginative thread that runs through the woof of Irish nature in every rank and condition of life—more conspicuous, probably, in the very humblest—imparted an intense pleasure to hearing and listening to her; and she, on her side, roused and stimulated by the adventurous character of the incident, the strange wild spot, the simple people, their isolation and their innocence, spoke with a warmth and an enthusiasm that were perfectly captivating.

She had seen much of the peasantry,—known them in the most unfrequented tracts, remote from all their fellow-men,—in far-away glens, by dreary mountains, where no footpaths led; but anything so purely simple and unsophisticated as these poor people she had never met with. The sons had been—and that rarely, too—on the mainland, but the children and their mothers had never left the Brannocks; they had never beheld a tree, nor even a flower, save the wild crocus on their native rock. With what eager delight, then, did they hear Mary describe the gardens of the castle,— pictures that glowed with all the gorgeous colors of a fairy tale. "You shall

all come and see me, some of these days. I'll send you a messenger, to say the time," said Mary; "and I'll promise that what you 'll witness will be far above my description of it!"

It was a sad moment when Mary arose to say good-bye. Joan, too, was to accompany her, and the grief at parting with her was extreme. Again and again the children clung round her, entreating her not to leave them; and she herself half faltered in her resolution. That lonely rock, that rude cabin, had been her refuge in the darkest hour of her life, and she felt the superstitious terror of her class at now deserting them.

"Come, come, dear Joan, remember that you have a home now that you can rightfully return to," whispered Mary. "It is not in shame, but in honor, that you go back to it."

It was already dark ere they left the Brannocks: a long, heavy swell, too, the signs of a storm, coming from the westward, made the boatmen eager to hasten their departure. As yet, however, the air was calm and still, but it was with that oppressive stillness that forebodes change. They hoisted their sail, but soon saw that they must, for a while at least, trust to their oars. The unbroken stillness, save by the measured stroke of the rowers, the dense dark atmosphere, and the reaction, after a day of toil and an event of a most moving kind, so overcame Mary that, leaning on Joan's shoulder, she fell off fast asleep. For a while Joan, proud of the burden she supported, devoted all her care to watch and protect her from the night air; but at last weariness stole over herself, and she dropped off to slumber.

Meanwhile the sea was rising; heavy waves struck the boat, and washed over her in sheets of spray, although no wind was stirring.

"We 'll have rain, or a gale of wind before long," said one of the men.

"There 's some heavy drops falling now," muttered another.

"Throw that sail over Miss Mary, for it will soon come down heavily."

A loud clap of thunder burst forth, and as suddenly, like a torrent, the rain poured down, hissing over the dark sea, and filling the air with a dull, discordant noise. Still they slept on, nor heard nor felt aught of that gathering storm.

"There now, sure enough, it 's coming," cried a boatman, as the sail shook tremulously; and two great waves, in quick succession, broke over the bow.

"We'll have to run for Innishmore," said another, "and lucky if we get there before it comes on worse."

"You ought to wake her up, Loony, and ask her what we are to do."

"I 'll make straight for the harbor of Kilkieran," replied the helmsman. "The wind is with us, and she's a good sea-boat. Take in the jib, Maurice, and we'll shorten all sail on her, and—"

The rest of his speech was drowned in the uproar of a tremendous sea, which struck the boat on her quarter and nearly overset her. Not another word was now uttered, as, with the instinct of their calling, they set about to prepare for the coming conflict. The mainsail was quickly lowered and reefed, the oars and loose spars secured, and then, seating themselves in the bottom of the boat, they waited in silence. By this time the rain had passed over, and a strong wind swept over the sea.

"She's going fast through the water, anyway!" said one of the men. But though the speech was meant to cheer, none felt or acknowledged the encouragement.

"I 'd rather than own Cro' Martin Castle Miss Mary was safe at home!" said Loony, as he drew the rough sleeve of his coat across his eyes, "for it's thicker it's getting over yonder!"

"It would be a black day that anything happened her!" muttered another.

"Musha! we've wives and childer," said a third, "but she's worth a thousand of us!"

And thus, in broken whispers, they spoke; not a thought save of her, not a care save for her safety. They prayed, too, fervently, and her name was in all their supplications.

"She's singing to herself in her sleep," whispered Loony. And the rough sailors hushed to hear her.

Louder and louder, however, grew the storm, sheets of spray and drift falling over the boat in showers, and all her timbers quivering as she labored in the stormy sea. A sailor whispered something in Loony's ear, and he grumbled out in reply,—"Why would I wake her up?"

"But I *am* awake, Loony," said Mary, in a low, calm voice, "and I see all our danger; but I see, too, that you are meeting it like brave men, and, better still, like good ones."

"The men was thinking we ought to bear up for Innish-more, Miss Mary," said Loony, as though ashamed of offering on his own part such counsel.

"You'll do what you think best and safest for us all, Loony."

"But you were always the captain, miss, when you were aboord!" replied he, with an effort to smile.

"And so I should be now, Loony, but that my heart is too full to be as calm and resolute as I ought to be. This poor thing had not been here now, but for *me*." And she wrapped her shawl around Joan as she spoke. "Maybe it's anxiety, perhaps fatigue, but I have not my old courage to-night!"

"Faix! it will never be fear that will distress you!" said he.

"If you mean for myself and my own safety, Loony, you are right. It is not for me to repine at the hour that calls me away, but I cannot bear to think how you and others, with so many dear to you, should be perilled just to serve *me!* And poor Joan, too, at the moment when life was about to brighten for her!" She held down her head for a minute or two, and then suddenly, as it were, rallying, she cried out, "The boat is laboring too much for'ard, Loony; set the jib on her!"

"To be sure, if you ordher it, Miss Mary; but she has more sail now than she can carry."

"Set the jib, Loony. I know the craft well; she 'll ride the waves all the lighter for it. If it were but daylight, I almost think I 'd enjoy this. We 've been out in as bad before."

Loony shook his head as he went forward to bend the additional sail.

"You see she won't bear it, miss," cried he, as the boat plunged fearfully into the trough of the sea.

"Let us try," said she, calmly. "Stand by, ready to slack off, if I give the word." And so saying, she took the tiller from the sailor, and seated herself on the weather-gunwale. "There, see how she does it now! Ah, Loony, confess, I am the true pilot. I knew my nerve would come back when I took my old post here. I was always a coward in a carriage, if I was n't on the box and the reins in my hands; and the same at sea. Sit up to windward, men, and don't move; never mind baling, only keep quiet."

"Miss Mary was right," muttered one of the men; "the head-sail is drawing her high out of the water!"

"Is that dark mass before us cloud, or the land?" cried she.

"It's the mountains, miss. There to the left, where you see the dip in the ridge, that's Kilkieran. I think I see the lights on shore now."

"I see them now myself," cried Mary. "Oh, how the sight of land gives love of life! They called earth truly who named her mother!" said she to herself. "What was that which swept past us, Loony?"

"A boat, miss; and they're hailing us now," cried he, peeping over the gunwale. "They've put her about, and are following our course. They came out after us."

"It was gallantly done, on such a night as this! I was just thinking to myself that poor old Mat Landy would have been out, were he living. You must take the tiller now, Loony, for I don't understand the lights on shore."

"Because they're shifting every minute, miss. It's torches they have, and they 're moving from place to place; but we 'll soon be safe now."

"Let us not forget this night, men," said Mary, in a fervent voice. And then, burying her face within her hands, she spoke no more.

It was already daybreak when they gained the little harbor, well-nigh exhausted, and worn out with fatigue and anxiety. As for Mary, wet through and cold, she could not rise from her seat without assistance, and almost fainted as she put her foot on shore. She turned one glance seaward to where the other boat was seen following them, and then, holding Joan's hand, she slowly toiled up the rocky ascent to the village. To the crowd of every age that surrounded her she could only give a faint, sickly smile of recognition, and they, in deep reverence, stood without speaking, gazing on her wan features and the dripping garments which clung to her.

"No, not to the inn, Loony," said she, to a question from him. "The first cabin we meet will shelter us, and then—home!" There was something of intense sorrow in the thought that passed then through her mind, for her eyes suddenly filled up, and heavy tears rolled along her cheeks. "Have they got in yet?" said she, looking towards the sea.

"Yes, miss; they're close alongside now. It's the revenue boat that went after us."

"Wirra, wirra! but that's bad news for her now," muttered a boatman, in conversation with an old woman at his side.

"What's the bad news, Patsey?" said Mary, overhearing him.

But the man did not dare to answer; and though he looked around on every side, none would speak for him.

"You used to be more frank with me," said Mary, calmly. "Tell me what has happened."

Still not a word was uttered, a mournful silence brooded over the crowd, and each seemed to shun the task of breaking it.

"You will make me fear worse than the reality, perhaps," said she, tremulously. "Is the calamity near home? No. Is it then my uncle?" A low faint cry burst from her, and she dropped down on her knees; but scarcely had she joined her hands to pray, than she fell back, fainting, to the ground.

They carried her, still insensible as she was, into a fisherman's cabin, till they went in search of a conveyance to take her to the cottage.

CHAPTER XXXII
LETTER FROM MASSINGBRED

"Martin Arms, Oughterard

"In spite of all your reasonings, all your cautions, and all your warnings, here I am once more, Harry, denizen of the little dreary parlor whence I first looked out at Dan Nelligan's shop something more than a year since. What changes of fortune has that brief space accomplished I what changes has it effected even in my own nature! I feel this in nothing more than in my altered relations with others. If the first evidence of amendment in a man be shame and sorrow for the past, I may probably be on the right road now, since I heartily grieve over the worthless, purposeless life I have led hitherto.

"I am well aware that you would not accept the reason I gave you for coming here. You said that, as to taking leave of my constituents, a letter was the ordinary and the sufficient course. You also hinted that our intercourse had not been of that close and friendly nature which requires a personal farewell, and then you suggested that other and less defensible motives had probably their share in this step. Well, you are right, perfectly right; I wanted to see the spot which has so far exerted an immense influence over me; I wanted—if you will have the confession—to see *her* too,—to see her in the humble station she belongs to, in the lowly garb of the steward's daughter. I was curious to ascertain what change her bearing would undergo in the change of position; would she conform to the lowlier condition at once and without struggle, or would her haughty nature chafe and fret against the obstacles of a small and mean existence? If you were right in guessing this, you are equally wrong in the motive you ascribe to me. Not, indeed, that you palpably express, but only hint at it; still I cannot endure even the shadow of such a surmise without a flat and full denial. Perhaps, after all, I have mistaken your meaning,—would it were so! I do indeed wish that you should not ascribe to me motives so unworthy and so mean. A revenge for her refusal of me! a reprisal for the proud rejection of my hand and fortune! No, my dear Harry, I feel, as I write the words, that they never were yours. You say, however, that I am curious to know if I should think her as lovable and attractive in the humble dress and humble station that pertain to her, as when I saw her moving more than equal amongst the proudest and haughtiest of Europe. To have any doubt on this score would be to distrust her sincerity of character. She must be what I have ever seen her, or she is an actress. Difference of condition, different associates, different duties will exact different discipline, but she herself must be the same, or she is a falsehood,—a deception.

"And then you add, it is perhaps as well that I should 'submit to the rude test of a disenchantment.' Well, I accept the challenge, and I am here.

"These thoughts of self would obtrude in the very beginning of a letter I had destined for other objects. You ask me for a narrative of my journey and its accidents, and you shall have it. On my way over here in the packet, I made acquaintance with an elderly man, who seemed thoroughly acquainted with all the circumstances of the Martins and their misfortunes. From him I ascertained that all Scanlan had told me was perfectly correct. The reversion of the estate has been sold for a sum incredibly small in proportion to its value, and in great part the proceeds of gambling transactions. Martin is, therefore, utterly, irretrievably ruined. Merl has taken every step with all the security of the best advice, and in a few months, weeks perhaps, will be declared owner of Cro' Martin. Even in the 'fast times' we live in, such rapid ruin as this stands alone! You tell me that of your own college and mess associates not more than one in five or six have survived the wreck of fortune the first few years of extravagance accomplish, and that Manheim, Brussels, and Munich can show the white-seamed, mock-smartened-up gentilities which once were the glories of Bond Street and the Park; but for poor Martin, I suspect, even these last sanctuaries do not remain,—as I hear it, he is totally gone.

"From the very inn where I am staying Merls agents are issuing notices of all kinds to the tenants and 'others' to desist and refrain from cutting timber, quarrying marbles, and what not, on certain unspeakable localities, with threats in case of non-compliance. Great placards cover the walls of the town, headed 'Caution to all Tenants on the Estate of Cro' Martin.' The excitement in the neighborhood is intense, overwhelming. Whatever differences of political opinion existed between the Martins and the people of the borough, whatever jealousies grew out of disparity of station, seemed suddenly merged in sympathy for this great misfortune. They are, of course, ignorant of the cause of this sudden calamity, and ask each other how, when, and where such a fortune because engulfed.

"But to proceed regularly. On my reaching Dublin, after a hurried visit to my father, I drove off to Mr. Repton's house. You may remember his name as that of the old lawyer, some of whose bar stories amused you so highly. I found him in a spacious mansion of an old neglected street,—Henrietta Street,—once the great aristocratic quarter of Ancient Dublin, and even to this day showing traces of real splendor. The old man received me in a room of immense proportions, furnished as it was when Flood was the proprietor. He was at luncheon when I entered; and for company had the very same stranger with whom I made acquaintance in the packet.

"Repton started as we recognized each other, but at a sign or a word, I'm not certain which, from the other, merely said, 'My friend was just speaking of his having met you, Mr. Massingbred.' This somewhat informal presentation over, I joined them, and we fell a chatting over the story of Cro' Martin.

"They were both eager to hear something about Merl, his character, pursuits, and position; and you would have been amazed to see how surprised they were at my account of a man whose type we are all so familiar with.

"You would scarcely credit the unfeigned astonishment manifested by these two shrewd and crafty men at the sketch I gave them of our Hebrew friend. One thing is quite clear,—it was not the habit, some forty or fifty years ago, to admit the Merls of the world to terms of intimacy, far less of friendship.

"'As I said, Repton,' broke in the stranger, sternly, 'it all comes of that degenerate tone which has crept in of late, making society like a tavern, where he who can pay his bill cannot be denied entrance. Such fellows as this Merl had no footing in our day. The man who associated with such would have forfeited his own place in the world.'

"'Very true,' said Repton, 'though we borrowed their money we never bowed to them.'

"'And we did wisely, sir,' retorted the other. 'The corruption of their manners was fifty times worse than all their usury! The gallant Hussar Captain, as we see here, never scrupled about admitting to his closest intimacy a fellow not fit company for his valet. Can't you perceive that when a man will descend to such baseness to obtain money, there is no measuring the depth he will go to when pressed to pay it?'

"'I am intimate with Martin,' said I, interrupting, 'and I can honestly assure you that it was rather to an easy, careless, uncalculating disposition he owes his misfortunes, than to anything like a spendthrift habit.'

"'Mere hair-splitting this, sir,' replied he, almost rudely. 'He who spends what is not his own, I have but one name for. It matters little in my estimation whether he extorts the supply by a bill or a bullet.'

"I own to you, Harry, I burned to retort to a speech the tone and manner of which were both more offensive than the words; but the stranger's age, his venerable appearance, and something like deep and recent sorrow about him, restrained me, and I caught, by a look from Repton, that he was grateful for my forbearance.

"'Come, sir,' said he, addressing me, 'you say you know Captain Martin; now let me ask you one question: Is there any one trait or feature of his character to which, if his present misfortunes were to pass away, you could attach a hope of amendment? Has not this life of bill-renewing, these eternal straits for cash—with all the humiliations that accompany them,—made him a mere creature of schemes and plots,—a usurer in spirit, though a pauper in fact?'

"'When I say, sir, that you are addressing this demand to one whom Captain Martin deems his friend, you will see the impropriety you have fallen into.'

"'My young friend is right,' broke in Repton. 'The Court rules against the question; nor would it be evidence even if answered.'

"I was angry at this interference of Repton's. I wanted to reply to this man myself; but still, as I looked at his sorrow-struck features, and saw what I fancied the marks of a proud suffering spirit, I was well satisfied at not having given way to temper; still more so did I feel as he turned towards me, and, with a manner of ineffable gentleness, said, 'I entreat you to pardon me, sir, for an outburst of which I am already ashamed. A rude life and some bitter experiences have made me hard of heart and coarse in speech; still, it is only in moments of forgetfulness that I cease to remember what indulgence he owes to others who has such need of forgiveness himself.'

"I grasped his hand at once, and felt that his pressed mine like a friend's.

"'You spoke of going down to the West,' said he, after a brief pause. 'I start for that country to-night; you would do me a great favor should you accompany me.'

"I acceded at once, and he went on. 'Repton was to have been of the party, but business delays him a few days in town.'

"'I'll join you before the end of the week,' said Repton; 'by that time Mr. Massingbred will have expended all his borough blandishments and be free to give us his society.'

"Though the old lawyer now tried, and tried cleverly, to lead us away to lighter, pleasanter themes, the attempt was a failure; each felt, I suspect, some oppressive weight on his spirits that indisposed him to less serious talk; and again we came back to the Martins, the stranger evidently seeking to learn all he could of the disposition and temper of the young man.

"'It is as I thought,' said he, at last. 'It is the weak, sickly tone of the day has brought all this corruption upon us! Once upon a time the vices and follies of young men took their rise in their several natures,—this one gambled, the other drank, and so on,—the mass, however, was wonderfully sound and healthy; the present school, however, is to ape a uniformity, so that each may show himself in the livery of his fellows, thus imbibing wickedness he has no taste for, and none be less depraved and heartless than those around him. Let the women but follow the fashion, and there 's an end of us, as the great people we boasted to be!'

"I give you, so well as I can trust my memory, his words, Harry, but I cannot give you a certain sardonic bitterness,—a tone of mingled scorn and sorrow, such as I never before witnessed. He gave me the impression of being one who, originally frank, generous, and trustful, had, by intercourse with the world and commerce with mankind, grown to suspect every one and disbelieve in honesty, and yet could not bring his heart to acknowledge what his head had determined. In this wise, at least, I read his character from the opportunities I had of conversing with him on our journey. It was easy to see that he was a gentleman,—taking the word in the widest of its acceptations,—but from things that dropped from him, I could gather that his life had been that of an adventurer. He had been in the sea and land services of many of those new states of Southern America, had even risen to political importance in some of them; had possessed mines and vast tracts of territory one day, and the next saw himself 'without a piastre.' He had conducted operations against the Indians, and made treaties with them, and latterly had lived as the elected chief of a tribe in the west of the Rocky Mountains. But he knew civilized as well as savage life, had visited Spain in the rank of an envoy, and was familiar with all the great society of Rome, and the intrigues of its prince-bishops. The only theme, however, on which he really warmed was sport. The prairies brought out all his enthusiasm, and then he spoke like one carried away by glorious recollections of a time when, as he said himself, 'heart and hand and eye never failed him.'

"When he spoke of family ties or home affections, it was in a spirit of almost mockery, which puzzled me. His reasoning was that the attachments we form are only emanations of our own selfishness. We love, simply to be loved again. Whereas, were we single-hearted, we should be satisfied to know that those dear to us were well and happy, and only seek to serve them without demonstration or display.

"Am I wearying you, Harry, by dwelling on the traits of a man who, for the brief space I have known him, has made the most profound impression upon me? Even where I dissent—as is often the case—from his views, I have to own to myself that were I *he*, I should think and reason precisely as he does. I fancied at first that, like many men who had quitted civilized life for the rude ways of the 'bush,' he would have contrasted the man of refinement unfavorably with the savage, but he was too keen and acute for such a sweeping fallacy; he saw the good and evil in both, and sensibly remarked how independent of all education were the really strong characteristics of human nature. 'There is not a great quality of our first men,' said he, 'that I have not found to exist among the wild tribes of the Far West, nor is there an excellence of savage nature I have not witnessed amidst the polished and the pampered.'

"From what I can collect, he is only here passingly; some family matter has brought him over to this country; but he is already impatient to be back to his old haunts and associates, and his home beside the Orinoco. He has even asked me to come and visit him there; and from all I can see I should be as likely to attain distinction among the Chaymas as in the House of Commons, and should find the soft turf of the Savannahs as pleasant as the Opposition benches. In fact, Harry, I have half promised to accept his invitation; and if he renew it with anything like earnestness, I am resolved to go.

"I am just setting out for the Hendersons', and while the horses are being harnessed I have re-read your letter. Of course I have 'counted the cost,'—I have weighed the question to a pennyweight! I could already write down the list of those who will not know me at all, those who will know me a little, and the still fewer who will know my wife! Can you not see, my dear friend, that where one drags the anchor so easily, the mooring-ground was never good? The society to which you belong by such slender attachments gives no wound by separation from it.

"My anxiety now is on a very different score: it is that she will still refuse me. The hope I cling to is that she will see in my persistence a proof of sincerity. I would not, if I could, bring any family influence to my aid, and yet, short of this, there is nothing I would not do to insure success.

"I wish I had never re-opened your letter; that vein of sarcastic coolness which runs through it will never turn me from my purpose. You seem to forget, besides, that you are talking to a man of the world, just as hackneyed, just as 'used up' as yourself. I should like to see you assume this indolent dalliance before La Henderson! Take my word for it, Harry, you 'd be safer with the impertinence amongst some of your duchesses in Pall Mall. You say that great beauty in a woman, like genius in a man, is a kind of brevet nobility, and yet you add that the envy of the world will never weary of putting the possessor 'on his title.' How gladly would I accept this challenge! Ay, Harry, I tell you, in all defiance, that your proudest could not vie with her!

"If I wanted a proof of the vassalage of the social state we live in, I have it before me in the fact that a man like yourself, wellborn, young, rich, and high-hearted, should place the judgments and prejudices of half a dozen old tabbies of either sex above all the promptings of a noble ambition—all the sentiments of a generous devotion. Your starling cry of 'the Steward's daughter,' then, does not deter, it only determines the purpose

"Of yours faithfully,

"Jack Massingbred."

"You 'll see by the papers that I have accepted the Chiltern Hundreds. This is the first step.—now for the second!"

CHAPTER XXXIII
A DINNER AT "THE LODGE"

While the "Morning Post" of a certain day, some twenty years ago, was chronicling the illustrious guests who partook of his Majesty's hospitalities at Windsor, the "Dublin Evening Mail," under the less pretentious heading of "Viceregal Court," gave a list of those who had dined with his Excellency at the Lodge.

There was not anything very striking or very new in the announcement. Our *dramatis personæ,* in this wise, are limited; and after the accustomed names of the Lord Chancellor and Mrs. Dobbs, the Master of the Rolls and Mrs. Wiggins, Colonel Somebody of the 105th, Sir Felix and Miss Slasher, you invariably find the catalogue close with an un-der-secretary, a king-at-arms, and the inevitable Captain Lawrence Belcour, the aide-de-camp in waiting!—these latter recorded somewhat in the same spirit that the manager of a provincial theatre swells the roll of his company, by the names of the machinist, the scene-painter, and the leader of the band! We have no peculiar concern, however, with this fact, save that on the day in question our old friend Joseph Nelligan figured as a vice-regal guest. It was the first time he had been so honored, and, although not of a stamp to attach any great prize to the distinction, he was well aware that the recognition was intended as an honor; the more, when an aide-de-camp signified to him that his place at table was on one side of his Excellency.

When this veracious history first displayed young Nelligan at a dinner-party, his manner was shy and constrained; his secluded, student-like habits had given him none of that hardihood so essential in society. If he knew little of passing topics, he knew less of the tone men used in discussing them; and now, although more conversant with the world and its ways, daily brought into contact with the business of life, his social manner remained pretty nearly the same cold, awkward, and diffident thing it had been at first. Enlist him in a great subject, or call upon him on a great occasion, and he could rise above it; place him in a position to escape notice, and you never heard more of him.

The dinner company on this day contained nothing very formidable, either on the score of station or ability,—a few bar celebrities with their wives, an eccentric dean with a daughter, a garrison colonel or two, three country squires, and a doctor from Merrion Square. It was that interregnal period between the time when the castle parties included the first gentry of the land, and that later era when the priest and the agitator became the favored guests of vice-royalty. It is scarce necessary to say it was, as regards agreeability, inferior to either. There was not the courtly urbanity and polished pleasantry of a very accomplished class; nor was there the shrewd and coarse but racy intelligence of Mr. O'Connell's followers.

The Marquis of Reckington had come over to Ireland to "inaugurate," as the newspapers called it, a new policy; that is, he was to give to the working of the relief bill an extension and a significance which few either of its supporters or opposers in Parliament ever contemplated. The inequality of the Romanist before the law he might have borne; social depreciation was a heavier evil, and one quite intolerable. Now, as the change to the new system required considerable tact and address, they intrusted the task to a most accomplished and well-bred gentleman; and were Ireland only to be won by dinner-parties, Lord Reckington must have been its victor.

To very high rank and great personal advantages he united a manner of the most perfect kind. Dignified enough always to mark his station and his own consciousness of it, it was cordial without effort, frank and easy without display. If he could speak with all the weight of authority, he knew how to listen with actual deference; and there was that amount of change and "play" in his demeanor that made his companion, whoever for the moment he might be, believe that his views and arguments had made a deep impression on the Viceroy. To those unacquainted with such men, and the school to which they belong, there might have appeared something unreal, almost dramatic, in the elegant gracefulness of his bow, the gentle affability of his smile, the undeviating courtesy which he bestowed on all around him; but they were all of the man himself,—his very instincts,—his nature.

It had apparently been amongst his Excellency's instructions from his government to seek out such rising men of the Roman Catholic party as might be elevated and promoted on the just claims of their individual merits,—men, in fact, whose conduct and bearing would be certain to justify their selection for high office. It could not be supposed that a party long proscribed, long estranged from all participation in power, could be rich in such qualifications. At the bar, the ablest men usually threw themselves into the career of politics, and of course by strong partisanship more or less prejudiced their claims to office. It was rare indeed to find one who, with the highest order of abilities, was satisfied to follow a profession whose best rewards were denied him. Such was Joseph Nelligan when he was first "called," and such he continued to the very hour we now see him. Great as had been his college successes, his triumphs at the bar overtopped them all. They who remembered his shy and reserved manner wondered whence he came by his dignity; they who knew his youth could not imagine how he came by his "law."

Mr. M'Casky, the castle law-adviser, an old recruiting-serjeant of capacities, who had "tipped the shilling" to men of every party, had whispered his name to the Under-Secretary, who had again repeated it to the Viceroy. He was, as M'Casky said, "the man they wanted, with talent enough to confront the best of the opposite party, and wealthy enough to want nothing that can figure in a budget." Hence was he, then, there a favored guest, and seated on his Excellency's left hand.

For the magic influence of that manner which we have mentioned as pertaining to the Viceroy, we ask for no better evidence than the sense of perfect ease which Joe Nelligan now enjoyed. The *suave* dignity of the Marquis was blended with a something like personal regard, a mysterious intimation that seemed to say, "This is the sort of man I have long been looking for; how gratifying that I should have found him at last!" They concurred in so many points, too, not merely in opinions, but actually in the very expressions by which they characterized them; and when at last his Excellency, having occasion to quote something he had said, called him "Nelligan," the spell was complete.

Oh dear! when we torture our brains to legislate for apothecaries, endeavoring in some way or other to restrict the sale of those subtle ingredients on every grain or drop of which a human life may hang, why do we never think of those far more subtle elements of which great people are the dispensers,—flatteries more soothing than chloroform, smiles more lulling than poppy-juice! Imagine poor Nelligan under a course of this treatment, dear reader; fancy the delicious poison as it insinuates itself through his veins, and if you have ever been so drugged yourself, picture to your mind all the enjoyment he experienced.

By one of those adroit turns your social magician is master of, the Viceroy had drawn the conversation towards Nelligan's county and his native town.

"I was to have paid a visit to poor Martin there," said he, "and I certainly should have looked in upon *you*."

Nelligan's cheek was in a flame; pride and shame were both there, warring for the mastery.

"Poor fellow!" said his Excellency, who saw the necessity of a diversion, "I fear that he has left that immense estate greatly embarrassed. Some one mentioned to me, the other day, that the heir will not succeed to even a fourth of the old property."

"I have heard even worse, my Lord," said Nelligan. "There is a rumor that he is left without a shilling."

"How very shocking! They are connections of my own!" said the Viceroy; as though what he said made the misery attain its climax.

"I am aware, my Lord, that Lady Dorothea is related to your Excellency, and I am surprised you have not heard the stories I allude to."

"But perhaps I am incorrect," said the Marquis. "It may be that I *have* heard them; so many things pass through one's ears every day. But here is Colonel Mas-singbred; he 's sure to know it. Massingbred, we want some news of the Martins—the Martins of—what is it called?"

"Cro' Martin, my Lord," said Nelligan, reddening.

"I hold the very latest news of that county in my hand, my Lord," replied the Secretary. "It is an express from my son, who writes from Oughterard."

Nelligan stood, scarcely breathing, with impatience to hear the tidings.

Colonel Massingbred ran his eyes over the first page of the letter, murmuring to himself the words; then turning over, he said: "Yes, here it is,—'While I write this, the whole town is in a state of intense excitement; the magistrates have sent in for an increased force of police, and even soldiery, to repress some very serious disturbances on the Martin property. It would appear that Merl—the man who assumes to claim the property, as having purchased the reversion from young Martin—was set upon by a large mob, and pursued, himself and his friends, for several miles across the country. They escaped with their lives, but have arrived here in a lamentable plight. There is really no understanding these people. It was but the other day, and there was no surer road to their favor than to abuse and vilify these same Martins, and now they are quite ready to murder any one who aspires to take their place. If one was to credit the stories afloat, they have already wreaked a fatal vengeance on some fellows employed by Merl to serve notices on the tenantry; but I believe that the outrages have really gone no further than such maltreatment as Irishmen like to give, and are accustomed to take.'"

Here his Excellency laughed heartily, and Joe Nelligan looked grave.

Massingbred read on: "'Without being myself a witness to it, I never could have credited the almost feudal attachment of these people to an "Old

House." The Radical party in the borough are, for the moment, proscribed, and dare not show themselves in the streets; and even Magennis, who so lately figured as an enemy to the Martins, passed through the town this morning with his wife, with a great banner flying over his jaunting-car, inscribed "The Martins for Ever!" This burst of sentiment on his part, I ought to mention, was owing to a most devoted piece of heroism performed by Miss Martin, who sought out the lost one and brought her safely back, through a night of such storm and hurricane as few ever remember. Such an act, amidst such a people, is sure of its reward. The peasantry would, to a man, lay down their lives for her; and coming critically, as the incident did, just when a new proprietor was about to enforce his claim, you can fancy the added bitterness it imparted to their spirit of resistance. I sincerely trust that the magistrates will not accede to the demand for an increased force. A terrible collision is sure to be the result, and I know enough of these people to be aware of what can be done by a little diplomacy, particularly when the right negotiator is employed. I mean, therefore, to go over and speak to Mr. Nelligan, who is the only man of brains amongst the magistrates here.'"

"A relative, I presume," said his Excellency.

"My father, my Lord," replied Joe, blushing.

"Oh! here is the result of his interview," said Massing-bred, turning to the foot of the page. "'Nelligan quite agreed in the view I had taken, and said the people would assuredly disarm and perhaps destroy any force we could send against them. He is greatly puzzled what course to adopt; and when I suggested the propriety of invoking Miss Martin's aid, told me that this is out of the question, since she is on a sick-bed. While we were speaking, a Dublin physician passed through on his way to visit her. This really does add to the complication, for she is, perhaps, the only one who could exert a great influence over the excited populace. In any other country it might read strangely, that it was to a young lady men should have recourse in a moment of such peril; but this is like no other country, the people like no other people, the young lady herself, perhaps, like no other young lady!'"

By a scarcely perceptible movement of his head, and a very slight change of voice, Colonel Massingbred intimated to the Viceroy that there was something for his private ear, and Lord Reckington stepped back to hear it. Nelligan, too deeply occupied in his own thoughts to remark the circumstance, stood in the same place, silent and motionless.

"It is to this passage," whispered the Secretary, "I want to direct your Excellency's attention: 'All that I see here,' my son writes,—'all that I see here is a type of what is going on, at large, over the island. Old families uprooted, old ties severed; the people, with no other instinct than lawlessness, hesitating which side to take. Their old leaders, only bent upon the political, have forgotten the social struggle, and thus the masses are left without guidance or direction. It is my firm conviction that the Church of Rome will seize the happy moment to usurp an authority thus unclaimed, and the priest step in between the landlord and the demagogue; and it is equally my belief that you can only retard, not prevent, this consummation. If you should be of *my* opinion, and be able to induce his Excellency to think with us, act promptly and decisively. Enlist the Roman Catholic laity in your cause before you be driven to the harder compact of having to deal with the clergy. And first of all, make—for fortunately you have the vacancy,—make young Nelligan your solicitor-general.'"

The Viceroy gave a slight start, and smiled. He had not, as yet, accustomed his mind to such bold exercise of his patronage. He lived, however, to get over this sensation.

"My son," resumed Massingbred, "argues this at some length. If you permit, I 'll leave the letter in your Excellency's hands. In fact, I read it very hurriedly, and came over here the moment I glanced my eyes over this passage."

His Excellency took the letter, and turned to address a word to Joe Nelligan, but he had left the spot.

"Belcour," said the Viceroy, "tell Mr. Nelligan I wish to speak to him. I shall be in the small drawing-room. I 'll talk with him alone. Massingbred, be ready to come when I shall send for you."

The Viceroy sat alone by the fire, pondering over all he had heard. There was, indeed, that to ponder over, even in the brief, vague description of the writer. "The difficulties of Ireland," as it was the fashion of the day to call them, were not such as government commissions discover, or blue books describe; they lay deeper than the legislative lead-line ever reaches,—many a fathom down below statutes and Acts of Parliament. They were in the instincts, the natures, the blood of a people who had never acknowledged themselves a conquered nation. Perhaps his Excellency lost himself in speculations, mazy and confused enough to addle deeper heads. Perhaps he was puzzled to think how he could bring the Cabinet to see these things, or the importance that pertained to them; who knows? At all events, time glided on, and still he was alone. At length the aide-de-camp appeared, and with an air of some confusion, said,—"It would appear, my Lord, that Mr. Nelligan has gone away."

"Why, he never said good-night; he did n't take leave of me!" said the Viceroy, smiling.

The aide-de-camp slightly elevated his brows, as though to imply his sense of what it might not have become him to characterize in words.

"Very strange, indeed!" repeated his Excellency; "is n't it, Belcour?"

"Very strange, indeed, your Excellency," said the other, bowing.

"There could have been no disrespect in it," said his Lordship, good-humoredly; "of *that* I'm quite certain. Send Colonel Massingbred here."

"He's gone off, Massingbred," said the Viceroy, as the other appeared.

"So I have just learned, my Lord. I conclude he was not aware—that he was unacquainted with—"

"Oh, of course, Massingbred," broke in the Viceroy, laughing, "the fault is all with my predecessors in office; they never invited these men as they ought to have done. Have you sounded M'Casky as to the appointment?"

"Yes, my Lord; he thinks 'we might do worse.'"

"A qualified approval, certainly. Perhaps he meant we might select himself!"

"I rather opine, my Lord, that he regards Nelligan's promotion as likely to give offence to Mr. O'Connell, unless that he be himself consulted upon it."

"Then comes the question, Who is it governs this country, Colonel Massingbred?" said the Marquis; and for the first time a flash of angry meaning darkened his cheeks. "If I be here,"—he stopped and hesitated,—"if you and I be here only to ratify appointments made by irresponsible individuals,—if we hold the reins of power only to be told where we 're to drive to,—I must own the office is not very dignified, nor am I patient enough to think it endurable."

"M'Casky only suggested that it might be advisable to see O'Connell on the subject, not, as it were, to pass him over in conferring the appointment."

"I cannot at all concur in this view, Massingbred," said the Marquis, proudly; "there could be no such humiliation in the world as a patronage administered in this wise. Write to Nelligan; write to him to-night. Say that his abrupt departure alone prevented my making to him personally the offer of the solicitorship; add that you have my directions to place the office in his hands, and express a strong wish, on your own part, that he may not decline it."

Massingbred bowed in acquiescence, and after a pause his Excellency went on:—

"There would be no objection to your adding something to the effect that my selection of him was prompted by motives in which party has no share; that his acknowledged eminence at the bar,—a character to which even political opponents bear honorable testimony,—in fact, Massingbred," added he, impatiently, "if the appointment should come to be questioned in the House, let us have it on record that we made it solely on motives directed to the public service. You understand me?"

"I think so, my Lord," said Massingbred, and withdrew.

If it were not that other cares and other interests call us away, we would gladly linger a little longer to speculate on the Viceroy's thoughts as he reseated himself by the fire. His brow was overcast and his features clouded. Was it that he felt he had entered the lists, and thrown down the glove to a strong and resolute opponent? Had he before him a vista of the terrible conflict between expediency and honor that was soon to be his fate? Had he his doubts as to the support his own Cabinet would afford him? Was his pride the ruling sentiment of the moment, or did there enter into his calculations the subtle hope of all the eager expectancy this appointment would create, all the disposable venality it would lay at his discretion? Who can answer these questions? who solve these doubts? Is it not very possible that his mind wandered amidst them all? Is it not more than likely that they passed in review before him? for when he rejoined his company his manner was more absent, his courtesy less easy than usual.

At length Mr. M'Casky came forward to say goodnight.

"Colonel Massingbred has told you of those disturbances in the West, has he not?" asked the Viceroy.

"Yes, my Lord," replied the other.

"And what opinion—what advice did you give?"

"To let matters alone, my Lord; to be always a little behind time, particularly in sending a force. 'Never despatch the police to quell a riot,' said John Toler, 'unless one of the factions be completely beaten, otherwise you 'll have them both on your back;' and I assure your Excellency, Ireland has been very successfully governed under that maxim for years past."

"Thank you, M'Casky; thank you for the advice," said his Excellency, laughing, and wished him good-night.

CHAPTER XXXIV
AN HONORED GUEST

It was a time of unusual stir and bustle at the Martin Arms; the house was crammed with company. Messengers—some mounted, others on foot—came and went at every moment; horses stood ready saddled and harnessed in the stables, in waiting for any emergency; in fact, there was a degree of movement and animation only second to that of a contested election. In the midst of this confusion a chaise with four smoking posters drew up at the door, and a sharp, clear voice called out,—"Morrissy, are my rooms ready?"

"No, indeed, Mr. Repton," stammered out the abashed landlord; "the house is full; there's not a spot in it to put a child in."

"You got my letter, I suppose?" said Repton, angrily.

"I did, sir, but it was too late; the whole house was engaged by Mr. Scanlan, and the same evening the company arrived in two coaches-and-four."

"And who is the precious company you speak of?"

"Mr. Merl, sir," said the other, dropping his voice to a whisper, "the new owner of Cro' Martin; he's here, with two or three great lawyers and one or two of his friends. They came down to serve the notices and give warning—"

"Well, what is to be done? where can I be accommodated?" broke in Repton, hastily. "Isn't Mr. Massing-bred in the house?"

"No, sir, he had to move out, too; but, sure enough, he left a bit of a note for you in the bar." And he hastened off at once to fetch it.

Repton broke open the seal impatiently, and read:—

"My dear Mr. Repton,—I regret that you 'll find the inn full on your arrival; they turned me out yesterday to make room for Mr. Merl and his followers. Happily, Mr. Nelligan heard of my destitution, and offered me a quarter at his house. He also desires me to say that he will deem it a very great favor if you will accept the shelter of his roof, and in hopeful anticipation of your consenting, he will wait dinner for your arrival. From my own knowledge, I can safely assure you that the offer is made in a spirit of true hospitality, and I sincerely wish that you may accept it.

"Yours very faithfully,

"J. Massingbred."

"Where does Mr. Nelligan live?" asked Repton, as he refolded the letter.

"Just across the street, sir. There it is."

"Set me down there, then," said Repton. And the next moment he was at Nelligan's door.

"This is a very great honor, sir," said old Dan, as he appeared in a suit of decorous black. "It is, indeed, a proud day that gives me the pleasure of seeing you here."

"My dear sir, if you had no other distinction than being the father of Joseph Nelligan, the honor and the pride lie all in the opposite scale. I am sincerely glad to be your guest, and to know you where every true Irishman is seen to the greatest advantage,—at the head of his own board."

While Nelligan conducted his guest to his room, he mentioned that Massingbred had ridden over to Cro' Martin early in the morning, but would be certainly back for dinner.

"And what's the news of Miss Martin? Is she better?"

"They say not, sir. The last accounts are far from favorable."

"Sir Henry Laurie saw her, did n't he?"

"Yes, sir; he passed all Sunday here, and only returned to town yesterday. He spoke doubtfully,—I might even say, gloomily. He said, however, that we cannot know anything for certain before Friday or, perhaps, Saturday."

"It is fever, then?"

"Yes, he told my wife, the worst character of typhus."

"Brought on, as I've been told, by exposure to wet and cold on that night at sea. Is n't that the case?"

"I believe so. Mrs. Nelligan went over the next morning to the cottage. She had heard of poor Mr. Martin's death, and thought she might be of some use to Miss Mary; but when she arrived, it was to find her in fever, talking wildly, and insisting that she must be up and away to Kyle-a-Noe to look after a poor sick family there."

"Has Mrs. Nelligan seen her since that?"

"She never left her,—never quitted her. She relieves Henderson's daughter in watching beside her bed; for the old housekeeper is quite too infirm to bear the fatigue."

"What a sad change has come over this little spot, and in so brief a space too! It seems just like yesterday that I was a guest at Cro' Martin,—poor Martin himself so happy and light-hearted; his dear girl, as he called her, full of life and spirits. Your son was there the night I speak of. I remember it well, for the madcap girls would make a fool of me, and insisted on my singing them a song; and I shall not readily forget the shame my compliance inflicted on my learned brother's face."

"Joe told me of it afterwards."

"Ah, he told you, did he? He doubtless remarked with asperity on the little sense of my own dignity I possessed?"

"On the contrary, sir, he said, 'Great as are Mr. Rep-ton's gifts, and brilliant as are his acquirements, I envy him more the happy buoyancy of his nature than all his other qualities.'"

"He's a fine fellow, and it was a generous speech; not but I will be vain enough to say he was right,—ay, sir, perfectly right. Of all the blessings that pertain to temperament, there is not one to compare with the spirit that renews in an old man the racy enjoyment of youth, keeps his heart fresh and his mind hopeful. With these, age brings no terrors. I shall be seventy-five, sir, if I live to the second of next month, and I have not lived long enough to dull the enjoyment life affords me, nor diminish the pleasure my heart derives upon hearing of a noble action or a generous sentiment."

Nelligan gazed at the speaker in mingled astonishment and admiration. Somehow, it was not altogether the man he had expected; but he was far from being disappointed at the difference. The Valentine Repton of his imagination was a crafty pleader, a subtle cross-examiner, an ingenious flatterer of juries; but he was not a man whose nature was assailable by anything "not found in the books."

Now, though Nelligan was himself essentially a worldly man, he was touched by these traits of one whom he had regarded as a hardened old lawyer, distrustful and suspicious.

"Ay, sir," said Repton, as, leaning on the other's arm, he entered the drawing-room, "a wiser man than either of us has left it on record, that after a long life and much experience of the world, he met far more of good and noble qualities in mankind than of their opposite. Take my word for it, whenever we are inclined to the contrary opinion, the fault lies with ourselves."

While they sat awaiting Massingbred's return, a servant entered with a note, which Nelligan, having read, handed over to Repton. It was very brief, and ran thus:—

"My dear Mr. Nelligan,—Forgive my not appearing at dinner, and make my excuses to Mr. Repton, if he be with you, for I have just fallen in with Magennis, who insists on carrying me off to Barnagheela. You can understand, I 'm sure, that there are reasons why I could not well decline this invitation. Meanwhile, till to-morrow, at breakfast,

"I am yours,

"Jack Massingbred."

If there was a little constraint on Nelligan's part at finding himself alone to do the honors to his distinguished guest, the feeling soon wore away, and a frank, hearty confidence was soon established between these two men, who up to the present moment had been following very different roads in life. Apart from a lurking soreness, the remnants of long-past bitterness, Nelligan's political opinions were fair and moderate, and agreed with Repton's now to a great extent. His views as to the people, their habits and their natures, were also strikingly just and true. He was not over-hopeful, nor was he despondent; too acute an observer to refer their faults to any single source, he regarded their complex, intricate characters as the consequence of many causes, the issue of many struggles. There was about all he said the calm judgment of a man desirous of truth; and yet, when he came to speak of the higher classes, the great country gentry, he displayed prejudices and mistakes quite incredible in one of his discernment. The old grudge of social disqualification had eaten deep into his heart, and, as Repton saw, it would take at least two generations of men, well-to-do and successful, to eradicate the sentiment.

Nelligan was quick enough to see that these opinions of his were not shared by his guest, and said, "I cannot expect, Mr. Repton, that you will join me in these views; you have seen these people always as an equal, if not their superior; they met *you* with their best faces and sweetest flatteries. Not so with us. They draw a line, as though to say, go on: make your fortunes; purchase estates; educate your children; send them to the universities with our own; teach them our ways, our instincts, our manners, and yet, at the end of all, you shall remain exactly where you began. You shall never be 'of us.'"

"I am happy to say that I disagree with you," said Repton; "I am a much older man than you, and I can draw, therefore, on a longer experience. Now the change that I myself have seen come over the tone and temper of the world since I was a boy is far more marvellous to me than all the new-fangled discoveries around us in steam and electricity. Why, sir, the man who now addresses you, born of an ancient stock, as good blood as any untitled gentleman of the land, was treated once as Jack Cade might be in a London drawing-room. The repute of liberal notions or politics at that day stamped you as a democrat and atheist If you sided with a popular measure, you were deemed capable of all the crimes of a 'Danton.'

"Do I not remember it!—Ay, as a student, young, ardent, and high-hearted, when I was summoned before the visitors of the university, and sternly asked by the dark-browed Lord Chancellor if I belonged to a society called the 'Friends of Ireland,' and on my acknowledging the fact, without inquiry, without examination, deprived of my scholarship, and sent back to my chambers, admonished to be more cautious, and menaced with expulsion. I had very little to live on in those days; my family had suffered great losses in fortune, and I disliked to be a burden to them. I took pupils, therefore, to assist me in my support. The Vice-Provost stepped in, however, and interdicted this. 'Young men,' he said, 'ran a greater chance of coming out of my hands followers of Paine than disciples of Newton.' I starved on till I was called to the bar. There fresh insults and mortifications met me. My name on a brief seemed a signal for a field-day against Jacobinism and infidelity. The very bench forgot its dignity in its zeal. I remember well one day, when, stung and maddened by these outrages, I so far forgot myself as to reply, and the Court of King's Bench was closed against me for twelve long years,—ay, till I came back to it as the first man in my profession. It was a trumpery cause,—I forget what; a suit about some petty bill of exchange. I disputed the evidence, and sought to show its invalidity. The Chief Justice stopped me, and said, 'The Court is aware of the point on which you rely; we have known evidence of this nature admitted in cases of trial for treason,—cases with which Mr. Repton, we know, is very familiar. I stopped; my blood boiled with indignation, my temples throbbed to bursting, to be thus singled out amongst my brethren—before the public—as a mark of scorn and reprobation. 'It is true, my Lord,' said I, with a slow, measured utterance, 'I am familiar with such cases. Who is there in this unhappy land that is not? I am aware, too, that if I stood in that dock arraigned on such a charge, your Lordship would rule that this evidence was admissible; you would charge against me, sentence, and hang me; but the present is an action for eleven pounds ten, and, therefore, I trust to your Lordship's lenity and mercy to reject it.'

"That reply, sir, cost me twelve years of exile from the court wherein I uttered it. Those were times when the brow-beating judge could crush the bar; nor were the jury always safe in the sanctuary of the jury-box. Now, such abuses are no longer in existence; and if we have made no other stride in progress, even that is considerable."

"In all that regards the law and its administration, I am sure you are correct, sir," said Nelligan, submissively.

"At the period I speak of," resumed Repton, who now was only following out his own thoughts and reminiscences, "the judges were little else than prefects, administering the country through the channel of the penal code, and the jury a set of vulgar partisans, who wielded the power of a verdict with all the caprice of a faction; and as to their ignorance, why, sir, Crookshank, who afterwards sat on the bench, used to tell of a trial for murder at Kells, where the 'murdered man' was two hours under cross-examination on the table! Yes, but that is not all; the jury retired to deliberate, and came out at length with a verdict of 'manslaughter,' as the prisoner was 'a bad fellow, and had once stolen a saddle from the foreman.' You talk of law and civilization; why, I tell you, sir, that the barbaric code of the red man is a higher agent of enlightenment than the boasted institutions of England, when thus perverted and degraded. No, no, Mr. Nelligan, it may be a fine theme for declamation, there may be grand descriptive capabilities about the Ireland of sixty or seventy years ago, but be assured, it was a social chaos of the worst kind; and as a maxim, sir, remember, that the inhabitants of a country are never so much to be pitied as when the aspect of their social condition is picturesque!"

Repton fell into a musing fit when he had finished these observations, and Nelligan felt too much deference for his guest to disturb him, and they sat thus silent for some time, when the old lawyer suddenly arousing himself, said, — "What's all this I hear about disturbances, and attacks on the police, down here?"

"There's nothing political in it," rejoined Nelligan. "It was resistance offered by the people to the service of certain notices on the part of this London Jew—Merl, I think they call him."

"Yes, that's the name," quickly responded Repton. "You are aware of the circumstances under which he claims the estate?"

"I had it from Brierley, who was told by Scanlan, that he purchased, or rather won at play, the entire and sole reversion."

Repton nodded.

"And such is a legal compact, I presume?" said Nelligan.

"If the immoral obligation be well concealed in the negotiation, I don't see how it is to be broken. The law, sir," added he, solemnly, "never undertakes the charge of fools till a commission be taken out in their behalf! This young fellow's pleasure it was to squander his succession to a princely estate, and he chanced to meet with one who could appreciate his intentions."

"Massingbred told me, however, that some arrangement, some compromise was in contemplation; that Merl, knowing that to enforce his claim would subject him to a trial and all its disclosures, had shown a disposition to treat; in fact, Massingbred has already had an interview with him, and but for Scanlan, who desires to push matters to extremity, the affair might possibly be accommodated."

"The Jew possibly sees, too, that an Irish succession is not a bloodless triumph. He has been frightened, I have no doubt."

"I believe so; they say he took to his bed the day he got back here, and has never quitted it since. The people hunted them for four miles across the country, and as Merl couldn't leap his horse over the walls, they were several times nearly caught by the delay in making gaps for him."

"I'd have given fifty pounds to be in at it," broke out Repton. Then suddenly remembering that the aspiration did not sound as very dignified, he hemmed and corrected himself, saying, "It must, indeed, have been a strange spectacle!"

"They started at Kyle's Wood, and ran them over the low grounds beside Kelly's Mills, and then doubling, brought them along the foot of Barnagheela Mountain, where, it seems, Magennis joined the chase; he was fast closing with them when his gun burst, and rather damaged his hand."

"He fired, then?"

"Yes, he put a heavy charge of slugs into Merl's horse as he was getting through the mill-race, and the beast flung up and threw his rider into the stream. Scanlan dismounted and gathered him up, discharging his pistol at some country fellow who was rushing forward; they say the man has lost an eye. They got off, however, and, gaining the shelter of the Cro' Martin wood, they managed to escape at last, and reached this about six o'clock, their clothes in tatters, their horses lamed, and themselves lamentable objects of fatigue and exhaustion. Since that, no one but the doctor has seen Merl, and Scanlan only goes out with an escort of police."

"All this sounds very like 'sixty years ago,'" said Repton, laughing.

"I'm afraid it does, and I half dread what the English newspapers may say under the heading of 'Galway Barbarities.'"

"By Jove! I must say I like it; that is," said Repton, hesitating and confused, "I can see some palliation for the people in such an outburst of generous but misdirected feeling. The old name has still its spell for their hearts; and even superstitions, sir, are better than incredulity!"

"But of what avail is all this? The law must and will be vindicated. It may cost some lives, on the road, but Mr. Merl must reach his journey's end, at last."

"He may deem the sport, as I have known some men do tiger-hunting, not worth the danger," said Repton. "You and I, Mr. Nelligan, acclimated, as I may say, to such incidents, would probably not decline the title to an estate, whose first step in possession should be enforced by the blunderbuss; but make the scene Africa, and say what extent of territory would you accept of, on the compact of enforcing your claim against the natives? Now, for all the purposes of argument, to this cockney's appreciation, these countrymen of ours are Africans."

"I can well understand his terror," said Nelligan, thoughtfully. "I 'm sure the yell that followed him through the gap of Kyle-a-Noe will ring in his heart for many a day. It was there the pursuit was hottest. As they came out, a stranger, who had been here during the winter,—a Mr. Barry—"

"What of *him*? What did *he* do?" broke in Repton, with great eagerness.

"He stood upon an old wall, and hurrahed the people on, calling out, 'Five gold guineas to the man who will hurl that fellow into the lake.'"

"He said that?" cried Repton.

"Yes, and waved his hat in encouragement to the mob! This was deposed in evidence before the bench; and Scanlan's affidavit went on to say, that when the temper of the people seemed to relent, and the ardor of their pursuit to relax, this man's presence invariably rallied all the energies of mischief, and excited the wildest passions of the populace."

"Who or what is he supposed to be?" asked the lawyer.

"Some say, a returned convict,—a banker that was transported thirty years ago for forgery; others, that he is Con O'Hara, that killed Major Stackpoole in the famous duel at Bunratty Castle. Magennis swears that he remembers the face well; at all events, there is a mystery about him, and when he came into the shop below stairs—"

"Oh, then, you have seen him yourself?"

"Yes; he came in on Monday last, and asked for some glazed gunpowder, and if we had bullets of a large mould to fit his pistols. They were curiosities in their way; they were made in America, and had a bore large as your thumb."

"You had some conversation with him?"

"A few words about the country and the crops. He said he thought we had good prospects for the wheat, and, if we should have a fine harvest, a good winter was like to follow. Meaning that, with enough to eat, we should have fewer outrages in the dark nights, and by that I knew he was one acquainted with the country. I said as much, and then he turned fiercely on me, and remarked, 'I never questioned you, sir, about your hides and tallow and ten-penny nails, for they were *your* affairs; please, then, to pay the same deference to *me* and *mine*.' And before I could reply he was gone."

"It was a rude speech," said Repton, thoughtfully; "but many men are morose from circumstances whose natures are full of kindliness and gentleness."

"It was precisely the impression this stranger made upon me. There was that in his manner which implied a hard lot in life,—no small share of the shadiest side of fortune; and even when his somewhat coarse rebuke was uttered, I was more disposed to be angry with myself for being the cause than with him who made it."

"Where is he stopping just now?"

"At Kilkieran, I have heard; but he has been repeatedly back and forward in the town here during the week, though for the last few days I have not seen him. Perhaps he has heard of Scanlan's intention to summons him for aiding and abetting an assault, and has kept out of the way in consequence."

"*He* keep out of the way!" cried Repton; "you never mistook a man more in your life!"

"You are acquainted with him, then?" said Nelligan, in amazement.

"That am I, sir. No one knows him better, and on my knowledge of the man it was that I apologized for his incivility to yourself. If I cannot say more, Mr. Nelligan, it is not because I have any mistrust in your confidence, but that my friend's secret is, in his own charge, and only to be revealed at his own pleasure."

"I wish you would tell him that I never meant to play the spy upon him,—that my remark was a merely chance observation—"

"I promise you to do so," broke in Repton. "I promise you still more, that before he leaves this you shall have an apology from his own lips for his accidental rudeness; nay, two men that would know how to respect each other should never part under even a passing misunderstanding. It is an old theory of mine, Mr. Nelligan, that good men's good opinions of us form the pleasantest store of our reminiscences, and I 'd willingly go a hundred miles to remove a misconception that might bring me back to the esteem of an honorable heart, though I never were to set eyes again on him who possessed it."

"I like your theory well, sir," said Nelligan, cordially.

"You 'll find the practice will reward you," said Repton.

"I confess this stranger has inspired me with great curiosity."

"I can well understand the feeling," said Repton, musing. "It is with men as with certain spots in landscape, there are chance glimpses which suggest to us the fair scenes that lie beyond our view! Poor fellow! poor fellow!" muttered he once or twice to himself; and then starting abruptly, said, "You have made me so cordially welcome here that I am going to profit by every privilege of a guest. I 'm going to say good-night, for I have much before me on the morrow."

CHAPTER XXXV
HOW DIPLOMACY FAILED

Repton was up at daybreak, and at his desk. Immense folios littered the table, and even the floor around him, and the old lawyer sat amidst a chaos that it was difficult to believe was only the growth of an hour or two. All the intentness of his occupation, however, did not prevent him hearing a well-known voice in the little stable-yard beneath his window, and opening the sash he called out, "Mas-singbred, is that you?"

"Ah, Mr. Repton, are you stirring so early? I had not expected to see you for at least two hours to come. May I join you?"

"By all means; at once," was the answer. And the next moment they were together. "Where's Barry? When did you see him last?" was Repton's first question.

"For a moment, on Tuesday last; he came up here to learn if you had arrived, or when you might be expected. He seemed disappointed when I said not before the latter end of the week, and muttered something about being too late. He seemed flurried and excited. I heard afterwards that he had been somehow mixed up with that tumultuous assemblage that resisted the police, and I offered to go back with him to Kilkieran, but he stopped me short, saying, 'I am not at Kilkieran;' and so abruptly as to show that my proposal was not acceptable. He then sat down and wrote a short letter, which he desired me to give you on arriving; but to deliver it with my own hand, as, if any reply were necessary, I should be ready to carry it to him. This is the letter."

Repton read it rapidly, and then, walking to the window, stood pondering over the contents.

"You know this man Merl, don't you, Massingbred?" asked Repton.

"Yes, thoroughly."

"The object of this letter is to try one last chance for an arrangement. Barry suspects that the Jew's ambition for Irish proprietorship may have been somewhat dashed by the experience of the last few days; that he will be likely enough to weigh the advantages and disadvantages with a juster appreciation than if he had never come here, and, if such be the case, we are ready to meet with a fair and equitable offer. We'll repay him all that he advanced in cash to young Martin, and all that he won from him at play, if he surrender his reversionary claim. We'll ask no questions as to how this loan was made, or how that debt incurred. It shall be the briefest of all transactions,—a sum in simple addition, and a check for the total."

"He'll refuse,—flatly refuse it," said Massingbred. "The very offer will restore any confidence the last few days may have shaken; he'll judge the matter like the shares of a stock that are quoted higher in the market."

"You think so?"

"I'm sure of it. I'm ashamed to say, Mr. Repton, that my knowledge of the Herman Merl class may be greater than yours. It is the one solitary point in the realm of information wherein I am probably your superior."

"There are others, and of a very different order, in which I would own you the master," said Repton. "But to our case. Suppose,—a mere supposition, if you like,—but suppose that it could be demonstrated to Mr. Merl that his claim will be not only resisted, but defeated; that the right on which he relies is valueless,—the deed not worth the stamps it bears; that this offer is made to avoid a publicity and exposure far more injurious to him than to those who now shrink from it. What think you then?"

"Simply that he'd not believe it! He'd say, and many others would say, 'If the right lay so incontestably with these others, they 'd not give some twenty thousand pounds to compromise what they could enforce for the mere cost of a trial.'"

"Mr. Massingbred, too, would perhaps take the same view of the transaction," said Repton, half tartly.

"Not if Mr. Repton assured me that he backed the opposite opinion," said Jack, politely.

"I thank you heartily for that speech," said the old man, as he grasped the other's hand cordially; "you deserve, and shall have my fullest confidence."

"May I ask," said Jack, "if this offer to buy off Merl be made in the interest of the Martins, for otherwise I really see no great object, so far as they are concerned, in the change of mastery?"

"You'll have to take *my* word for that," said Repton, "or rather, to take the part I assume in this transaction as the evidence of it; and now, as I see that you are satisfied, will you accept of the duty of this negotiation? Will you see and speak with Merl? Urge upon him all the arguments your own ingenuity will furnish, and when you come, if you should be so driven, to the coercive category, and that you want the siege artillery, then send for *me*. Depend upon it, it will be no *brutum fulmen* that I 'll bring up; nor will I, as Pelham said, fire with 'government powder.' My cannon shall be inscribed, like those of the old volunteers, independence or—"

At any other moment Jack might have smiled at the haughty air and martial stride of the old man, as, stimulated by his words, he paced the room; but there was a sincerity and a resolution about him that offered no scope for ridicule. His very features wore a look of intrepidity that bespoke the courage that animated him.

"Now, Massingbred," said he, laying his hand on the young man's arm, "it is only because I am not free to tell another man's secret that I do not at once place you fully in possession of all I myself know of this transaction; but rely on it, you shall be informed on every point, and immediately after the issue of this negotiation with Merl, whatever be the result, you shall stand on the same footing with myself."

"You cannot suppose that I exact this confidence?" began Jack.

"I only know it is your due, sir," said Repton. "Go now,—it is not too early; see this man, and let the meeting be of the briefest, for if I were to tell you my own mind, I'd say I'd rather he should reject our offer."

"You are, I own, a little incomprehensible this morning," said Massingbred, "but I am determined to yield you a blind obedience; and so I'm off."

"I 'll wait breakfast for you," said Repton, as he reseated himself to his work.

Repton requested Mr. Nelligan's permission to have his breakfast served in his own room, and sat for a long time impatiently awaiting Massingbred's return. He was at one time aroused by a noise below stairs, but it was not the announcement of him he looked for; and he walked anxiously to and fro in his chamber, each moment adding to the uneasiness that he felt.

"Who was it that arrived half an hour ago?" asked he of the servant.

"Mr. Joe, sir, the counsellor, has just come from Dublin, and is at breakfast with the master."

"Ah! he 's come, is he? So much the better," muttered Repton, "we may want his calm, clear head to assist us here; not that we shall have to fear a contest,—there is no enemy in the field,—and if there were, Val Repton is ready to meet him!" And the old man crossed his arms, and stood erect in all the consciousness of his undiminished vigor. "Here he comes at last,—I know his step on the stair." And he flung open the door for Massingbred.

"I read failure in your flushed cheek, Massingbred; failure and anger both, eh?"

Massingbred tried to smile. If there was any quality on which he especially prided himself, it was the bland semblance of equanimity he could assume in circumstances of difficulty and irritation. It was his boast to be able to hide his most intense emotions at moments of passion, and there was a period in which, indeed, he wielded this acquirement. Of later times, however, he had grown more natural and impulsive; he had not yet lost the sense of pain this yielding occasioned, and it was with evident irritation that he found Repton had read his thoughts.

"You perceive, then, that I am unsuccessful?" said he, with a faint smile. "So much the better if my face betrays me; it will save a world of explanation!"

"Make your report, sir, and I'll make the tea," said Repton, as he proceeded to that office.

"The fellow was in bed,—he refused to see me, and it was only by some insistence that I succeeded in gaining admittance. He has had leeches to his temples. He was bruised, it seems, when he fell, but far more frightened than hurt. He looks the very picture of terror, and lies with a perfect armory of pistols beside his bed. Scanlan was there, and thought to remain during our interview; but I insisted on his withdrawing, and he went. The amiable attorney, somehow, has a kind of respect for me that is rather amusing. As for Merl, he broke out into a vulgar tirade of passion, abused the country and the people, cursed the hour he came amongst them, and said, if he only knew the nature of the property before he made his investment, he 'd rather have purchased Guatemala bonds, or Santa Fé securities.

"'Then I have come fortunately,' said I, 'for I bring you an offer to reimburse all your outlay, and to rid you of a charge so little to your inclination.'

"'Oh! you do, do you?' said he, with one of his cunningest leers. 'You may not be able, perhaps, to effect that bargain, though. It's one thing to pay down a smart sum of money and wait your time for recovering it, and it's another to surrender your compact when the hour of acquisition has arrived. I bought this reversion—at least, I paid the first instalment of the price—four years ago, when the late man's life was worth twenty years' purchase. Well, he 's gone now, and do you think that I 'm going to give up my claim for what it cost me?'

"I gently insinuated that the investigation of the claim might lead to unpleasant revelations. There were various incidents of the play-table, feasible and successful enough after a supper with champagne, and in the short hours before day, which came off with an ill-grace on the table of a court of justice, with three barons of the exchequer to witness them. That I myself might prove an awkward evidence, if unhappily cited to appear; that of my own knowledge I could mention three young fellows of good fortune who had been drained to their last shilling in his company. In fact, we were both remarkably candid with each other, and while *I* reminded *him* of some dark passages at *écarté, he* brought to *my* memory certain protested bills and dishonored notes that 'non jucundum esset meminisse.' I must say, for both of us, we did the thing well, and in good breeding; we told and listened to our several shortcomings with a temper that might have graced a better cause, and I defy the world to produce two men who could have exchanged the epithets of swindler and scamp with more thorough calm and good manners. Unhappily, however, high as one rises in his own esteem by such contests, he scarcely makes the same ascent in that of his neighbor, and so we came, in our overflowing frankness, to admit to each other more of our respective opinions than amounts to flattery. I believe, and, indeed, I hope, I should have maintained my temper to the end, had not the fellow pretty broadly insinuated that some motive of personal advantage had prompted my interference, and actually pushed his insolence so far as to insinuate that 'I should make a better thing' by adhering to his fortunes."

Repton started at these words, and Massingbred resumed: "True, upon my honor; I exaggerate nothing. It was a gross outrage, and very difficult to put up with; so I just expressed my sincere regret that instead of being in bed he was not up and stirring, inasmuch as I should have tried what change of air might have done for him, by pitching him out of the window. He tugged violently at the bell-rope, as though I were about to execute my menace, and so I left him. My diplomacy has, therefore, been a sad failure. I only hope that I may not have increased the difficulty of the case by my treatment of it."

"You never thought of *me* at all, then?" asked Repton.

"Never, till I was once more in the street; then I remembered something of what you said about coercive means, but of what avail a mere menace? This fellow is not new to such transactions,—he has gone through all the phases of 'bulleydom.' Besides, there is a dash of Shylock in every Jew that ever breathed. They will 'have their bond,' unless it can be distinctly proved to them that the thing is impossible."

"Now then for our breaching battery," said Repton, rising and pacing the room. "This attempt at a compromise never had any favor in my eyes; Barry wished it, and I yielded. Now for a very different course. Can you find a saddle-horse here? Well, then, be ready to set out in half an hour, and search out Barry for me. He'll be found at Kilkieran, or the neighborhood; say we must meet at once; arrange time and place for the conference, and come back to me."

Repton issued his directions with an air of command, and Massingbred prepared as implicitly to obey them.

"Mr. Nelligan has lent me his own pad," said Massingbred, entering soon after, "and his son will accompany me, so that I am at your orders at once."

"There are your despatches," said Repton, giving him a sealed packet. "Let me see you here as soon as may be."

CHAPTER XXXVI
A GREAT DISCOVERY

About an hour after Massingbred's departure for Kilkieran, Mr. Repton set out for Cro' Martin Castle. The inn had furnished him its best chaise and four of its primest horses; and had the old lawyer been disposed to enjoy the pleasure which a great moralist has rated so highly, of rapid motion through the air, he might have been gratified on that occasion. Unhappily, however, he was not so minded. Many and very serious cares pressed upon him. He was travelling a road, too, which he had so often journeyed in high spirits, fancying to himself the pleasant welcome before him, and even rehearsing to his own mind the stores of agreeability he was to display,—and now it was to a deserted mansion, lonely and desolate, he was turning! Death and ruin both had done their work on that ancient family, whose very name in the land seemed already hastening to oblivion!

Few men could resist the influence of depression better than Repton. It was not alone that his temperament was still buoyant and energetic, but the habits of his profession had taught him the necessity of being prepared for emergencies, and he would have felt it a dereliction of duty were his sentiments to overmaster his power of action.

Still, as he went along, the well-known features of the spot would recall memories of the past. There lay a dense wood, of which he remembered the very day, the very hour, poor Martin had commenced the planting. There was the little trout-stream, where, under pretence of fishing, he had lounged along the summer day, with Horace for his companion; that, the school-house Mary had sketched, and built out of her own pocket-money. And now the great massive gates slowly opened, and they were within the demesne,—all silent and noiseless. As they came in sight of the castle, Repton covered his face with his hands, and sat for some minutes thus. Then, as if mastering his emotion, he raised his head and folded his arms on his chest.

"You are true to time, I perceive, Dr. Leslie," said he, as the chaise stopped at the door and the venerable clergyman came forward to greet him.

"I got your note last night, sir, but I determined not to keep you waiting, for I perceive you say that time is precious now."

"I thank you heartily," said Repton, as he shook the other's hand. "I am grateful to you also for being here to meet me, for I begin to feel my courage fail me as to crossing that threshold again!"

"Age has its penalties as well as its blessings, sir," said Leslie, "and amongst these is to outlive those dear to us!" There was a painful significance to his own desolate condition that made these words doubly impressive.

Repton made no reply, but pulled the bell strongly; and the loud, deep sounds rung out clearly through the silent house. After a brief interval a small window above the door was opened, and a man with a blunderbuss in his hand sternly demanded their business.

"Oh, I ax pardon, sir," said he, as suddenly correcting himself. "I thought it was that man that 's come to take the place,—'the Jew,' they call him,—and Mr. Magennis said I was n't to let him in, or one belonging to him."

"No, Barney, we are not his friends," said Dr. Leslie; "this is Mr. Repton."

"Sure I know the Counsellor well, sir," said Barney. "I 'll be down in a minute and open the door."

"I must go to work at once," said Repton, in a low and somewhat broken voice, "or this place will be too much for me. Every step I go is calling up old times and old scenes. I had thought my heart was of sterner stuff. Isn't this the way to the library? No, not that way,—that was poor Martin's own breakfast-room!" He spoke hurriedly, like one who wished to suppress emotion by very activity of thought.

While the man who conducted them opened the window-shutters and the windows, Repton and his companion sat down without speaking. At last he withdrew, and Repton, rising, said,—"Some of the happiest hours of my life were passed in this same room. I used to come up here after the fatigues of circuit, and, throwing myself into one of those easy-chairs, dream away for a day or two, gazing out on that bold mountain yonder, above the trees, and wondering how those fellows who never relaxed, in this wise, could sustain the wear and tear of life; for that junketing to Harrow-gate, that rattling, noisy steamboating up the Rhine, that Cockney heroism of Swiss travel, is my aversion. The calm forenoon for thought, the pleasant dinner-table for genial enjoyment afterwards,—these are true recreations.

And what evenings we have had here! But I must not dwell on these." And now he threw upon the table a mass of papers and letters, amongst which he sought out one, from which he took a small key. "Dr. Leslie," said he, "you might have been assured that I have not called upon you to meet me to-day without a sufficient reason. I know that, from certain causes, of which I am not well informed, you were not on terms of much intimacy with my poor friend here. This is not a time to think of these things; *you*, I am well assured, will never remember them."

Leslie made a motion of assent; and the other went on, his voice gradually gaining in strength and fulness, and his whole manner by degrees assuming the characteristic of the lawyer.

"To the few questions to which I will ask your answers, now, I have to request all your attention. They are of great importance; they may, very probably, be re-asked of you under more solemn circumstances; and I have to bespeak, not alone all your accuracy for the replies, but that you may be able, if asked, to state the manner and even the words in which I now address you.—You have been the incumbent of this parish for a length of time,—what number of years?"

"Sixty-three. I was appointed to the vicarage on my ordination, and never held any other charge."

"You knew the late Darcy Martin, father of the last proprietor of this estate?"

"Intimately."

"You baptized his two children, born at the same birth. State what you remember of the circumstance."

"I was sent for to the castle to give a private baptism to the two infants, and requested that I would bring the vestry-book along with me for the registration. I did so. The children were accordingly christened, and their births duly registered and witnessed."

"Can you remember the names by which they were called?"

"Not from the incident in question, though I know the names from subsequent knowledge of them, as they grew up to manhood."

"What means, if any, were adopted at the time to distinguish the priority of birth?"

"The eldest was first baptized, and his birth specially entered in the vestry-book as such; all the witnesses who signed the entry corroborating the fact by special mention of it under their signature. We also heard that the child wore a gold bracelet on one arm; but I did not remark it."

"You have this vestry-book in your keeping?"

"No; Mr. Martin retained it, with some object of more formal registration. I repeatedly asked for it, but never could obtain it. At length some coolness grew up between us, and I could not, or did not wish to press my demand; and at last it lapsed entirely from my memory, so that from that day I never saw it."

"You could, however, recognize it, and be able to verify your signature?"

"Certainly."

"Was there, so far as you could see, any marked distinction made between the children while yet young?"

"I can remember that at the age of three or four the eldest boy wore a piece of red or blue ribbon on his sleeve; but any other mark I never observed. They were treated, so far as I could perceive, precisely alike; and their resemblance to each other was then so striking, it would have been a matter of great nicety to distinguish them. Even at school, I am told, mistakes constantly occurred, and one boy once received the punishment incurred by the other."

"As they grew up, you came to recognize the eldest by his name?"

"Yes. Old Mr. Darcy Martin used to take the elder boy more about with him. He was then a child of ten or eleven years old. He was particular in calling attention to him, saying, 'This fellow is to be my heir; he 'll be the Martin of Cro' Martin yet'"

"And what name did the boy bear?"

"Godfrey,—Godfrey Martin. The second boy's name was Barry."

"You are sure of this?"

"Quite sure. I have dined a number of times at the castle, when Godfrey was called in after dinner, and the other boy was generally in disgrace; and I could remark that his father spoke of him in a tone of irritation and bitterness, which he did not employ towards the other."

"Mr. Martin died before his sons came of age?"

"Yes; they were only nineteen at his death."

"He made a will, I believe, to which you were a witness?"

"I was; but somehow the will was lost or mislaid, and it was only by a letter to the Honorable Colonel Forbes, of Lisvally, that Martin's intentions about appointing him guardian to his elder boy were ascertained. I myself was named guardian to the second son, an office of which he soon relieved me by going abroad, and never returned for a number of years."

"Godfrey Martin then succeeded to the estate in due course?"

"Yes, and we were very intimate for a time, till after his marriage, when estrangement grew up between us, and at last we ceased to visit at all."

"Were the brothers supposed to be on good terms with each other?"

"I have heard two opposite versions on that subject. My own impression was that Lady Dorothea disliked Barry Martin, who had made a marriage that was considered beneath him; and then his brother was, from easiness of disposition, gradually weaned of his old affection for him. Many thought Barry, with all his faults, the better-hearted of the two."

"Can you tell what ultimately became of this Barry Martin?"

"I only know, from common report, that after the death of his wife, having given his infant child, a girl, in charge to his brother, he engaged in the service of some of the Southern American Republics, and is supposed yet to be living there,—some say in great affluence; others, that he is utterly ruined by a failure in a mining speculation. The last time I ever heard Godfrey speak of him was in terms of sincere affection, adding the words, 'Poor Barry will befriend every one but himself.'"

"So that he never returned?"

"I believe not; at least I never heard of it."

"I have written down these questions and your answers to them," said Repton; "will you read them over, and if you find them correct, append your signature. I am expecting Mr. Nelligan here, and I'll go and see if there be any sign of his arrival."

Repton just reached the door as Mr. Nelligan drove up to it.

"All goes on well and promptly to-day," said the old lawyer. "I have got through a good deal of business already, and I expect to do as much more ere evening sets in. I have asked you to be present, as a magistrate, while I examine the contents of a certain closet in this house. I am led to believe that very important documents are deposited there, and it is in your presence, and that of Mr. Leslie, I purpose to make the inquiry. Before I do so, however, I will entreat your attention to a number of questions, and the answers to them, which will be read out to you. You will then be in a better position to judge of any discovery which the present investigation may reveal. All this sounds enigmatically enough, Mr. Nelligan; but you will extend your patience to me for a short while, and I hope to repay it."

Nelligan bowed in silence, and followed him into the house.

"There," said Mr. Leslie, "I have written my name to that paper; it is, so far as I can see, perfectly correct."

"Now, let me read it for Mr. Nelligan," said Repton; and, without further preface, recited aloud the contents of the document. "I conclude, sir," said he, as he finished, "that there is nothing in what you have just heard very new or very strange to your ears. You knew before that Darcy Martin had two sons; that they were twins; and that one of them, Godfrey, inherited the estate. You may also have heard something of the brother's history; more, perhaps, than is here alluded to."

"I have always heard him spoken of as a wild, reckless fellow, and that it was a piece of special good fortune he was not born to the property, or he had squandered every shilling of it," said Nelligan.

"Yes," said Leslie, "such was the character he bore."

"That will do," said Repton, rising. "Now, gentlemen, I'm about to unlock this cabinet, and, if I be correctly informed, we shall find the vestry-book with the entries spoken of by Mr. Leslie, and the long missing will of Darcy Martin. Such, I repeat, are the objects I expect to discover; and it is in your presence I proceed to this examination."

In some astonishment at his words, the others followed him to the corner of the room, where, half concealed in the wainscot, a small door was at length discovered, unlocking which, Repton and the others entered a little chamber, lighted by a narrow, loopholed window. Not stopping to examine the shelves loaded with old documents and account-books, Repton walked straight to a small ebony cabinet, on a bracket, opening which, he drew forth a square vellum-bound book, with massive clasps.

"The old vestry-book. I know it well," said Leslie.

"Here are the documents in parchment," continued Repton, "and a sealed paper. What are the lines in the corner, Mr. Nelligan,—your eyes are better than mine?"

"'Agreement between Godfrey and Barry Martin. To be opened by whichever shall survive the other.' The initials of each are underneath."

"With this we have no concern," said Repton; "our business lies with these." And he pointed to the vestry-book. "Let us look for the entry you spoke of."

"It is easily found," said Leslie. "It was the last ever made in that book. Here it is." And he read aloud: "'February 8th, 1772. Privately baptized, at Cro' Martin Castle, by me, Henry Leslie, Incumbent and Vicar of the said parish, Barry and Godfrey, sons of Darcy Martin and Eleanor his wife, both born on the fourth day of the aforesaid month; and, for the better discrimination of their priority in age, it is hereby added that Barry Martin is the elder, and Godfrey the second son, to which fact the following are attesting witnesses: Michael Keirn, house-steward; George Dorcas, butler; and Catharine Broon, maid of still-room.'"

"Is that in your handwriting, sir?" asked Repton.

"Yes, every word of it, except the superscription of the witnesses."

"Why, then it would appear that the eldest son never enjoyed his rights," cried Nelligan. "Is that possible?"

"It is the strict truth, sir," said Repton. "The whole history of the case adds one to the thousand instances of the miserable failures men make who seek by the indulgence of their own caprices to obstruct the decrees of Providence. Darcy Martin died in the belief that he had so succeeded; and here, now, after more than half a century, are the evidences which reverse his whole policy, and subvert all his plans."

"But what could have been the object here?" asked Nelligan.

"Simply his preference for the younger-born. No sooner had the children arrived at that time of life when dispositions display themselves, than he singled out Godfrey as his favorite. He distinguished him in every way, and as markedly showed that he felt little affection for the other. Whether this favoritism, so openly expressed, had its influence on the rest of the household, or that really they grew to believe that the boy thus selected for peculiar honor was the heir, it would be very difficult now to say. Each cause may have contributed its share; all we know is, that when sent to Dr. Harley's school, at Oughterard, Godfrey was called the elder, and distinguished as such by a bit of red ribbon in his button-hole. And thus they grew up to youth and manhood,—the one flattered, indulged, and caressed; the other equally depreciated and undervalued. Men are, in a great measure, what others make them. Godfrey became proud, indolent, and overbearing; Barry, reckless and a spendthrift Darcy Martin died, and Godfrey succeeded him as matter of course; while Barry, disposing of the small property bequeathed to him, set out to seek adventures in the Spanish Main.

"I am not able to tell, had you even the patience to hear, of what befell him there; the very strangest, wildest incidents are recorded of his life, but they have no bearing on what we are now engaged in. He came back, however, with a wife, to find his brother also married. This is a period of his life of which little is known. The brothers did not live well together. There were serious differences between them; and Lady Dorothea's conduct towards her sister-in-law, needlessly cruel and offensive, as I have heard, imbittered the relations between them. At last Barry's wife died, it was said, of a broken heart, and Barry arrived at Cro' Martin to deposit his infant child with his brother, and take leave of home and country forever.

"Some incident of more than usual importance, and with circumstances of no common pain, must now have occurred; for one night Barry left the castle, vowing nevermore to enter it. Godfrey followed, and tried to detain him. A scene ensued of entreaty on one side, and passionate vehemence on the other, which brought some of the servants to the spot. Godfrey imperiously ordered them away; they all obeyed but Catty. Catty Broon followed Barry, and never quitted him that night, which he spent walking up and down the long avenue of the demesne, watching and waiting for daybreak. We can only conjecture what, in the violence of her grief and indignation, this old attached follower of the house might have revealed. Barry had always been her favorite of the two boys; she knew his rights; she had never forgotten them. She could not tell by what subtleties of law they had been transferred to another, but she felt in her heart assured that in the sight of God they were sacred. How far, then, she revealed this to him, or only hinted it, we have no means of knowing. We can only say that, armed with a certain fact, Barry demanded the next day a formal meeting with his brother and his sister-in-law. Of what passed then and there, no record remains, save, possibly, in that sealed packet; for it bears the date of that eventful morning. I, however, am in a position to prove that Barry declared he would not disturb the possession Godfrey was then enjoying. 'Make that poor child,' said he, alluding to his little girl, your own daughter, and it matters little what becomes of *me*.' Godfrey has more than once adverted to this distressing scene to me. He told me how Lady Dorothea's passion was such that she alternately inveighed against himself for having betrayed her into a marriage beneath her, and abjectly implored Barry not to expose them to the shame and disgrace of the whole world by the assertion of his claim. From this she would burst out into fits of open defiance of him, daring him as an impostor; in fact, Martin said, 'That morning has darkened my life forever; the shadow of it will be over me to the last hour I live!' And so it was! Self-reproach never left him: at one time, for his usurpation of what never was his; at another, for the neglect of poor Mary, who was suffered to grow up without any care of her education, or, indeed, of any attention whatever bestowed upon her.

"I believe that, in spite of herself, Lady Dorothea visited the dislike she bore Barry on his daughter. It was a sense of hate from the consciousness of a wrong,—one of the bitterest sources of enmity! At all events, she showed her little affection,—no tenderness. Poor Godfrey did all that his weak and yielding nature would permit to repair this injustice; his consciousness that to that girl's father he owed position, fortune, station, everything, was ever rising up in his mind, and urging him to some generous effort in her behalf. But you knew him; you knew how a fatal indolence, a shrinking horror of whatever demanded action or energy overcame all his better nature, and made him as useless to all the exigencies of life as one whose heart was eaten up by selfishness.

"The remainder of this sad story is told in very few words. Barry Martin, from whom for several years before no tidings had been received, came suddenly back to England. At first it had not been his intention to revisit Ireland. There was something of magnanimity in the resolve to stay away. He would not come back to impose upon his brother a renewal of that lease of gratitude he derived from him; he would rather spare him the inevitable conflict of feeling which the contrast of his own affluence with the humble condition of an exile would evoke. Besides, he was one of those men whom, whatever Nature may have disposed them to be, the world has so crushed and hardened that they live rather to indulge strong resentments and stern duties than to gratify warm affections. Something he had accidentally heard in a coffee-room—the chance mention by a traveller recently returned from Ireland—about a young lady of rank and fortune whom he had met hunting her own harriers alone in the wildest glen of Connemara, decided him to go over there, and, under the name of Mr. Barry, to visit the scenes of his youth.

"I have but to tell you that it was in that dreary month of November, when plague and famine came together upon us, that he saw this country; the people dying on every side, the land until led, the very crops in some places uncut, terror and dismay on every side, and they who alone could have inspired confidence, or afforded aid, gone! Even Cro' Martin was deserted,—worse than deserted; for one was left to struggle alone against difficulties that the boldest and the bravest might have shrunk from. Had Barry Martin been like any other man, he would at once have placed himself at her side. It was a glorious occasion to have shown her that she was not the lone and friendless orphan, but the loved and cherished child of a doting father. But the hard, stern nature of the man had other and very different impulses; and though he tracked her from cottage to cottage, followed her in her lonely rambles, and watched her in her daily duties, no impulse of affection ever moved him to call her his daughter and bring her home to his heart. I know not whether it was to afford him these occasions of meeting her, or really in a spirit of benevolence, but he dispensed large sums in acts of charity among the people, and Mary herself recounted to me, with tears of delight in her eyes, the splendid generosity of this unknown stranger. I must hasten on. An accident, the mere circumstance of a note-book dropped by some strange chance in Barry's room, revealed to him the whole story of Captain Martin's spendthrift life; he saw that this young man had squandered away not only immense sums obtained by loans, but actually bartered his own reversionary right to the entire estate for money already lost at the gaming-table.

"Barry at once set out for Dublin to call upon me and declare himself; but I was, unfortunately, absent at the assizes. He endeavored next to see Scanlan. Scanlan was in London; he followed him there. To Scanlan he represented himself as a money-lender, who, having come to the knowledge of Merl's dealings with young Martin, and the perilous condition of the property in consequence, offered his aid to re-purchase the reversion while it was yet time. To effect this bargain, Scanlan hastened over to Baden, accompanied by Barry, who, however, for secrecy' sake, remained at a town in the neighborhood. Scanlan, it seems, resolved to profit by an emergency so full of moment, and exacted from Lady Dorothea—for Martin was then too ill to be consulted—the most advantageous terms for himself. I need not mention one of the conditions,—a formal consent to his marriage with Miss Martin! and this, remember, when that young lady had not the slightest, vaguest suspicion that such an indignity could be offered her, far less concurred in by her nearest relatives! In the exuberance of his triumph, Scanlan showed the formal letter of assent from Lady Dorothea to Barry. It was from this latter I had the account, and I can give you no details, for all he said was, 'As I crushed it in my hand, I clenched my fist to fell him to the ground! but I refrained. I muttered a word or two, and got out into the street. I know very little more.'

"That night he set out for Baden; but of his journey I know nothing. The only hint of it he ever dropped was when, giving me this key, he said, 'I saw Godfrey.'

"He is now back here once more; come to insist upon his long unasserted rights, and by a title so indisputable that it will leave no doubt of the result.

"He is silent and uncommunicative; but he has said enough to show me that he is possessed of evidence of the compact between Godfrey and himself; nor is he the man to fail for lack of energy.

"I have now come to the end of this strange history, in which it is not impossible you yourselves may be called to play a part, in confirmation of what you have seen this day."

"Then this was the same Mr. Barry of whom we spoke last night?" said Nelligan, thoughtfully. "When about to describe him to you, I was really going to say, something like what Mr. Martin might look, if ten years older and white-haired."

"There is a strong resemblance still!" said Repton, as he busied himself sealing up the vestry-book and the other documents. "These I mean to deposit in your keeping, Mr. Nelligan, till they be called for. I have sent over Massingbred to Barry to learn what his wishes may be as to the next legal steps; and now I am ready to return with you to Oughterard."

Talking over this singular story, they reached the town, where Massingbred had just arrived a short time before.

"I have had a long chase," said Jack, "and only found him late in the afternoon at the cottage."

"You gave him the packet, then, and asked when we should meet?" asked Repton, hurriedly.

"Yes; he was walking up and down before the door with the doctor, when we rode up. He scarcely noticed us; and taking your letter in his hand he placed it, without breaking the seal, on a seat in the porch. I then gave him your message, and he seemed so lost in thought that I fancied he had not attended to me. I was about to repeat it, when he interrupted me, saying, 'I have heard you, sir; there is no answer.' As I stood for a moment or two, uncertain what to do or say, I perceived that Joe Nelligan, who had been speaking to the doctor, had just staggered towards a bench, ill and fainting. 'Yes,' said Barry, turning his eyes towards him, 'she is very—very ill; tell Repton so, and he'll feel for me!'"

Repton pressed his handkerchief to his face and turned away.

"I'm afraid," said Massingbred, "that her state is highly dangerous. The few words the doctor dropped were full of serious meaning."

"Let us hope, and pray," said Repton, fervently, "that, amidst all the calamities of this sorrow-struck land, it may be spared the loss of one who never opened a cabin door without a blessing, nor closed it but to shut a hope within."

CHAPTER XXXVII
A DARK DAY

A mild, soft day, with low-lying clouds, and rich odors of wild-flowers rising from the ground, a certain dreamy quiet pervading earth and sky and sea, over which faint shadows lingered lazily; some drops of the night dew still glittered on the feathery larches, and bluebells hung down their heads, heavy with moisture; so still the scene that the plash of the leaping trout could be heard as he rose in the dark stream. And yet there was a vast multitude of people there. The whole surface of the lawn that sloped from the cottage to the river was densely crowded, with every age, from the oldest to very infancy; with all conditions, from the well-clad peasant to the humblest "tramper" of the high-roads. Weariness, exhaustion, and even hunger were depicted on many of their faces. Some had passed the night there; others had come long distances, faint and footsore; but as they sat, stood, or lay in groups around, not a murmur, not a whisper escaped them; with aching eyes they looked towards an open window, where the muslin curtain was gently stirred in the faint air.

The tidings of Mary Martin's illness had spread rapidly: far-away glens down the coast, lonely cabins on the bleak mountains, wild remote spots out of human intercourse had heard the news, and their dwellers had travelled many a mile to satisfy their aching hearts.

From a late hour of the evening before they had learnt nothing of her state; then a few words whispered by old Catty to those nearest the door told "that she was no better,—if anything, weaker!" These sad tidings were soon passed from lip to lip; and thus they spent the night, praying or watching wearily, their steadfast gaze directed towards that spot where the object of all their fears and hopes lay suffering.

Of those there, there was scarcely one to whom she was not endeared by some personal benefit. She had aided this one in distress, the other she had nursed in fever; here were the old she had comforted and cheered, there the children she had taught and trained beside her chair. Her gentle voice yet vibrated in every heart, her ways of kindness were in every memory. Sickness and sorrow were familiar enough to themselves. Life was, at least to most of them, one long struggle; but they could not bring themselves to think of *her* thus stricken down! She! that seemed an angel, as much above the casualties of such fortune as theirs as she was their superior in station, — that *she* should be sick and suffering was too terrible to think of.

There was a stir and movement in the multitude, a wavy, surging motion, for the doctor was seen to issue from the stable-yard, and lead his pony towards the bridge. He stopped to say a word or two as he went. They were sad words; and many a sobbing voice and many a tearful eye told what his tidings had been. "Sinking, — sinking rapidly!"

A faint low cry burst from one in the crowd at this moment, and the rumor ran that a woman had fainted. It was poor Joan, who had come that night over the mountain, and, overcome by grief and exhaustion together, had at last given way.

"Get a glass of wine for her, or even a cup of water," cried out three or four voices; and one nigh the door entered the cottage in search of aid. The moment after a tall and handsome girl forced her way through the crowd, and gave directions that Joan might be carried into the house.

"Why did ye call her my Lady?" muttered an old hag to one of the men near her; "sure, she's Henderson's daughter!"

"Is she, faith? By my conscience, then, she might be a better man's! She's as fine a crayture as ever I seen!"

"If she has a purty face, she has a proud heart!" muttered another.

"Ayeh! she'll never be like *her* that's going to leave us!" sighed a young woman with a black ribbon in her cap.

Meanwhile Kate had Joan assisted into the cottage, and was busily occupied in restoring her. Slowly, and with difficulty, the poor creature came to herself, and gazing wildly around, asked where she was; then suddenly bursting out in tears, she said, — "Sure, I know well where I am; sure, it's my own self, brought grief and sorrow under this roof. But for *me* she 'd be well and hearty this day!"

"Let us still hope," said Kate, softly. "Let us hope that one so dear to us all may be left here. You are better now. I 'll join you again presently." And with noiseless footsteps she stole up the stairs. As she came to the door, she halted and pressed her hands to her heart, as if in pain. There was a low murmuring sound, as if of voices, from within, and Kate turned away and sat down on the stairs.

Within the sick-room a subdued light came, and a soft air, mild and balmy, for the rose-trees and the jessamine clustered over the window, and mingled their blossoms across it. Mary had just awoke from a short sleep, and lay with her hand clasped within that of a large and white-haired man at the bedside.

"What a good, kind doctor!" said she, faintly; "I'm sure to find you ever beside me when I awake."

"Oh, darlin', dear," broke in old Catty, "sure you ought to know who he is. Sure it 's your own—"

"Hush! be silent!" muttered the old man, in a low, stern voice.

"Is it Tuesday to-day?" asked Mary, softly.

"Yes, dear, Tuesday," said the old man.

"It was on Thursday my poor uncle died. Could I live till Thursday, doctor?"

The old man tried to speak, but could not.

"You are afraid to shock me," said she, with a faint attempt to smile, "but if you knew how happy I am,—happy even to leave a life I loved so well. It never could have been the same again, though—the spell was breaking, hardship and hunger were maddening them—who knows to what counsels they 'd have listened soon! Tell Harry to be kind to them, won't you? Tell him not to trust to others, but to know them himself; to go, as I have done, amongst them. They 'll love him *so* for doing it. He is a man, young, rich, and high-hearted,—how they 'll dote upon him! Catty used to say it was my father they 'd have worshipped; but that was in flattery to me, Catty, you always said we were so like—"

"Oh dear! oh dear! why won't you tell her?" broke in Catty. But a severe gesture from the old man again checked her words.

"How that wild night at sea dwells in my thoughts! I never sleep but to dream of it. Cousin Harry must not forget those brave fellows. I have nothing to requite them with. I make no will, doctor," said she, smiling, "for my only legacy is that nosegay there. Will you keep it for my sake?"

The old man hid his face, but his strong frame shook and quivered in the agony of the moment.

"Hush!" said she, softly; "I hear voices without. Who are they?"

"They're the country-people, darlin', come from Kiltimmon and beyond Kyle-a-Noe, to ax after you. They passed the night there, most of them."

"Catty, dear, take care that you look after them; they will be hungry and famished, poor creatures! Oh, how unspeakably grateful to one's heart is this proof of feeling! Doctor, you will tell Harry how *I* loved *them* and how *they* loved *me*. Tell him, too, that this bond of affection is the safest and best of all ties. Tell him that their old love for a Martin still survives in their hearts, and it will be his own fault if he does not transmit it to his children. There's some one sobbing there without. Oh, bid them be of good heart, Catty; there is none who could go with less of loss to those behind. There—there come the great waves again before me! How my courage must have failed me to make this impression so deep! And poor Joan, and that dear fond girl who has been as a sister to me,—so full of gentleness and love,—Kate, where is she? No, do not call her; say that I asked for her—that I blessed her—and sent her this kiss!" She pressed a rose to her hot, parched lips as she spoke, and then closing her eyes seemed to fall off to sleep. Her breathing, at first strong and frequent, grew fainter and fainter, and her color came and went, while her lips slightly moved, and a low, soft murmur came from them.

"She's asleep," muttered Catty, as she crouched down beside the bed.

The old man bent over the bed, and watched the calm features. He sat thus long, for hours, but no change was there; he put his lips to hers, and then a sickly shuddering came over him, and a low, deep groan, that seemed to rend his very heart!

Three days after, the great gateway of Cro' Martin Castle opened to admit a stately hearse drawn by six horses, all mournfully caparisoned, shaking with plumes and black-fringed drapery. Two mourning-coaches followed, and then the massive gates were closed, and the sad pageant wound its slow course through the demesne. At the same moment another funeral was approaching the churchyard by a different road. It was a coffin borne by men bareheaded and sorrow-struck. An immense multitude followed, of every rank and age; sobs and sighs broke from them as they went. Not an eye was tearless, not a lip that did not tremble. At the head of this procession walked a small group whose dress and bearing bespoke their class. These were Barry Martin, leaning on Repton; Massingbred and the two Nelligans came behind.

The two coffins entered the churchyard at the same instant The uncle and the niece were laid side by side in the turf! The same sacred words consigned them both to their last bed; the same second of time heard the dank reverberation that pronounced "earth" had returned "to earth." A kind of reverential awe pervaded the immense crowd during the ceremony, and if here and there a sob would burst from some overburdened heart, all the rest were silent; respecting, with a deference of true refinement, a sorrow deeper and greater than their own, they never uttered a word, but with bent-down heads stole quietly away. And now by each grave the mourners stood, silently gazing on the little mounds which typify so much of human sorrow!

Barry Martin's bronzed and weather-beaten features were a thought paler, perhaps. There was a dark shade of color round the eyes, but on the whole the expression conveyed far more of sternness than sorrow. Such, indeed, is no uncommon form for grief to take in certain natures. There are men who regard calamity like a foe, and go out to meet it in a spirit of haughty defiance. A poor philosophy! He who accepts it as chastisement is both a braver and a better man!

Repton stood for a while beside him, not daring to interrupt his thoughts. At length he whispered a few words in his ear. Barry started suddenly, and his dark brow grew sterner and more resolute.

"Yes, Martin, you must," said Repton, eagerly, "I insist upon it. Good heavens! is it at such a time, in such a place as this, you can harbor a thought that is not forgiveness? Remember he is poor Godfrey's son, the last of the race now." As he spoke, passing his arm within the other's, he drew him gently along, and led him to where a solitary mourner was standing beside the other grave.

Barry Martin stood erect and motionless, while Repton spoke to the young man. At first the words seemed to confuse and puzzle him, for he looked vaguely around, and passed his hand across his brow in evident difficulty.

"Did you say here, in this country? Do I understand you aright?"

"Here, in this very spot; there, standing now before you!" said Repton, as he pushed young Martin towards his uncle.

Barry held out his hand, which the young man grasped eagerly; and then, as if unable to resist his emotions longer, fell, sobbing violently, into the other's arms.

"Let us leave them for a while," said Repton, hurrying over to where Massingbred and the Nelligans were yet standing in silent sorrow.

They left the spot together without a word. Grief had its own part for each. It is not for us to say where sorrow eat deepest, or in which heart the desolation was most complete.

"I'd not have known young Martin," whispered Nelligan in Repton's ear; "he looks full twelve years older than when last I saw him."

"The fast men of this age, sir, live their youth rapidly," replied the other. "It is rarely their fortune to survive to be like me, or heaven knows what hearts they would be left with!"

While they thus talked, Massingbred and Joe Nelligan had strolled away into the wood. Neither spoke. Massingbred felt the violent trembling of the other's arm as it rested on his own, and saw a gulping effort by which more than once he suppressed his rising emotion. For hours they thus loitered along, and at length, as they issued from the demesne, they found Repton and Mr. Nelligan awaiting them.

"Barry Martin has taken his nephew back with him to the cottage," said Repton, "and we 'll not intrude upon them for the rest of the evening."

CHAPTER XXXVIII
REPTON'S LAST CAUSE

We have no right, as little have we the inclination, to inflict our reader with the details by which Barry Martin asserted and obtained his own. A suit in which young Martin assumed to be the defendant developed the whole history to the world, and proclaimed his title to the estate. It was a memorable case in many ways; it was the last brief Val Repton ever held. Never was his clear and searching intellect more conspicuous; never did he display more logical acuteness, nor trace out a difficult narrative with more easy perspicuity.

"My Lords," said he, as he drew nigh the conclusion of his speech, "it would have been no ordinary satisfaction to me to close a long life of labor in these courts by an effort which restores to an ancient name the noble heritage it had held for centuries. I should have deemed such an occasion no unfitting close to a career not altogether void of its successes; but the event has still stronger claims upon my gratitude. It enables me in all the unembellished sternness of legal proof to display to an age little credulous of much affection the force of a brother's love, — the high-hearted devotion by which a man encountered a long life of poverty and privation, rather than disturb the peaceful possession of a brother.

"Romance has its own way of treating such themes; but I do not believe romance can add one feature to the simple fact of this man's self-denial.

"We should probably be lost in our speculations as to the noble motives of this sacrifice, if our attention was not called away to something infinitely finer and more exalted than even this. I mean the glorious life and martyr's death of her who has made a part of this case less like a legal investigation than the page of an affecting story. Story, do I say! Shame on the word! It is in truth and reality alone are such virtues inscribed. Fiction cannot deal with the humble materials that make up such an existence, — the long hours of watching by sickness; the weary care of teaching the young; the trying disappointments to hope bravely met by fresh efforts; the cheery encouragement drawn from a heart exhausting itself to supply others. Think of a young girl — a very child in the world's wisdom, more than a man in heroism and daring, with a heart made for every high ambition, and a station that might command the highest—calmly consenting to be the friend of destitution, the companion of misery, the daily associate of every wretchedness; devoting grace that might have adorned a court to shed happiness in a cabin, and making of beauty that would have shed lustre around a palace the sunshine that pierced the gloom of a peasant's misery! Picture to yourself the hand a prince might have knelt to kiss, holding the cup to the lips of fever; fancy the form whose elegance would have fascinated, crouched down beside the embers as she spoke words of consolation or hope to some bereaved mother or some desolate orphan!

"These are not the scenes we are wont to look on here. Our cares are, unhappily, more with the wiles and snares of crafty men than with the sorrows and sufferings of the good! It is not often human nature wears its best colors in this place; the spirit of litigious contest little favors the virtues that are the best adornments of our kind. Thrice happy am I, then, that I end my day where a glorious sunset gilds its last hours; that I close my labors not in reprobating crime or stigmatizing baseness, but with a full heart, thanking God that my last words are an elegy over the grave of the best of The Martins of Cro' Martin.'"

The inaccurate record from which we take these passages—for the only report of the trial is in a newspaper of the time—adds that the emotion of the speaker had so far pervaded the court that the conclusion was drowned in mingled expressions of applause and sorrow; and when Repton retired, he was followed by the whole bar, eagerly pressing to take their last farewell of its honored father.

The same column of the paper mentions that Mr. Joseph Nelligan was to have made his first motion that day as Solicitor-General, but had left the court from a sudden indisposition, and the cause was consequently deferred.

If Val Repton never again took his place in court, he did not entirely abdicate his functions. Barry Martin had determined on making a conveyance of the estate to his nephew, and the old lawyer was for several weeks busily employed in that duty. Although Merl's claim became extinguished when young Martin's right to the property was annulled, Barry Martin insisted on arrangements being made to repay him all that he had advanced,—a course which Repton, with some little hesitation, at last concurred in. He urged Barry to reserve a life-interest to himself in the property, representing the various duties which more properly would fall to his lot than to that of a young and inexperienced proprietor. But he would not hear of it.

"He cannot abide the place," said Repton, when talking the matter over with Massingbred. "He is one of those men who never can forgive the locality where they have been miserable, nor the individual who has had a share in their sorrow. When he settles his account with Henderson, then he 'll leave the West forever."

"And will he still leave Henderson in his charge?" asked Jack.

"That is as it may be," said Repton, cautiously. "There is, as I understand, some very serious reckoning between them. It is the only subject on which Martin has kept mystery with me, and I do not like even to advert to it."

Massingbred pondered long over these words, without being able to make anything of them.

It might be that Henderson's conduct had involved him in some grave charge; and if so, Jack's own intentions with regard to the daughter would be burdened with fresh complications. "The steward" was bad enough; but if he turned out to be the "unjust steward" — "I 'll start for Galway to-night," thought he. "I 'll anticipate the discovery, whatever it be. She can no longer refuse to see me on the pretext of recent sorrow. It is now two months and more since this bereavement befell her. I can no longer combat this life of anxiety and doubt. — What can I do for you in the West, sir?" asked he of Repton, suddenly.

"Many things, my young friend," said Repton, "if you will delay your departure two days, since they are matters on which I must instruct you personally."

Massingbred gave a kind of half-consent, and the other went on to speak of the necessity for some nice diplomacy between the uncle and his nephew. "They know each other but little; they are on the verge of misunderstandings a dozen times a day. Benefits are, after all, but sorry ties between man and man. They may ratify the treaty of affection; they rarely inscribe the contract!"

"Still Martin cannot but feel that to the noblest act of his uncle's generosity he is indebted for all he possesses."

"Of course he knows, and he feels it; but who is to say whether that same consciousness is not a load too oppressive to bear. I know already Barry Martin's suggestions as to certain changes have not been well taken, and he is eager and pressing to leave Ireland, lest anything should disturb the concord, frail as it is, between them."

"By Jove!" exclaimed Massingbred, passionately, "there is wonderfully little real good in this world; wonderfully little that can stand the test of the very basest of all motives, — mere gain."

"Don't say so!" cried Repton. "Men have far better natures than you think; the fault lies in their tempers. Ay, sir, we are always entering into heavy recognizances with our passions, to do fifty things we never cared for. We have said this, we have heard the other; somebody sneered at that, and some one else agreed with him; and away we go, pitching all reason behind us, like an old shoe, and only seeking to gratify a whim, or a mere caprice, suggested by temper. Why do people maintain friendly intercourse at a distance for years, who could not pass twenty-four hours amicably under the same roof? Simply because it is their natures, and not their tempers, are in exercise."

"I scarcely can separate the two in my mind," said Jack, doubtingly.

"Can't you, sir? Why, nature is your skin, temper only your great-coat." And the old lawyer laughed heartily at his own conceit. "But here comes the postman."

The double knock had scarcely reverberated through the spacious hall when the servant entered with a letter.

"Ah! Barry Martin's hand. What have we here?" said Repton, as he ran his eyes over it. "So-so; just as I was saying this minute, only that Barry has the good sense to see it himself. 'My nephew,' he writes, 'has his own ideas on all these subjects, which are not mine; and as it is no part of my plan to hamper my gift with conditions that might impair its value, I mean to leave this at once.

"'I have had my full share of calamity since I set foot in this land; and if this rugged old nature could be crushed by mere misfortune, the last two months might have done it. But no, Repton, the years by which we survive friends serve equally to make us survive affections, and we live on, untouched by time!

"'I mean to be with you this evening. Let us dine alone together, for I have much to say to you.

"' Yours ever,

"'Barry Martin.

"'I hope I may see Massingbred before I sail. I 'd like to shake hands with him once again. Say so to him, at all events.'"

"Come in to-morrow to breakfast," said Repton; "by that time we'll have finished all mere business affairs." And Massingbred having assented, they parted.

CHAPTER XXXIX
TOWARDS THE END

Repton was standing at his parlor window, anxiously awaiting his friend's arrival, when the chaise with four posters came to the door. "What have we here?" said the old lawyer to himself, as Barry assisted a lady dressed in deep mourning to alight, and hurried out to receive them.

"I have not come alone, Repton," said the other. "I have brought my daughter with me." Before Repton could master his amazement at these words, she had thrown back her veil, revealing the well-known features of Kate Henderson.

"Is this possible?—is this really the case?" cried Repton, as he grasped her hand between both his own. "Do I, indeed, see one I have so long regarded and admired, as the child of my old friend?"

"Fate, that dealt me so many heavy blows of late, had a kindness in reserve for me, after all," said Barry. "I am not to be quite alone in this world!"

"If *you* be grateful, what ought not to be *my* thankfulness?" said Kate, tremulously.

"Leave us for a moment together, Kate," said Barry; and taking Repton's arm, he led him into an inner room.

"I have met with many a sore cut from fortune, Repton," said he, in the fierce tone that was most natural to him; "the nearest and dearest to me not the last to treat me harshly. I need not tell you how I have been requited in life; not, indeed, that I seek to acquit myself of my own share of ill. My whole career has been a fault; it could not bring other fruit than misery." He paused, and for a while seemed laboring in strong emotion. At last he went on:—

"When that girl was born—it was two years before I married—I intrusted the charge of her to Henderson, who placed her with a sister of his in Bruges. I made arrangements for her maintenance and education,— liberally for one as poor as I was. I made but one condition about her. It was that under no circumstances save actual want should she ever be reduced to earn her own bread; but if the sad hour did come, never—as had been her poor mothers fate—never as a governess! It was in that fearful struggle of condition I first knew her. I continued, year after year, to hear of her; remitting regularly the sums I promised,—doubling, tripling them, when fortune favored me with a chance prosperity. The letters spoke of her as well and happy, in humble but sufficient circumstances, equally remote from privation as from the seductions of a more exalted state. I insisted eagerly on my original condition, and hoped some day to hear of her being married to some honest but humble man. It was not often that I had time for self-reproach; but when such seasons would beset me, I thought of this girl, and her poor mother long dead and gone—But let me finish. While I struggled—and it was often a hard struggle—to maintain my side of the compact, selling at ruinous loss acquisitions it had cost me years of labor to obtain, this fellow, this Henderson, was basely betraying the trust I placed in him! The girl, for whose protection, whose safety I was toiling, was thrown by him into the very world for which I had distinctly excepted her; her talents, her accomplishments, her very graces, farmed out and hired for his own profit! Launched into the very sea where her own mother met shipwreck, she was a mere child, sent to thread her way through the perils of the most dissipated society. Hear her own account of it, Repton. Let *her* tell you what is the tone of that high life to which foreign nobility imparts its fascinations. Not that I want to make invidious comparisons; our own country sends its high tributaries to every vice of Europe! I know not what accident saved her amidst this pollution. Some fancied theory of popular wrongs, she thinks, gave her a kind of factitious heroism; elevating her, at least to her own mind, above the frivolous corruptions around her. She was a democrat, to rescue her from being worse.

"At last came a year of unusual pressure; my remittance was delayed, but when sent was never acknowledged. From that hour out I never heard of her. How she came into my brother's family, you yourself know. What was her life there, she has told me! Not in any spirit of complaint,—nay, she acknowledges to many kindnesses and much trust. Even my cold sister-in-law showed traits for which I had not given her credit. I have already forgotten her wrongs towards myself, in requital of her conduct to this poor girl."

"I'll spare you the scene with Henderson, Repton," said he, after a long pause. "When the fellow told me that the girl was the same I had seen watching by another's sickbed, that she it was whose never-ceasing cares had soothed the last hours of one dearer than herself, I never gave another thought to him. I rushed out in search of her, to tell her myself the tidings."

"How did she hear it?" asked Repton, eagerly.

"More calmly than I could tell it. Her first words were, 'Thank God for this, for I never could love that man I had called my father!'"

"She knows, then, every circumstance of her birth?"

"I told her everything. We know each other as well as though we had lived under the same roof for years. She is my own child in every sentiment and feeling. She is frank and fearless, Repton,—two qualities that will do well enough in the wild savannahs of the New World, but would be unmanageable gifts in the Old, and thither we are bound. I have written to Liverpool about a ship, and we shall sail on Saturday."

"How warmly do I sympathize in this your good fortune, Martin!" said Repton. "She is a noble creature, and worthy of belonging to you."

"I ask for nothing more, Repton," said he, solemnly. "Fortune and station, such as they exist here, I have no mind for! I'm too old now to go to school about party tactics and politics; I'm too stubborn, besides, to yield up a single conviction for the sake of unity with a party,—so much for my unfitness for public life. As to private, I am rough and untrained; the forms of society so pleasant to others would be penalties to *me*. And then," said he, rising, and drawing up his figure to its full height, "I love the forest and the prairie; I glory in the vastness of a landscape where the earth seems boundless as the sky, and where, if I hunt down a buffalo-ox, after twenty miles of a chase, I have neither a game-law nor a gamekeeper nor a charge of trespass hanging over me."

"There's some one knocking at the door," said Repton, as he arose and opened it.

"A thousand pardons for this interruption," said Mas-singbred, in a low and eager voice, "but I cannot keep my promise to you; I cannot defer my journey to the West. I start to-night. Don't ask me the reasons. I 'll be free enough to give them if they justify me."

"But here is one who wishes to shake hands with you, Massingbred," said Repton, as he led him forward into the room.

"I hope you are going to keep your pledge with me, though," said Barry. "Have you forgotten you have promised to be my guest over the sea?"

"Ah," said Jack, sighing, "I 've had many a day-dream of late!"

"The man's in love," said Repton. "Nay, prisoner, you are not called on to say what may criminate you. I 'll tell you what, Barry, you 'll do the boy good service by taking him along with you. There 's a healthful sincerity in the active life of the New World well fitted to dispel illusions that take their rise in the indolent voluptuousness of the Old. Carry him off then, I say; accept no excuses nor apologies. Send him away to buy powder and shot, leather gaiters, and the rest of it. When I saw him first myself, it was in the character of a poacher, and he filled the part well. Ah! he is gone," added he, perceiving that Martin had just quitted the room. "Poor fellow, he is so full of his present happiness,—the first gleam of real sunshine on a long day of lowering gloom! He has just found a daughter,—an illegitimate one, but worthy to be the rightful-born child to the first man in the land. The discovery has carried him back twenty years of life, and freshened a heart whose wells of feeling were all but dried up forever. If I mistake not, you must have met her long ago at Cro' Martin."

"Possibly. I have no recollection of it," said Jack, musing.

"An ignoble confession, sir," said Repton; "no less shocked should I be were she to tell me she was uncertain if she had ever met Mr. Massingbred. As Burke once remarked to me, 'Active intelligences, like appropriate ingredients in chemistry, never meet without fresh combinations.' It is then a shame to ignore such products. I 'd swear that when you did meet you understood each other thoroughly; agreed well,—ay, and what is more to the purpose, differed in the right places too."

"I'm certain we did," said Jack, smiling, "though I'm ungrateful enough to forget all about it."

"Well," said Martin, entering, "I have sent for another advocate to plead my cause. My daughter will tell you, sir, that she, at least, is not afraid to encounter the uncivilized glens beside the Orinoco. Come in, Kate. You tell me that you and Mr. Massingbred are old friends."

Massingbred started as he heard the name, looked up, and there stood Kate before him, with her hand extended in welcome.

"Good heavens! what is this? Am I in a dream? Can this be real?" cried Jack, pressing his hands to his temples, and trembling from head to foot in the intensity of his anxiety.

"My father tells me of an invitation he has given you, Mr. Massingbred," said she, smiling faintly at his embarrassment, "and asks me to repeat it; but I know far better than he does all that you would surrender by exile from the great world wherein you are destined to eminence. The great debater, the witty conversationalist, the smart reviewer, might prove but a sorry trapper, and even a bad shot! I have my scruples, then, about supporting a cause where my conscience does not go along with me."

"My head on't, but he 'll like the life well," said Barry, half impatiently.

"Am I to think that you will not ask me to be your guest?" said Jack, in a whisper, only audible by Kate.

"I have not said so," said she, in the same low tone. "Will you go further, Kate," muttered he, in tremulous eagerness, "and say, 'Come'?" "Yes!" said she. "Come!"

"I accept!" cried Jack, rushing over, and grasping Martin's hands between his own. "I 'm ready,—this hour, this instant, if you like it."

"We find the prisoner guilty, my Lords," said Repton; "but we recommend him to mercy, as his manner on this occasion convinces us it is a first offence."

We have now done with the Martins of Cro' Martin. Should any of our readers feel a curiosity as to the future fortunes of the estate, its story, like that of many another Irish property, is written in the Encumbered Estates Court. Captain Martin only grew wiser by the especial experience of one class of difficulties. His indolent, easy disposition and a taste for expense led him once again into embarrassments from which there was but one issue,—the sale of his property. He has still, however, a handsome subsistence remaining, and lives with Lady Dorothea, notable and somewhat distinguished residents of a city on the Continent.

We cannot persuade ourselves that we have inspired interest for the humbler characters of our piece. Nor dare we ask the reader to hear more about Mrs. Cronan and her set, nor learn how Kilkieran fared in the changes around it.

For Joseph Nelligan, however, we claim a parting word. He was the first of an order of men who have contributed no small share to the great social revolution of Ireland in late years. With talents fully equal to the best in the opposite scale of party, and a character above all reproach, he stood a rebuking witness to all the taunts and sarcasms once indiscriminately levelled at his class; and, at the same time, inspired his own party with the happy knowledge that there was a nobler and more legitimate road to eminence than by factious display and popular declamation.

We do not wish to inquire how far the one great blow to his happiness — the disappointment of his early life — contributed to his success by concentrating his ambition on his career. Certain is it, no man achieved a higher or more rapid elevation, and old Dan lived to receive at his board the Chief Justice of the Queen's Bench in the person of his own son.

Poor Simmy Crow! for if we would forget him, he has taken care that oblivion is not to be his fate. He has sent from the Rocky Mountains, where he is now wandering with Barry Martin, some sketches of Indian Life to the Irish Art Exhibition.

If it be a pleasure to trace in our friends the traits we have admired in them in youth, and remark the embers of the fires that once wanned their hearts, Simmy affords us this gratification, since his drawings reveal the inspirations that first filled his early mind. The Chief in his war-paint has a fac-simile likeness to his St. John in the Wilderness; and as for the infant the squaw is bathing in the stream, we can produce twelve respectable witnesses to depose that it is "Moses."

We are much tempted to add a word about the Exiles themselves, but we abstain. It is enough to say that all the attractive prospects of ambition held out by friends, all the seductions of generous offers from family, have never tempted them to return to the Old World; but that they live on happily, far away from the jarring collisions of life, the tranquil existence they had longed for.